D0301286

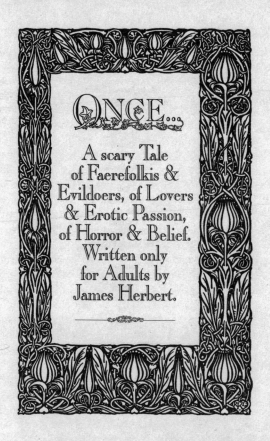

# ONCE...

A scary Tale
of Faerefolkis &
Evildoers, of Lovers
& Erotic Passion,
of Horror & Belief.
Written only
for Adults by
James Herbert.

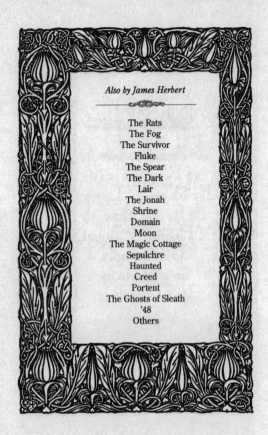

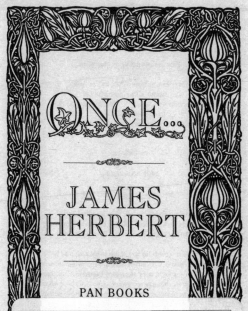

# ONCE...

## JAMES HERBERT

PAN BOOKS

First published 2001 by Macmillan

This edition published 2002 by Pan Books
an imprint of Pan Macmillan Ltd
Pan Macmillan, 20 New Wharf Road, London N1 9RR
Basingstoke and Oxford
Associated companies throughout the world
www.panmacmillan.com

ISBN 0 330 37613 6

5 7 9 8 6

A CIP catalogue record for this book is available from
the British Library.

Typeset by SetSystems Ltd, Saffron Walden, Essex
Printed and bound in Great Britain by
Mackays of Chatham plc, Chatham, Kent

'... there is enough (evidence of fairies)
already available to convince any
reasonable man that the matter is not one
which can be readily dismissed ...'

THE COMING OF THE FAIRIES
Sir Arthur Conan Doyle

'... fairies are not tiny; they also
come in medium (brownies) and full sizes
(beautiful human-sized fairies) ...'

THE COMPLETE BOOK OF
DEVILS AND DEMONS
Leonard R. N. Ashley

'Fairy tales can come true
it can happen to you ...'

YOUNG AT HEART
Johnny Richards and Carolyn Leigh

in aspect and daunting on overcast days when its stone turned dull and brooding. It rose three storeys high, but located on the flat roof, with its fortress ramparts and terrace, was another floor, much smaller in area, almost a garret, although grander in design and purpose. This in turn had its own roof with ramparts and substantial chimney towers at each corner.

The sanguine edifice of Castle Bracken had mellowed even more with time and weather, and was mottled with lighter patches where surfaces had worn away. Several wide grey steps led up to the imposing front door of solid oak that was set into the roof-tall centre porch, and sinuous vines of dead, leafless wisteria crept around it and high up into the stonework above. They should have been cut down long ago, for now they were nothing but naked clinging parasites that refused to give up their host. The many windows, nearly all of equal size, their rectangular frames divided by stone mullions, were dark and impenetrable, as if their glass was a barrier to the sunlight rather than a portal for it to enter.

It should have felt like coming home, but it didn't. That, Thom hoped, would come later when he finally reached the cottage.

---

Even before he drew up to the steps, the front door opened and the almost portly figure of Hugo Bleeth was hurrying down, one hand held high in greeting. Thom noticed the shadowy figure inside the doorway behind him and assumed it was Bracken's household servant and, nowadays, general factotum, a frighteningly thin, aloof man who had been with the Bleeth family for as long as Thom could remember. When they were kids, Thom and Hugo had called him 'Bones', but naturally, never to his face for, servant though he might be, there nevertheless had always been a menacing air of superiority about him.

'Thom! So bloody good to see you,' the Bleeth heir called out as he scurried round to the driver's side of the Jeep. 'So bloody, bloody good!'

Thom stuck a hand out through the open window and Hugo took it with relish. Despite the apparent enthusiasm though, the hand Thom held was limp, the palm moist, and it was he who had to pump it.

'Hugo,' he said, his grin wearied by the long journey.

'How the bloody hell are you?' Hugo's eyes, normally protuberant, now looked as if they might pop from their sockets. He had always faintly reminded Thom of Toad of Toad Hall – the enthusiasm, the impatience, and yes, the silliness – and as with Kenneth Grahame's fictional character, there was something immensely likeable about him.

'Yeah, good,' Thom replied.

Hugo regarded him doubtfully. 'Journey not too tiring? You know, you really should have taken the train up from London. Or better yet, I could have sent Hartgrove down in the old Bentley to fetch you. Arrive in style, eh?'

Hartgrove – Bones – had stepped from the shadows to appear at the top of the stairs. His cadaverous features remained unmoved as he looked down at Thom, even though they had not seen each other in many years. Thom gave a small wave of his hand through the windscreen, perhaps expecting a warm – all right, a warm*ish* – acknowledgement, but none was forthcoming.

Hartgrove – not even Hugo knew his first name – no longer wore the standard butler's uniform of black coat over pinstripe trousers and grey waistcoat that Thom remembered so well – something of an anachronism in this day and age, he considered, and perhaps even then, when Thom was a boy – but instead was attired in a three-buttoned charcoal-coloured suit that appeared just one size too large for him. Even the top of his white shirt collar overlapped where the tie knot squeezed it tight around his scrawny neck.

'Good to see you too,' Thom muttered under his breath.

Hugo had already yanked open the Jeep's door and was reaching in to take Thom's elbow.

'Hey, I'm not an invalid,' he protested with a smile. Because he was tired, Thom had to give thought to releasing the steering wheel with his left hand: gripping objects was no longer a problem after months of physical rehabilitation, but sometimes – particularly when he was weary – releasing them could still be something to think about. He eased himself out of the vehicle, allowing his friend to keep his grip on his arm out of appreciation for the concern. Turning back, he pulled a walking-stick from the passenger side.

'Oh no? Not an invalid? So what's this then?' Hugo regarded the cane with undisguised regret in his watery brown eyes. 'Mind you, chum, I expected you to be on crutches.'

Thom gave a short laugh. 'Look, I've told you more than once that I'm fine. The first few days after the stroke were tricky – or so they tell me; I was pretty much out of it – but I'm making good progress, and that's official. And don't forget, I've had almost four months of rehab.'

'Yes, yes, of course. All the same, you're not quite a hundred per cent, otherwise you wouldn't need all this convalescence.'

'Rest, not convalescence. And the stick's only because my left leg gets tired easily and tends to go a bit wobbly.'

'Call it what you like, dear one, but a haemorrhage to the old brain-box is hardly a couple of aspirins and a few days in bed stuff.' Hugo had let go of Thom's elbow and stood with a hand on his hip, one knee bent forward, an effeminate pose he adopted sometimes merely for effect. Even his voice rose a nannyish octave that went with the stance.

Thom chuckled. 'That pose is beginning to look natural on you Hugo,' he warned.

But there was nothing prissy about his friend, even though he often enjoyed acting that way. Hugo was just below average height, stocky, with a paunch that was a little more overhanging than the last time Thom had seen it. He remembered Hugo arriving at the hospital a day after the stroke had almost snuffed his light, Hugo with metaphorical cheque in hand ('the very best for you, Thom, the finest specialist money can buy') and a scared, haunted look on his sweat-shined chubby face. His light curly hair – springy, golden locks when he was a boy – was already thinning, patches of pink scalp showing through like the lighter mottles on the sandstone wall behind him. He wore an unbuttoned camel waistcoat over a pale blue open-necked cotton shirt; red braces supporting grey flannel trousers (Thom caught a glimpse of them every time his friend breathed out and the parting in the waistcoat expanded) that bagged around his ankles. The turn-ups were snaggled over incongruous, stained Timberland boots. The hurried descent of Bracken's stone steps had left him a little breathless and the swollen pouches under his eyes indicated either lack of sleep or too-frequent alcohol binges (he wondered if his old friend was still on the absinthe). Same old Hugo, Thom mused: out of condition, out of style, and probably still out of a proper job.

By profession, Hugo Bleeth had been a Lloyd's underwriter, occupying a 'box' at the insurance corporation's Lime Street headquarters until his unwitting (?) involvement in the great mid-eighties insurance scandal had scuppered his career before it had properly begun.

Without warning, Hugo threw his arms around him in an embrace that squeezed breath from his lungs.

'So, so *bloody* good to see you!' he all but exclaimed in Thom's ear. 'I was worried, old mate, I don't mind telling you now. You looked so deathly lying there in the hospital bed. Could hardly believe my own eyes – I mean, when we had our reunion drink the week before, you looked marvellous. Tip-top, in fact.'

As his friend prattled on, Thom noticed Hartgrove over Hugo's shoulder: the manservant was staring down at them, face an expressionless mask, but his pale eyes as hard as flint. As a boy, Thom had always been wary of the man – no, he'd been plain bloody frightened of him – with his cadaverous features and long, skinny, dry neck emerging from stooped shoulders, and the dark tones of his uniform, that made him look like some human vulture. Thom always seemed to be catching Hartgrove watching him with those pale, cold eyes, watching him as though resenting his presence in the Big House, this tutor's son, who would have been a pauper were it not for the munificence of his master. Perhaps he had been waiting to catch Thom slipping some tiny ornament or one of Hugo's toys into his pocket. Perhaps he thought Thom might soil the furniture.

Despite the passage of time, Thom felt a familiar shiver run through him. With some deliberation, he managed to divert his attention.

'Hey, c'mon Hugo, you're going mushy on me,' he said through tight lips.

Hugo immediately broke away and grinned. 'Can't help it. It's just so . . . so . . .'

'Bloody good to see me,' Thom finished for him.

'Right.' Hugo lightly punched his shoulder.

Thom looked up at the house again, but this time avoiding the gaze of the sombre manservant, who still loitered at the top of the steps. His eyes swept up towards the rooftop and the house, with its dark windows and tall, jutting bays, seemed to loom over him.

'How is he, Hugo?'

Hugo glanced back, following Thom's gaze. 'Not so good. Some days Father perks up a little, others . . . well, other days he seems to sink as far as a person can go without actually dying. Even in these advanced times nothing much can be done for a diseased heart and I'm afraid the trauma of a transplant would kill him off more quickly in his present weak condition. Sod's law, it seems. He's not strong enough to withstand the op, but without it his health will never improve. Perhaps if they'd caught it sooner things might be different. As you know, the old boy has never been in what you might call mint condition, so we failed to notice the change in him right away . . .' Hugo's voice trailed off as though it was too upsetting to continue.

For as long as Thom could remember, Hugo's father, Sir Russell Bleeth, had been a figure to revere. His sharp manner and equally sharp temper had always made the young Thom nervous, and the man's overbearing presence seemed to govern Castle Bracken even when he was absent from the place. The deaths of his first, then second wife, later followed by the loss of his eldest son, who while serving as a British Army officer in Belfast had been blown to pieces by an IRA bomb before Thom was born, may have contributed to his aloofness, but only Hugo would ever talk to Thom of these tragic events; others in the Bleeth employ, including his mother, Bethan, were discreet to the point of secrecy where these tragedies were concerned.

Now Sir Russell had an illness that would eventually finish him off and, although Thom had never had any fondness for the man – how was it possible to like someone you feared so much? – he could not help the sadness that spoiled his mood.

'He should be in a hospital, where they can take care of him properly, ease his pain for him.' Thom lowered his gaze to Hugo, who remained looking upwards.

'You think we haven't tried? He won't leave his eyrie.' Hugo said with such regret in his voice that Thom thought his friend might start to weep. 'Lord knows I've begged him, but, well you know how stubborn he is . . . He loves it up there because he can view everything he owns right there from his bed. The room was probably designed for that very purpose, just so the original lord of the manor could indulge his own vanity. I never imagined it would become my father's death chamber.' He turned back to Thom and gave a brisk shake of his head as if to shed the mood. 'He moderates the worst of his pain himself with an intravenous morphine drip controlled by a button at his side, but it can do strange things to him. Sometimes he raves or speaks of odd things. He also insists that before he is buried, his throat is cut, just to be sure he's dead. He has a morbid fear of being buried alive.' Hugo shrugged. 'It's a matter of time, Thom, but let's not dwell on it today. We should be celebrating the wanderer's return.'

He managed a smile and allowed his pleasure to reassert itself, a seemingly inherent ability that Thom had often wished he, himself, possessed. 'How about a beer, or something stronger? You *must* have a thirst after your long drive.'

Thom didn't like to tell his friend that following his stroke he had lost much of his appetite for alcohol.

'Thanks, but no,' he said, clasping Hugo's shoulder with an appreciative hand, anxious not to offend. 'I'd kinda like to get to the cottage and settle in. We can catch up tomorrow.'

'Or later tonight?' Hugo suggested hopefully.

'We'll see. I'm not quite up to strength yet and as you say, it's been a long drive.'

'Well . . . okay. But at least let me get Hartgrove to drive you over and help you unpack.'

Thom glanced at the manservant, who still watched from the top step. 'You kidding?'

They both grinned at each other knowingly.

'You know what I'd really like to do?' Thom said. 'I'd like to walk from here. It's funny, but that was all I dreamt of when I was laid up in hospital, recovering from the . . .' he hated the word '. . . from, the, uh, stroke. I just wanted to stroll through the woods again, you know? Come up on the cottage as I remembered it.'

'Alone?'

Thom nodded.

'Understand perfectly, old son. If that's your wish . . .'

There was no direct road suitable for vehicles to Little Bracken; to take the Jeep would mean going back to the main road and finding the rutted track that led directly to it.

'Leave the Jeep and I'll get old Eric to drive it over later. It'll give you time to get used to the place again.'

Eric Pimlet along with Hartgrove and Mrs Boxley, the cook who came in once a day from the nearby village of Much Beddow to serve lunch and evening meals, were the manor house's only permanent staff; gardeners and cleaners were employed on a once-a-week basis nowadays.

'It'll be good to see old Eric again,' Thom said.

'I'm sure he'll be pleased to see you, too. Now look, I've had your larder filled with essentials, plus a few goodies you'll like. And someone will pop over from time to time to help keep you stocked up. Unfortunately, I haven't had the phone line switched back on yet, but I can—'

'No need.' Thom patted a jacket pocket. 'I've got my mobile.'

'Hmn ... reception's not always that good in this part of the world, but I can get Eric to look in on you every morning.'

'Not necessary, Hugo. I'll be fine – honestly. The doctors haven't quite given me the all-clear yet, but they're amazed at my progress. Besides, I'll have a physio working me over three times a week in the cottage to make sure I get back to strength. A kind of buy-your-own-torture scheme that the doctors insist upon.'

'Well, if you're sure ...'

'Hugo, believe me, I am.' Thom reached out to his friend's shoulder again. 'Listen, you've been great. You know I appreciate all you've done.'

Hugo's face reddened and for a second or two his already watery eyes became even more liquid. He cleared his throat and looked towards the distant woodlands.

'Don't mention it, Thom,' he said, a little hoarsely. 'We've been pals a long time ...'

He left it at that and Thom grinned. 'Who else would put up with you?' Thom said, dropping his hand away. He, too, looked towards the lush woodlands in the distance. 'Best be on my way. I've been looking forward to this.'

'I can imagine, laid up in hospital like that. You still love the old place, don't you, Thom?'

He hesitated. 'I'm not sure if that's true. There was a time when I hated it.'

'When Bethan . . .? Hugo brought himself to a halt. Insensitive though he could be sometimes, even Hugo understood how hard the premature loss of his mother had hit Thom all those years ago; so hard, in fact, the grief had not yet faded entirely. He reached into his trouser pocket and drew out a long, worn iron key, which he thrust at Thom. Its rounded head was made up of three simple, flat circles resembling a metal shamrock. The bit was hidden behind Hugo's fleshy fingers, but Thom easily remembered the solid plain pattern of its ward cuts.

Thom reached for the key and, as he did so, felt a frisson of . . . of what? He couldn't be sure. Excitement? Yes, there was that, but there was something else also. Relief? Yes, that too. But this, paradoxically, was mixed with . . . it couldn't be fear, could it? No, not quite that. Apprehension was more correct. For just a moment, he had experienced a fluttery nervousness in his stomach, paranoid butterflies with hard-edged wings. Could he really be nervous of going back to the home he had loved so much as a child? Was it the thought of its emptiness, the absence of the mother he had lost so many years ago? Since the illness Thom had realized that his emotions were more frail, that tears seemed never far away, and he had assumed it was because of a barely suppressed self-pity. Well, maybe it was exactly that. Yet this . . . this *apprehension* . . . seemed to emanate from outside himself, as though it tainted the very air between the two outstretched hands.

Then he had the long key in his palm and the disquiet dissolved, was merely a passing sensation.

The key seemed to become warm against his flesh as he

33

looked at it and something inside him . . . his spirit? . . . lifted once more. Bemused, he smiled at Hugo.

'It's good to be back,' he said.

And at that time, he honestly meant it.

# Chapter : Third

# A WALK THROUGH THE WOODS

H E WALKED away from the Big House, descending the gentle slope to the wide path that led towards the river and concentrating on keeping his left foot from turning inwards, another symptom of the damage he had suffered. At this stage, his walking-cane was merely a prop; before he completed the journey to the cottage, however, and his left leg was even more wearied, it would become a necessity. Half-way down the hill he turned to see Hugo still watching him, hands in his pockets, the distance too far to read his expression. He waved the stick and his friend raised an arm to wriggle his plump fingers in response. Thom's smile faltered when he noticed Hartgrove – Bones – remained by the front door, as still and watchful as a black bird of prey. Jesus, what was it about the man that made his flesh creep? Was it the incident in the cellar? Was that why he still had nightmares about the man? With an effort, Thom dismissed the manservant from his mind and went on his way.

He soon reached another path that entered a leafy tunnel

and that would take him to the old stone bridge crossing the river. A coolness settled over his shoulders, the sun's rays barely penetrating the thick ceiling of leaves; a breeze came off the fast-flowing river to meet him. Once, long ago, he had relished the sudden drop in temperature when his mother had brought him across the great sunshine-filled meadow (didn't the sun always shine its hardest when you were little?) from the opposite direction, where she had pointed out insects and grey butterflies barely visible to the human eye, flowers with exotic names, and even animal droppings, evidence of creatures who preferred to hide from view; now though, the coolness was almost unpleasant, for it seemed to freeze the perspiration on his brow, and today the river sounded angry rather than swift.

The short straight bridge had been built from greystone soon after Castle Bracken was finished, and the mortar had become either crumbly or filled with moss; a greenness tainted the stone, deeper near the water that rose and faded wash-like as it reached the jutting parapet. Thom paused towards the middle and peered down into the agitated foam below, its rush caused by a sudden dip in levels beneath the dark arch itself, a singular rapid that increased the river's flow. He thought of the many times he and Bethan – how his heart softly ached for her – had lingered at this same spot as she had dropped a leaf or small twig into the froth and they had watched it being washed downstream, a fragile craft tossed and swirled by the currents, Thom laughing and pointing a finger, Bethan smiling indulgently. He smiled now, seeing in his mind's eye the valiant little vessel fighting against the bullying waters, bobbing to the surface again and again every time it was immersed, finally becoming too far away to see any more. The air was always damp here on the bridge no matter how bright the sun, invisible droplets of moisture filling the shade offered by the trees and shrubbery on either bank. Indeed, long twisting branches reached across the river to meet their counterparts on the other side, leafy fingers intertwining so that the span was in a permanent gloom, even the winter sun finding it difficult to penetrate the naked but dense interlacing.

Pushing himself away from the wall by his elbows, Thom moved on, following the wide track through the wooded area on the far side of the bridge, the sound of the river's flow receding behind him, the air gradually warming with each step he took until the trees ended and he was confronted by a rickety wooden gate and fence. The barrier was there to keep in the deer, a few horses, and other, less obvious, animal life that wandered or skipped the meadows and pastures beyond. The gate was kept shut by a simple but heavy metal latch.

Again he lingered, taking time to view the broad expanse of coarse, browning grass beyond, searching towards the thick fringes of woodland on the other side, and his spirit lifted afresh, something within escaping its shell to soar high into the deep summer sky. His smile became a grin and his breath became an appreciative murmur.

He quickly pressed down on the latch, leaning hard to disengage it, and then he was through, carefully closing the gate after him. Wary of the grass snakes that always appeared to be in abundance in this particular field, he strode purposefully into the longish grass, walking-stick held under his arm, his leg steady enough. He suddenly felt happier than at any other time since the stroke, including when he had received the good news that, if he was careful – cut out the smokes, easy on the booze – and if he obeyed and worked with the therapist, then there should be no recurrence, he would be just fine. Thom felt oddly unburdened, as free as he had been as a boy, chasing through this same meadow, clapping his hands and giggling at butterflies or startled rabbits, his mother's caring eyes on him at all times. Perhaps he sensed that same protection now; maybe he was reminded of a glorious era when he was cherished and guarded, when he was invincible against the bad things; a time when his soul was light and his mind untroubled, his young body bothered neither by weakness nor pain.

It stayed with him for a while, this dreamy glow; stayed with him until he approached the woods and his leg began to ache.

---

It was as if he were entering another world, a hushed world, a world that was shaded and cool, shafts of sunlight angling through its twilight in long, shimmering beams, the silence only occasionally interrupted by a falling branch somewhere out of sight, or a rustle of undergrowth as some hidden animal, aware of his presence, broke for home. Thom followed the path he and Bethan and all past visitors to Little Bracken, from one century to the next, had taken. There were other paths running through the woods, not as obvious as this one, and as a boy he had explored most of them; he wondered now how many such tracks had been lost to time and neglect, untrodden and so reclaimed by the forest. Did any one walk these woods anymore? Who would bother unless they knew of its 'magic', the serenity within? But then, who would have access anyway? Eric Pimlet, of course; it was part of his job. But Thom could not imagine old Bones venturing into such wilderness. Nor Hugo – certainly *not* Hugo. No nature-lover he, nor one to enjoy strenuous exercise – *any* exercise, for that matter. And Sir Russell had been too frail for years and was now too ill.

It was a waste and a shame; but he was glad, for it meant that the little kingdom belonged to him alone. Thom was aware that this was a fancy, but the notion was not new to him, it was something in which he had *always* indulged since the early days of running through the trees, surrounding himself with imaginary friends, invisible beings who were never too tired or too busy to play.

Even then he was aware that he was considered an odd,

solitary child, whose only real companion was Hugo Bleeth. But Hugo was older and under Bethan's tutelage; he was also the boss's son and Thom had constantly been reminded he was to be treated as such (though never by Hugo, himself). But Thom – and his mother – knew better. He had never been lonely here, not when imagination and fantasy were his true friends. Or perhaps, his *mentors*. It was they who had given him a life that was far from empty, a time when his thoughts were boundless, his imageries true. And the woodland, itself, had invoked its own treasures, *mind* treasures, which could be explored and experienced, and relished and *owned*. For an instant – and only an instant – the childhood memories became a reality, became *now*, and he felt the same excitement, the same soaring blissfulness that could only come from a special kind of innocence and a willingness to believe.

A nightingale, singing somewhere deep within the woods, diverted his attention for a moment and the sweet call was not an interruption to his thoughts but somehow an endorsement of the remembered happiness. Thom listened a while, then pressed on, even keener to reach his old home.

He passed by shade-loving flowers along the side of the trail, sanicle, archangel, yellow pimpernel, flora that usually waited for late summer to bloom, but here – as ever – they had arrived early. He heard the low pitch of warblers singing to each other, while a blackcap swooped down into a glade off to his right, disappearing briefly into a tangle of hawthorn and rooting around until it found the insect noticed from the air. A flurry of wings took the bird back above the treetops. Because of his profession, Thom took a more than usual interest in the trees themselves, noting their condition, their texture and robustness, the slight 'sheen' of the silver birch, taking pleasure in naming aloud each variety.

He came upon a huge oak, one easily remembered because of its age and sheer scariness. Its gnarled bark seemed to contain images, carvings that were not quite discernible but that resembled grotesque, twisted figures and tortured faces; its great thick branches spread outwards as if ready to grab anything that might pass by. To allay his fear, Bethan had explained that such ancient trees were invaluable in nature, for they supported the perfect life cycle: their leaves, bark, acorns eaten by animals and insects, which in turn were prey to others; their remains passed on as droppings or simply discarded to be broken down by bacteria and so replenishing the earth itself. A fine system, unless you were first in the chain. The big old oak also provided the perfect home for small creatures – animals, insects and birds – who lived inside the trunk or the deep channels of its bark, or simply nested among the boughs.

He went on, delighting in the colours along the way, their random display exhilarating, the perfumes almost intoxicating, and, for a time, the trauma of the last few months was completely forgotten. But soon – too soon – his aching leg began to weary and a numbness began to spread down his arm like a creeping frost. Thom knew he was abusing his weakened body, ignoring the doctors' advice to take things easy for a while, to exercise every day but *not* to overdo it; and after months of therapy, he still needed time to build up his strength and impatience could be his worst enemy. That very day he had driven all the way from London and, although the left side of his body had barely come into play, the journey had taken its toll. Then to walk from the Big House to the cottage (not on a whim, it had to be said, but on a self-promise) might have been pushing himself too far. Nevertheless, he did not regret his decision, even if his breathing was becoming a little laboured and he had consciously to lift his left foot from the ground, a sweat beginning to break out on his forehead once more: the air was too fresh and scented, the forest and its flora too beautiful, for him to worry over fatigue and physical discomfort.

In a clearing ahead he saw the jagged trunk of a tree that had been struck by lightning, its base still firm in the ground but rising like a blackened spire pointing darkly towards the sky. The top half lay by its side, leafless branches withered and dry. There were other fallen trees in the forest, but this one struck Thom as particularly unsightly, as though the drama of its felling had left its sickly aura. He wondered if he bore a similar aura, the suddenness and fierceness of the attack on his own body similar in its way to the lightning strike on the tree. No. He was still alive and the tree was dead. Such comparison was as foolish as it was self-pitying. He shrugged off the idea, only too aware of his persistently delicate emotional state.

Leaf mulch beneath his feet softened his footsteps, yet still his left leg seemed unusually heavy. The cane's tip sank further into the earth each time he leaned on it, an indication of his increasing dependency. When he spied another toppled tree trunk close by the path, this one nothing more than a thick log obviously undisturbed for many a year, the scars where branches had been lopped off covered by lichen, he decided to rest awhile. Trudging through long grass, he made his way over to the natural bench and sat down.

The faint challenge of a cuckoo came to him from somewhere in the heart of the woodland. A breeze shifted through leaves overhead. Something small, perhaps an acorn from a nearby oak, dropped to the forest floor, the sound soft but singular in the near-silence. And then another noise, one he did not recognize, as faint as the cuckoo's call, yet closer.

Thom held his breath and listened. Was it in his own imagination? It wasn't the common sound of the forest, it was neither a bird, nor an animal – yet inexplicably, it seemed natural enough to the environment. The noise stopped, but he continued to hold his breath.

It began again, a soft . . . whistling. A high-pitched, almost gentle . . . whistling-ringing.

He turned towards the sound, puzzled, expectant, and saw nothing. That is, he saw nothing unusual. The woods were perfectly still. Normal.

The queer yet sweet whistling-ringing persisted, but he could not recognize its source: it was somehow melodious, but with no fixed tune, like tiny faraway wind chimes caught in a draught. It was like nothing he had ever heard before. And yet . . . and yet it seemed familiar to him, as though it might have originated from some forgotten dream. Then it occurred to him that this was not a noise at all, but some kind of weird, unreal tintinnabulation that emanated from within his inner ear, a sensation rather than a real sound. Another belated surprise thrown at him by the stroke, blood-flow through the ears distorting the vibrations that are turned into the electrical impulses we know as sound? It wouldn't have surprised him – it wouldn't be the last nasty shock the illness had in store for him, no matter how well he was progressing, he was sure of that.

He mentally kicked himself. Give it up, he silently chastised, you can't blame everything on the stroke. Some things in life just happen naturally, and with no dire consequences. A peculiar whistling-ringing in his ears was nothing to get stressed about. It would pass. How many times in his life had he thought he'd developed tinnitus before, only for it to disappear again in less than a minute?

Then a strange thought occurred and he had no idea where it had sprung from: maybe this noise was something that connected with the subconscious before it reached the conscious; maybe it was only a vibration that gave off a peculiar sound. For some reason, the theory was perfectly rational to him at that moment. Even so, it had to have a source . . .

Eyes narrowing, he peered into the thicket from where the – now he had no idea of what to call it, so settled for his first recognition – the *whistling-ringing* appeared to emanate. It could have been in his own mind, or a breeze might have been the cause, but were the leaves shivering? Remaining on the log, he leaned forward and realized that they truly were disturbed and in a way that no air current could sustain, for the thicket quivered in a regular rhythm while nothing else in the area moved at all.

The first of the tiny lights appeared.

Initially, he reasoned that they were fireflies, but common sense and country wisdom told him that such creatures were only visible at twilight or night-time; besides, such insects were more prevalent on the Continent that in England, so it would have been a doubly rare occurrence. And anyway, the many glows from these lights were different from anything he had ever before witnessed. They seemed to range through an unusual spectrum, from bright silver to violet, from white to pale green, iridescent and twinkling as though their image could not be maintained; nor did they move in the way insects might, for their flight was swift and smooth, but by no means erratic.

Thom realized he was still holding his breath and he let it go in one long astonished rush. Even from this distance and in bright sunlight – the thicket stood in the centre of the glade – the dancing lights sparkled. There were at least five – no, six, no, now there were *seven* of them – and they winked in and out of his vision, little glimmerings as bright as diamonds and looking as delicate as snowflakes. Forgetting his heavy leg and numbed arm for the moment, he slowly began to rise, afraid any sudden movement might frighten these skittish creatures away – or spoil the illusion, for an illusion they might well be. But still they flitted in and out of the leaves, occasionally alighting on one as an insect might rest on a smooth surface. Cautiously, taking each step with great care, he moved towards the phenomena, his breath held once more within a tight chest.

The sounds (for he suddenly understood that there were many high-pitched whistling-ringings making up the whole) were the equivalent of the collective hum of bees, and the colours had become even more diverse – blues, yellows, greens, purples and red, all dazzling to his eyes. He thought they might be some minute and uncommon breed of luminescent butterfly, but the shapes were too indistinct and swift to tell. Their noise became a light but busy clamour inside his head as amazement gripped him. His gaze became intense, his footsteps faltered . . .

He hadn't noticed the rut in the ground, its edge raised only slightly but enough to catch his left foot, which by now had become difficult to raise without conscious effort. He stumbled forward, his weakened leg giving way, the cane unable to help him keep his balance. Thom fell, landing on hands and knees on the mulchy forest floor, mercifully unhurt, but with the wind knocked from him in a surprised cry.

When he raised his head again to look, the thicket was just a thicket, the leaves empty and unmoving in the sunlight. The images were gone. And so was the sound.

# Chapter : Fourth

## LITTLE BRACKEN

THE BLUEBELLS were a surprise. Normally they would bloom from late April to early June, but here they were in late July, stretching across the path that had widened into a sun-dappled clearing.

Thom scarcely wondered about the late blooming, for he could only gaze towards the building beyond. Little Bracken, standing in the centre of the glade, was just as he remembered, a sandstoned, octagonal-shaped, two-storey building, a turret – this, too, eight-sided – rising beside it, pointed bell-tower at its top like an open umbrella beneath a clear blue sky. This turret would have been a ridiculous appendage to such a small building had it not been skilfully integrated into the whole structure and made from the same red sandstone, the square, leaded windows with frames of grey stone copying those of the main section. It was as if the architect responsible for the grim Castle Bracken had decided to design its very antithesis, a glorious summerhouse (or folly) that resembled a miniature faerytale castle. Towards the late sixteenth century such banqueting towers, built at a distance from the main house, were extremely popular among wealthy landowners, and Sir Edward Bracken had been no exception to the trend: he had commissioned Little Bracken for the purpose of entertaining guests after their main meal at Castle Bracken, having them driven to the summerhouse by coach or, if the weather was clement, encouraging them to make the journey on foot (what better way to renew the appetite for the treats to come?), there to indulge in desserts usually comprising sweetmeats, fancy sugar moulds, fruits, and spiced wines. Afterwards they might take in the panoramic views over the woodland from the *banquet's* flat, balustraded roof.

It was rumoured that in later years, various lords of the manor kept their mistresses at Little Bracken, away from their poor long-suffering, yet mostly resigned, wives, out of sight, but close enough for frequent visits. Latterly, estate workers had used the place as a tied cottage, but then it had lain empty for many, many years until Bethan Kindred, tutor to Sir Russell Bleeth's somewhat dim-witted youngest son, Hugo, had taken up residence, eventually giving birth to her own son there.

Memories flooded back to Thom as he stood there and were almost overwhelming: skipping ahead of Bethan through the little flowerbeds either side of the short, flag-stoned path, laughing as she called out to him to wait for her, he might get lost (even though she knew he would never lose himself in this beloved woodland that he knew so well). He recalled the animals – deer, squirrels, rabbits, and even shy hedgehogs – that would wait by the front door or beneath a window, lingering there until receiving a scrap of food or just attention; the birds that settled on the windows-ills and doorstep, chirping for cake crumbs and pieces of bread.

Thom felt suddenly dizzy as the thoughts assailed him.

Dark winter nights, huddled around an open log fire,

front scorched, back frozen, while his mother read adventure stories or told him of nature, sometimes explaining the ways of a puzzling world or just singing simple songs in her sweet soft voice; answering all his questions, save one – the mystery of his absent father; acting out little plays to each other, playing charades, giggling over silly verses and rhymes. The memories came, faster and faster, little snatches, picture snippets, all joyful but none staying long in his mind. He saw faces, always fleeting, never focused long enough to register, and there was merriment and laughter, all the things that were good, so that a warm flush filled his body, touched his heart . . .

He reached out and held a branch to steady himself as more and more thoughts threatened to engulf him and his head began to spin. The sensation soon passed, leaving him to wonder at the mental barrage and its effect; maybe physical tiredness had made it difficult for his brain to cope with the overload. He needed to rest, catch his breath again. He needed to calm himself.

Leaning heavily on the cane, he approached Little Bracken, glancing up at the rooftop as he did so. He had the feeling of being observed, so was not surprised to see the magpie watching him from the thick rail of the stone parapet.

Thom had never warmed to the crow family as a species, but for some reason among them he particularly disliked the magpie, despite its sleek shape and beautiful black and white plumage and the glossy tail that in certain lights shone like a rainbow. The magpie had always been regarded as a bird of bad omen by countryfolk who, on sight of one – 'one for sorrow, two for joy' – would spit three times over their right shoulder and say: 'Devil, Devil, I defy thee.' All nonsense, the towny in Thom told himself, yet he still felt uneasy under its black-eyed gaze. Perhaps it was because he knew there was something devious about its kind, who stole eggs from other birds and sometimes took away the nestlings.

Thom approached the big, green-painted door to the

47

cottage, a stained and rusted (and rarely used in his childhood because the door was always open in daytime) bell
on the wall next to it, reaching into his jacket pocket for
the long key that Hugo had given him as he did so. It lay
heavy in the palm of his hand and felt warm to the touch, as
though the heat of the day had seeped through the material
of his jacket to take the chill from the metal. Holding the
flat shamrock-shaped head between thumb and crooked
finger, he pushed it into the door's lock and turned it to the
right.

Nothing happened. It felt as if the key were in a void, an
empty space that offered no resistance, the long shaft turning
effortlessly but uselessly. Round, and round again; the lock
did not catch, the door did not open.

Thom withdrew the key and stared at the bit as if it
might reveal the problem. He tried the lock again.

And felt heat run through the warm metal into his
fingers, then up as far as his wrist. The bit caught, the catch
clicked.

The door opened.

⁂

It opened smoothly. No creaks, no expected squealing of
rusty hinges. A nice, easy movement, as if the painted oak
door were gliding weightlessly on oiled bearings.

A stale and malodorous wave of air swept past him as
though it had been waiting centuries to make its escape,
rushing out into the freshness behind him, submission to
something purer the price of release. Thom stepped back,
an involuntary reaction to an unexpected and physically
intangible pressure. The stink of decay and waiting was
quickly gone, the remnants chased away by the sweet air
that now wafted through the open doorway. Its fresh,
scented breath revived further childhood memories, for

the smell, itself, *was* part of his childhood: nature's own fragrance, a hint of Bethan, the aroma of a house filled with wild flowers and traces of other, unnameable balms and bouquets. But this time, mindful of the dizziness before, he did not allow such tumbling thoughts to occupy his mind: he confined them to distant quarters.

Thom took his first step for many a year inside Little Bracken, pausing a while on the threshold, leaning forward and quickly scanning the interior as if expecting to find some biding intruder inside.

He saw the oak table in the middle of the room, its sturdy legs and round top etched with marks and writing that Bethan had encouraged the young Thom to make, for they – the scratched names, dates, even the games such as hangman and noughts and crosses, together with little clumsily rendered drawings – gave the wood an extra dimension, turned it into a receptacle for Thom's earliest energies, his imagination, his raw but enthusiastic carvings, such efforts absorbed by grain and fibre and sealed within to create a scrapbook of scratchings, a wooden time-capsule of early impressions.

He ventured further into the room to stand immobile, as if in awe, taking it all in: the large, pine dresser pressed against the whitewashed wall to his left, its long shelves bereft of the delicately patterned crockery he remembered so well, now replaced by plain, functional plates and dishes and an equally plain set of cups and saucers. A couple of striped mugs provided the only colour.

The black, iron range that had once served as oven, grill, hotplate – even though there was an elderly, enamel-chipped electric cooker standing at the end of kitchen units almost opposite – and fireplace was set into the broad soot-stained chimney-breast, metal saucepans and other cooking utensils cluttering its shadowed top. (He noticed that the fire had been laid with kindling and small, chopped logs, presumably by old Eric, who in the past had always taken a reserved but kindly interest in the welfare of the boy and his mother. A dusty bucket of slow-burning coal rested in the hearth itself.)

The bookshelves on either side of the chimney-breast, built into the slants of the octagonal-shaped walls with timber from the forest were filled with weary-looking titles that mostly had to do with nature and gardening, poetry and travel books; the lower reaches, however, were stacked with tales of adventure and olden-time chivalry, while at the very top were ancient leather-bound editions, dreary-looking tomes that had no appeal to a young boy who could not even reach that high.

The deep, old-fashioned porcelain sink, beneath one of the arched windows that framed the woodland beyond, was big enough for him to have been bathed in when he was very small, solid enough for him to have stood in and flannelled himself down when he was a little older, the makeshift tub filled with water from saucepans warmed on the nearby range. (With regard to at least some modernity, an electric water-heater had been fitted over the wooden draining board, its thin, metal arm and spout swung over the sink itself, and he fondly remembered the day it had been installed, his and Bethan's delight at their bold advance so late into the twentieth century. Now he wondered at how sparse their living conditions had been – and how gloriously cosy they were.) He was still smiling as he took in more details, finding himself both amused and bemused. No central heating here; no TV, either, just an elderly radio that had hissed and squawked with atmospherics (atmos-hysterics, Bethan had called them). And no telephone for a long while, no car (shopping meant a bus ride into Much Beddow), and scarcely any money (Bethan's tuition fees for Hugo had been minimal, for Sir Russell considered rent-free accommodation plus the bird and rabbit regularly shot and delivered by Eric Pimlet added to the weekly wage as remuneration enough).

Yet the penury, if it could be called that, hardly mattered – *no*, it mattered *not* at all. They had been happy together, Thom and his mother, and although he had sometimes seen sadness in her face, a sudden unannounced melancholy in her eyes, most of their days had been filled with the magic of their environment and the simple pleasure of being alive. They were wonderful, safe times, when love and isolation had been both his security and his sanctuary.

How cruel then, when it was all snatched away.

Thom's expression darkened and he immediately pushed this last potentially lachrymose thought away: he'd endured enough self-imposed self-pity over the past few months to last a lifetime. Time to move on, live for today. Then why the return to Little Bracken? He straightened his shoulders. To convalesce, why else? And to get some of that happiness back into his life.

He smiled again, turning around on the quarry-tiled floor, muddied boots scuffing the stone, taking it all in one more time. It was beginning to work already. Joy was soaking through his very skin; a lightness was filling his whole being.

Thom stopped turning and closed his eyes. He allowed the relief to flood his senses.

---

Using his right hand, he lifted the iron latch to the interior door, this one as big as the front door itself, although unpainted, the grainy wood unpolished and interesting. The staircase beyond spiralled round the interior of the stunted tower that gave the cottage its unique appearance. It wound its way up to a landing outside the cottage's single bedroom before continuing another flight to the door that led out on to the flat lead-covered roof.

The space at the foot of the stairs contained a broom closet which also housed an electric meter and small boiler. Next to this, a tiny combined bathroom and toilet, whose tub, were fitted in directly beneath the winding stairs, was only long enough to sit upright in; a small basin with mirror above took what little room was left. Thom peeked in, pulling down on the hanging switch as he did so. The little room was filled with light, the abrupt environmental change paralysing a huge black spider that had found itself trapped in the bathtub. Even though his earliest years had been spent in the countryside where insects and spiders were part of everyday life, Thom could not help but shudder. He hated the buggers. Hated their long spindly legs that ran so scaringly fast, hated their furry bodies and malevolent eyes. Hated them for the evil thoughts he always imagined they were thinking.

In disgust and, he had to admit to himself, in fear, he reached for both taps and turned them on, then quickly grabbed the new-looking plastic lavatory cleaner someone had thoughtfully provided for his visit. He used the bristled end to push the spider into the whirlpool around the bath's plughole. The spider desperately tried to swim for it, but it was quickly sucked into the miniature maelstrom. To Thom's dismay, however, it was too big to be flushed through the gaps in the outlet's ring. The spider's cotton-thin legs scrabbled at the edges as its body wedged into one of the openings and irrationally – God, he knew he was being stupid – the sight caused him to panic. He had only meant to wash the spider away and prevent its return by placing the chained rubber plug on the outlet, but now he had to beat at the wriggling creature and push it through and the very thought made him feel physically sick. 'Wuss,' he accused himself and jabbed at the struggling spider with the brush. He fancied the creature was screaming, calling up at him to *stop, please, leave me alone, I'm only little*, and cursed his own overcharged imagination.

He paused from the pounding to turn the taps full on, intent on drowning the bloody thing if it wasn't already crushed to death, poking with the brush again and again until the soft, pulpy mess suddenly disappeared from view into the pipe, one of its black legs remaining stuck (or clinging?) like a pubic hair to the metal ring around the hole. To his relief, the stubborn limb soon followed the mashed body and Thom quickly hung the plug above the swirling water, then let it drop home lest the crushed spider minus one leg miraculously rise up again against the deluge.

'Bloody hell . . .' he whispered to himself as he leaned back against the bathroom wall, shaken by and ashamed of his panic. It was only a defenceless spider whose long skinny legs made it appear larger than it really was. What the hell was wrong with him? He was supposed to be a grown-up now, not some snivelling kid afraid of creepy-crawlies. No other such creatures, insects or beasts, had unduly disturbed him as a child – not even the occasional rat that might find its way into the house – but there had always been something about spiders that had turned his legs to jelly and sent his heart racing. His mother had often patiently explained that every creature had its part to play in nature, none of less value than the next, but the young Thom had never been truly convinced. Spiders had always remained abhorrent to him. He shuddered as he peeped over the edge of the bath, half-expecting to find the rubber plug wobbling in its metal setting as thin spider's legs pushed through from underneath . . . *Jesus, cut it out!*

Over-tired and over-wrought, he told himself. Get a grip.

Replacing the makeshift plastic bully-stick, he backed out of the bathroom, still eyeing the puddle of brownish water at the bottom of the tub, heart skipping a beat when a single air bubble escaped the side of the plug. The plug remained firmly in place though.

At another time he might have smiled at his own nervousness, but today wasn't the day: he was too vulnerable, his homecoming was too emotional. He closed the bathroom door and began to climb the creaky wooden stairs, his left hand brushing over the newel post, the thick trunk around which the staircase spiralled. More memories came with the touch and in his mind he was a child again, in a time when his knees rose high to mount the steps that were thin at one end, broad at the other, his small hand pressed against the circular newel for balance, his head tilted upwards to look into the shadows above: on the first floor landing, the door leading off to the bedroom he had shared with his mother, as big and sturdy as the two below, as if they all had come as a job lot; the leaded window set high in the curved wall, too high for him to look through unless he was on the stairs just past it, always a pot of bright seasonal flowers or a plant sitting on its oak sill . . .

There were no flowers and no plant there now, just an empty vase, one that was unfamiliar to him. He could see through the window as soon as he reached the first step beneath it.

The bedroom door was already open and he peered in without entering, noting that this, too, had hardly changed: the same oak four-poster bed, large enough to accommodate himself and his mother, the dark brown sideboard with separate mirror on top that served as a dressing-table for Bethan, the stone fireplace with its heavy duty wooden lintel, the six-panelled windows on three of the angled walls, these too, leaded, their number ensuring the room was always bright, even on the dullest of days. He didn't linger too long, for it was the rooftop with its panoramic views over the surrounding woodland that he wished to revisit most of all.

There were even more cracks and holes in the stair-boards than he remembered, some of those holes as large as old penny pieces, and he recalled shining torchlight down them all those years ago. Somehow the beams had never been able to penetrate the seemingly endless darkness, even though the backing board could not have been more than a foot away. It was eerie then, the thought of it eerie now.

Yet that kind of thing had been part of Little Bracken's fascination: its warmth in summer, when doors and windows could be left open all night, its winter coldness; its security and sometimes – *only* sometimes – its bleakness; its interesting nooks and crannies, built-in cupboards and bell-less belltower, places where a little boy could play hide-and-seek with an indulgent mother. Then there were the mysterious scrapes and bumps late at night, the distant yet somehow close-by sounds that would wake him from sleep, or interrupt one of Bethan's night-time stories as he lay by her side in the broad four-poster bed they shared, noises that would cause his eyes to widen and his shoulders to stiffen. Always his mother would give a little laugh at his fear, or perhaps just smile as she cuddled him close and told him there was never, *ever*, anything to be afraid of, not in this place, and not with her beside him. And sometimes, when he pulled away to look at her face for extra reassurance, her soft features rendered even softer by the candlelight she always kept burning through the night on the mantelshelf opposite, he would catch a certain knowing look in her light-blue eyes, as if she was only too aware of the sound's cause and it secretly amused her. She would explain it was probably a woodmouse rummaging around the kitchen below, or some other little creature from the forest that had found its way inside the cottage, or perhaps a bird or bat settling down in the eaves of the belltower's roof. Even the quiet clank of pot against pan, or the shifting of something across a worktop or table below failed to alarm her, and her unshakeable confidence would soon draw him in so that he was no longer afraid. Never once, though, did he suggest they go down to investigate, and never once did his mother show any curiosity herself.

Thom resumed the climb, boards creaking noisily beneath his feet. Normally, spiral staircases in castles and fortresses twisted to the right so that soldiers defending their ground had room to swing swords or thrust pikestaffs at advancing intruders whose own sword arms were disadvantaged, but Little Bracken's original architect obviously had only peaceful purposes in mind when he designed the *banquet* and its copycat tower, hence these stairs turned to the left. However, that non-military consideration had not prevented the boy Thom from engaging imaginary foes in battle there, his own short reach and wooden weapon unencumbered by the vagaries of architecture, the invisible villains easily beaten back by his ferocious attack.

He was smiling yet again as he quickly reached the short landing where the newel post ended and two thick horizontal rails served as a balustrade. Directly above him was the empty – save for stout crossbeams – conical-shaped space beneath the lead apex which, in truth, was never meant to house a bell. To his right on the landing was another door, this one considerably smaller than those below, which opened out on to the cottage's roof, and Thom lifted the latch, then pushed outwards.

The breeze hit him instantly, refreshing him and clearing the mustiness (compliments of the disused cottage) from his nose. Before he had even stepped through he was dazzled not just by sunlight, but by the view itself, and he gave a small gasp of pleasure.

It was still as beautiful as he remembered; time had neither enhanced nor diminished the reality. The thousand hues of green were the same, the pale blueness of the distant, low hills was unchanged, the sheer vastness of the clear, open sky was just as impressive.

He walked out on to the flat rooftop, pausing each time to lift his left foot over the lead ridges, and approached the thick open stone balustrade that ran round seven sides of the octagonal deck, the tower wall and door taking up the eighth angle. Thom leaned forward, resting both hands on the balustrade's wide coping, and gazed out at the landscape.

Below, the woodland was like a deep, bumpy carpet stretching far into the distance, its shades ranging from an intense jade to an exuberant lime and beyond this fields and grassland rising to gentle hills. Easily visible on its own rise was Castle Bracken, its walls washed almost golden by afternoon sunlight that was beginning to mellow. Yet although from this viewpoint and in the scenic grandeur of its setting it truly did resemble a castle from a child's storybook, Thom could not remember ever having been in awe of it. Perhaps even as a boy there had been a dark side to his imagination, an aspect of his nature that had picked up on the misery contained within those stone walls and high-ceilinged halls. A sadness seemed to pervade the very air, as if past tragedies tainted everything that was to follow. In those days he had pitied his friend Hugo, for the older boy seemed crushed by the austere, even grim, atmosphere, and afraid of his own father.

Sir Russell had lost two wives in this place, his first dying swiftly from throat cancer, the second – Hugo's mother – even more quickly in a fall down the central hall's main staircase. (Apparently she was a heavy drinker – or had *become* a heavy drinker since her marriage to the knight – who had many bitter arguments with her husband. She had tripped at the top of the long staircase during a particularly heavy binge and after an especially nasty quarrel.) Then, Hugo's elder stepbrother, the son from Sir Russell's first marriage, had been blown to pieces by a booby-trapped bomb planted by the IRA while he was serving with the British Army in Northern Ireland. It was little wonder that Castle Bracken seemed burdened by grief, shadowed with gloom, and not surprising that Sir Russell himself presented such a gruff, embittered figure. Only when he and Thom had played together outside in the grounds or down by the bridge had Hugo truly come to life, his humour and unbridled enthusiasm infectious, so that Thom, himself, would become boisterous and joyous, revelling in the companionship. The only minor hitch in their relationship was that Hugo would never enter the woods, no matter how much he was begged by Thom, who knew there were even greater adventures to be had and secrets to be discovered there. But Hugo had been forbidden by his father ever to wander into the forest, intimations that he would become hopelessly lost and that nasty animals roamed the wildwoods enough to discourage the boy if Sir Russell's order alone was not sufficient.

Thom wondered how his old friend would cope with the latest in a long line of tragedies that haunted Castle Bracken: the impending death of his father. Would he succumb to the grief? Would he be lost without his father's – overbearing? – guidance? Or would he feel liberated, would he at last become his own man? It remained to be seen.

Thom heard a car's engine growing louder and looked below to see his Jeep emerging from the lane almost opposite, its wheels bumping over the rough unmade road, bodywork jolting as it passed over the deeper holes. He caught sight of Eric Pimlet through the windscreen and raised a hand to wave, but realized the gamekeeper was concentrating too much on handling the vehicle to notice.

The Jeep came to a halt close to the front door and the horn sounded twice, upsetting a bird settled in a nearby bush. It took to the air, complaining loudly, and, as Thom turned from the balustrade to make his way back across the leaded roof, he noticed another bird perched on the lip of the belltower.

The magpie studied him coolly – *seemed* to watch him coolly – apparently not at all intimidated by his closeness, and Thom felt sure it was the same one who had watched him approach the cottage earlier. There was something eerie about its unblinking gaze, as if the bird were thinking dark thoughts, all of them about Thom. He suddenly clapped his hands together, sharp and hard, hoping to make the bird take flight. It didn't. The magpie did not even flinch. It continued to watch.

For a few moments longer, man and bird stared at each other, and it was Thom who broke first. *Eric's waiting below*, he reasoned, somewhat ruefully, *and here am I trying to face down a bloody bird!*

He shook his head and passed beneath the magpie into the open doorway. The bird made a short *hacking* sound and Thom muttered, 'Yeah, and fuck you too,' as he began to descend the stairs.

Of course, it was in his own imagination, but the next cry he heard sounded like a challenge, as if the magpie were warning him off its territory.

*Stupid, Thom*, he admonished himself, *very, very stupid*.

# Chapter: Fifth

## NIGHT-TIME AT LITTLE BRACKEN

H E HAD no idea what had roused him. A noise? He didn't think so. His sleep had been deep and he was sure that only a sound as loud as thunder would have woken him. It had been a tiring day – the drive up from London, the walk through the woods and the re-exploration of the cottage, then later helping Eric unload his gear from the Jeep and chatting with the old gamekeeper over steaming mugs of coffee, reliving past times, chuckling at most of them, until the sun had turned golden and begun to slip away.

For some reason, it had been a relief to find the gamekeeper had scarcely changed – perhaps it was because he represented a kind of constant in Thom's own changing life. In fact, whenever Thom looked back on passing years, he always saw Eric as 'old', so that now the most that could be said was that the gamekeeper had 'grown' into his proper age: his abundant head of hair was overall white rather than a patchy grey as Thom remembered, his pale blue eyes, a little watery these days, rheumy even, squinting so much more that they were almost slits, and the lines and wrinkles of his face, especially the 'crow's feet' that ran from the corners of his eyes to large, stick-out ears, had deepened, become more established rather than increased; thread-veins splayed his ruddy cheeks and hooked nose, and his thin lips were now a purplish colour with clefts at each side. Even Eric's clothes appeared to be the same – baggy brown corduroy trousers held up by a thick leather belt, green tweed jacket with patched elbows and cuffs over woollen check shirt, knitted brown tie worn on all occasions, and green Wellington boots – although the major items must have worn out over the years to be replaced by exact copies which, due to the nature of his work, must have quickly worn in. Thom knew that Eric had been married once long ago and that his wife had died before Thom was born. He knew also that Eric was the last in a long line of Bracken gamekeepers, for he had no heir of his own, either male or female, to follow on the tradition.

After Eric had left, he had eaten one of those sad pre-packed dinner-for-ones cooked in the mini-microwave he'd brought up with him, followed by a bath, knees and shoulders well above the waterline in the short tub and, finally, he'd taken the weary climb up the creaking stairs to bed.

If he had needed reminding he was still a convalescent, then the busy day had done the trick. When he'd pulled back the bedsheets he had been almost dead to the world. After taking his routine medication – aspirin to thin his blood, a mild and, by now, probably unnecessary dose of pravastatin to reduce his cholesterol level; he decided the diothiepin to help him sleep and ease any anxiety wasn't needed (night-time was always bad for stroke victims, for death was always closest when others slept and shadows seemed to beckon the invalid), because he was too exhausted not to sleep – Thom had turned off the bedside lamp, laid his head on the pillow, and had been instantly out.

If he had dreamed, he could not remember, for the sudden awakening had wiped the dream-slate clean.

He regarded the underneath of the four-poster's sagging canopy, the corner curtains and pelmets restricting his view of some of the room, then lifted his head to glance towards the stone fireplace opposite the end of the bed. There was enough moonlight to tell there was no intruder – unless he was hiding, of course. But although he was tense, he could not feel another's presence, there was no shift in the atmosphere, no sneaking scuffles. There were, however, faint reflections on the part of the ceiling close to one of the stone-framed windows.

Subtle hints of colour gently moved against the greyness overhead, as if someone outside were playing weak lights through the leaded glass.

Thom rose from the bed, a slow and awkward movement because of the stiffness in his left arm and leg – it always took a little time for the muscles in both to loosen up, even after only a short nap. He shuffled to the window behind the bed and peered out, his feet cold against the bare floorboards. He blinked rapidly to clear his vision, not quite believing what he saw a short distance away.

A half-moon waxed in the night sky, providing enough silvery light to see the stretch of grass and scrub directly below, but it was what lay just beyond at the dark edge of the surrounding forest that had drawn his attention . . .

Thom pressed closer to the window so that his nose almost touched the glass; his breath misted the thin barrier between himself and the night.

He quickly cleared the vapour with a wipe of his flattened hand and looked again, this time holding his breath and squinting his eyes.

It was hard to tell from this distance, but the cores of the dancing lights seemed very small, only the halos around them initially making them appear larger than they were. These surely were the same tiny creatures – *beings* – he had come upon in the woods earlier that afternoon, only now their colours were more intense, sharper, vivid – more beautiful. And there seemed to be many more of them, all weaving and diving in arcs and loops, with no regular pattern, yet without collision, their movement exquisitely synchronized.

The spectacle – the greens, the blues, the purples, and now the denser colours, the mauves, indigos, the deep blues – was astonishing ... and *breath*taking. His chest was tight, his lungs frozen sacs, and he had to force himself to exhale, the glass before him immediately clouding once more. Again he rubbed at the window with the palm of his hand and the tiny gemstone lights reappeared, dancing among the shadows, some now flitting crazily, while others hovered, their light strong but flickering, as though it was movement that gave them puissance, their energy generating the luminescence.

Thom was unaware that he was smiling in the shadowy room, his face lit both by moonlight and the auroral ballet below, colour tinges fluttering across his whitened skin in faint playful shades, only the reflections in his eyes sharp and stunning.

Occasionally, he breathed a sigh or murmured a sound of wonder as if observing some splendid but silent pyrotechnic display, and soon he lost all sense of time itself. And next morning, he neither recalled dawn's arrival, nor leaving the window to climb back into bed.

## Chapter : Sixth

# NELL QUICK

SOMETHING BANGED against the front door below. Then the iron bell-pull grated rustily and he heard the dull, wasted *clunk* of the long-neglected bell itself.

Thom had awakened only moments earlier, sunlight pouring through the bedroom's windows, dust motes dancing in the brilliant shafts. He had lain there pondering the lights, his face creased in puzzlement, bedsheet pushed down to his waist, not even the numbness tormenting the left side of his body distracting the thoughts. Twice he had seen them, these tiny glittering orbs, and he could only wonder at their source. If he hadn't come across them in broad daylight, he might well have thought he'd only dreamed them last night.

Another bang against the front door, someone using the old brass knocker this time and, momentarily forgetting his condition, Thom attempted to whip back the sheet. He winced as the stiffness turned to a stab of pain and became still again, waiting impatiently.

An even sharper knock on the door now, as if someone was frustrated by the lack of response. He thought he heard a voice calling.

'Okay, okay,' Thom muttered, easing his legs over the side of the bed. He sat on the edge. *'Okay!'* he said aloud and irritably as yet another *clunk* of the bell, this time a looser sound, almost but not quite, a *clank*, came from below.

Leaning forward with a groan – Jesus, it felt like he had a hangover – he grabbed the cargoes draped over the arm of the two-seater settle close by the bed, mumbling curses as he dragged them on. One foot got caught up in a leg and he had to wriggle his ankle to free it, his curses becoming louder and more angry. Finally, he stood and hauled the stone-coloured trousers over his hips, snapping them shut easily because of the weight he'd lost recently, then reached for the white linen shirt hung over the opposite arm of the settle. Shrugging the shirt over his shoulders and slipping his arms into the sleeves, he limped across the room to the door.

As he began to descend the winding stairs, right hand slipping round the newel to steady himself, creaking floor-boards cool beneath his bare feet, the bell rang yet again, *clank* becoming a hoarse *clang*. Light streaming from the stairway's window momentarily blinded him and he almost stumbled, saving himself by bracing his arms against the curved wall and newel post. He blinked rapidly, and as the haze cleared he thought he saw something small scurry across the ground floor landing to disappear through the slightly opened bathroom door.

Thom blinked again, not quite believing what he had seen. Imagination? Still half-dreaming? No, he was sure he'd caught sight of something scooting across the floor. Maybe a mouse. No, too big. Some kind of animal from the forest then. Oh God, not a rat. Please not a rat. Maybe it was to be expected, with the place being empty all these years. Who knew what other creatures had set up home inside the cottage in the absence of human occupation?

He reached the foot of the stairs, the big oak door to the living-room in front of him, the doors to the cupboard and bathroom to his right. Cautiously, he pushed the bathroom door further open and peered inside. The little room was in darkness and he tugged at the hanging light-switch. A heavy double-click and light vanquished most of the shadows. There was nothing amiss though, nothing unusual, nothing out of place. Thom was about to step inside and search the nooks and crannies, anywhere a smallish animal could hide, when there was more rapping and ringing at the front door.

Torn between further investigation and answering the door, Thom bit into his lower lip, did another quick scan of the tiny room, then backed out, leaving the light on but the door closed behind him. He could do a thorough search later.

He called out as he went through into the octagonal-shaped room and the sounds outside ceased. Drawing back the bolt at the bottom of the painted door (he hadn't bothered with the top one) and turning the long key in its lock, Thom yanked the front door open, ready to give the impatient caller a piece of his mind. Instead, he stood there open-mouthed.

She was stunning. Not quite beautiful in the conventional way, but nevertheless stunning. So stunning, in fact, that he gawped a moment or two more.

Long black hair fell in wild tangles to her shoulders, and her eyes, set wide above high cheekbones, matched its darkness. Hollowed cheeks led to a firm but gently pointed jaw and her nose, while still feminine, was strong, the nostrils slightly flared. It was a striking face, handsome rather than pretty, and sensual perhaps rather than beautiful. She was smiling at him and there was an implicit challenge, one that went with the gentle, amused mocking in her dark, gypsy eyes.

'Good morning, Thom,' she said, tilting her head to one shoulder to scrutinize his face. Just in those three words he could detect the slight Shropshire lilt that betrayed the county's closeness to Wales, this mixed with the faintest burr of the south-west counties, a fine, comfortable blend that was pleasant to the ear.

'Uhh . . .' was all he could find to say.

She gave a laugh that came from deep within her throat, so that it sounded like a chuckle.

'Not quite awake then?' she said. 'I thought you might still be sleepin', s'why I banged on the door so hard and kep' at the bell.' The missing letters in her speech hardly mattered at all, for there was still something soft and pleasing in her accent. 'S'gone nine, you know.'

Her smile seemed to drink him in, the look in her eyes a little too knowing. It was seductive though, God, her *whole* persona was seductive.

She stood about five foot six and he guessed her to be in her late twenties, maybe early thirties. Her high breasts swelled against a plain, buttoned blouse and her skirt was long and loose, flimsy and gaily patterned. The blouse was short-sleeved and her bare arms were tanned a tawny-gold; that same colouring in her face enhanced the whiteness around her pupils – which he now realized were so darkly brown that they appeared black – and the perfect flash of her smile. She carried a large wicker basket, a red-chequered teacloth covering its contents.

'Hugo told me about your illness, but he never explained you had no tongue in your head.' She stuck a fist against her hip, her other arm looped under the basket's handle.

He brushed a lock of hair from his forehead, embarrassed and a little perplexed. 'Hugo didn't tell me anyone was . . .' He stopped, vaguely remembering that Hugo had

67

mentioned something about looking in on him occasionally. He lightly slapped his head. 'Sorry, he did say ... I just didn't expect...' He was surprised, and annoyed, at his reaction.

'Uh, won't you come in?' He stood aside, waved a hand at the room behind him.

'Can't fix your breakfast without comin' in, can I?'

Still smiling, she brushed past him and dumped the obviously heavy basket on the centre table, while Thom remained by the doorway as if transfixed. There was a certain arrogant vanity about her, but then who could blame her for that? He had caught her scent as she went by and, although he was no connoisseur, it was unlike any he had ever known. It wasn't subtle, nor was it particularly distinct; it wasn't teasing, but it was ... it was strangely intoxicating, as though some mild stimulant was part of its mix. The perfume hinted at fresh forest air and musk, plus one other indefinable ingredient, Lord knows what.

Forgetting to close the door, Thom followed after the woman, noticing the thonged sandals she wore, the pleasing shape from lower calf to slim ankle. She was still smiling as she unpacked the wicker basket – fresh bread, two milk cartons, fruit, and other items to which he could pay no attention.

Glancing up at him, the woman said, 'Name's Nell Quick, and I'm very pleased to meet you, Thom.' Her voice was low-keyed, husky in a whisky-and-cigarettes way. She stopped her task for a moment to study his face.

At least he had finally remembered to close his mouth.

'You look very tired,' she said in her soft lilt. 'Is it the illness or didn't you sleep well on your first night home? I s'pose the cottage will take some time gettin' used to again.'

He returned her smile, even though he felt mildly uncomfortable under her bold, almost mocking gaze. Was she flirting with him?

As if to answer his unspoken question, Nell Quick

allowed her eyes to rove down his bare chest, a deliberate action he was sure was meant to be interpreted as such. He began buttoning up his shirt, the fingers of his left hand fumbling awkwardly.

'Let me do that for you,' she said immediately, stepping round the table and reaching forward.

'No.' A little too sharply.

She froze, but the smile remained on her lips and in her eyes.

'Uh, sorry,' he said quickly. 'I can manage. Got to get use to it. My physio told me the more I persist, the easier it'll become.' He shuffled his feet as if the stone floor was cold. 'Look, thanks for the food. I . . .'

'Oh, I'm here to cook for you. Hugo wants me to build you up again. He told me you used to be quite athletic when you two were boys. I bet you both got into mischief, didn't you?'

'Honestly, I can manage. I don't need a nursemaid.' It came out with more annoyance than he intended; he hadn't meant to snub such kind consideration.

If she took any offence, it didn't show. 'Nobody's nursemaidin' you, Thom. I'm just bein' a good neighbour, is all.'

He raised his eyebrows in surprise. 'You live close by?'

She had already turned towards the cooker to switch on its grill and a ring. 'Not far,' she replied over her shoulder. 'Now, how would bacon and eggs suit you? You could cut the loaf if you want to be helpful. Have some fruit first – there's apples, plums, all nice and freshly picked. We'll soon have you feelin' well again.'

He could only watch helplessly as Nell busied herself by taking two eggs and plastic-sealed bacon from the fridge, which had been well stocked – by her? – before his arrival yesterday. Once preparations were under way, she pulled a small transistor radio from the basket and placed it on the table, pressing a button so that music instantly filled the cottage with new and, because the set was pre-tuned to Classic FM, unobtrusive life. She adjusted the volume so that the music was background noise that would not interfere with conversation.

Realizing resistance was pointless, Thom said, 'I think I'll just wash and shave first.'

Again smiling, and with that same amused little gleam in her dark eyes, she waved a dismissive hand. 'Don't be takin' too long now, you should always eat breakfast nice and hot. Put some shoes or slippers on too – this stone floor will still be mornin' cold.'

Thom backed towards the door, aware of the silly grin on his face, but unable to rid himself of it for the moment, a hand unconsciously flicking hair away from his forehead again.

As he closed the door behind him and paused outside, he heard the music's volume turned up again. Nell Quick was a great surprise to him and he wasn't sure if he should be annoyed or grateful for Hugo's presumption that he would need a nursemaid. He decided he could only be bemused.

He crowded into the bathroom – it was so compact that one person did, indeed, constitute a crowd – and stood over the toilet, his combats unzipped in the two strides it took to get there. As he relieved his bladder, which had been protesting dully throughout the morning's exchange, Thom remembered the creature he thought he had seen dashing for cover earlier. He looked at the floor around him as he peed, squinting into the darker corners and niches. He was soon wondering if he had imagined the whole thing. After all, he'd been roused from a deep sleep by the persistent knocking at the door and in truth had not been properly awake as he'd staggered down the stairs, half-blinded by sunlight, and brain busy with other thoughts. Maybe it had been a trick of the light, maybe just a figment of his over-stretched imagination, or a remnant of whatever dream he'd been having. He would make a thorough search later, see if there were any holes in the floorboards or skirting that a small house pest could squeeze into. But had it been *that* small? He thought not, but nevertheless dismissed the matter from his mind. By the time he had finished shaving and washing, the episode was almost forgotten.

He went back up to the bedroom, most of the stiffness gone from his arm and leg, and slipped on a pair of soft moccasins he'd bought from a pricey Covent Garden shop.

He was still sitting on the unmade bed running fingers through his untidy hair when he heard footsteps on the landing outside the door. Then Nell Quick was leaning against the door-frame, one fist on her hips as before.

'Christ . . .' he said, with a start.

'I called, but you obviously didn't hear me.' Same full, slightly lascivious smile, same veiled intention in her eyes.

'You shouldn't have—' he began to say, but she interrupted with a laugh.

'I'm used to lookin' after people, Thom, 'specially men. I'm a trained nurse, didn't Hugo tell you? I've been carin' for Sir Russell some time now.'

'Maybe so, Ms Quick—'

'You jus' call me Nell.'

'Okay – Nell. But what I'm trying to say is, I enjoy my privacy. That's why I came up here to Little Bracken, to get away from all the friends and acquaintances who think I need mollycoddling.'

''Specially the girls, I bet.' Her eyes shone challengingly.

'No, not particularly. Well, maybe one or two, but that's not the point.' He rose from the bed and spoiled his next assertion somewhat by reaching for his cane. 'I'm quite fit, actually, well on the mend.'

She eyed the aid and he cringed, silently cursing himself.

'It's just the mornings,' he hastily explained. 'Leg's a bit stiff until I really get going. Gets tired quite easily, too, but I'm working on that.'

'I can help you there.' By now she had stepped into the

room, shortening the gap between them. 'I'm good at easin' men's stiffness.'

He did a double take.

'Know how the muscles work, y'see,' she went on, letting the smile fall away when he had expected an even more licentious one. 'I have my own herbs and balms that can do wonders for ailin' limbs and bodies. Natural cures, mostly forgotten now, but effective, you jus' wait and see.'

She was less than a foot away, deliberately invading his space, her deep eyes studying his. His discomfort began to turn to irritation once more.

And yet . . .

And yet he could feel the tension – the sexual tension – between them and, for the first time since the outset of his illness, Thom felt a stirring, a reaction in his body over which he had no command. Her coquetry was plain and, at another time, would have been exciting, even welcome; but this morning, and in these circumstances – so fast, so unexpected – he could only be confused. And anxious, for he had been celibate for some time, even before his stroke, and right then he was not sure of his own adequacy, how much damage his system had sustained. Nell Quick was certainly alluring, gloriously so, in fact, and another man might have grabbed the opportunity to prove himself to himself. Not right then, though. No, he wasn't ready. And, he had to admit, he was too scared.

He went to the sideboard and pretended to search for something, but in truth, putting distance between himself and this unsettling woman.

'Dammit, always losing my comb,' he muttered, as if he had been oblivious to the interplay between them a moment before. Nell could not know, of course, that he rarely used a comb to tidy his hair anyway, but she certainly wasn't fooled by the ploy.

She gave a short, fruity laugh. 'Your breakfast's on the warmer, but you don't want to let it get too dry, do you?'

Turning from him in a smooth, gliding movement she disappeared through the doorway.

Thom took a deep breath as he listened to her retreating footsteps and looked at himself in the free-standing mirror on the sideboard.

'Bloody hell,' he said, blushing deeply.

He followed after her and avoided her eyes as he sat at the table. One plate had been laid and Nell busied herself cutting into the bread.

'Er, won't you join me?' Thom asked out of politeness only.

'Oh, I never eat a big breakfast,' she replied, laying two slices on a bread plate. 'Usually just some fruit or a yogurt, enough to get me through the mornin'. I drink gallons of coffee though.'

He could smell the coffee aroma and saw a percolator close to the electric kettle on a worktop beside the cooker. He hadn't noticed either of them before – there had been too much to take in yesterday, and his nightcap had been a rare can of beer from the six-pack he'd found in the fridge – and again, he was grateful for Hugo's thoughtfulness. Thom began to eat and, with the first mouthful, realized how hungry he was. His newfound appetite was a delightful surprise.

He felt suddenly cheered as he buttered a slice of bread, this small improvement in his condition giving him hope that he really was on the mend. He could only hope it wasn't temporary.

'White with?'

The knife stayed over the bread as he looked up at her. 'Sorry?'

'Milk and sugar with your coffee?' Nell Quick was leaning back against the worktop, arms folded, her pelvis thrust forward slightly. She was probably one of those unconsciously sexy women who had no idea of the effect she had on men. *Oh really?* a dry little inner voice that frequently spoke up for the cynical side of his nature insinuated. *Seems to me she knows* exactly *what she's doing, pal.*

Whatever, it was good to know some of his old libido was returning – it had been a while since he'd looked at a woman in this way. God bless good, fresh, country air and decent exercise.

'Yeah, both please. One sugar.' His grin was genuine.

'Comin' up. Mind if I join you in a drink?'

Thom would have preferred his privacy, but that might have been churlish after all she had done for him that morning. As he waved a hand at the chair opposite him, he wondered if it was Nell Quick who had cleaned the cottage from top to bottom for his homecoming.

He studied her back while she poured the coffee, enjoying the sight of her lushly dark hair which fell between narrow but firm shoulders, its wild ringlets reaching midway down her back. Gentle music filled the room and a breeze drifted in from the open doorway, bringing with it forest smells that mingled with the stronger coffee aroma, and the sounds of birds calling, a distant cuckoo louder and more distinctive than the rest. A bee buzzed in, explored the new territory in a figure-eight flight plan, and buzzed right back outside again.

Nell Quick placed a mug of steaming coffee in front of Thom and took a seat opposite him. She raised her steaming mug to her lips, a forearm leaning on the table-top, and took a long sip.

She looked deeply into his eyes, the smile still there at the corner of her lips, her gaze intense as if she were seeing through to his very soul.

'Did you . . . did you sleep well last night?'

It sounded like *lasnigh'*, and her slight hesitation seemed to give the question more significance than probably was intended.

His own hesitation did the same for his reply. 'I . . . uh . . . I don't know. I think so. Can't remember to be honest.'

'Nothing disturbed you, then?'

'Like what?'

74

Her long fingers flicked the air between them. 'Anythin'. Place's been empty a long time. All kinds of things could've moved in from the woods.'

'The cottage has been kept locked up, right?'

She shrugged. 'Little creatures have ways of gettin' in, 'specially into places that are warm and cosy.'

He was about to tell her he thought he'd seen something scurry across the landing only a short time ago, but for some reason – he really had no idea why – he decided not to. Instead, he raised the coffee mug to his lips.

'Shiii—'

Thom quickly set down the mug and put his fingers to his scalded lips.

'Oh, I should have warned you it was hot.' Nell was already on her feet and grabbing for a tea towel. Folding it first, she thrust a corner under the cold tap over the sink, soaking it thoroughly before bringing it to Thom.

'Here, press it against your lips, it'll take away some of the sting,' she said, putting it to his face herself.

He took the wet towel and applied it to his mouth, the pain already beginning to throb. 'Thanks,' he mumbled, mentally calling himself a fool for not being more cautious. For Christ's sake, he had seen the hot steam rising from the mug, was aware it had been freshly made. Stupid, stupid – but wait a minute. Hadn't he seen Nell Quick drinking the coffee a moment before?

'It didn't burn you,' he said, almost accusing, his complaint awkward through numbed lips.

She didn't appear concerned – why should she be? It was *his* lips – and reached into the wicker basket for a canvas bag lying at the bottom. From the open bag she took a small, round, red pot and thumbed off its plastic lid.

'Always carry salves and healing unguents with me. Never know when one or another will be useful. This is good for insect stings as well as burns.'

She dabbed her middle fingertip into the pot and it came

out with a gobbet of yellowish greyish cream. Thom flinched away when she prepared to smear his mouth with the stuff.

'Come on, don't be a baby,' she scolded playfully. 'It's only a mixture of coriander leaf and thorn-apple juice, with a few secret ingredients of my own. It's the pig's grease it's boiled up with that makes it look and smell like this. Come on, it'll work, I promise. The pain will soon go and we'll stop any inflammation before it starts. Got to go on straight away though, otherwise it'll be no good.'

'Cold water will do,' he protested, turning his head away.

'No, it won't. Trust me, Thom, this will get rid of the pain and heal the burn at the same time.'

Her voice was soothing and, for some reason he could not fathom, hard to resist. Reluctantly, he faced her and allowed her to smear the sickly smelling unguent over his lips.

The relief was instant, and he straightened in surprise. The pain was gone the moment she touched him with the substance. Her face was only inches away from his as she leaned over him, her finger still poised over his mouth. Her pupils were large within their irises so that her eyes really were almost totally black. In them he could see the reflections of his own image.

He could feel the salve sinking deeper into his lips, as though it were chasing after any lingering pain or infection. With her face so close, her breath warm on his cheek, and her smell – like some sweet musky incense carried on a breeze – so puissantly sensual, Thom felt a warm flush course through him and the room began to spin, fading as it did so until it felt like only he and the woman existed in the world; there was a hush between them that seemed full of unspoken meaning.

She drew even closer and he could not be sure if he hadn't leaned towards her himself. He was mystified but drawn by her allure. He had no wish to resist. Her lips were only inches from his own and he noticed they glistened and were so deeply red, so enticing . . .

An excitement made him shiver. His lips brushed against hers and just as they both began to exert equal pressure, the spell – how appropriate that word, he was to learn later – was broken.

He jerked away – she merely stiffened – when something smashed against the flagstone floor.

# Chapter: Seventh

# A HASTY DEPARTURE

THOM JUMPED to his feet in shock, forcing Nell to take two startled steps backwards. As one their heads snapped round, their eyes searching.

A plate lay shattered nearby on the stone floor in a crazy jigsaw of white pieces.

The silence that followed was only a little less disturbing than the explosive crash that had preceded it and Thom quickly understood why: the birds outside had ceased their babel, as though they, too, had been frightened; even the breeze now seemed reluctant to enter. But stranger than all this, the radio had become silent too.

Thom slowly took his gaze from the broken plate and shifted it to the woman. He was not so much confused as bewildered, for the plate apparently had *flown* from the dresser shelf as if self-propelled. It hadn't just dropped; it was too far from the dresser for that. And its force must have been immense for it to shatter into so many pieces.

And what was this expression on Nell Quick's face? It

wasn't shock and it wasn't curiosity. No, there was anger in her eyes. And ... and ... was that fear?

Now her eyes sought his, as if to gauge *his* reaction.

'What the hell is that all about?' Perhaps he hoped she might have an answer.

A long pause before she replied, the air frighteningly still around them. 'All sorts of things can happen in old places like this,' she offered unconvincingly. 'Old timber and stone grow weary, they shrink, then expand. Pressures build.' She shrugged. 'Strange things happen.' Then, as if anxious to reassure him: 'P'raps a wind knocked it down.'

Sure, he thought to himself. Feasible if the whole row of plates had taken to the air. Besides, he had felt no *wind* and he was pretty sure she hadn't either. And for a plate to sail across the room like that, the gust would have had to have been really fierce. He realized she was still watching him closely and there seemed to be a skittishness to her body language, a flick of a hand, a twitch of her shoulders; even her pupils had contracted ...

The music from the radio suddenly started up again, making them both start. A welcome breeze drifted through the door once more.

The moment was gone.

As if nothing untoward had happened, Nell said, 'I'd best be on my way. Lots to do today. Must look in on Sir Russell ...' She retrieved the pot of ointment from the table and dropped it into her bag, then went to the small radio, switched it off and this, too, was dumped unceremoniously into the canvas bag.

Confused, Thom watched. She is more shocked than I am, he thought. She's acting, pretending. Jesus, she can't wait to get out.

'Dustpan and brush are under the sink.' She was pointing back, already on her way to the door. 'No time to clear up for you, must be gettin' on ... Don't forget your breakfast now, it's gettin' cold.'

'What about your coffee? Not going to finish it?' It was his turn for a little innocent mockery. Why *was* she so scared?

She stopped in the doorway and for a moment there was a hard glint in her eyes, as if she recognized his tone and did not like it.

'Hope you sleep well again tonight,' was all she said, but there seemed to be a hint of malice behind her words. Then she left.

A light *clunking* from behind him made him turn anxiously towards the dresser again. He was just in time to notice a row of cups hanging by their handles from hooks underneath the shelf that held the plates – plates minus one – settling after another stiff breeze (hopefully a genuine one) had disturbed them.

He also noticed that in her haste to leave the cottage, Nell Quick had left the wicker basket under the table.

# Chapter : Eighth

## THE LAKE AND
## AN ENCOUNTER

ABOUT AN hour later, after finishing the lukewarm breakfast and tepid coffee, then completing some gentle but necessary therapeutic exercises – it would get tougher when the therapist turned up in a day or two – Thom left the cottage without locking the front door behind him (he and his mother never had in the past, so why start now?). Although the air was still a little fresh, he now wore minimal clothing – dark straight-legged joggers, tan boots, and grey lightweight armless gilet – sure that the day would quickly warm up. Hairs on his bare arms prickled as a light wind rushed at him from the trees and he zipped up the gilet almost to the neck to protect his stomach and chest. That brief gust brought with it more fragrances from the forest and he savoured them all as they cued more memories, his spirits immediately rising. He sucked in a great gasp of air, cleansing the confusion of Nell Quick's speedy departure and flying crockery from his mind. Only when his lungs had expanded to their limit did he let go, controlling the breath so that it flowed outwards in a steady stream.

He took his time sauntering down the short path, noting that he would have to do something about the grass sprouting between the cracks as he went. The woods were less than twenty yards away, ferns, bramble, and wild flowers occupying much of the space in between, the shadows beneath trees no longer deep, nor mysterious in daylight; vibrant shafts of sunlight created little oases of brightness beyond the treeline. The woodland that had appeared impenetrable last night was now irresistibly inviting.

Thom regarded the carpet of late bluebells with appreciation rather than the curiosity of yesterday as his eyes swept over this splendidly private view. Again his thoughts dwelt on the life cycle for, like the old oak he had come upon along the trail, the soil itself and the covering flora provided a ceaseless order of survival, animals, insects, organisms, all replenished the earth just as they took from it, nothing ever remaining the same, but not one single life form ever becoming nothing at all. Every individual kind of life had its purpose, which was to sustain all else, and the notion was comforting to Thom, who had faced his own untimely metamorphosis so recently and somehow cheated it. And it was with this reasoning that he realized it was not death he feared, but what lay beyond, what came next.

Continuing to look around him, considering which direction to take for his morning walk, he spied a certain familiar break in the trees. The path there led to a small lake deep within the woods, a quiet place he had once thought was the centre of the world, possibly of the universe too. His mother had also loved this beautiful haven, with its deep, still waters where willows dipped their leaves and animals came to drink without fear, for it was there that she brought him as a reward for being particularly good or working hard at the minor chores she gave him. It had seemed to hold a special magic for her, for while he played along the grassy banks and in and out of the trees, Bethan could sit by the lake's edge, watching its placid surface, occasionally closing her eyes as if her thoughts were deep within herself and of things she never divulged to him. Sometimes he would find her quietly weeping and his arms would encircle her shoulders so that he could hold her tight, the child giving comfort to the mother.

The overgrown trail was easy enough for him to pick out, because he had passed that way so many times as a boy, and he even recognized many of the more mature trees along the way and mentally greeted them as if they were old friends: the multi-trunked oak he had climbed so often as a boy, its middle section a broad junction of thick boughs offering a discreet platform from where he could snoop on unwitting animals below – the fox, the squirrel, even the occasional deer, and best of all, at dusk the badger, whose sett was close by; there was the silver birch whose lower white bark he once had carefully peeled away to denude the trunk – the bark had returned over the years, but its discoloured diamond-shaped patches were not as dark, nor as numerous as those in the higher reaches; the beech body he had rested against, the hard-to-rot leaves it had shed in past seasons providing an inches-deep rug beneath him while he read books and comics (the latter loaned from Hugo), or carved wood with Eric's gift. He spotted tiny, coloured moths that were almost invisible to the human eye as they flitted among leaves. There were the flowers, the nightshade, forget-me-not, red campion, columbine – varieties and colours that never failed to make him catch his breath. The familiar sounds – the birdcalls, the rustlings of undergrowth, a single cry that might have been bird or beast.

He saw everything through the eyes of a recovering invalid: all was fresh, new to him, colours vivid, intense, everything appeared more sharply focused. Even sounds were keener, scents more distinctive. Thom experienced it all in the same way he had as a child, before time had dulled senses.

Deeper into the woods he went, every so often touching his lips with tentative fingertips, surprised there was no pain and no blisters from the scalding coffee. But then, hadn't Bethan used similar salves to treat his scrapes and burns years ago? Colds and fevers had been defeated by potions and broths, chicken-pox and measles by herbs and mixtures, tried and tested cures known to countryfolk for centuries, passed on from generation to generation, but mostly forgotten in this new age of science and genetics. Not forgotten by Nell Quick though, it seemed . . .

His thoughts lingered on his slightly odd but attractive visitor that morning. Why had she fled the cottage so quickly when the plate had smashed to the floor? And just before that incident they had been about to kiss. There was no question that she had flirted with him from the moment she'd arrived and he had to wonder why. They were complete strangers to each other, so why would she move in so fast? It wasn't a regular occurrence for him, that was for sure. Maybe she was just the friendly type.

He grinned to himself. Yep, no question there.

Then he remembered that she had known immediately where the dustpan and brush were kept. Did that mean she'd visited the cottage before? Was she the one who had prepared the place for his arrival? If so, he wished Hugo had warned him about her. Maybe then he wouldn't have been so unprepared.

He trekked on, moving ferns and thin branches aside with the cane as he went, musing on that morning's – and the previous night's events. Occasionally, he disturbed some small creature on the ground and would wait patiently until it had scuttled away to safety; or a bird would fly across his path, shrieking a warning to watch himself in its territory. Not once, though, did he feel himself to be a trespasser: no, this was *his* territory as much as theirs and he relished the feeling of being home. The magic of it all was still the same; only his childhood innocence was missing.

Butterflies caught his attention – Browns, Yellows, Vanessids, and others – as they flitted about woodland strawberries, and birdsong began to fill his head. He looked for and soon found the tree along the trail where an owl used to live, the creature not at all shy when the boy ambled by its roosting hole and hooted or '*kewick-kewicked*' up at it, merely returning a round-eyed expressionless stare as it waited for dusk to give way to night, the beast walking below too large for consumption and not large enough to fear. Thom wondered if the tawny owl was still in residence, or had died long ago in his absence. Perhaps it had been replaced by another of its breed, maybe its own offspring. Thom sucked in a great draught of air, appreciating, after so many years of city life, just what fresh air really *tasted* like.

It took another twenty minutes to reach the lake (a boyhood journey of no more than seven minutes of breathless running) and when he came upon it he stood perfectly still, favouring his right leg, unaware of the smile that had lit up his face, the shine that was in his eyes.

Nothing had changed, except that the lake seemed to be smaller. But then, wasn't everything big when *you* were little? It was still a sleepy, tranquil paradise, with trees rimming the banks, a golden willow overhanging the water, water lilies floating on its surface. Flowering plants filled the edges like herbaceous borders, wasps *bizzing* around them and sounding like miniature chainsaws in the morning quietness. Tiny circles softly rippled the lake's placid surface here and there as fish below snatched floating food; swifts and swallows dashed over the mirror face, wings creating hardly a stir as the birds hunted flies. In colours of green, ochre and glittering blue, dragonflies hovered low like humming birds, poised to strike and, having struck, disappeared from sight, their speed the secret of their implausible vanishing act.

The lake was irregular in shape, reeds and the floating water lilies sometimes concealing its natural shoreline. From the far bank there came the metallic *twicking* of yellowhammers. A breeze rippled the flat water, and perhaps it was the sweet aroma of willowherb that came with it that reminded him of a time when life was simple and insecurity an unknown thing. Or maybe it was the warm breath of air against his cheek, so like the sensation that preceded his mother's kiss, that brought the feeling to him.

Something distracted him and at first he could not be sure if it had been a sound or a sudden sense of no longer being alone. Inexplicably, and worryingly, a mist descended *behind* his eyes and dizziness almost sent him to his knees. He leaned heavily on his cane, saving himself, and the sensation, as well as the illusory mist, quickly passed. And then he most definitely heard something, a disturbance that was close by.

But when he looked around, he saw nothing unusual. Nothing about the blissful scene before him was different. Yet all had changed. He felt disorientated, as if he had just arrived at a place he knew, but from a different approach so that nothing seemed the same as he remembered.

The sound he heard was vaguely familiar though: it was the high-pitched yet mellifluous whistling that had come to him as he walked through the woods towards Little Bracken only yesterday.

He leaned towards its source, his eyes squinting. The foliage was dense, but through the gaps he saw what looked like flickering lights. They had to be tiny, for none filled the holes through which they could be seen, and perhaps they did not flicker but merely gave that illusion as leaves wavered before them. They shone just as brightly as they had last night.

Thom knew they were those same lights, akin to fireflies only in that they glowed as they flitted to and fro, something telling him, something he *sensed* telling him, that they bore no relation to any physical insect, that they were not a natural species – and that they could not possibly be *real*. Twice before he had observed them but now, as if with the familiarity, their sound was more distinct, more defined. Thom realized that it was a kind of singing that he could hear, faint, tiny voices unlike any he had ever heard before – or, *if* he had, he had forgotten – that rose and ebbed in a weird but euphonic flutey harmony. As if mesmerized, he took robot-like steps towards the bushes that screened them, cane forgotten in his hand, limp imperceptible.

His footsteps were soundless on the mushy forest floor and his breath was held so that his approach was almost silent. His eyes were focused only on the lights as they flashed behind the broken wall of leaves ahead; his ears no longer acknowledged any extraneous noises, for his attention was centred purely on what lay beyond the leafy cover.

His feet narrowly missed brittle twigs which, if broken, might have announced his presence; the tip of his cane was raised inches above any exposed tree root that might have caught it; breathing was held in abeyance. As he drew closer to the rough barrier, his free hand began to stretch forward. His fingertips touched the leaves and gently, and so very slowly, drew them apart.

His quick gasp for air was barely audible.

---

Although the lights were mostly a candescent white at their nucleus, their peripheries appeared to take in every hue of the spectrum, from purples to violets, greens to blues, reds to oranges, yellows and golds, and they sparkled as they zipped through the air like brilliant insects in spectacular display. Like the dragonflies he had watched over the lake, they sometimes hovered, their brightness momentarily subdued, and it was then that Thom could just make out the blur of their tiny, almost pellucid, wings.

But his astonishment turned to awe when he realized these delicately beautiful creatures were the darting satellites of a quite ethereal reclining figure whose flesh appeared so white it might have been the purest marble. Pallid colours reflected off their host as the creatures' gossamer wings brushed its smooth surfaces, and it was only when it slowly moved that Thom understood it was human, a living, breathing *human*. And when he leaned closer still and shaded his eyes against the dazzling lights, he saw then that it was a woman – no, no, a *girl*, for her skin was unblemished, her curves subtly rounded, her naked breasts small. He thought then that she was the most sensual female he had ever set eyes on.

She lay back between the two stout roots of a large oak, the thick, gnarled limbs spread like welcoming arms around her before sinking into the ground. Long yellow hair tumbled about her small face, with its finely pointed chin and high cheekbones, falling over her narrow shoulders in a cascade of wild, golden locks; closed eyes were slightly tilted, their lashes long and dark; her lips parted and they were pink and moist, for she was in passion. She drew in soft hasty gasps and her slender body writhed languidly; he realized her eyes were closed in ecstasy.

Her body was slight and her breasts, although small and their tips pubescently pink with no visible areola, were mature and beautifully formed. She began to tease their rising nipples, stroking them with her fingertips, the movement tender, unhurried.

Thom felt a stirring of his own body, blood beginning to rush to his centre so that for the first time since his illness had struck, he grew hard and the muscles of his stomach and groin became uncomfortably taut. He felt no shame for the voyeurism – his senses were too much in turmoil, his fascination too overwhelming. Maybe the guilt would come later, but right then the eroticism of the moment was too powerful, impossible to resist.

She continued to coax those little darkening tips into thrusting peaks, pressing and kneading the soft flesh around them, using fingers, the palms of her hands, drawing the nipples out with gentle fingertips, sighing with the pleasure of it, her body quivering. Her other hand slid down over the slight ⸱roundness of her stomach, reaching down, down, diverting to one softly-defined hip, then to the other on the way, as if every part of her needed to be felt, touched, aroused, then further down to the hairless – hairless, not shaven, for there was no shadow – place between her thighs where her long fingers paused, soothed, fondled, before delving, sinking into the parting fissure, one finger, the middle one and the longest, disappearing into the fleshy folds of her cleft, re-emerging again slick with glistening, returning, her legs widening, accommodating, the pressure of her hand gentle at first but increasing the urgency and adding firmness as inner juices began to flow, collecting some of that wetness to smear the insides of her thighs, the plain area where curls of blonde hair should have grown, sinking again, this time two fingers entering to part around the little risen protuberance that afforded so much delight if served correctly, lovingly ...

... the tiny lights became frenzied, as if sharing her ecstasy, their high peal reaching a new pitch, their colours almost blinding ...

... and she gave out a small moan and her face tilted so that broken sunlight dappled her cheeks, blazed the fringes of her hair, and blessed her closed eyelids ...

... while the frenetic light show continued around her, a number of the shining things alighting on the white plains of her skin, where they used their busy wings to delight her with delicate, rhythmic strokes. A few went to her erect nipples and excited them further ...

... as her hand left her breasts to join its partner between her legs. Her moans became a long sigh and her small tongue darted out between perfect white and slightly pointed teeth to wet her lips even more before retreating with another sigh that to Thom sounded like a musical note . . .

He could see the flying creatures more clearly now, as though their excitement somehow made the forms stronger, less vague: within the glows, there appeared to be diminutive human forms, these themselves somehow lit from within. He could just make out their tiny limbs, but their heads were too small to discern features of any kind. He did not study them long, for it was difficult to keep his eyes off the girl, whose rising frenzy was becoming uncontrolled, causing her to cry out.

Her age remained indeterminate to him, as was her true size given the reclining position. He was sure she was not tall though, perhaps a fraction less than five feet. And even though she appeared to possess no pubic hair, there was something about her – which had nothing to do with this unconcealed wantonness – that convinced him this was no child. Certainly she was young, for no lines or flaws spoiled her milky skin, and there was something about her expression – even beyond lascivious blissfulness – that was all too knowing for an innocent . . .

. . . now both sets of fingers had entered her body joining to enhance her pleasure, delving deep, then playing around the pouting lips, teasing herself, fingers quickening, their metre swift but regular, buried deep again, then appeasing, conciliating, *gratifying* the very entrance to her well once more, the high-pitched musical sounds and the dashing lights of her tiny cohorts almost as hypnotizing – as intoxicating – as the sight of this lovely young girl herself, the oscillations about her so brightly intense that they created a vibrant aura, a melded glow that pulsed and charged itself with some unworldly energy, a kind of spectral spectrum . . .

. . . and all the while Thom gazed in awe, seduced and stirred by the sight, although not sure if he were hallucinating . . .

. . . as this wondrously sexual female squirmed and

uttered sighs and moans in the discreet sun-dappled clearing, her golden hair, now damp at its edges, falling over her face, lank tips touching her little breasts, her smooth stomach heaving with exertion and pleasure, her sleek thighs opening and closing around her hands as if to pressure them. Her chin came down, teeth biting into her lower lip, her breathing strained, muscles taut; but these were merely initial paroxysms, her climax still approaching...

... her head twisted from side to side, her hair flicking across eyes that were now half open, but revealing only white, their pupils lost behind the upper lids for the moment. More lights joined the others on her flesh, using their flimsy butterfly wings to titillate nerve points just beneath the surface, their flutterings like the softest of feathers, tickling, intensifying the sensitivity...

... her eyes closing again in rapture, her mouth yawning wide as if in rictus, the muscles of her neck stretched tight, as her fingers worked quickly, her thrusts not so deep, lavishing their attention mostly on and around the small hard protuberance high inside the silky-wet cavity between her thighs...

... and he was almost in a delirium himself, his mind stunned, but his senses in turmoil, his desire barely suppressed...

... as she arched her back, her shoulders pressing into the rough bark of the tree behind. Her heels dug into the soil as her hands hurried, then slowed, hurried, then slowed, the thrusts harder, more measured, yet beyond proper control. A long, quiet, hissing scream escaped her as inner juices surged, her body now feverish, her skin shiny with perspiration, rapture reaching its glorious peak...

... before subsiding in great shudders and hushed quivering moans...

... and the bright entities around her blinked and twinkled, and quietly faded, became dulled...

... as the girl sank between the arms of the giant tree

and into the earth, her petite breasts, with their tiny engorged tips rising and falling with the joyful exhaustion that follows perfect orgasm.

Soft murmurs came from her as her excitement calmed, her body relaxed. One knee was raised at an angle, her other leg straight before her, her fine slim hands remaining at her centre as if for comfort and certainly not for modesty. Her eyes were closed once more as she raised her face to the sun and her breathing gradually slowed, became less laboured.

Thom was silent and he tried to keep perfectly still, although his heart continued to race and blood seemed to roar in his ears. He had no idea of what to do next. Skulk away? Wait until she left? Now he did begin to feel the shame. He was trembling.

And then the girl lowered her chin and lazily opened her eyes as she turned her head to look towards his hiding-place. He saw that they were, indeed, almond-shaped, saw that they glittered silver . . .

. . . as they looked directly into his . . .

# Chapter : Ninth

## A CHASE

THE GUILT flooded over him. He felt something else, too, something he could not define.

It was in her eyes, those startling glittering eyes. Those wonderfully oblique eyes.

He saw something in them – sensed something in them – that alarmed him . . . yet drew him in. He felt a *frisson* of emotion that had nothing to do with her allure or his desire. It was . . . a connection. Thom thought it might even be a recognition. But that would be impossible: he had never seen this beautiful girl in his life before.

If he thought he might detect some sense of shame also in their expression, or even embarrassment at having been caught in such privately intimate circumstances, he was wrong. The naked girl merely returned his stare, while a slow smile filtered through to her lips. Now she looked at him from beneath her lashes, chin tilted downwards, neither coy, nor coquettish, just a little shy.

Thom could only remain open-mouthed, not sure what

he should do, what he should say. *If* he should say anything at all. The hand that held back the leaves before him was shaking fiercely by then.

The girl, this lovely abandoned, apparently shameless, creature began to laugh, a small, delicious sound that contained no mockery or derision, only delight, and he felt his heart lift, his senses spin in a different, happier way. His body had calmed, erection already waning, yet there was a yearning in him, a different and purer kind of desire replacing the previous lust. Thom wanted to speak to her but, for the moment, he was speechless.

And then it was too late.

The girl's companions, those strange, ethereal satellites of light, were settling around her, some drifting lethargically as others lay on her body or found leaves to fall upon; but almost immediately they began to stir again as if alerted to his presence. Their odd but sweet whistlings took on a new tone that was not unlike the sound made by agitated insects. Their inner lights brightened again but the colours were somehow fiercer than before, no longer lustrous, flashing violently instead. Thom began to fear rather than wonder.

They rose as one into the air, dashing to and fro, several sweeping towards him, but retreating after a few feet in the way that certain animals might to warn off their foe. His ears began to ring with the sound and his heart seemed to take on a fresh beat, one that was less regular than before.

Something he could not see crashed into the other side of the bush he was hiding behind and Thom staggered backwards, surprised and not a little dismayed. His heel caught a root or bump in the ground and he fell awkwardly, the cane dropping from his hand. He floundered on his back and the angry sound rose in volume, drew closer. He felt a sting on his cheek as a light whipped across his face and he held up a hand to ward it off. But others arrived and flew around his head, their excited buzzing becoming hard to bear, the noise increasing his panic.

'*What* . . .?' was all he managed to cry out.

There was more movement around him, but this came from the debris of the woodland floor itself, a lifting of dead leaves and soil as though things underneath were pushing through.

Impossible, he told himself. Just impossible. The disturbance wasn't only in one location but in several scattered moving mounds, brittle leaves slithering off them. 'What . . .?' He murmured the question this time. It was like one of those late-night horror movies on TV where rotting arms and fleshless fingers burst through the soil and the observer can only watch in frozen horror: too bloody daft to show earlier in the evening and only good after a few pints in the pub beforehand and you are ready for a good laugh. Only this wasn't funny. This was for real.

He twisted round, got a knee under him. Crouched . . .

A brown, grimy bump emerged from the earth nearby, clots of dirt crumbling away from it. And then – oh, dear God, and then – a pair of eyes.

A nose followed the eyes – the glaring, malevolent slitted eyes – and it was a nose that started high on the forehead, and was large and pointed, the nostrils swelling to fill half the creature's face. The head tossed and wriggled, the thin neck stretched and strained, as the thing worked its way out of the earth like a small beast struggling to escape a tight womb, and all the while its yellow glare was fastened on Thom.

Thom yelped when the claws of a minuscule, scaly hand – a monkey's paw of a hand – dug into his own, which was flat against the ground, fingers splayed to support himself as he knelt. So fixed were his eyes on the emerging thing a few feet away that he had failed to notice another creature rising beside him. In astonishment, he watched as beads of blood seeped through the skin where the nails had scratched him. Instantly, in a reaction that required no further thought, he was on his feet, and when he saw other pygmy heads with baleful eyes focused solely on him, mounds of earth – ten, a dozen, Christ – *twenty, twenty at least!* – rising from the ground around him, he broke into a run, but came to a halt almost immediately when a brown head mounted on narrow scrawny shoulders blocked his way. He took a different direction, but stopped again as yet another thing rose in front of him, the creature's mouth downturned, almost mournful, its teeth like needles, its expression wicked.

As he hesitated, the lights attacked him, diving and swooping, tearing across his path, stinging his face and raised hands, their drone piercing, the noise itself seeming to cut into his head, confusing him, increasing his panic. He headed in another direction, this time leaping over the next minikin creature, whose skinny arms and claws reached out to scratch at him, the rest of its runty little body still trapped in the earth. Thom ran and kept running, without looking back, without realizing his limp had gone, sheer fright and the desire to leave this bad dream far behind driving him onwards.

But the nightmare followed. Indeed, it even preceded him, for he began to see things ahead and around him in his beloved woodland never before encountered, nor imagined.

A tangle of spiky brambles and intertwined branches appeared to be a shadowy tumble of limbs and faces, entwined bodies, from which evil-looking eyes peered out at him. An old oak that had fascinated him as a child, with its rough and rutted trunk, its gnarled bumps and whorls that invoked myriad images of faces, now seemed sinister. Its great branches contorted to reach down for him, perhaps to grab him as he ran by and crush him in a cruel embrace. The faces he had once imagined were really there now, features pronounced and mouths grinning at him, calling silently, eyes of wrinkled bark blind but somehow seeing him. Little figures that sat in the grass beside the trail turned doll-sized heads to watch his flight and although he did not return their stares – he was concentrating too hard on the way ahead – he caught impressions of narrow faces with mouths too wide, long pointed ears that resembled wings, mean sloping eyes and noses that were too large, or too small, or no noses at all but slitty apertures that must have been nostrils. Most appeared to be naked, their flesh pale, coloured green or muddy, some even blue. Others had bodies so misshapen, limbs so tortured, and countenances so wickedly cunning, they could only be described as grotesques.

Although startling, it was fleeting, for Thom had no wish to slow his pace, no desire to linger in this terrible place that once had been so wonderful for him.

Shapes with wings – these were not the shiny little creatures of earlier, for they were larger and with no incandescence – fluttered against his face like attacking bats, and their touch was harsh, sharp, like razorblades. He swiped them away with frantic hands, expecting his flesh to be cut to ribbons but, although the skin stung where he made contact, there were no wounds or blood. The assailants quickly fell away and he thought he heard – perhaps he imagined – fading laughter.

He staggered onwards, stumbling occasionally over the uneven ground or tree roots, creeping trailers across the path or fallen branches, and he had the crazy notion that these things were deliberately trying to trip him. That ridiculous thought led him to wonder if the haemorrhage to his brain had not done even more damage than was originally thought; had the damage created all sorts of post-chemical malfunctions inside his head, disruptions that created hallucinations? Maybe it was something to do with the drugs they had fed him in the aftermath of the stroke. Maybe he was just going crazy.

He kept moving, hobbling now, left foot already turned inwards, left arm, bent at the elbow, hand dangling, held to his side. His gait had become ungainly, a clumsy lope.

Thom tried to focus on the uncertain path, ignoring sly

movements in the undergrowth on either side and the low whispering and giggling that seemed to be following him, just as he had decided to ignore his own nagging questions. It matters not at all if all this was mere illusion: the fear was genuine, as was the desperate need to get back to Little Bracken where he had always been safe, where Bethan had promised him nothing nasty could ever enter . . .

But it was a long way home, an awful long way. And he was already beginning to flag.

As he passed beneath a low-hanging tree branch, something grabbed at his hair. He uttered a single cry as steely fingers curled into the roots, and a shout of pain followed the cry as he pulled away and stumbled on, sure that hair had been yanked from his scalp. Thom thought he heard someone snicker, a coarse, throaty kind of closed cackle that terrorized him even more, because it contained so much threat.

Panic, haste, pumping adrenaline, made his vision almost kaleidoscopic, a jumbled medley of colours and movement and his breathing was difficult, the exertion spoiling its rhythm. Glancing behind him did not help his confusion and he had to look again because, even though his sight was muddied, there were no pursuers, the trail behind was empty.

The surprise sent him veering off the path, crashing into undergrowth and nearly smacking into the thick trunk of an elm. His flailing hand caught something attached to a low bough as he went down. He rested there on hands and knees, shocked and winded, shoulders heaving as he sucked in air, and something flashed across his downturned face. He heard a sharp buzzing sound that was different from before and another tiny flying thing – although it could have been the same one – skimmed across his cheek. Suddenly there were more than one or two, suddenly there was a swarm of them and he quickly understood that these were not the same as the creatures that had chased him from the lake, these were far less exotic, and certainly not hallucinatory. They were bees – no, they were *wasps* – and he realized that the earthy mound that his hand had clipped on the low-hanging bough was the hardened pulp of a wasps' nest. He had frightened them into believing they were under attack and now they were reacting instinctively, they were countering-attacking, defending their queens and their home. Within seconds the air around him was filled with long black and yellow-striped bodies and the sound of their fury.

He felt the first sting, quickly followed by the second, then a third, then – he lost count. Their poisoned barbs stabbed the skin of his face and waving hands, his bare arms, his neck – anywhere that was exposed. Thom gasped at the sudden needle-pricks of agonizing pain, some of the wounds already going numb, beginning to swell, and he scrabbled to his feet and kept moving, afraid that if he fell again he would be at their mercy, pain and exhaustion would render him helpless. He knew he had to find refuge and quickly. Had to get home . . .

An eyelid half-closed, the sharpness of the sting making him cry out. Thom held his hands up to his face, frightened that he might be blinded and completely defenceless. He slapped at the little whining bodies, feeling them reel from the blows, but never for long, always they came back at him, attacking, stinging, for these were the female wasps, the dangerous kind, who would not give up their attack until each one was exhausted and the enemy vanquished.

He had never been inordinately sensitive to wasp stings – as a boy he had suffered more than a few – but with so many of them injecting their venom into him, he feared that he might go into allergic shock and that in his debilitated state, it might even kill him. He screamed at them, still flailing with his arms, staggering into bushes, glancing off trees, the agony of their jabs driving him on rather than dragging him down, each separate stab causing an involuntary spasm. He knew that if he fell, if he tripped or fatigue brought him to his knees, then he would be in serious trouble. They would not leave him alone until their anger was sated and the threat eliminated.

Thom stumbled onwards with no idea of direction, just desperate to get as far away from their nest as possible. He could feel them inside his now open gilet, could feel them at his ankles and on his bare arms, the agonizing punctures becoming one massive hurt, and when he cried yet again, he felt one enter his mouth.

He spat it out, but too late: the inside of his cheek exploded with a fiery pain that almost made him faint. With sheer force of will, Thom remained upright and he used his own anger, the thought that such vicious little bastards could torment him this way, to drive himself on. He needed to find shelter, and find it fast, but he had no idea how far away he was from Little Bracken, nor even if he was going the right way, for he had to hold his hands to his eyes to protect them, the throbbing left eyelid already shut tight of its own accord. So he just loped onwards, foot dragging, praying for the attack to stop, tempted to lie down and curl into a tight ball, using his shirt and arms to cover his head and face, but he knew the wasps would be relentless, that they would keep up their attack until he was unconscious, and, if that did happen, if he passed out, then he would be entirely at their mercy.

Then, through the gaps between his protective swelling fingers, he glimpsed a sight that was completely unexpected. Only a few yards ahead was a broad expanse of calm water. Somehow he had arrived back at the lake. Blindness and agony had driven him in a wide circle so that he had unwittingly, but oh so fortunately, returned to the lake.

There was a barrier of undergrowth and shrubbery between him and the great expanse of cool, placid water, but it wasn't a problem. Thom smashed his way through, brushing away obstacles with his hands, treading down leafy plants, the air around him almost black with the swarm, and then he was in the clear, staggering down the gentle incline of the bank until his boots were squelching mud and splashing water. Before it was even up to his knees, Thom dived, his lean body stretched, straightened right arm breaking the surface. The lake closed over him, but he kept going, kicking and thrashing, plunging down until he was sure that every part of himself was covered by the water.

And there he waited in the mud-swirling darkness, lying in sludge, praying for deliverance, until his breath ran out. Only then, and with much reluctance, did he push himself upwards.

The wasps were waiting.

# Chapter : Tenth

# THE WAY BACK

I T MIGHT have been the pain that roused him. Or it might just have been time for consciousness to reassert itself. Could have been both.

Thom felt as though his body – his *whole* body – was on fire. No, it was worse than that: he felt as if his blood was on fire, molten streams coursing through his veins, carrying the broiling lava to every part, every extremity. Even the inside of his mouth burned white heat. He groaned and barely heard his own sound, for his senses were still gathering themselves. He tried to move and the movement was stiff, clumsy, as if his limbs were fettered. His fingers curled into soft damp soil.

He took his time, allowed the thoughts to assemble, to consider his predicament, to puzzle how and when he had escaped both a watery grave and the wrath of the wasps. But he could not remember a thing, only the merciful plunge into the lake. Just blackness after that. Wait . . . a hazy vision filtering through. Rising again, but heavy, pressure pushing at him from all around, the lake's smooth, bright ceiling above him, broken only by the silver bubbles of his own air escaping from his deflating lungs. Pushing through ... sunlight in his eyes ... a swirling horde, a mass of droning things waiting for him ... inches from his upturned face. Then ... nothing.

Now he was on the lake's muddy bank and he had no idea how he had got there.

Only one of his eyes was open; the eyelid of the other, his left, felt as if something heavy were glued to it. It throbbed painfully and Thom remembered he had been stung there.

Nevertheless, he forced the eyelid open, using a trembling finger, wincing as he did so, and succeeding only partially. The vision there was blurred, as though a thin liquid layer covered the pupil. He took his hand away and rested his head against his forearm, lying there on his stomach in the greasy soil, his breathing unsteady, his whole body shivering. He could smell the moist earth, could hear birdsong around him. The sun burned his cheek, aggravating the stings even more. Thom moaned and attempted to turn on to his side.

He managed, but it took effort and the pain was intense. Lifting his head a few inches from the mud, he looked towards the trees, not sure what he expected to see. Those flying lights? The young ... girl? He prayed it wouldn't be the wasps swarming again. All was clear though, all was quiet. Save for the birds. And the mild breeze that whispered through leaves and grass. Everything appeared to be normal. Everything except the bizarre images that continued to crowd his mind.

'Insane,' he mumbled to himself, aloud because he needed to hear his own voice. 'Crazy,' he added, as if the first word was not enough. 'Must ... be ... going ... crazy...' He knew he wasn't though. He was sure of himself enough to know he hadn't imagined everything that had happened before the wasps had attacked. It might have seemed like fantasy right then, but Thom knew what he had witnessed was real. He was no lunatic, and the illness had not turned him into one. The neurologists had assured him that, as far as they could tell, there had been no serious damage to his brain, otherwise his recovery would not be progressing so swiftly. The MRI scan had revealed nothing abnormal inside his head, and a lumbar puncture had shown that his brain fluids were clear ('like gin', they had told him). They *might* be wrong, they had admitted, there was always the chance of something showing up later, but they didn't think so. And neither did he. He was *okay*. His mind was *fine*.

Then explain it, Thom. *Explain it!*

He was aware that his thoughts were rambling and his body was beginning to shake violently. He was going into shock and if he didn't move soon he would probably lie here for the rest of the day and night. And if that were the case, then he'd really be in trouble.

'Have to get home,' he instructed himself, speaking aloud because he felt it was necessary. 'Get back, use the phone.' Thom cursed himself for not bringing the mobile with him. He'd wanted to get away from everything and everyone, find his own space, enjoy the absence of well-meaning but interfering people. Wanted to reclaim his life in his own way. Big mistake today, pal. Oh yeah, big one.

Thom struggled to get to his feet, his head groggy, balance all out of kilter, the pain excruciating. Wanting to lie back down again, but scared of its implication, Thom rested with his hands on his knees, waiting for the dizziness to pass and, hopefully, take the nausea with it. He swayed there for a few moments before taking the dare and staggering over to the double trunk of an alder, the nearest tree to him. He held on to it with one hand, his body bent, other hand on a knee, resting there until he got his breath back. He began to retch, but nothing pumped up from his stomach except a clear drool that hung from his mouth in a slick stream.

After a few moments that could easily have stretched out a lot longer, Thom willed himself to straighten up. The collar of his sleeveless shirt seemed to bite into his neck when he turned his head to search around and he uttered a sharp cry; he tried again, but more slowly this time. He had no idea what he was searching for: he knew he was alone in the woods, that there was no one around to help him. He felt like weeping, nothing unusual for him these days, but now it was more in frustration and pain than self-pity.

He wasn't going to make it. The poisons were racing through his body, their combined strength weakening him, making him feel sick, tightening his chest so it was difficult to breathe, causing a reaction in his blood ... blood that flowed to his brain ... Oh shit, what kind of damage was that going to do?

Thom pushed away from the tree, forcing himself to stand straight and draw in deep shuddering breaths, despite the restriction in his chest. After wiping drool from his mouth with a shaking hand, he made to walk towards the trail that had brought him here to the lake.

It was an optimistic move, far too bold for one in his state, and his legs, particularly the left one, almost gave way beneath him. He managed to catch himself, halting for a second or two, just long enough to regain his balance. Then on again, foot dragging, bent arm rigid against his stomach, moving woodenly but determinedly closing his mind to the swellings, the unreasonable sense of venom rushing through veins and arteries, concentrating on the way ahead.

He lost count of how many times he fell and picked himself up again, and he lost all sense of time. He lost all sense of reality also, the woodland around him a confusing place, the hot pain of his entire body all-consuming, making him feverish. One clear image kept him moving though, a light that danced ahead of him, never within catching distance, always just beyond reach, and his tormented mind told him he might as well follow it, follow the star, for he had nothing better to do, nowhere else to go, and as long as his stiffening legs kept moving and his one good eye, the other no more than a Popeye squint, kept seeing the floating light, the pretty, oh so pretty, little light, then sure, he would follow, because for God's sake, at the moment this was the only friend he had in this lonely wilderness: the insects didn't like him, and the trees, these trees on either side of the path, well, they didn't like him, because they were scowling and their branches were trying to scratch him as he went by, and maybe they were trying to grab him like before, and maybe the trees were in league with those little monkey-monsters that lived in the earth, the horrible midget-things which had tried to catch him and which had sent the wasps after him, bastard little venomous wasps that had tried to sting him to death, but he'd been too smart for them, he'd jumped into the lake, the lake ... where he'd first seen the girl ... the beautiful, wondrous girl ... who had – he *knew* she had – sent him ... the light ... little dancing light ... to guide him ... home ...

In his delirium, Thom failed to notice that he had strayed from the original path and had wandered off on to one that was even more obscure, a way that perhaps could only be familiar to woodland creatures. A path that – although he was not yet to know this – led more quickly to Little Bracken.

# Chapter : Eleventh

## AWAKENING

THE AFTERNOON, the evening, the night – the *whole* of the night – passed as a blur. Thom remembered finding himself on the doorstep of the cottage and the front door was wide open as if he had been expected.

Nothing more then. He could not remember entering, nor climbing the stairs to the bedroom; he could not remember undressing, but did remember waking later in his bed, naked beneath a single sheet. He thought there had been someone else in the room with him, but could not recall seeing anyone. He was sure though, that he had felt soothing hands on his body, gentle applications of creams or ointments to his wounds and swellings, the coolness seeping through to dampen their heat, sinking deep into the poisons to weaken their hold and blunt agony's sharp edge.

He remembered glimpsing a face close above his own, that same sweet face he had been mesmerized by in the woods, golden hair hanging loose to brush against his

107

cheeks, his forehead. The softest fingertips touching his swollen eyelid, more lotions being applied, the mist – and the pain – lifting from the injured eye. Yet he had been unable to speak, unable to express gratitude ... unable to ask who she was.

He also thought he had witnessed the tiny lights once more, this time gliding around the bedroom, leaving and entering by an open window, but he could not be sure, it might have been part of the delirium, an evocation of his fevered mind. Whatever they were, real or imaginary, they had made him feel wonderfully peaceful with their subtle hues and their graceful flight.

There had seemed to be occasional voices, sweet sounds that were easy on the ear – and sometimes there came that high flutey whistling, the speech of the lights. Thom could be sure of none of this, though: it could all have been a fever-induced dream. Possibly he had found his own way home, had climbed the spiral staircase and put himself to bed, all the rest in his own imagination. But he did not think so, because it wouldn't have made sense. The attack had left him too weak, too full of poison, the combined stings enough maybe even to fell a horse or a cow. So much injected into a human could have proved terminal. He had gone into some kind of anaphylactic shock and there was no way he could have got himself upstairs, shed his clothes and climbed into bed. Just no way.

Then there was the liquid he had been coaxed into drinking. He was certain of that, could easily recall its cool, syrupy taste, someone – the girl, it had to be the girl, he could still remember her fragrance that was of flowers and fresh air and nature itself – lifting his head from the pillow, delicate fingers cushioning the back of his neck, the liquid she proffered yellow in colour, like honey, but less viscid, flowing smoothly into his parched throat. The sound of her voice came back to him, for it could not easily be forgotten, even though the words might. Gentle, tender – *magical*. The voice of an angel. But angels did not masturbate in the woods. Did they?

He put a hand to his forehead, aware that he was going nowhere with this line of thought. There was a dull ache in both temples, but otherwise there was no pain and, as he stretched his legs beneath the sheet, apparently no stiffness. He still felt tired, but not exhausted, which presented another mystery: with all he had been through, he should have felt totally drained even after a good day and night's sleep. That was the natural law of things. There was always an aftermath, even if only brief.

Thom began to explore his face with his fingertips, cautious at first, touching lightly, feeling for the tender inflammation and swelling capped by blisters that should have been there. He felt only his own skin and overnight stubble on his chin. He already knew before touching the left eyelid that there would be no injury, his vision was clear in both eyes, and there was no weight on the lid that had been stung. What the hell was going on?

Thom studied his hands, the palms, their backs: there were no marks, scabs or punctures, nothing at all to indicate the harm they had suffered when he had tried to beat away the swarming wasps. Throwing back the bedsheet from his waist, he lifted his head to look at his legs and in particular, his ankles. Nothing. God, he did not even feel anything.

He leapt from the bed and went over to the free-standing swivel mirror on the oak sideboard. Tilting it so that he could examine his face, Thom released a long, slow breath. Apart from the two small shallow scars on his cheek and lower lip, he was unblemished, completely unmarked.

Thom straightened, eyes staring straight ahead, yet seeing nothing. He felt dazed, confused. But most of all, he felt wonderfully well.

Thom hurriedly donned cargoes and short-sleeved sweat-shirt, pondering the events of the day before as he did so, the fact that at least *some* of it had happened given credence by the condition of the clothes he had worn, the joggers and gilet, which were lying together over one arm of the sofa. They were sodden and muddy, the armless shirt torn in several places. He examined the damp tan boots, picking one up and turning it over in his hand to examine the undersole. Mud was caked between its ridges. And there, leaning against a windowsill close to the bed, was the walking-stick he had lost during his flight from the horror near the lake. He shook his head in puzzlement.

Bundling clothes and boots together, Thom carried them downstairs and laid them on a kitchen worktop for attention later. His bare feet were cooled by the flagstone floor. It was only when Thom glanced at the old wind-up clock on the windowsill that he realized how late it was: fifteen past ten. The sun's position through the bedroom window should have given him a hint earlier. He rarely slept so late, but obviously his body knew it needed the rest. A yawn escaped him as though prompted and he stretched his arms wide and high, arching his back, letting go of the last sleepy remnants, feeling unusually well. He froze mid-yawn when he spotted the bowl of fresh fruit on the centre table.

Beside it was a jug of cloudy liquid – it looked like opaque apple juice – and Thom strolled over, puzzled, his arms now folded, hands clamped around his upper arms beneath the short sleeves of his light grey sweatshirt in a gesture of calm but reluctant acceptance. He was already too mystified by events to be fazed by the unexpected offering of food and drink. That someone had tended him through the afternoon and night, then left him breakfast the next day was fine; what really troubled him was *who* that someone could be.

He remembered the beautiful face close to his own as he lay in fever, the golden hair brushing his face, the tenderness in her eyes. The vision became sharper. Those lovely, doe-like eyes, tilted at the corners, their colour ... their colour changing from silver-blue to an astonishing soft shade of violet! The memory stunned him and he could only stand by the table and stare into space, his mind reeling once more. *Who was she?*

His thoughts then went to his first sight of her, naked in the small clearing by the lake, touching herself in that most intimate way, the tiny lights driven to a frenzy around her, helping her with her pleasure, titillating her body with their movement and glances, and memory revived that same desire he had felt when he had been innocent voyeur to her personal moment, hidden observer to solitary (apart from the tiny lights) passion.

His erection swelled against his clothing and, despite himself, it felt good, was, in fact, a relief to him, for such reaction had been absent too long and the absence had caused him anguish. His mouth became dry, his hardening almost painful, as the eroticism he had been witness to filled his mind and senses. He cupped a hand to himself as if to stay the tide of passion, but the touch merely increased the sensation, made him give out a small groan. It had been a long time since ...

Jesus! No. You're not that bloody desperate!

With a sigh of frustration, Thom wheeled around and strode determinedly from the kitchen into the bathroom beneath the stairs where he whipped off the sweatshirt and doused his face and chest with cold water from the tap. Still dripping, he steadied himself by gripping the sides of the porcelain sink with both hands, elbows locked, arms straight, and stared into the wall mirror.

The soul-wearying tiredness that had reflected back at him for so long was gone; in its place was a fresh vitality, a sharp-edged keenness in his eyes that was marred only slightly by the confusion in them. Thom suddenly found himself smiling at his own image.

With a rueful shake of his head he reached for his electric razor.

---

Thom sat at the oak table and took a huge dark plum from the bowl, pouring himself a tumbler-full of apple juice, or whatever it was, from the jug before biting into it. He warily took a sip first, taste buds sampling the juice before swallowing.

It *was* apple juice; and yet it wasn't. It had a flavour all its own, one that was unfamiliar to him, a sweetness that was refreshing rather than sickly. It tasted like nectar – not that he'd *ever* tasted nectar, nor knew anyone who had. But it was his idea of what nectar would be like if he had the chance. Deep, satiating, somehow filling his chest first before his stomach, the flavour almost addictive. This from one small sip. He took a larger gulp, nearly draining the tumbler.

If the drink was good, then the fruit was an ideal complement. The plum *was* a plum, looked like a plum, tasted like a plum. But oh God, it was the finest and biggest plum he had ever eaten. And the apple that he tried next was the finest apple he'd ever eaten, as were the berries he tried afterwards. It was as if he could physically feel their goodness, their nourishment, entering his system, to revive and energize. Thom was well aware that senses could be heightened after a long illness, but this was different. It was as though this was the first fruit he had ever eaten and the very first juice he had ever drunk. Neither tasted strange, but both were unique.

With renewed relish, Thom sat at the table and feasted.

---

Sometime later, after exercising (which he had tackled with uncharacteristic enthusiasm) and completing what little unpacking was still left to do, he heard the sound of a car's engine approaching the cottage. Assuming that either Eric Pimlet was paying another visit, or that Nell Quick had returned, this time by car, Thom went to the open front door.

The small, sickly green, two-door VW Polo had pulled up beside his Jeep by the time he reached the doorstep and a bespectacled young woman was opening the driver's door.

'Hi!' she called out, stepping from the Volkswagen and giving him a cheery wave. 'Tried to reach you on your mobile yesterday, but it must have been switched off. Unless I was given the wrong number, of course.'

She wore trainers and tight-fitting black cycle shorts, a white T-shirt and an open, hooded zip-up; as she stretched back into the car to retrieve something from the passenger seat, he saw that her legs were long and lightly tanned (just a few shades off their natural colour), white ankle-socks enhancing their tone. Quickly, she was upright again, slamming the car door with one hand, a large canvas sports bag in the other. She came towards Thom, her smile as cheery as her greeting, her free hand now stretched towards him, fingers straight, thumb cocked.

'Katy Budd,' she announced. 'Your new rehab physiotherapist, here to get you fighting fit again.'

Thom offered his own hand and she shook it a lot less robustly than he thought she might, probably in deference to his condition, whatever she assumed that to be. Her tawny-flecked eyes behind the round thin-rimmed glasses were already appraising him.

Thom was undertaking his own appraisal: probably in her late twenties, just slightly overweight, heavy-breasted and bra-less it seemed, for her nipples were pleasingly pronounced; her blonde hair contained lighter streaks that looked sun-blessed rather than beauty-fashioned, and her face was appealing rather than pretty. She had an engaging smile and lively expression.

'You weren't easy to find,' she was saying as he considered all this. 'Luckily, I went to the big place – Castle Bracken? – first and they directed me here.' He detected Home Counties in her accent rather than anything local.

'Sorry I missed your phone call,' he apologized. 'Could've made it easier for you.'

'No problem. I'm here now. Can we discuss the torture?'

He grinned, but only weakly; he knew the kind of 'torture' she had in mind.

'Sure. Come in. Can I get you coffee?'

'Fruit juice would be nicer.'

'Ah. I've got just the thing.'

He led the way inside without bothering to close the door behind them.

As she placed the sports bag on the floor her eyes swept round the octagonal-shaped room.

'This is such a cute place,' she said with unconcealed delight. 'It looks like some tiny faerytale castle as you approach. Is it your holiday home? The agency told me you lived in London.'

'No, I was born here.'

She looked at him in surprise.

'I went south when I was a kid. Stayed down there after I left college.'

'I see,' she said, but he could tell she didn't quite; she probably thought he was loaded, with a place in London and a retreat up here.

'You said juice rather than coffee? I could make tea.' Was he suddenly reluctant to share the nectar?

'Oh no, juice is fine.'

He mentally slapped his own wrist. Selfish with fruit juice? Come *on*.

Thom took a glass tumbler from the dresser and poured

from the jug, saving just a little for his own glass. He caught her watching his hands, no doubt looking for signs of poor finger extension; generally, it wasn't gripping objects that stroke victims had trouble with, but releasing them, extending fingers enough to let go. They sat opposite each other and exchanged generalities before discussing the main topic – his illness and the exercise regime she proposed to help get him back to normal.

'Basically it's this,' she said, taking leaflets and notebook and pen from her bag. 'These are for you . . .' she pushed the leaflets across the table at him. 'You probably know everything about having a stroke and what it does to your body – not to mention your mind – and I know you've already been through a lot of physiotherapy, but these will just refresh your memory. That particular one . . .' she indicated the leaflet he was flicking through '. . . will explain the exercises I've planned and how they'll help your body get completely back to normal. In your case, because the stroke was relatively minor and because you're still young, I think we can achieve that. Tell me how you're feeling now, after what is it, three months . . .?'

'Four.'

'Okay. How fit do you feel you are and what physically is bothering you the most?'

Thom gave her a quick rundown on his present condition, mentioning the ongoing weakness to the left side of his body, and the physiotherapist made notes, nodding her head and making sympathetic noises as she did so. Naturally having no wish for the state of his mind to be brought into question, he made no mention of yesterday's little adventures, the naked girl in the forest, the floating lights, the attack of the wasp swarm (how the hell would he explain the lack of marks and bruising to his body?), and the loathsome things that had tried to crawl from the earth itself. No, he wasn't that crazy – at least not crazy enough to tell anyone else.

As he talked, he noticed she was constantly laying down her pen to take more and more frequent sips of the drink he had given her, until finally she said:

'What *is* this stuff? It's delicious. At first I thought it was apple juice, but now I'm not so sure.'

For some reason unbeknown even to himself he lied. 'Apple juice mixed with mango.' The invented ingredients almost seemed reasonable, given the unusual taste.

The therapist screwed up her face and held up the glass to examine the last dregs. 'You could've fooled me. Doesn't taste like that.'

Again, he lied, and again, he wondered why. 'Well, I've added something a little extra of my own. Secret recipe, you know?'

She gave him a mean smile and shook her head. 'So I can't get it in Tesco's or my local health shop?'

He laughed with her.

The therapist took a few more notes as he resumed informing her of how he felt generally until finally she flipped the notebook shut and laid it on the table.

'Good,' she said with another reassuring smile. 'I think you might be one of my easy clients. I've got to say, you already look pretty fit to me.'

'Uh, one thing . . .'

Her eyebrows rose askance.

'Did . . . have . . . have any other patients or, er, clients of yours – those who've suffered strokes, that is – have any had problems with, well, with their mind?'

Her attractive face became serious. 'I'm not sure what you mean. Most – no, not most, *all* – have been a lot older than you, and some have become somewhat vague or slurred their words. Sorry, I know you want me to be frank. Not all recovered their full mental faculties after their original attack. But only one or two had second and third attacks, if that's what concerns you.'

'No, I really meant mental problems.' There, he'd said it.

'I'm sure your doctor has told you that often there can be speech impediment, or that simple things like reading or tying up shoelaces have to be relearned. A stroke can wipe clean certain parts of a person's memory, but they're likely to recover over a period of time. Time and patience, Mr Kindred, that's what it's all about. And exercise, of course – can I call you Thomas?'

'You could, but the name's Thom, with an *h*, but no *as*.'

'Mine's Katy, with a *y*. And Budd has two *d*s. So, listen, we'll make a start day after tomorrow, but now I want to do a few simple tests.' She reached into the sports bag by her feet and drew something out.

He was surprised to see it was a small dartboard.

She quickly looked around and spied the coat hook on the door leading to the spiral staircase. 'That'll do,' she said, rising and taking the dartboard over to it. She hung it on the hook and returned to the bag, dipping into it again and bringing out a transparent box containing three feathered darts.

'D'you mind standing . . .' she mentally measured a distance from the dartboard and pointed to a spot on the flagstone floor '. . . just about there.'

He did as she asked, bemusedly taking the offered arrows.

'Aim for the centre,' Katy told him. 'Get me a nice bullseye.'

Thom suddenly understood the point of the exercise, for he'd tried something similar for his last therapist.

'Left hand, I suppose,' he said.

'I've read your notes, but I've forgotten. The infarct was in the right hemisphere, wasn't it?'

He nodded.

'So the left side of your body is the problem, right? I ask because it isn't noticeable to me.'

'Not today, it isn't.' He was surprised himself, especially after all he had been through two days ago.

117

'Your previous therapist has done a terrific job,' Katy commented.

He didn't reply, raising the dart to eye level with his left hand instead. Depending on which side of the brain the haemorrhage took place, the recovering victim would favour a particular direction when throwing an object. In his case, when aiming for centre the dart would probably strike the right-hand side of the board. He released the arrow after only one flexing of his arm and it almost hit bullseye.

'Hey!' Katy exclaimed. 'Good shot. Another.'

The second arrow was only slightly less accurate.

'Another!'

The third hit dead centre.

Katy clapped her hands, but not in a patronizing way; he could tell she was genuinely pleased.

'The next test seems hardly necessary,' she said, still smiling. 'Walk the line for me, please.'

She was pointing at one of the long joins in the flagstone floor and Thom obediently paced it, aware that his tester was watching for left 'foot-lift' and perhaps anticipating a drift off course.

'Okay, great,' she said when he reached the other side of the kitchen without deviation from the line, 'foot-drag', or left foot turning inwards. She quickly put him through a few other exercises – foot extensions, outwardly rotating arm movements, shoulder protraction, upper arm and leg extensions, hand and finger extension – all of which he passed with flying colours, again even surprising himself.

Katy watched his breathing, made him stand on his toes, then his heels, tested his reflexes, and finally asked him to close his eyes and extend his arms at shoulder level. After a full minute she allowed him to open his eyes again and he saw for himself that both arms were still level, the left had not drifted downwards.

'I'm not even going to ask you to climb on a chair, or watch you get into your car,' she said with a further satisfied smile as she took down the dartboard and put it back into the bag, 'because everything tells me your gross motor skills are fine. I understood from the medical notes they sent me that you still had some way to go. If you do, I can't see it.'

'This seems to be a particularly good day,' he replied almost sheepishly.

'Well, we'll see how you do next time. I think I'm going to work you quite hard, so be prepared.'

She produced a card from a pocket in her zip-up. 'Here's my number and address should you need to get in touch urgently. Mobile's on there too. I'm just on the outskirts of Shrewsbury, so I can get over in no time at all. Do you think I could check your mobile number in case I have to reach you?'

As Thom wrote the number down on a scrap of notepaper he wondered if she offered the same service to all her clients; she wasn't a GP after all.

Katy lifted the sports bag and glanced around the room again.

'It has a lovely atmosphere,' she remarked. 'Quite peaceful. Serene, sort of. You're a lucky man, Thom.'

Yeah, he thought, as if the notion had only just struck him. Yeah, I am. He smiled back at her and it turned into a grin.

'I'm very lucky,' he said.

# Chapter : Twelfth

## RETURN TO THE BIG HOUSE

THE WEATHER had turned. Rain clouds had gathered in the east to be carried by stiff westerly winds across the country, now settling over the county in one scarcely drifting grey blanket. The climate was uncomfortably warm though, even humid, the occasional spot of rain having little effect, and Thom rested his elbow on the sill of the Jeep's open window as he drove towards Castle Bracken so that fresh air blew into his face.

Questions continued to plague him, questions not only concerning the weird and exciting events just passed, but also as to why exactly he had lied to the physiotherapist, Katy Budd. That particular answer came soon enough: *Because you didn't want her to think you were going nuts.*

Who would believe such a story? No one, and you're sane enough to know that. So why let them think that the stroke caused some brain damage when you know it hasn't?

*You do know that, don't you?*

You're not mad, you're not suffering dementia (even if

you are talking to yourself like this; that's something you've always done, and long before the illness, right?).

'Right,' he said aloud.

Thom steered across the road and took the Jeep into the rutted lane between the trees. So if you're not crazy, he continued to ask himself, what the hell was it all about yesterday and the day before?

Of course, no answer came, but for the moment Thom was not unduly worried. He felt good. He felt healthy. He felt better than he had for four long, wearying months. Air coming through the open windows tangled his hair and ruffled the soft collar of the white short-sleeved polo shirt he wore over straight-legged jeans and soft loafers.

The Jeep bounced and bumped over the rutted surface, but was soon through the open gates and on to the smoother road leading up to Castle Bracken.

When he arrived at the front steps, Thom was surprised to see a black vintage bicycle resting against them, a shopping basket affixed to the handlebars and no crossbar to its frame; it also lacked alternative gears and appeared sturdy enough to bear a circus elephant. A real relic, Thom mused as he stepped from the Jeep. Hugo's Range Rover was some distance away near the edge of the parking quadrangle, so he assumed his friend was at home. The old Bentley, no doubt, was parked inside the garage at the rear.

Thom climbed the steps up to the front door without realizing he had left the walking-stick behind in the vehicle, propped up against the passenger seat; he even failed to notice there was not the slightest hint of a limp to his stride. His thoughts were more concerned with the dilapidated state of the big manor house itself, something that had not quite sunk in the first day of his return. Certainly he had noticed the patchwork discoloration of the edifice, but not the crumbling of the stonework's pointing, the cracked and flaking window-frames, nor the chipped and damaged mouldings. The stone steps, too, had hairline cracks, and their surfaces were worn, uneven, as if trodden by too many generations of feet; faint hues of green mould discoloured them. The mansion was becoming shamefully run down, which was a great pity, for although as a child he had feared the place, he was equally in awe of it. Now Castle Bracken was losing its grandeur, growing old without grace. The change saddened him.

He was about to press the bell when the great door swung open and Hugo's broad grinning face beamed out at him.

'Hello, Thom. Saw you pull up. Wasn't expecting you. Everything all right?'

Thom took the outstretched hand and shook it. Always formal on any occasion, his friend Hugo.

'Everything's fine,' he said stepping over the threshold. 'I just thought I'd pay my respects to Sir Russell.'

'Ah. I see. Might be awkward, old son. Father's resting right now.'

Bracken's large entrance hall was in gloom, the long windows over the wide sweeping staircase north-facing, its unpolished oak-panelled walls aiding and abetting the lacklustre atmosphere. Thom remembered that the high chandelier was rarely lit during daytime, no matter how overcast the weather. Sombre portraits of previous tenants decked the walls and their faces appeared to be peering out from mysterious shadows. The stale mausoleum smell was instantly familiar and he wasn't surprised he had always hated the place as a child – it had little appeal to him now.

Black and white tiles decorated the floor, although the white squares had turned a miserable yellowish-grey over the years, and many closed doors led off from the hall (he remembered how Sir Russell had always insisted that doors be left open. A proud man, he would never admit to anyone that he suffered from claustrophobia – he loathed confined spaces, and everyone knew it), a few plinths bearing small statues or busts standing against the walls between them. A long oak settle with threadbare cushions nestled in the space under the stairway, the plain door next to it the entrance to the enormous cellar area built into the foundations of the house. Thom remembered how, when they were boys, he and Hugo once – and only *once* – had played hide-and-seek down there. Many years ago. God, a lifetime ago, it seemed ...

———

It had been Hugo's idea to use the labyrinth of underground rooms and corridors for the game, even though the basement was strictly out of bounds to both of them. But its mystery was appealing and Hugo's entreaties had quickly overcome Thom's trepidation. Given the 'privilege' of hiding first, he was sent on ahead, Hugo holding the door open for him and pointing challengingly at the darkness below. All the light-switches to the cellar area were conveniently banked together on a panel just inside the doorway and Hugo flicked them all on so that the darkness, though not all of the shadows, was immediately vanquished.

Warily, Thom went down the creaky stairway while Hugo, his face a mask of innocence, remained by the door; Thom caught his friend's sly smile when he glanced back but, regardless, continued the descent, reluctant to be thought afraid, eager to impress. A long corridor led back beneath the house and doorless entrances to various chambers were set in the rough brick walls. Dusty naked lightbulbs dangled from twisted flexes and the smell of must and dirt that permeated the air seemed to penetrate his very skin.

Although hesitant at first, the sound from above of his friend's slow count to a hundred urged Thom to venture further into the labyrinth. He was half-way down the corridor, peering through openings, seeking a suitable place to hide, when all the lights blinked off. From behind he heard the muted sound of Hugo's laughter.

Thom's natural impulse was to scoot back upstairs, feeling the corridor's unfinished walls for guidance, but fear of Hugo's teasing and his own determination drove him on. Okay, let Hugo find me in the dark if he has the nerve, Thom said to himself with forced bravado as he touched his way along the corridor. In truth, his heart felt frozen inside his chest and he had almost cried out, almost *shrieked*, when the lights had gone out. Now he was fighting to control his terror by withdrawing into himself, going into that inner retreat Bethan had told him of, the personal place, where nothing outside could ever enter, nothing else could ever touch, because it was the secret home of his true spirit, his true *self*. It was untouchable to anything beyond himself, she had said, because it was not part of this Earth, even though it governed everything he did and thought. His mother had never properly explained it, but had assured him that the bigger he grew, the older and wiser he got, and the more he believed in its presence, so he would begin to understand for himself. Only life itself, with all its outward influences, could dim the knowledge. He had been only six years old when Bethan had told him of this, and four years later – barely a month before she had killed herself – her words were still strong within him.

He moved further into the umbra, his hand feeling the cracks and the crumbling mortar in the wall, fingers floating in the terrifying empty space whenever he passed an open doorway, making his way towards an eerie light source that glimmered faintly up ahead.

By the time he reached the opening at the end of the corridor his eyes had grown used to the blackness around him and the pale beacon seemed clearer, stronger, with each step. He had began to wrinkle his nose at the coal dust in the air long before he reached the doorless end-chamber and when he stood at the portal he was able to discern a great hill of black rubble rising against a wall to his right. At its peak was a sliver of daylight, the light source itself, a vertical crack that was the centre parting of a coal hatch. The coal fell away in a steep slope, its foothills held back by a five-foot-high partition wall and as Thom peered further into the vast room he could just make out a huge metal boiler, lifeless now, the fire that should have raged inside allowed to burn itself out so that maintenance work could be done on the piping. He saw the rectangle of its open coal flap, black and empty, as if the boiler's soul had fled without closing it.

A noise behind him, Hugo beginning his search. Thom nervously looked around, seeking a place to hide. Gingerly he moved into the boiler-room, hands outstretched before him, afraid he might trip over some discarded tool or piece of junk on the floor, reaching for the top of the partition wall, then crawling around and behind it, crouching on the lower slopes of the coal hill. He tried to steady his breathing, his nostrils already clogged with black dust, tried to calm the rushed beating of his now unfrozen heart, afraid the sound might give him away. He didn't like this game any more. In fact, it was a rotten game. And this was a rotten, dirty, smelly cellar. Even so, a jittery giggle escaped him when he heard footsteps coming along the corridor outside the boiler-room.

The footsteps grew louder, treading the stone floor with slow precision, as though Hugo knew exactly where to look for Thom, but was taking time to peer into each opening along the way just in case he was wrong. Thom wondered why his friend had not switched on the lights again, but when he stood to take a quick peek over the top of the partition, he saw a dull but warm glow coming from the corridor; it became brighter as the footsteps became even louder. In his nervous excitement, Thom failed to realize that those steps were far heavier than any boy, even one of Hugo's plumpness, could make.

Suddenly they stopped and Thom could not help but giggle yet again at the thought of Hugo, candle in hand, pausing just outside the boiler-room, perhaps unsure now, or disinclined to enter such a nasty smelly place. He clapped a hand to his mouth to suppress the sound and ducked back behind the partition.

In the quietness that followed, Thom heard breathing, heavy stuff, slightly laboured, and unlike the kind a boy would make somehow. *Older* breathing.

Thom's eyes widened in the darkness. It wasn't Hugo out there. Hugo would be giggling himself by now. And Hugo hadn't had a candle when Thom had left him at the top of the stairs. And Hugo wouldn't breathe like that. Or walk like that. And, in truth, Hugo would *never* go down into a horrible dark cellar without first making sure it was well lit . . .

Thom felt his body trembling from tip to toe.

A rock of coal shifted beneath his feet and he breathed a small sharp gasp, the tendons of his neck stretching as his head sprang up an inch or so.

He heard the person outside moving again and the ceiling above the partition brightened. Whoever held the candle, whoever's footsteps were louder than any boy's, whoever's breathing was heavier too, had entered the boiler-room. Another pause and the candlelight's reflection shifted on the ceiling, as though the seeker were looking around. Thom scrunched into himself as the footsteps grated against the stone floor and the deep shadow that protected him began to glide down the hill of coal. The light was not only coming closer, but it was also being raised higher.

He tucked his head between his hunched shoulders, his breath held, his body taut although still trembling, as the mantle of covering darkness shrank away.

Thom heard the wooden partition he hid behind creak as if someone on the other side were pressing against it. He sensed a presence looming over him, felt eyes inspecting his cowering body, saw the coal around him glinting warm diamonds of light. The breathing was drawn out, a slight raspiness to its edges.

Slowly, unwillingly, Thom lifted his eyes, afraid to look

and afraid not to. Hugo had once told him that rich people kept mad or grotesquely deformed relatives locked in attics or cellars, hidden away from those who would have them incarcerated in special asylums. Hugo's daddy was rich. And Hugo had had a brother who was supposed to be dead . . .

Who *would* be wandering the cellars by candlelight?

Against his own will, he forced his gaze up the partition.

Thom shrieked and fell back against the coal rubble when he caught sight of the long cadaverous face watching him from the top of the wooden wall, its eyes dead, expressionless, tiny candle flames reflected in them, its lipless mouth set grim.

Bones – Hartgrove – had not spoken a word, Thom recalled. Instead, a thin hand, fingers extended like the claws of a funhouse lucky dip crane, had reached over to grasp him by the hair and raise him up, the pressure immense, the fingertips against his scalp icy cold. The iron grip had drawn him around the partition so that he was exposed, shivering before the tall, but stooped, thin man. In silence, Bones, who had obviously been down in the cellars before the lights had gone out using candlelight rather than electricity – the old, always frugal, manservant had odd opinions on wasting power), had released him and pointed towards the open doorway.

Thom had fled the boiler-room, not even stopping when he bumped into Hugo outside in the corridor, pocket-torch in hand. Ignoring his friend's calls, Thom had scrambled up the creaky wooden staircase and burst out into the hallway, where he had continued to run, making for the main door. He had flung it open, then dashed down the stone steps, gathering momentum on the gentle slope that led to the bridge, thin legs barely under control, the sun bright in his eyes, the fresh warm air taking the chill from his flesh, but not from his heart.

Thom had not stopped running until he was through the woods and back inside the cottage, in the safe arms of his startled mother. He still had recurring nightmares about that incident – his fear of Bones since out of all proportion – but he had got his revenge on Hugo a week later.

---

'Mornin', Thom.'

The surprise of hearing her voice brought Thom back to the present with a jolt. She was standing in the doorway of one of the reception rooms off the hallway.

'Ms Quick . . .' he said as a reaction.

'I told you to call me Nell. It's much more friendly, isn't it?'

There was no lack of composure today, neither in her stance – she leaned against the door-frame, one hand on her hip, her smile as mockingly challenging as the moment he had first set eyes on her – nor in her voice. She may have fled the cottage in near-panic when the plate had smashed to the stone floor two days ago, but apparently the incident caused no embarrassment now. She wore the same long and flimsy skirt as before, its hem loose around her calves, but the thonged sandals had been replaced by more sensible brogues with broad heels. Her blouse was more formal too, even though one too many top buttons had been left undone, but her raven-dark hair was only partially tamed by a bow tied at the back.

'Yes, you've met Nell, haven't you, Thom?' Hugo was beaming, as though taking great pleasure from the re-introduction. 'I told you someone would be looking in on you from time to time, but I bet you didn't imagine it would be a ravishing creature like Nell.'

Nell Quick shook her head at Hugo in mock reproach.

'Actually, Nell's job is to take care of Father. And a fine job she makes of it too.'

'Oh, Sir Russell's not much trouble.' She strolled from the doorway to come close to Thom. 'Poor man sleeps for most of the day. Rarely at night-time though. It's funny how the dying are afraid to fall asleep at night.' The soft tones of her accent belied the cruelty of the remark.

Thom frowned. There was something about this woman . . .

'Thom would like to see Sir Russell,' Hugo said, apparently oblivious to Nell's tactless remark. 'What d'you think, Nell? Is my father up to it today?'

'I don't see why not,' Nell told him, her eyes remaining on Thom. 'It can't do any harm, even though Sir Russell might not be aware of anythin' around him. It's the drugs, they dull his mind. But what would be the point of cuttin' down on them – the poor thing would only suffer more.'

'I'll take you up, Thom,' Hugo interjected briskly. 'Be prepared though, won't you? It isn't a pleasant experience.'

A deep feeling of gloom pushed aside his previous overwhelming sense of wellbeing as Thom followed his friend to the sweeping staircase. On impulse, just before he began to climb, he turned his head to glance back at Nell Quick.

That same mocking smile was on her lips, but a scarcely disguised hardness had replaced the seductiveness of those dark eyes.

# Chapter : Thirteenth

# THE EYRIE

IT WAS a long haul up to Castle Bracken's top floor, to
the peculiar self-contained eyrie imagined and con-
structed by the mansion's first tenant, who had been inspired
by the wonderful views from the rooftop. Once a romantic
overlook, it had now become one man's self-designated
death-chamber. The thought made Thom Kindred shiver.

The building's inner staleness seemed to saturate the
atmosphere and Thom's dread deepened with every step:
stagnation was its essence, corruption an element. Even
though he had never liked the place, Thom could not
remember the aversion ever being this fierce. Perhaps the
old man's imminent demise was part of the tainting, just as
long ago Sir Russell's powerful presence had lent the mansion a kind of driving vigour, his rigid discipline holding
sway over family and staff alike until infirmity had slowly
begun to take over. What would it be like now to witness the
complete draining of that power, to see the man he had

feared as much as respected enfeebled and so near to death? Thom was tormented by the coming moment.

The long dusty drapes of the first-floor windows were half-closed against the dismal light from outside, making the gloom almost sepulchral. A worn rug, colours faded to a grey murkiness, stretched the entire length of the hallway at the top of the stairs, and tapestries, their colours also muted, but by time rather than wear, adorned the oak-panelled walls. Every door, be it to bedrooms or other reception rooms, was closed here, as if sealed against enquiry, and at the far end of the hallway a tall longcase clock, its casing made of walnut and olivewood, dial engraved brass, ticked away with deep, sonorous strokes. As Thom glanced towards it, the elongated minute hand shifted and he heard the solid *clunk* of the movement; the hour was way behind the actual time and he had no doubt that the wheels and springs within were worn and neglected – like the house itself. In fact, to Thom the clock seemed to symbolize not only the winding down of Castle Bracken, but of its master, too, the vitality slowly ebbing away, the heartbeat, like the tick of the clock, becoming leaden.

He thumped the banister rail with the flat of his hand to check himself as he and Hugo started up the next flight of stairs.

'You all right, old son?' Hugo was looking curiously over his shoulder at him.

'Sorry. Just bad thoughts catching up on me again. I was warned that depression would get to me from time to time.'

'Well I'm afraid what you're about to see won't help. Sure you want to go on?'

Thom nodded and said nothing more until they reached the second-floor landing, which was even gloomier than the first. Here, the curtains were completely closed.

'I don't get it, Hugo. Why are you treating the place like a mausoleum?'

His friend paused on the landing to catch his breath. 'It's

not intentional, Thom,' he said, leaning back against the rail. 'It's just that this floor isn't used any more. Hartgrove has his room up here – as you know, in the old days it used to be mainly the servants' quarters – which is useful, because he can be close to Father during the night. Must admit though, you've got a point. Place does look and smell like a bloody crypt. I suppose I've never really noticed, too busy running backwards and forwards to tend Father. Must've got used to it.'

He looked about him, wrinkling his nose. There was no oak panelling here, only faded wallpaper that might easily have been put up half a century ago, perhaps even longer. There were no adornments – no pictures or tapestries, no pieces of furniture. All the doors, whose paintwork was chipped and cracked, were closed as below, but here the wide corridor branched off midway towards another, plainer, staircase. Both men headed towards it, Hugo breathing a little harder than normal.

'We should have installed a lift from the ground to the top a long time ago, but you remember my father's problem with confined spaces,' Hugo complained as they began to climb once more. 'Unfortunately, money's a bit tight these days to spend on such expensive contraptions and it wouldn't be much use to him anyway. Not now, it wouldn't. It'd save my poor old legs though. And Hartgrove's. The old boy's up and down like a yo-yo. Devoted servant and all that.'

Thom was surprised to hear that the Bleeths' financial resources were less than buoyant; he had always imagined that Sir Russell's wealth was boundless.

As if reading his thoughts, Hugo said: 'Father's remaining stake in his import companies has been cut drastically since his retirement. And the continual fluctuation of sterling's value has affected trade terribly over the past few decades. Strong one moment, weak the next, making advance planning difficult, y'know. Whatever shares he retained are worth a bit if only he'd cash them in. We're by no means up shit creek, as they say, but income ain't what it used to be.'

Thom was curious. 'Why didn't you get involved in the company yourself? Surely you could have taken over from Sir Russell?'

'Unfortunately, nepotism ain't what it used to be either.' Hugo stopped, one foot on a higher step, a hip leaning against the rail. 'I don't think Father *ever* had any faith in me as a businessman. He certainly blocked every move I made to become part of the old firm. God, I'd have started as a teaboy if he had only allowed it, then I'd have worked my way up, Thom, climbed the ladder by my own efforts. Ha! But no, Father wasn't having any of it. Afraid he didn't have much faith in either of his sons.'

Thom shook his head more in sympathy than dismay. Had Sir Russell really lost all belief in Hugo after the Lloyd's insurance scandal in the late eighties? Even after all these years?

'I know what you're thinking, Thom, but a lot of good people went under because of Lloyd's, and ridiculously Father acted as if it were all my fault. I ask you, one of the biggest insurance debacles of all time and he thought I was a major player.'

'I'm sure he didn't, Hugo.' Thom rested against the rail opposite his friend, but a couple of steps below so that he had to look upwards. His left leg was beginning to feel heavy, and he was aware his foot was beginning to turn inwards slightly. He consciously straightened it, feeling disappointed with himself because he had felt so unbelievably well earlier on.

'Oh, I can assure you, he did. Dishonour to the family name and all that. A lot of sound people were bankrupted, poor saps who were suckered into investing in the insurance market with promises of decent returns with very little actual outlay and, of course, the prestige that went with being a

Name. Many were personal friends and business acquaintances of his – in fact, it was Father who introduced them to me – and two of them committed suicide because they couldn't face the shame of losing everything. Fortunately, Father took his own losses stoically—'

'He was a Name, too?'

'Yes, didn't you know? I was the one who invited him to join the 404 Syndicate, the one that became involved with all those asbestosis claims. I thought you were aware at the time.'

Thom shook his head. 'How could I? I was away at college.'

'Well, it was just something else to blame me for, although he was more concerned for his pals in the City than himself. His personal losses were severe, but at least he wasn't bankrupted, otherwise . . .' he waved his hand around '. . . all this would have gone too. I don't think he ever forgave me, though.'

'But that was years ago and you'd only just started out. He can't have continued to blame you.'

Although he had been a mere youth at the time, Thom still remembered the great Lloyd's of London insurance scandal, mainly because Hugo had been one of the younger underwriters, insignificant and inexperienced enough to be used as a convenient scapegoat by the senior and more 'knowing' members. Incompetence and what at best could be described as sharp practice had resulted in thousands of trusting but, in hindsight, gullible outside investors placing their entire wealth and assets as security for a relatively small investment in the insurance market.

Unfortunately, those investors, known as Names, were not informed of the horrendous number of claims, dating back some thirty to forty years, against insurance companies, most of them concerning asbestosis suffered by employees who had been employed in the manufacture of asbestos, or who had come into contact with the fibrous material in construction work. There had also been a record worldwide rise in disasters and calamities – sinking oil tankers and the pollution they caused, oil rig and gas sea platform fires, airline crashes, as well as earthquakes, forest fires, even urban riots – all escalating in the latter half of the century to catastrophic proportions for the insurance business. Colossal losses were predicted when all claims were finally agreed and processed, most of which affected the leading and longest-serving insurance institution of them all, the once-great Lloyd's of London.

While the Lloyd's overlords were speedily recruiting or accepting new Names, loosening the previously restrictive requirements and conditions in order to do so, a number of underwriters and brokers were frantically spreading their risks by reinsuring over and over again, creating ever-widening circles that eventually arrived back with their own syndicates, a questionable if not fraudulent practice known as 'spiralling'. It should never have happened and the new Names should never have been 'duped' into joining without being warned of the tremendous losses about to be incurred (even though all were warned they were liable for everything they possessed, including the shirt on their back, should things go wrong, this was generally done with a metaphorical nudge of an elbow and the wink of an eye).

Before very long, and after many, many novice Names had been added to the Lloyd's list, the fan had been hit and the renowned institution's reputation for honesty and competence had been irrevocably tarnished. Lives also had been ruined. Only the fact that a large number of Members of Parliament were caught in the Names' trap prevented a government-instigated public inquiry (bankruptcy would have lost those MPs their seats in the House), and a deal was brokered so that the unfortunate investors had to pay only a percentage – albeit a *large* percentage – of their losses (many of those investors claimed that institutional extortion – 'blackmail' might have been a more appropriate word – was used to force them to pay up).

Matters eventually cooled down and Lloyd's itself escaped complete collapse by the skin of its teeth (although never again would its word be trusted as its bond). But before this was so, scapegoats had to be found, sacrificial lambs had to be slaughtered. Hugo Bleeth had always claimed that he was one such offering.

It was Hugo who broke the silence that had developed between them. He swung round on the stairs and continued to climb. 'Come on, Thom. No more post-mortems, please. It's a part of my past I long to forget. Life moves on, old chum.'

Thom caught up with him, using the rail on his side to pull himself up. He was surprised at how tired he had become.

The stairway opened up to a kind of antechamber to the main quarters, a long room with deep, curtained windows and a single door leading out on to the mansion's flat roof. A round table stood in a corner opposite the stairs, a tall free-standing cupboard unit next to it. Various cartons and pill-boxes were neatly set out on the table top and Thom guessed that other medical supplies and instruments were stored inside the cupboard, along with drugs necessary to treat Sir Russell's illness and alleviate pain. The general staleness prevailed, but the atmosphere felt defiled by something extra, something less palpable than dust and lack of clean air, something Thom couldn't quite ... Then he had it. There was the pervasive intimation of approaching death.

'Let's be very quiet, shall we? Sir Russell sleeps most of the day.' Hugo was standing by a double door, a hand on one of the tarnished brass doorknobs. A stubby finger was raised unnecessarily to his pursed lips.

Thom steeled himself, afraid of what he might find behind the closed doors. The lasting memory he had of Sir

Russell Bleeth was of a man still brisk with energy, a serious man, someone of moderate build but whose back was always ramrod straight, his shoulders always squared. His sharp intelligent eyes had never revealed the sadness surely lodged within, but an anger seemed to be permanently simmering just beneath the surface; when that anger erupted, it was more often than not directed at Hugo, the youngest, remaining son, who always seemed to disappoint. Sir Russell's thinning hair had been jet-black then, as was the narrow line of his moustache, and although his brow was deeply furrowed and wrinkles ran from the corners of his eyes, the flesh of his face was tight and cleanly defined, with no sagging of jowls or chin, no pouches below those clear blue eyes.

When Hugo quietly turned the doorknob and eased one side of the double doors open, Thom closed his eyes and drew in a deep breath. Then he was ready. He followed his friend into the room.

His first sight was a complete surprise. He had expected the room to be darkened like the hall outside and the floor they had just left below, with curtains closed or half-closed, shadows dominant. Instead it was full of brightness, daylight, grey though it might be, streaming in through the big plate-glass windows all around the room. Of course, he should have known. It seemed that even in illness Sir Russell preferred open spaces. Beyond the windows, Thom could see the rooftop's terrace and parapet, and beyond that the low hills and woodlands of the Shropshire countryside. It was a magnificent view, the distant hills almost a faint blue against the dull sky, with forest and fields between. He turned his head towards the great four-poster bed and the frail figure that lay within, the bed itself set between two windows that offered easterly views.

Sir Russell Bleeth was propped up on a mountain of pillows, his hands by his sides on top of the sheets, acutely thin wrists and long, gnarled hands protruding from white pyjamas. Tubes and wires of an IV and an electrocardiogram sprang from his body like thin exterior organs and the lump by his hip beneath the bedsheets suggested he was also hooked up to a colostomy bag. Oddly, the four solid, carved bedposts at each corner bore no canopy, the overhead frame bare, as if any such covering had been deliberately removed along with its drapery. Thom could only assume that Sir Russell had ordered the furnishings taken away so that nothing would obstruct his views of the countryside beyond the windows nor enclose him. The bedroom was wonderfully bright, apart from the sickbed itself only a medical trolley giving evidence of its present purpose, which was an intensive care room for the terminally ill; that and the reek of body degeneration.

It was hard to take his attention from the frail figure and, when Hugo moved towards the bed, Thom went with him. As they drew closer, he took in the transparent plastic oxygen mask that covered the lower portion of the sick man's face and then the tube that ran from it to the chrome cylinder on its wheeled stand between the bed and the medical trolley. He saw the slight movement of Sir Russell's chest as the old man drew in the pure air.

'Father . . .?' he heard Hugo say, both of them treading cautiously as if any sudden noise might startle the patient. 'Father, are you awake? I've brought someone to see you . . .'

Hugo stopped beside the bed and glanced back at Thom. 'I think he's asleep.'

Even as he spoke both men heard a faint sound from Sir Russell, perhaps a murmur, or just the clearing of his dry old throat.

Hugo quickly leaned forward, looking directly into his father's face. 'Are you awake?' he repeated. 'Look, a friend has come to visit, someone you haven't seen for a long time.' He motioned Thom to come nearer, then moved himself out of the way.

Legs pressed against the side of the bed, Thom bent over the frighteningly thin figure and almost drew back again at the sickly sweet stench that seemed to rush at him; this was the nucleus of the room's general malodour. But it was the sight of Sir Russell, his one-time benefactor, that shocked him the most, for, although he had prepared himself for the worst, the close-up actuality was even more distressing than he had expected.

The master of Castle Bracken and its vast estate was little more than a shrunken ruin, his body painfully emaciated, his mottled scalp almost hairless save for a few long white strands. There was a disturbing blue tinge to his flesh and lips, and the lines and wrinkles of his shrivelled face were now deeply etched, dark ravines that had multiplied beyond belief. Heavy pouches beneath his half-closed eyes were like layered folds of blanched latex, the pallid pupils above – what could be seen of them through the slitted lids – seemingly adrift in a creamy, liquid substance; they moved a little when Thom drew closer, but he wasn't sure if they were merely reacting to his shadow, the change in light, or if, through the moist haze of their vision, they had registered his presence.

Thom thought – or imagined – he saw the faintest flicker of recognition in them.

'Sir Russell,' he said, almost in a whisper, 'it's me, Thom. Thom Kindred.'

The gaunt head jerked slightly, as if the sick man was making a effort to turn towards him, and for a few all too brief moments, the eyes sharpened and Thom thought he saw some emotion in them, something more than mere recognition. It might have been joy, but it was too distant to tell, too lost in the mists of drugs and weariness. One of Sir Russell's skeletal hands moved, then rose an inch or so; weak, cold fingers closed around Thom's wrist and he felt ashamed for wanting to pull away. Somehow this ... this thing . . . in the bed was no longer the man, the vital, active man, he had once known; that person had transmuted into this withered wreck, all skin and bones and stinking flesh.

Oh, dear God, forgive me . . .

The cold fingers dropped away. The eyes closed completely, as if to shut out whatever it was they had observed in Thom's own eyes. As ill and as drugged as he was, Sir Russell had felt, had sensed, the younger man's revulsion.

In that instant Thom hated himself, and he reached for the withdrawn hand again to squeeze it gently in apology for his cruel but involuntary reaction.

But the old man's eyes remained closed and, despairingly, Thom saw a single tear seep from the corner of Sir Russell's left eyelid. It welled, then trickled down into the sparse white hair at his temple, a faint, weak stream that caused Thom deep shame.

He straightened and looked round at Hugo, his expression one of appeal, as if begging to be told what he might do. His friend was momentarily embarrassed and gave a shrug of his shoulders, a small shake of his head.

'I doubt he knows you're here, old chum,' Hugo said as if to reassure him. 'He's like this most of the time these days. I'm sure he can't even hear us, Thom.'

Thom studied Sir Russell's worn pallid face until Hugo cleared his throat and said, 'Best be going, eh? Let him rest.'

'There must be something more that can be done for him.' Thom was almost pleading with Hugo.

'Everything that could be done has been. My father has had the very best advice and treatment on offer, all to no avail. We might *think* that medical care has taken huge leaps forward but we're wrong. Ask any honest practitioner or surgeon and they'll tell you that half the time they're making educated guesses. Not very comforting, I know, but unfortunately, that's the strength of it. Now let's leave him, Thom.'

Thom could only acquiesce. He had hoped to talk with Sir Russell, perhaps convey some of the gratitude he felt for his patronage over the years, perhaps even find out what *he* could now do for *him*. Mostly he wanted Sir Russell to know that he was there, that he cared about his condition, that he would stay and help nurse him, would do anything that might ease the discomfort, if not the pain. He had always been afraid of Sir Russell and in a way he still was, despite the fact that the old man was a mere husk of what once he had been; but now it was his, Thom's, turn to give whatever support he could. Thom knew that Bethan would have wanted this.

'Can I come back and see him, Hugo?' he asked his friend, who was hovering anxiously by the bed. 'Maybe when he's more alert? I think he really would like to know I'm around.'

'Not sure there'd be much point, Thom. You see how he is. He just drifts in and out, hardly aware of his surroundings, it seems to me, although when he's up to it he spends much of his time gazing out the windows.'

Thom automatically looked towards the nearest window and felt his heart lift at the wonderful scene. From this position, Sir Russell was able to see the fields and wood-lands, the distant hills. He squinted his eyes. And yes, there, the turret just rising above the treetops ... It was Little Bracken, a reddish smudge among all the greenery. He wondered if the old man could see the tower too. For some reason, he hoped so.

Distractedly, he walked around the bed and went to one of the long windows. The skies remained overcast, the day grey and uninteresting; yet the view was still magnificent, the myriad greens outside deepened by the lack of sunshine. He was tempted to go out on to the terrace, to breathe in the clean, fresh country air, the room he was in almost stifling in its foulness, but even as he considered it, a bird landed on the roof's parapet opposite the window. It was a magpie, and when its wings had settled, the bird securely perched, it cocked its head and looked directly at him.

Thom had the strange notion that this was the same magpie he had found on the top of Little Bracken's fake belltower, the one that had not even flinched when he had clapped his hands at it. Nonsense, of course – there was more than one magpie in the neighbourhood. But even so, the way this one watched him was equally disconcerting.

The bird continued to stare through the window at him, cool and detached, showing no fear at all when Thom tapped on the glass. He scowled, somehow irritated by the creature's boldness.

Thom suddenly felt a presence behind him and assumed Hugo had come over to see why he was tapping on the window. But when he turned his head, ready to point at the bird outside and explain, he was startled to find Hartgrove – old Bones – standing behind him. The manservant must have been in the room all the while, sitting silent and unnoticed in a corner, keeping a solitary vigil for his master, Sir Russell Bleeth.

Dark, expressionless eyes looked past Thom to see what had caught his attention, and those matt eyes suddenly took on some life – what was it? Curiosity, anger, *fear?* – when Hartgrove saw the magpie perched on the parapet. Without saying a word, Hartgrove went to the door that led on to the roof and opened it. He stepped outside. In surprise, Thom watched as the manservant strode purposely towards the parapet, clapping his hands loudly as he went.

The magpie had nerve, Thom had to give it that, because it waited until the last moment before lifting into the air. Hartgrove swiped at it with a long arm, but the bird was too swift and too cunning. Its flight took it backwards a few feet before it rose high into the air and finally swooped away.

Thom looked around at Hugo, who was walking towards him, obviously wondering what the fuss was about. When he reached the window, both men exchanged looks of bewilderment before returning their attention to the tall, dark figure outside.

Hartgrove stood perfectly still, hands by his sides, just watching the bird's flight. And when he turned to face them a few moments later they saw a deep rage on his cadaverous face.

Once again, Thom and Hugo swapped glances. It was Thom who spoke, and it was in a whisper.

'What the hell was *that* all about?' he said.

# Chapter : Fourteenth

## NELL'S PLACE

'STIFFENER, THOM? Even better, stay for a spot of lunch, eh? Cook'll soon rustle up something for us both.'

Thom and Hugo were back downstairs in Castle Bracken's main hallway, both of them relieved to have left the rooftop eyrie, although neither one would have admitted it. A place of beautiful views had become death's waiting-room and the transformation was deeply unpleasant.

'I don't think so, Hugo. To be honest, I'm not that hungry.'

'Made you lose your appetite did it? Well, I did warn you it'd be disagreeable. It's a shock to see Father in that condition, I know, but come on, you've got to eat, old chum.'

'I'll have something back at the cottage.'

'You're quite sure? I can't persuade you?' Hugo's eye-brows were raised, the palms of his hands displayed.

'Yeah, I'm sure. Thanks for the offer though.'

Together, they walked to the front door, but just as Hugo

opened it for Thom, a voice from one of the nearby doorways halted them.

'Oh, Thom, I've been waitin' for you.'

They turned to see Nell Quick emerging from the drawing-room, a light raincoat over her arm and a plastic shopping-bag in her hand. Her smile sent a rush through Thom despite himself.

'I meant to leave earlier, but when I got outside I found my bicycle had a puncture.' She planted herself directly in front of Thom, her back to Hugo. 'Could you drop me off at my place on your way home?'

He wanted to make an excuse, say he was going on into town, but found it hard to resist those deep brown eyes that looked so intensely into his. And the smile ... oh, God, the smile ...

'Um ...' was all he managed.

'Good. It's not far out of your way, only a couple of minutes.' She turned to Hugo. 'You'll make sure Sir Russell takes his special medication, won't you? It's all prepared and waitin' on the kitchen table for you. Mrs Baxley is complainin' again, but don't you stand for any of her nonsense. We both know Sir Russell won't touch any proper food, 'specially not the kind she wants to force on him. It'd jus' be wasted on your father, stubborn old thing that he is.'

Thom was surprised at the casual way the 'carer' spoke to his friend, although Hugo did not seem to mind. He merely nodded his head and smiled as if eager to please.

'I'll be back later,' Nell Quick went on, 'to give him his next dose. Sometimes I think it's only my medicines that's keepin' him alive.'

'I'll do as you say, Nell.' Hugo had opened the front door for them.

'If you need me sooner, jus' call. You know I'm on hand, night or day.'

A look passed between them and Thom frowned. Am I missing something here? he silently asked himself. Is there

# JAMES HERBERT

something going on between these two? Nell was an attractive woman, and Hugo . . . well, Hugo had to be lonely here at the great manor house. But she was his father's nurse. Surely Hugo wouldn't be involved with her?

'Shall we go, Thom?' Nell was smiling at him again – no, it was more than just a smile. Her expression was both seductive and mocking at the same time, as if she were playing some secret game with him. He was beginning to be irritated by it.

'Fine,' he said. 'I need to be getting back. Things to do.'

She lowered her chin, looking up at him questioningly. Things to do? He was supposed to be convalescing, so what *would* he have to do? She seemed to enjoy his small lie.

They descended the steps together and Thom, feeling eyes on his back, glanced over his shoulder. But Hugo had already closed the front door.

'There, you see.' Nell was pointing at the old Raleigh lying against the steps, its rear wheel tyre flat and useless. Her expression was curiously triumphant, as though she knew he had doubted her word.

He wondered why he had not noticed the puncture on his arrival, but said: 'We'll try and get it into the back of the Jeep. It should just about fit with a bit of manoeuvring and the backs of the rear seats down.'

'That's very kind of you, Thom. It deserves a reward of some kind.'

He ignored the glint in her eye, righting the heavy-framed bicycle and pushing it towards the Jeep, holding the rear wheel off the ground so that the flaccid tyre would not be further damaged. He suddenly became aware that his left foot was dragging, a sure sign he was becoming weary; he was beginning to limp too. He had felt so good earlier, healthy, fit, even strong. And now the tiredness, the numbness, was returning. His visit to Castle Bracken had left him in a state of depression and he wondered if that was part of the problem, bad memories, the wretched sight of Sir Russell, even the general deterioration of the once-great mansion itself, all these things preying on his mind, bringing him down, undermining his physical resistance.

He opened up the Jeep's tailgate and then adjusted the rear seats. There was just enough room for the hefty old bicycle once he had twisted the front wheel and handlebars. He had to push hard to get the tailgate closed again, but finally it was done.

Thom limped round and opened the door for his grateful passenger, and then moved on around the bonnet to the driver's side. He realized his arms were trembling slightly with the strain of lifting when he climbed into his seat and pushed the key into the ignition. He had broken out in a sweat and was relieved when he looked over at Nell to see perspiration on her brow too. It was still a humid kind of day, the air thick and sultry.

'This is kind of you, Thom,' Nell repeated flashing beautifully white teeth at him.

'No problem.' He leaned forward and turned the key, bringing the engine into life.

Out the corner of his eye, Thom saw the woman tug at her loose skirt, pulling it back over her knees so that its hem lay across her lower thighs. Her legs were smooth and a light brown colour as though she, too, like the physiotherapist earlier, had taken full advantage of the season's brilliant weather.

'It's so warm,' she murmured distractedly and as if unaware how provocative the sight of her legs were. ''S'pect there'll be a storm later. What you think, Thom?' She regarded him as though honestly interested in his opinion, her eyes wide and pupils jet black in the shadows of the Jeep.

He caught the faint muskiness of her natural odour – as far as he could tell, she wore no perfume – in the close confines and even through the sudden weariness that had come over him, he felt himself stirring.

'There might be,' he replied, swinging the Jeep round in an arc.

'It'll clear the air.' She lifted the hem of her skirt from her thighs, just an inch or so, as if to allow air to circulate.

Thom pretended not to notice.

'You saw Sir Russell?' she asked innocently, her hand bringing the skirt even higher up her legs.

'Yeah.' His mouth was dry.

'And . . .?

'And?'

'What did you think?'

'He's in a bad way.'

'I think he hasn't much longer.' The index finger of the hand holding the skirt played up and down the skin above her knee, each journey a little longer, but never beyond a certain point.

Thom tried to keep his eyes on the road ahead. 'Tell me something,' he said to get his mind back on track.

'Anything,' she replied before he could continue; she was obviously enjoying her tease.

'You're a qualified nurse? I mean, you've been trained, you've had practical training . . .?'

'Don't I seem like a nurse to you?'

'Frankly, no.'

She gave a small laugh.

'Do I take that as a compliment?'

He was beginning to get annoyed again and was grateful for that: it wasn't easy to switch off from this woman's flirting. 'It's just a question.'

'Well, I've had some trainin' and cared for many sick people over the years.'

'But you said you'd made up some medicine for Sir Russell . . .'

'Well, you could call it medicine. A lot of people come to me for my special brews and potions. Mostly country people who know the old ways, although there are others – townies – who've heard about my cures.'

Thom could hardly believe his ears. 'Are you kidding me? Sir Russell needs a professional nurse to look after him.'

'His doctor comes at least once a week and he seems perfectly satisfied. I've been shown how to use the medical equipment and it really isn't that difficult.'

'Surely he would insist that Hugo hires a proper nurse. Sir Russell—'

'Sir Russell is going to die, Thom. All the *professional* . . .' she emphasized the word '. . . help in the world can't alter the fact. So if my special mixtures can ease his suffering, then his doctor isn't going to complain, is he? Remember, Sir Russell has already received the best treatment money can buy, now it's just a matter of time.'

'Surely he needs proper medication, drugs or pills, sedatives – stuff to deal with the discomfort and pain.'

'They're all at hand. You must have seen them, for yourself. Hugo and I have been trained to administer them so it isn't a problem. I also bathe him, I clean his mess, I make his bed. I can do anythin' a hired nurse can do, so please stop your worryin'. When I'm not there, that old pile of bones Hartgrove is always around.'

Now she had become a little irate and, Thom noted with relief, had ceased teasing him. But, as though having just read his thoughts, she smiled at him again and leaned across to touch his arm.

'I know Sir Russell has been good to you, Thom – Hugo told me how he employed your mother, then saw to your education when she died – but he's looked after in every way, I can promise you that.'

By now they had passed through the estate gates and had reached the main thoroughfare. Thom glanced at her as he waited for several cars and lorries to go by. The apparent sincerity of her expression surprised him.

'Look, I'm sorry if—' he began to say.

She put a finger to his lips. 'I understand. You're concerned for him, but then so are we all. 'Specially Hartgrove – he scarcely leaves his master's bedside. Have a little faith, Thom, just a little faith. I promise you I'm doin' my best to keep Sir Russell as comfortable as possible.'

For a moment or two he could only look at her. The smile had gone and there was a faint crease in her brow; strangely it made her look even more attractive.

'Which way?' he said.

She straightened. 'What?'

'Which way to your place. Left or right?'

'Oh, left. Same direction as your cottage, but we turn off to the right before we reach your lane. I'll show you as we go.'

Nell sat back in her seat, leaning back against the raised headrest. The smile had returned, but this time it wasn't for him. It was a secret smile.

'Seatbelt,' he told her as he buckled up himself, then turned into the main road.

'Oh I don't worry 'bout that sort of thing,' she replied pleasantly, looking straight ahead.

He shrugged and pressed his foot down on the accelerator pedal.

---

It took only a few minutes to reach Nell Quick's home, which was situated at the end of a lane of similar-type cottages – redbrick, slate roofs, small front gardens. There was a good distance between each abode, the gardens bordered by low picket fences, with plenty of tall greenery between flower-beds to ensure a certain amount of privacy. There was also an interesting variation in maintenance, some of these small homes well kept, one or two even made to look chocolate-box pretty – Thom guessed these might be weekend retreats for wealthy city-types – while others were badly maintained, with peeling window-frames and front doors in need of a lick of paint, these no doubt occupied by locals who had probably been in residence for many more years than their upmarket neighbours.

From the outside it was difficult to tell into which category Nell Quick's cottage fell, for its walls and roof were covered in creepers, only small sections of its structure and windows spared. As instructed by his passenger, Thom pulled up in front of the short cracked path leading to the open porch. The small garden was a mess, with flowers slowly being strangled by weeds, shrubbery growing where it pleased, and the low fence rickety, with several uprights missing. There was no gate.

'Will you bring the bike in for me, Thom? I keep it in the porch.' Nell had already opened the passenger door and was climbing out without waiting for a reply.

'I'm pretty busy—'

But she was already gone, a hand delving into the plastic bag for her door key, raincoat draped over her arm. What was he going to say anyway? I've got to get home because I'm pretty busy doing nothing?

'Thom!' She was under the porch, at the front door. Her call was more like a command.

He quickly released his seatbelt and swung the door open. What the hell *was* wrong with him? The woman was indulging in a little flirting, that's all there was to it. My God, was he so vain that he imagined such a good-looker would be interested in him? Sure, he'd had a number of girlfriends in London, but his work was too important to him to let serious romance get in the way. And he was no stud, any female could see that. Nell was teasing him because she sensed his innate shyness, that was all. Probably did it to every man she met. Hugo certainly seemed taken by her. Thom remembered the way she had spoken to her employer and wondered again if anything was going on between them. Good luck to Hugo, if there was.

A tiny worry nagged at him. Hugo was soon to be a wealthy man despite the family's downturn in financial matters. When Sir Russell died, then as the only son and heir, Hugo would inherit everything. He'd be a fine catch for any woman . . .

By now, lost in his thoughts, Thom was at the back of the Jeep, hands on the tailgate catch. Only Nell's further call prompted him into action.

He quickly pressed the catch button and lifted the tailgate, then dragged the bicycle out. It bounced to the ground on its front wheel and he pushed it through the gateless opening in the fence, this time without bothering to lift the flat tyre; it made a *scudding* noise as he guided the bike along the worn path. By the time he reached Nell under the cover of the porch, she had opened the door to her cottage and pushed it wide. It seemed so dark inside, the shadows unnaturally deep, and Thom had a moment of unease. The door itself was of dark oak and was in two sections, a stable door whose lower section reached above his hips. He peered into the gloom, but could not make out much: wood flooring, wooden beams set in terracotta walls, a tall, plain chair-stool just inside the doorway.

'Leave the bike there, Thom, and come inside,' he heard her say as he leaned forward to see more. 'You look hot. S'pect you could do with a cool drink.'

He caught himself and straightened up. 'Uh, no, I'm fine. I'll just be on my way.' He leaned the Raleigh against the side of the porch.

'Nonsense. You come inside, let me repay your kindness.'

Without waiting for further dissent, Nell disappeared from sight, leaving him with no other choice but to follow.

It was cool inside, and shadowy, the small windows fringed with creepers that obscured much of the light from outside. *Compact* might have been an estate agent's description of the interior and *cluttered* was the word Thom would have added. There seemed scarcely an unfilled space in the room: dog-eared magazines and weary-looking books were piled high on chairs and windowsills, while straw containers and dried herbs hung from ceiling beams; astrological symbols were daubed on the brown terracotta walls between inset wooden beams and a round centre table was crowded with clay pots and jars, more books and magazines, pens, coloured inks, a vase of pink lilies, cotton reels of various colours, needles pushed into the threads, tiny ornaments, and a few metres of red ribbon. A large copper kettle, its bottom blackened by fire, stood on one of the brick shelves inside a large (so large it took up most of the wall opposite) inglenook fireplace, an old-fashioned black cooking-pot on the other side, along with tongs and poker; the thick wooden mantelshelf above held many more pots and jars. A rickety-looking staircase next to the inglenook led to the upstairs rooms, its first turn lit by a small window visible from where he stood; an open doorway on the other side of the fireplace went through to the kitchen – he could see part of a sink and draining board from this same spot. On a sideboard beneath the window overlooking the road was a remarkably erotic carving in dark brown polished wood of a naked woman, only her thighs but not her pubis covered by a fold of the drapery she reclined upon; the tips of her long breasts caught the daylight from behind and one hand was positioned provocatively close to the dip between her upper legs. Through the opposite window overlooking the back of the property, he saw a garden that was even more unkempt and overgrown than the front; the difference here, though, was that vivid splashes of colour fought valiantly against the tangled greenness, these being different specimens of flora. He could see the side of a ramshackle greenhouse, its windows filthy with grime.

Although there were shadowy corners in the over-crowded room, and its beamed ceiling was almost oppressively low, it was not quite as dark as he had expected from the outside with the creepers crowding the windows.

'So, Thom, what would you like your reward to be?'

Nell was standing by the lumpy sofa on which she'd dropped her coat and bag, one fist on her hip in a pose that was now familiar to him. She wore the same mocking (or was it provocative?) smile that he was also becoming used to.

'No, I've really got to get going.'

Why was *he* being so coy? he wondered. Maybe it was because there was something about this woman that instinctively he did not trust. *Or maybe you're afraid you might have to perform*, a sly little inner voice scorned. *Maybe you think you might not be up to it now. After all, it has been a long time, hasn't it? And your whole system has been knocked through a hoop.*

'Oh come on, just a lemonade, or a fruit juice,' she persisted, her voice coaxing. 'Something stronger, if you like. I've got gin. Or wine. Whatever you like.'

He sighed inwardly, knowing she would not give up until he acquiesced. 'Okay, just a lemonade then. That'd be fine.'

'Wasn't so hard, was it?' she teased before disappearing through the doorway into the kitchen. Before she did so, however, Nell glanced into a gilt-framed mirror on the wall and gave a little push here and there to her hair. Yeah, Thom mused. He'd been right: there was something vain about this woman. But again, why not? She had something to be vain about. 'Take a seat, Thom, make yourself at home,' she called back. 'Try the sofa – it doesn't look it, but it's very comfortable. Just dump my things on the floor.'

He went over to the sofa and placed the bag on the untidy table, then laid the light raincoat over the arm of the seat. He settled back.

Out of sight, Nell leaned against the kitchen dresser, disturbing the jars and pots standing on the middle shelf behind her. The shelves above and below were filled with more pots, some tall, others squat, and containers of various shapes and sizes. All were neatly labelled – basil, garlic, mint, marjoram, verbena, honey, and many more – while on the topmost shelf there were oils – thyme, lemon, lime, rose and geranium. Her eyes closed briefly and her smile was no longer mocking; her expression was one of secret pleasure. Her tongue licked her upper lip, just once, making it moist, and there was a light sheen of perspiration on her forehead, on her neck, between the cleft of her breasts. When she exhaled, there was a light trembling in her breath.

Nell could not be sure if it was the man himself that aroused her this way, or the thought of what she was to do to him. He was certainly handsome enough in a certain way, and his body, although perhaps a little wasted after his illness, was young and firm enough to make the seduction a pleasure. Nell pulled at her long, light skirt, raising the hem so that her bare legs were uncovered. She ran her fingertips along the length of her thigh, enjoying the touch, the skin moist from the humid heat of the day, before sliding her hand inside her cotton panties, delving into the coarse black hair between her legs. She drew in a sharp breath when her middle finger dipped into her vagina, slipping easily through the raised lips, using only gentle pressure to open herself further.

Another breath as she thought of Thom, only a few feet away on the other side of the wall and unaware of what she was doing to herself, and her body shuddered helplessly as juices inside her began to flow. She rubbed herself, but only gently, unwilling to take it too far, for she had other plans. Her first finger joined its companion in stroking her vaginal lips, occasionally dipping further, feeling her swelling clitoris, collecting the slickness there so that when she withdrew they were silky wet.

She allowed the hem of her skirt to fall, then held the fingers to her nose, sniffing their scent. Her breath was heavy by now, her breasts almost heaving with barely suppressed excitement. She ran the damp fingers around her neck, between her breasts, behind her ears, smearing herself with her own secretions, for they contained pheromones, the most natural but barely perceptible aphrodisiac. The chemicals mixed with those produced by her light perspiration, enhancing the effect. Male pheromones were generally more powerful than those of the female, but Nell was well aware of her own special allure.

Fully aroused, she reached into the kitchen's refrigerator and took out the lemonade bottle. Quickly filling a beaker, she returned to the other room where Thom was perched uncomfortably on the very edge of the sofa, studying a wicker cat that stood on a small sideboard at the other end of the room, the animal perhaps fashioned by Nell herself. He turned his attention to her and she saw the edginess in his eyes. It broadened her smile.

'Here, this should cool you down a little,' she said, handing him the full beaker, the innuendo not lost on him.

He took the drink with a murmured thank you and swallowed half the contents at once.

'I knew you were thirsty,' she remarked as she sat next to him. Thom had to move along the sofa to make room, but even so, their knees were almost touching.

'Aren't you lonely there, Thom, out in the woods, all by yourself?' she asked, leaning sideways so that her face was even closer to his, no hint of mockery or teasing in her eyes now.

A slight mustiness drifted across to him from her, a faint smell that was difficult to identify. It was not unpleasant.

'It's how I like it,' he replied before taking another sip of lemonade. 'The quietness makes a change from London and the solitude ... well, it gives me space to think.'

'Sometimes too much thought can be a bad thing. You start gettin' inside your own head and it's not always easy to get out again.'

It was a strange thing to say, but he thought he understood what she meant. Since the stroke and particularly in the early stages when he could only lie helpless in bed, he had often felt himself trapped inside a shell, his body no more than a mobile container for his mind – not his brain, but his *mind*. His eyes were merely the portals through which his mind gazed out at the world.

'I've pretty much kept myself occupied since I've been there.' An understatement if ever there was one. For a brief moment he was tempted to tell her all that had happened to him since arriving back at Little Bracken, but something – that little niggling voice again – warned him not to.

'You surprise me.' Her arm slid along the top of the sofa and, because he had leaned back, her hand brushed the nape of his neck. 'I wouldn't have thought there'd be anything to do there.'

'Well, I've got regular exercises to get me fit again, and I can take long walks through the woods. In a few days' time I intend to get back to some easy carpentry.'

'Ah yes, the master carpenter. Hugo told me how good you are.'

This last remark gave him the opportunity to turn the conversation around. 'Just how long have you known Hugo?'

'A year or so. I knew of him, of course – everybody hereabouts knows of the Bracken Estate – but we'd never met until he came to me for help one day.'

'When he was looking for someone to nurse Sir Russell?'

'No. Hugo came to me because of his warts.'

'What?' Thom almost spilt his drink and Nell laughed at his expression.

'You didn't know he had warts on his back?' She gave another short laugh.

Thom shook his head, wondering what Hugo's mild affliction had to do with anything.

'I'm a healer, didn't you know? Didn't Hugo explain that to you?' She looked genuinely surprised.

'Well, no. I just thought he'd hired you because you had some training as a nurse or carer.'

'And so I have. I worked in a health centre in Wales before an old aunt I never knew I had died and left me this place. I was her only living relative, so everything she possessed became mine.'

'You'd never met her?'

'Never met her and didn't even know she existed. My mother had never spoken of any family, so I'd always assumed there was nobody. Imagine my surprise when I learned we shared the same vocation. She was a healer too.'

'A nurse, you mean?'

'A healer, Thom. A herbalist, a homeopath. Some folk around here believed she was a witch.'

Again the laughter, but her eyes were fixed on Thom's.

He looked again at the astrological symbols painted on the brown walls, then, almost laughing at himself, at the rough broomstick leaning against a corner of the inglenook, the big black pot on the shelf inside which now, to him, resembled a cauldron.

Her laughter had stopped, and her expression was enigmatic. 'And they think I'm one, too,' she said.

His turn to grin. 'In this day and age?'

'You think there are no witches?'

'I've heard of people claiming to be so. I've always thought it's in their own heads. I suppose they're harmless enough as long as nobody takes them too seriously.'

'I won't argue with you, Thom. But I've always been able to heal.'

'That's a different thing. I can accept that. But magic spells and curses? No, I'll leave that to storytellers, the kind who write for children. What happened about the warts, by the way?'

He felt her fingers curl into the hair at the back of his neck and was aware of a slight tug as he leaned even further forward.

'Hugo had heard about me, how I could make old country cures, potions to help the troubled body and mind.'

'Potions? Sounds like you were carrying on your aunt's work.'

'I learned everything from my mother and she from her mother actually. The secret ways of the Wicca have always been known to my family even though we've never been accepted by those who call themselves true Wiccans.'

She caught the cynicism in his eyes and her grin made him uneasy.

'Don't believe in such things?' she scorned. 'And you from Little Bracken.'

There were all kinds of things implied in that last remark, but Thom kept quiet.

'It has nothing to do with belief anyway,' she went on. 'The Wiccan values, Thom. They value and celebrate the natural world, they have the feelin' for magic. They also value the natural ways, cures and remedies that aren't synthetic or chemical.'

'But you said you've never been accepted by them,' Thom interrupted.

'Some of us like the unnatural ways.' She laughed, a full throaty sound. He felt chilled for a moment.

Her laughter stopped abruptly and her sly charm returned. 'I could make you feel much better, Thom, if you'd let me.'

'I'll stick to mild pills and therapy.' Now he managed a smile.

'You don't believe I can make you better?'

'With herbs and potions?' His smile broadened.

'You don't believe me?'

He was blunt. 'It's a little far-fetched.'

'Ask Hugo about his warts. I made them disappear.'

This time he laughed. 'My illness is just a bit more severe.' He became serious again. 'I still don't understand why Hugo took you on as a nurse. Sir Russell is gravely ill and needs all the expert medical attention he can get.'

'I told you, Sir Russell is dyin' and the best doctors and nurses in all the world can't alter that. That's why Hugo wanted my help once he'd listened to me and learned to have faith.'

It seemed as if there were two small fires in those beautifully dark eyes of hers and somehow it made her even more startling. Jet-black curls framed her face, accentuating the high cheekbones, the vivid redness of her shiny lips. Thom felt himself tense, but it was a pleasurable tenseness, the arousing kind, the kind that sent blood rushing. Somehow, and without his noticing, she had moved even closer, her legs turned towards his so that their knees touched.

'Time and time again the medical profession lets us down, sometimes even killin' us with their stupid mistakes and ignorance, so people have no choice but to look for other ways to be cured.'

He could not prevent his eyes from taking in the fullness of her breasts beneath the blouse she wore, the undone top buttons providing almost intoxicating glimpses of bare flesh. Although he was not sure if he liked this woman or not, Thom could not deny he was attracted to her.

'I help Sir Russell with the pain. I use balms to soothe his nerves. I have my own preparations that can take the strain off his diseased old heart.'

'When I saw him this morning he seemed pretty much drugged.'

'I'm obliged to use the *normal* stuff on him, Thom ...' she made *normal* sound like a dirty word '. . . his own doctor insists on that, but I help him in other ways. Why don't you let me help you?'

'I told you, I need exercise, rest and the regular mild pill. It's what the doctors have ordered.'

The finger of her left hand rested on his knee as if to make a point. He felt its light pressure, but it wasn't localized: it seemed to spread along his thigh.

'I thought you understood me, Thom – doctors know very little, especially when it comes to the human psyche. My kind of healing deals with mind, body and spirit.'

Now her whole hand rested on his knee. He shifted, feeling uncomfortable, but she did not take her hand away. Her other hand found the back of his neck once more, and warm fingers slid beneath his shirt collar. It wasn't unpleasant. In fact, it felt electric, a gentle shock that hurried its way down his spine.

'I can calm your nerves, Thom,' Nell said quietly and, it seemed to him, sincerely. 'I can cure whatever ails you, those headaches . . .' her hand left his leg to touch his brow and her fingertips did feel wonderfully soothing '. . . I can give your leg strength again . . .' she must have noticed his limp and inward-turning left foot when he carried her bicycle to the Jeep '. . . make your arm strong again . . .' obviously she had noticed how he'd favoured his left arm when he'd lifted the bike '. . . and I can cleanse your spirit, Thom, I can make you feel safe inside your home . . .'

'What?' He took her hand away from his forehead, not forcefully, but firmly enough to make the message clear. 'Why shouldn't I feel safe there?'

She straightened and he thought he saw regret in her eyes, as though she blamed herself for breaking the mood.

'You haven't realized there's something wrong inside Little Bracken?' She regarded him with genuine curiosity.

'It's my home. There's nothing *wrong* with it.'

'Then how did that plate fly across the room and smash itself on the floor?'

'A wind came through the door. The door was open, remember?'

'I didn't feel any wind.' If she was annoyed, she did not show it. Rather, she spoke in sympathetic tones, as if concerned that he could not see the truth of it for himself.

'We were preoccupied at the time.'

At least she smiled as she remembered. She argued her point though. 'I've felt it before, each time I've visited.'

'You've been inside Little Bracken before I came back?'

'Only twice. Hugo asked me to dust and clean the place

for your return. I stocked your cupboards and fridge the second time. That was when I sensed something bad there.'

'In a cottage that had been empty for years?' He shook his head. 'I don't believe in that kind of stuff, and neither should you.'

'Why not? It's not uncommon for some places to have their own moods or atmospheres, 'specially if somethin' bad has happened in them. I don't think Little Bracken likes people.'

He could not help his wry grin.

'It's true, Thom. How did you feel inside the mansion today? Didn't you sense its misery?'

'Sir Russell is dying there. Anyone who knows that is bound to feel something is wrong.'

'It's much more than that. Every room feels wretched. But I'm worried about you, Thom.'

Again her fingers nestled in the hair at the back of his neck, while her other hand rested on his thigh. He felt its heat through the tough material of his jeans.

He did not resist. Why should he? But he did delay.

'Why . . . why would you be worried about me?'

'Because you're alone there.'

'There's nothing wrong with the place.'

'Oh, but there is . . .'

Nell was not one to be diverted. She pressed her lips against his.

Now Thom did resist, but only feebly. His mind was full of questions: What was the matter with Little Bracken? And so what if he were alone – what could harm him? And why was she so keen to seduce him? And why the hell was he playing so hard to get?

He suddenly matched her pressure, kissing Nell hard, his lips moistened by hers, her tongue darting between his teeth, seeking his. He felt her hand against his neck, drawing him forward so that their kiss became almost painful; he felt her other hand move on his thigh, travelling further as if she knew of his swelling, and was eager to touch. His own hand found the bare flesh of her arm and her skin was firm but so smooth. He smelled her odd muskiness and somehow it roused his passion even more. Her fingers moved to the top button of his jeans, pushing against the rise beneath them, skilfully pressing against it, arousing him even more. Even with his mouth hard against hers, he drew in a short sharp breath – her breath – as the button was released. He gave out a murmur . . .

And felt a tingling vibration against his thigh.

He was confused for a moment, the rising passion stalled. The vibration again, like a tiny and painless electric shock, stronger this time. And then the sound and the understanding came together. His cell phone, a Motorola that was small enough to tuck into his trouser pocket without feeling a dragging weight. Then its ringing tone began.

*Burrrp – burrrp.* Insistent. *Burrrrp – burrrrp.*

It was Nell who cursed under her breath when he broke away and delved into his pocket.

'Sorry,' he apologized, although he was strangely relieved. 'Might be important.' He flipped open the mobile's lid. 'Hello?'

Nell sank back into the sofa, folding her arms across her chest, looking mean.

'Thom? It's Katy Budd. We forgot to arrange a time for tomorrow.'

Thom was surprised: it didn't really matter to him what time he took his exercise, but he supposed the therapist had other clients to work around. (What he couldn't know was that Katy, unmarried and currently without a boyfriend, had taken a particular liking to Thom. He was young, not unattractive, and lived *alone* in a beautiful location.)

'Uh, yeah, so we did,' he said quickly. 'Any time's good for me.'

'How about nine thirty tomorrow morning?'

'It's really that urgent?'

'What?'

'Well, yeah, I can be there.'

'At the cottage? Of course.'

'Soon as possible then.'

'Sorry?'

'I'll be there.'

'Oh . . . right. Tomorrow then. Nine thirty.'

''Kay. 'Bye.'

Thom closed the flap and pushed the mobile back into his pocket.

'Gotta go,' he said.

'Thom, not right now . . .?'

'Yep. Sorry. Apparently, it's urgent.'

'Who was it? Is something wrong?'

'Oh no, it's nothing. Well, that is . . . I've got to get back, that's all. Arranged for something to be delivered. Seems I've got to sign for it.'

He was already on his feet buttoning up his combats.

'Are you runnin' away from me, Thom?' She looked angry, but the knowing smile was there, as was the mocking in her eyes.

'You're kidding. No, I've just got to be there, Nell. I told you.'

She rose and moved against him, her arms going around his waist. She pulled him tight and he felt the firmness of her stomach. Desire seemed to sharpen every nerve in his body once more, but something made him pull away. It was crazy, but he really *was* afraid of this woman, and he had no idea why. *Instinct*, his helpful, *canny*, little voice told him. *There's something dangerous about Nell Quick and you just haven't worked it out yet. But it'll come. Oh yes, it'll come.* He held her at arm's length, the action non-aggressive but adamant. By her expression, he could tell Nell was amused, as though this was just part of the game. She made no further move towards him.

'I'll see you soon, Nell,' he said, quickly turning away and heading for the front door.

'Will you be all right?' she asked after him.

That stopped him. He looked back at her, 'What d'you mean?'

'Will you be all right in the cottage? Will you be safe there?'

'Why shouldn't I be?' He was confused, perplexed. She was making him nervous again.

And perhaps that was what Nell wanted for, although the smile remained, there was something cruel about her eyes.

'No reason, Thom,' she said. 'Just a feelin' I have. *Instinct*, you might call it.' She said the word as though she had read his own thoughts about her. 'Be careful tonight, Thom. It's very isolated there in the woods.'

Thanks a lot, he thought, cold fingers tapping his spine.

'I'll be fine,' he said, then left, suddenly eager to be out in the open.

Nell followed him to the door and, shadowed by the porch, leaned against the door-frame to watch him walk away.

He realized he was limping very badly.

---

Thom switched on the engine and drove off, carrying on down the narrow lane so that he could turn the Jeep around at a suitable point. Nell Quick's house had been the last one in the row, only high hedges and fields further on. As he drove past on the return journey, he glanced at it and the windows were darkened, shadowed by the wild foliage around them. The place looked empty, bleak.

Thom suddenly felt drained of energy, as if he had overstretched himself. His left arm was numb, so he had to use the device on the steering-wheel with his right hand to take the turns, and his left foot kept slipping off the metal footrest. He concentrated hard to stop the foot turning inwards and silently cursed himself for his weakness.

Although tired, frustrated with himself, and perspiring freely, he was surprised to find he was not depressed; rather, his mood was edgy, his nerves taut, senses alive despite the weariness. It was almost like being on a caffeine overdose. And behind it all was a weird mood of expectancy.

But expecting what?

He had no idea. He did feel anxious, though, afraid even. He had the peculiar feeling that things were about to start happening, that events had suddenly shifted gear. It was inexplicable, but very real.

Something bad was impending, he just knew it. Something nasty was looming, but he couldn't imagine what or why.

Nell took a small earthenware vessel from a kitchen cupboard and went back to the sofa. Most of the lock of brown hair she had surreptitiously snipped from the back of Thom's neck with tiny nail scissors lay on the top edge of the cushion, directly behind where he had been sitting. The scissors, themselves, had been hidden in the palm of one hand when she had brought his lemonade, and it had been easy to rest them on the windowsill behind the sofa when they had done their job. Carefully she picked up the lock and dropped it into the bowl. Then, moving even closer, she searched for stray hairs, plucking each one from the sofa's coarse material and placing them in the bowl with the mother lock.

When Nell was satisfied that she had every last one, she turned and sat on the edge of the seat, elbows resting on her knees, the vessel held up before her. Once again, the smile. But this time there was a different gleam in her dark eyes. If Thom had witnessed it, he might have thought it evil.

A sound from outside distracted her, a flapping of wings against a windowpane. Nell looked across the room in the direction of the back garden where she grew her herbs and plants. The magpie had landed on the windowsill and was cocking its black hooded head sideways to look through the glass.

Nell left the sofa and made space on the crowded table for the stone vessel and its contents. Then she went to the window.

Opened it.

# Chapter : Fifteenth

## THE DREAM

WHEN THOM got back to Little Bracken it was all he could do to make himself a quick meal – a lasagna from the frozen packs stocked in the fridge, fairly tasteless but it filled the gap – before climbing the stairs, pulling off his clothes and all but collapsing on to the four-poster.

For a while he lay there, naked, staring up at the canopy over the bed and reflecting on the day's events: Sir Russell, an enfeebled old man just waiting to die; Hugo, a cheerful buffoon to some, but a loyal friend to him. Thom remembered with gratitude the day Hugo had walked into the private room at the hospital, flowers held in one chubby hand, a broad grin like the Cheshire cat's on his face, the cheer and optimism he had also brought with him. Hugo had taken care of all the medical expenses and waved a disdainful hand when Thom had promised to pay back every penny. He hadn't known then that the Bleeth family was no longer as wealthy as it once had been, yet Bleeth Senior had paid for him through college and here was Bleeth Junior,

Hugo, helping him with specialists' fees and God knows what else. Thom could have just about managed to handle his hospital bills, but it would have meant selling the workshop – even in the backwaters, London rates were extortionate – and perhaps even selling off well-crafted pieces cheaply for the revenue. Thom had already decided that not only would he repay Hugo, but he would make him something special, a writing desk or a secretaire bookcase, something for him to prize. Thoughts of Hugo led to thoughts of Nell Quick, and he pictured her with her wild black hair and dark eyes, the mocking smile, the soft lips . . .

What was going on between his friend and this woman? Again he thought of Hugo's inheritance, the house, the estate, whatever money Sir Russell had left. And if, as he suspected, they were engaged in an affair, then why would she come on so strongly to him?

His eyelids began to droop and his left arm and leg felt like lead weights on the bed. He had to make an effort just to pull the bedsheet over himself. More pictures, more thoughts, were whirling through his head. The wasp stings that had disappeared overnight, the beautiful girl by the lake, the wonderful lights, the weird grotesques . . .

He began to drift.

---

She was beautiful. She really was *fantastically* beautiful. The golden tresses caught by the sun, cascading around her petite face, reaching almost to her waist. The pale body, so slim but so wonderfully moulded with those small breasts and softly rounded hips, the long thighs whose beginnings bore no shade, no pubic hair, leading to her hidden, inner lips. Neck so graceful, limbs so sensual, hands so delicate in their intimate task, quickening as her pleasure increased, one hand leaving to touch the pink nipples of her little breasts. Tiny lights playing over her like incandescent butterflies.

This time he saw his own hardening, did not just feel it, for he was as naked as the mysterious girl, his body trembling, blood pounding beneath flushed skin. He was walking forward, going to her, and she did not seen afraid ... nor shy ... for her actions did not cease, they merely became more languid, enticing, her silver-violet eyes on his.

He knelt before her and watched, not daring, not *wanting*, to interrupt, and the lights around her frenzied, darting here and there, to and fro, touching *his* unclothed flesh, flailing him with swift almost-transparent wings, increasing his passion; and all the while she watched *him*, even though her eyes were now half-closed, heavy-lidded in delirium. One hand reached for him and he gladly took it in his own; but she did not draw him to her, did not invite him to lie with her, but instead came forward and gently pushed him back so that his shoulders touched the cool earth and his hips pressed against blades of grass.

She hovered over him, the lights between them brilliant in her shadow. Their reflections danced across her skin, bathing the soft points of her pendant breasts in different hues, washing her smooth stomach with spectral tints.

But before the breach between them closed, this inscrutably wondrous vision became something – *someone* – else. The golden hair turned to black, the delicate pink lips became scarlet, the slight breasts grew heavier, their tips darker, and it was Nell above him, lovely, lascivious Nell, who pressed close, her breasts cleaving to his chest, her nipples burning into his.

Her body was smothering his, her fleshy hips in touch with his hips, her stomach crushed against his stomach, the valley between her legs taking in his hardness. He felt the coarse hair at the top of her mound and knew it was as black as the hair that now fell over his face as she kissed his neck, her lips firm and at once firmer, becoming harsh, drawing nerve endings and tiny veins to the surface of his skin so that he gasped, an expression not only of surprise, but of delight also.

She trailed her mouth up to his face, nuzzling his chin, his nose, his brow, but not yet his lips. Nell raised her head to look down at him and her deep eyes studied his, her smile mocking as usual, but somehow adding to the exquisite tension. Something passed between them – a look, an indication of acquiescence on his part (but not yet submission, although that would soon come), a challenge on hers, and then she was upon him once more, her moist lips crushing his, her tongue forcing his lips apart, searching out his tongue. Tongues touched and pressed and slithered over each other's, and just when he was eager for more, his head lifted from the grass to push against her, she pulled away, lowering her lips to his neck once more, leaving him gasping and panting, his hardness now a solid rod between them.

Her lips did not linger: they descended slowly to his chest, taking each of his nipples in turn, dampening them, tensing them with her tongue, kissing them, making them engorged, before moving on, sinking to the firm muscles of his belly, leaving a trail of slickness in their wake, then downwards again, tongue dipping into the tangle of hair before finding the base of the penis that waited so impatiently.

And she did not stop there. Her lips and tongue were gliding up the long, smooth shaft, making it wet, making it throb, taking time, teasing but pleasing, until her mouth was at the tip. A beat. Anticipation screaming. Another beat. And then she took him in her mouth, into a hot cavern that was velvet at the edges and hard inside the entrance with teeth that caught his skin, but gently, never gripping, never biting. And the delight of her tongue when it closed on him to lap at his sticky flow, then around the shaft, coating it with her saliva, drawing on it, pushing against it, repeating the process, her mouth taking him in almost to the hilt, her throat accommodating, creating a sensation he had never before experienced, a swallowing of him he had never thought possible. His body arched, his shoulders burrowed into the soft earth, grass tickled his spine; but she rode him, never losing her precious hold, her mouth constantly working, a hand finding his genitals, cupping them gently, her middle finger finding his perineum, exerting easy pressure, heightening his pleasure and his desire for her, before moving on to the orifice behind. There her fingertip played around the sensitive edges, making him moan out loud. He gripped her breasts and it took self-control not to squeeze them hard; instead he kneaded them, drew out the long nipples from their dark surrounds, this time causing her to draw in a sharp gasp, before murmuring her own pleasure, for a moment losing him, but quickly swallowing him again to continue the strokes that were now becoming tighter, faster, fluids inside him racing to his centre where they seemed to boil as if in a cauldron; his hands left her breasts to grab her upper arms, so that he could control the rhythm, so that he could prolong the rapture . . .

And all the while she watched him, watched his head thrash from side to side, his eyes closed in bliss, watched his chest heave and sink, his skin sheened with sweat, watched him while his hips thrust against her, and never once losing him, the finger beneath him now probing, gently entering so that there was no pain, only sensual delight.

His movement slowed, but hers did not; his hips squirmed and thrust upwards, but she maintained her hold. His body was becoming rigid, a long moan escaping his open mouth, and she knew the signs and made ready for what was to follow.

He could no longer bear to contain the flood. He needed release, needed the final exultation. And it was not too far away . . .

His member was like iron between her lips, inside her

throat and still she worked, still her smooth action was relentless as she awaited the liberation of all those boiling fluids. She even tightened her velvet grip and increased the friction. She plunged with her finger, deeper into his anus, so that all his muscles spasmed, every part of him became taut ... yet out of control ...

And then he was in the euphoria of release and he spilled into her mouth. He cried out with the exhilaration and his eyelids sprung open so that he saw ...

So that he saw the fiend squatting between his legs, its great humped back bent over his groin, thick, enormous lips around his penis, massive head jerking erratically as it drained him of his semen.

# Chapter : Sixteenth

## THE SUCCUBUS

THOM SCREAMED and pulled away, scrabbling to the top of the bed and crouching there, legs drawn up, a shoulder against the headboard. *It couldn't be happening! He had to be dreaming this!* But no nightmare could be as clear and as real. Nor as terrifying, for the mind has its own way of protecting itself, even in sleep, and he would surely have wakened if this had been a dream.

The monster, deprived of its prey, slowly looked up at Thom, its huge head scrunched between crooked shoulders, Thom's semen drooling from its thick grinning lips.

'*No . . .!*' Thom screamed, as if denial would make the thing go away. '*No!*' he screamed again.

There was no soul behind its bulging black eyes.

Wood cracked as Thom pressed harder against the headboard. His feet dug troughs in the undersheet.

It was not a big creature, for although it squatted on the end of the bed, knees almost up to its scabrous chin, back arched in a great hump, it was easy to tell it would stand no more than three to four feet when upright (*if* it could stand upright); but its dark unclean body rippled with muscles and thick sinews. Its baleful eyes still on Thom, it reached for a beaker lying close by on the bed and held it up to its chin. It allowed the creamy fluid in its mouth to drip into the container, spitting to force every last drop from its lips, finally *hawking* to clear the stuff from its throat.

Then it appraised Thom, its open-mouthed leer revealing dozens of small, glistening, yellow, pointed teeth, four rows of them set in its upper and lower jaws. Without taking its black eyes off the horrified figure of Thom, who was trying to push through the headboard itself, the creature sealed the beaker with a matching cap. It twisted the lid tight.

Satisfied, it began to crawl towards Thom, its prize held close to its barrel chest.

---

'*Keep away!*' cried Thom, turning his face away from the advancing beast but with his eyes still riveted to it in a sideways stare. He tried to tell himself that it wasn't real, that he *was* dreaming, but it was no use – he *felt* the wood splintering under his weight, he could *smell* the creature's rancid odour as it drew closer, and he could *see* with fine definition every hair on its ponderous, monstrous body, every furrow in its enormous slanted forehead, every glint on its rows of pointed teeth. And he could *hear* every snuffling grunt it made.

Whether it was some kind of animal of simian origins, or a human mutant, he had no way of knowing – nor did he care at that particular moment; all he knew was that this ugly, frightening thing was of evil intent and he was to be the victim.

Naked, he sprang from the bed just as the beast reached out with its free – hand? paw? – to catch his ankle, and his legs became tangled in the bedsheet so that he lost balance and tumbled into a corner created by the end of the sideboard and the angled wall. His head cracked against stone, almost knocking him unconscious; only the adrenaline pumping through him – and of course, the terrible fear – kept him moving. Groggy from the bump, Thom pushed himself to his feet, kicking his legs free of the sheet, one hand on the sideboard, the other on the windowsill, both props helping him remain upright. His eyes cleared and he looked back at the rumpled bed.

The creature – *the ape, the mutant, the terrifying bloody thing!* – was squatting on the edge, so close, so *very* close, no more than four feet away, and it was . . . grinning? Could it be described as a grin, or was it just its natural – *unnatural* – countenance? Whatever the answer, it was looking at him with big prominent soulless eyes, bright moonlight from the open window reflected in both. And it *was* grinning, Thom was certain now, and it was a kind of . . . kind of . . . *lewd* grin, a kind of *licentious* grin, and its lips were shiny with the residue of Thom's semen.

It raised its head as it watched him and Thom noticed it had short, pointed ears. He also noticed that its great barrel chest came to hairy points, as if the creature had breasts. Good God, was this the female of whatever weird species it sprang from?

Beaker clutched between its tapered breasts, a leer stretching its thick, slimy lips, the thing remained perfectly still on the edge of the bed.

But then it began to tremble as if a huge rage were building inside. Its pitchy black eyes began to glare; its hair began to bristle; a snarling growl began to rise from some-where deep in its throat.

Thom could only cower in the corner, one arm raised across his face, his body paralysed by fear.

It shuffled on its haunches, as if making ready to leap at him. Thom wanted to move, he *tried* to move, but it seemed that his limbs were locked, that all power, all mobility had been drained from him, as if his lost semen had taken his strength with it. He found that, such was the stupefying fear, he could not even cry out any more. If only he could at least close his eyes against the horror . . .

The thing on the bed bunched its muscles, steadying itself. Its great multi-toothed mouth yawned wide.

But then another peculiar sight.

Through the open doorway to the spiral staircase there came a long, vertical . . . stick? Rod? Lance? What the hell *was* it?

For two seconds, perhaps more, Thom watched it dance closer in the bright moonlight, the lower end obscured by the side of the bed.

The creature's prominent eyes were too intent on its prey to notice. That is, until the length of wood whacked its head, a weird little helium voice screeching at the same time:

'*Begonesuccubusbegone!*'

The crack echoed all around the room, bouncing off the angled walls with a resonance whose sharpness was motivating for both man and beast.

The creature yowled as its large head dived further into its hunched shoulders, while Thom escaped his paralysis and leapt to his feet. Only then did he see the little head on the other side of the bed.

---

If the beast was the most awful thing that Thom Kindred had ever seen, then the tiny creature to whom the little head belonged was the most curious. Its tiny hands held the brush end of the broom firmly in their grip (the broom staff was like a great pole to this thing that was even too small to be a midget) as repeatedly it *thwacked* Thom's attacker over its gross-shaped head and shoulders, running around the bed as it did so, breaking off only to avoid the tall, corner bedpost.

It was then, when it paused briefly, that Thom saw it more clearly. It had a roundish face with a pointed chin and long pointed ears that stuck out from beneath a floppy brown cap. It was impossible to tell its skin colouring in the moonlight's bleaching, but it looked like tanned leather, and its eyes were tilted, almost Chinese-looking. Its sharp chin was beardless, but long black straggles of hair hung down from the rim of the cap, separating over the ears and dropping below to a long thin neck. A muddy-green tight-fitting coat covered its body, while knee breeches and stockings of a roughish material covered its short and very skinny legs. Thom was still unable to see its feet, for the little man – it *seemed* to be a man – was partially hidden by the end of the bed.

'*Begonebegone!*'

At least that was what its high-pitched cry seemed to be as it resumed its beating of the monster, which held up its arms to deflect the blows, yowling as it did so. Now the victim, the beast glared from Thom to the tiny man, and then back to Thom again.

'*Getawaygetaway!*'

It took a moment for Thom to realize his rescuer was calling to him now, the strange-sounding words all rolled into one. Instinct took over and he ducked around the corner of the sideboard, putting distance between himself and the cowering beast on the bed. But even as he did so, it reached a great paw and raked Thom's cheek with what felt like sharp claws. He uttered a cry at the sudden searing pain, but nevertheless kept moving, grabbing his jeans from the settle as he went, his nakedness only increasing his sense of vulnerability. As the little man – Thom could now see it/he was wearing boots with ridiculously long pointed toes – continued to distract the beast, he did a kind of backwards hopping shuffle, pulling up one leg as he went.

'*Getoutsuccubus!*'

The words somehow were plainer, but hardly made sense. Succubus?

The beast suddenly backed off, loping to the far end of the bed, where it sank to its haunches, cradling the beaker between its ugly breasts. It began to tense itself, its hair bristling, knotted muscles undulating, and Thom realized it was going to attack him again. It now seemed enraged by the unexpected assault and the deflection from its purpose, for it twisted its neckless head, waving it to and fro, shoulders moving in rhythm, and it yowled once more into the night and bellowed its wrath.

Streaking down the length of the bed, it launched itself at Thom who, both legs now in the jeans, ducked. The beast, hoisted by powerful leg muscles, sailed over his head to smash into the broad, stone fireplace behind. It screeched as it landed in a flurry of hump and limbs in the hearth below, and went on screeching as it scrabbled around trying to pick itself up. Meanwhile the beaker had fallen to the floor and was lying on its side.

*'Thegobletthegobletthegoblet!'*

Thom, on his knees and still trying to button his jeans, heard the strange little man's shouts, but couldn't understand their meaning.

Clutching the giant broom by its handle, the pint-sized defender hobbled over to Thom. He stared squarely into Thom's face and deliberately drew out the words.

*'Get-the-goblet!'*

His voice was like a slowed-down tape, for it became deeper, had more timbre.

'Get-the-goblet.'

Fear somehow numbed by the craziness of it all, Thom reacted. At once he had buttoned the jeans and was stretching his other hand towards the beaker – the goblet – whose contents were slowly seeping out on to the rug in front of the hearth. He managed to snatch it just before the creature tried to rake him with its claws again. Thom fell back against the end of the bed and for long moments, he and the beast stared at each other.

The diminutive man suddenly appeared between them, facing the crouching beast, the broom held across his tiny chest like a pikestaff. From behind, Thom could see that his narrow shoulders were trembling with fright.

Thom pushed himself to one knee, the knuckles of one hand against the floorboards for support, the other clutching the beaker. He expected the beast to rush at him.

But instead it ignored both Thom and his tiny champion, and began lapping at the spilled drool of semen as though it were cream. It did not appear to swallow.

'*Getyisselfdownstairs.*'

At first, Thom did not realize the little man was instructing him, for his eyes were still on the beast. The words, all rolled into one as they were, were difficult to understand as well.

'Get-yisself-downstairs.' He was told again, this time more slowly, the voice deeper as before.

Thom understood, but as he rose to tower over his pint-sized protector, so the beast slowly looked up from its lapping.

'*Run!*'

It was a high-pitched squeal and it came from the little man, but the meaning was very plain to Thom this time. He scooted for the door.

As he passed through the opening to be immersed in the deep shadows of the landing, he heard a shriek from behind, but still he did not stop. Moonlight shone through the stairway's only window, lighting his way as he hurried down. He heard a scuffling from behind.

So sure-footed was he as he rounded the stairs, one hand brushing against the central column, it was as if he had never been away. He could have been a small boy again, awakened by a nightmare, running down to seek comfort from his mother. Even the creaks and cracks of the stair-boards were familiar to him, and his fingertips on the newel post found old grooves and grains that he still remembered. For one mad moment – if anything else could be madder than the insanity just transpired – he was that boy again, and he believed in things that he had long forgotten, things that he had been told by Bethan, *things that he had seen for himself!* Faeries and elves and things. Magical creatures that faded from memory when he moved away and grew older. Creatures that no adult would – *could* – ever believe in. Not unless they were special, his mother had once told him. But even then, she had never spoken of monsters, had never frightened him with such tales. So why this beast in his bedroom now? Why this ugly, grotesque, semen-guzzling monster that was on the landing and about to chase after him? Was this all a dream? The throbbing of his cheek where the beast – the *succubus* – had slashed him told him otherwise. And he could feel his bare feet on the stairs, could feel the roughness of the wooden newel beneath his fingertips. And he could *hear* the beast following him. He could *hear* its snuffling and its snarls. No dream could ever be *this* real.

He did not stop when he reached the open kitchen door, but ran straight through into the moonlit room, putting the centre table between himself and the thing that was following.

He fell back against the refrigerator and its motor unit inside hummed as if nudged into action. His chest was heaving, his hands, one still holding on to the beaker, were shaking, and his eyes were wide with terror. The thing was a dark shape in the doorway.

It had come to a halt, as if it knew the prey was trapped. Why Thom had not run through the front door, which was wide open, and into the woods beyond, Thom did not know himself. Perhaps he feared the woods themselves, perhaps he was afraid of being chased through the concealing darkness there, with trees and thickets set to hinder him. The cottage was his sanctuary, the one true place of safety. He could hear the beast snorting, shuffling its clawed feet. The snorting became a snarling again, the snarling became a screeching. And the monster began to lumber around the table after him.

Thom waited until the last moment before swinging the fridge door open with all his might.

It crashed into the beast, stopping it in its tracks for a moment, and Thom ran off in the opposite direction.

Thom stayed on the other side of the table, wondering what the hell he was going to do now. The creature was too strong and too vicious to fight and Thom didn't give much for his chances out there in the woods. In the kitchen he might at least find something with which to fight this thing. If he could reach one of the carving knives in the drawer . . . on the other side of the kitchen . . . where the beast, stunned by the fridge door, was just pulling itself up, one horrible clawed paw on the back of a kitchen chair.

It was all so lucid in the moonlight that streamed through the kitchen's many windows, all so clear and real and all so nightmarishly unreal. The table, with its fruit bowl and oddments, the shelving filled with crockery, the units and sink, the crammed bookshelves – all so clear and all so ordinary, so commonplace. But the stunted creature just rising into view, the guttural sounds of its grunts and snarls – that was what the nightmare was made of.

Thom suddenly felt weak at the knees. *This* was not good for him. He was *supposed* to be convalescing, avoiding anything stressful. His doctors would be cross if they knew. Huh!

He realized that his mind, as if it were a voice, was gibbering. The creature was moving round towards him and Thom backstepped away, holding the beaker tight against his chest as if it were a prize, its contents liquid gold. Even as he did so he wondered why he was protecting his own semen. And what did this hideous creature want with it anyway?

Light footsteps on the stairs behind him, the little guy running through the doorway, broom apparently discarded. Across the table the beast-thing – the succubus – was shuffling to and fro, uncertain which way to chase Thom, who was also weaving about, trying to confuse his pursuer.

'*Don'tletitgitit!*'

Thom paused for just a second. 'What?'

The agitated pint-size was jumping on the spot – did he seem taller now? About eighteen inches high? A pint-and-a-half size? – pointing in turn at the beaker and the beast. He suddenly stood perfectly still and his almond-shaped eyes focused directly on Thom's. He seemed to be concentrating hard.

'Don't let the succubus git it,' he said, his voice slowing and dropping several octaves.

Thom shook his head uncomprehendingly. He knew he wasn't dreaming, but surely it wasn't the real world he was living in at this precise moment. Couldn't be. Creatures like these didn't exist in the proper world. Not the one he was used to. But it *was* happening and he *was* scared witless. Okay, maybe there was one thing he could do to bring some reality to the situation.

While keeping a wary eye on the bobbing head on the other side of the scarred kitchen table, he reached behind and swiped his hand down against the two light-switches by the front door. The moonlight immediately relinquished its right to the room and the kitchen and small landing next door were flooded with bright clarifying artificial light. Both oddities clapped hands or paws over their eyes as if blinded, the beast grunting and snarling, the little man giving out a sharp shriek of surprise.

If Thom hoped the abundant illumination would improve the situation he was wrong. He remained in a nightmare that wasn't a dream, still in his kitchen confronted by two of the most peculiar creatures he had ever laid eyes on, one a beast, the other a dwarf. The latter was more like ... more like a pixie or elf, not quite the same as those you saw in kids' storybooks but, he guessed, the closest thing to one. It was then that it occurred to Thom that his stroke, the impediment of blood to his brain, really had either killed off certain key cells – those dealing with reason maybe – or at least damaged them, made chemical and electrical charges, or whatever, act in a different way. In other words, caused hallucinations. Oh bloody hell!

Even so, something told him he could only go with it, ride the flow. If he didn't, then his abused mind might tell him this beast could actually harm him and, in believing it, it would be so. Thom fled to the other side of the table as the succubus, still blinking those awful black eyes against the new light, decided which way to give chase.

Stalemate once again. The beast halted before the open front door, while Thom staggered back against the tall bookshelf on the other side of the room. He felt a weight dragging on his leg and, looking down, found the little man clinging to him, his body trembling all over. To see such terror gave Thom no comfort at all.

Breathing heavily, its great shoulders heaving, the brute-beast turned its great head towards the open doorway through which a cooling night breeze blew. For one optimistic moment, Thom thought his pursuer might be making ready to bolt out into the darkness of the forest, its work here frustrated.

He couldn't have been more wrong.

Instead, the creature reached out a great paw and slammed the door shut.

Now Thom truly was trapped and he bitterly regretted not having escaped from the cottage when he had had the chance. So what if he had been hampered in the woods, tripped by a fallen branch, entangled in shrubbery, knocked out by a tree he had not seen coming – at least he would have stood some kind of chance. Now this. Shut inside his own kitchen with a gibbering sub-midget hugging his leg like a dog in heat. At the thought, he glanced down. Was he mistaken, or had his hopeless champion grown shorter again? He – it, whatever – was less than a foot high. Thom almost accepted the previous notion: he *was* going mad. That didn't mean he wasn't just as terrified though.

He had to get out. But the monster was guarding the door. Get up to the roof, try and hold the door shut when he was outside? No chance. The beast, as small and hunched as it was, was far too powerful to hold off – all muscle, sinew and mammoth shoulders – and the roof door opened inwards anyway. Besides, the door to the staircase was next to the front door, so the beast had them both covered. The windows? Closed. By the time he'd managed to get one open – *if* they still opened after all these years of disuse – he'd be caught. And to limit his options further, his attacker was lumbering towards the kitchen table, paws, or bloody claws, reaching out to push it across the room and trap him in a corner.

Thom looked around wildly. Oh shit.

Okay. Keep calm. A window was his only choice and he was going through one, open or not. He only hoped the old wooden frames were weak.

Its legs made a scraping-grinding noise against the stone floor as the heavy table came closer and Thom made ready to climb on to it, use its surface as a launching pad for his leap through the nearest window. But the little man was tugging at his leg.

'*Thebookthebookthebook!*'

It sounded like a squealing of, '*dabukdabukdabuk!*' but this time he understood what his terrified companion was shouting. Unfortunately, he had no idea what he actually meant.

'*What book?*' Thom yelled back.

The midget – had he grown taller once more? – was

pointing at the top shelf of the bookcase behind them. Again he forced himself to speak more slowly so that Thom understood his words more easily. '*Get the book!*'

Meanwhile, the big table was less then two feet away, its weight alone preventing it sliding across the floor to smash into Thom's legs. He barely had time to look at the row of books on the highest shelf, then back down at the little man's anxious face.

'*Pickmeup! Pick-me-up!*' Only a little slower, now, but coherent.

Still grasping the beaker in one hand, Thom scooped him up by the back of his coat and with his free hand held him against the top shelf. The little man weighed less than a one-year-old child, so holding him there required hardly any effort.

Thom gasped with pain as the edge of the table slammed into his lower right thigh and he fell across its top. The bowl of fruit, condiments, a table mat, a couple of magazines he had brought up from London with him, an empty coffee cup with spoon still inside – all the things he had not bothered to clear away earlier – came sliding towards him, some of them falling to the floor, the mug smashing. Hurt, eyes momentarily closed, he heard the beast's low-growling snarl. He looked up to see that it had jumped up on to the table, only the bowl, which had lost its top fruit, between them. Almost eyeball to eyeball, they stared at one another.

He could easily have been mistaken, so lacklustre were the black eyes of the beast, but Thom thought he saw a look of gloating triumph on the other's brutish face. The gaping mouth with its scores of jagged teeth seemed to be grinning at him.

Thom wanted nothing more than to close his eyes against the leering vision, perhaps even offer up the beaker with what was left of its contents, let the monster have his semen, even say, 'cheers', as it drank – if that's what it wanted to do.

He had no strength left, he wanted to rest, sleep, *escape* the nightmare. But no, fuck it, that wasn't what he was going to do.

Thom drew the beaker into himself, holding it beneath his chest as if it were the elixir of life itself, the plastic container a holy chalice. Which got the succubus *really* mad.

Squatting on the table, it lifted its great arms like a baboon and screeched and screeched and screeched.

So loud was the screeching that Thom felt the *thump* of the book rather than hearing its sound as it landed on the table next to his shoulder. He turned his head to look at it.

The little man was standing over it. 'Open-the-book,' he said slowly and evenly.

'Uh?'

'Open-the-book.' Even slower, but it still managed to sound like '*Uppendabuk*'.

Fortunately, as exhausted and as terrorized as he felt, Thom was becoming familiar with the strange talk. He reached out and flipped open the book just as the succubus started forward.

It fell open about half-way through and the rushing beast halted in its tracks. The big black deadpan eyes again took on a faint expression. Thom, who was cowering under the anticipated onslaught, could have sworn that the look was one of trepidation.

He followed the beast's gaze to the open book. It was a heavy-looking tome, the edges of its vellum leaves brown with age, the corners battered and turned. But from its yellowish pages there came a golden glow.

# Chapter : Seventeenth

## THE PORTAL

THEY WERE glorious. Tiny sprites of light – gold, silver, violet, all colours but predominantly these three. And dazzling. It almost hurt Thom's eyes to look as the illuminations poured from the open pages of the dusty book lying on the table. They flew high into the air as bright as any night star – no, far brighter – circling the ceiling lamp in a dazzling carousel of brilliance.

All other movement in the room stopped. They watched. Thom slack-jawed, eyes filled with wonder, fear forgotten for the moment. The succubus, stony-eyed, but dark body quivering. The little pixie-man, happiness beaming from his peculiarly wizened yet unlined face.

The ceiling shone with reflections thrown by the darting lights, in softer hues that were far easier to gaze at, the colours seemingly more various, but toned down: greens, blues and some soft shades of red were the dominant colours there. Thom knew that the lights themselves were the same as those he had witnessed on the first day he had returned to Little Bracken, the day he had left the Big House to walk through the woods. He *had* seen them the other night too, from his bedroom window. And of course, when he had spied on the naked girl in the woods. He also knew what they were, although his mind would not quite allow the word at that moment.

They hovered, they skimmed low, they flitted like moths around the ceiling light. And more and more came from the book, legions of them, spilling out and taking to the air like butterflies escaping a net. Their sounds came to him now, that familiar whistling-singing, high flutes, the highest notes of the harp, the tinkling of distant bells. And many of the lights grew larger even as he watched so that he saw their flickering wings, inside their radiances, silken wings so sheer they were almost invisible. And then their tiny lively bodies, a great number of them naked, while others wore wispy shifts that were as immodest as the nakedness. Minute heads, fully-formed though – little eyes, little noses, little mouths, little pointed ears. Most, but by no means all, had long flowing hair, some dark, some fair, some golden. They weaved and dived and their cries seemed far away, as if they were not in the same room, as if they were not truly in this *world*. Thom's own eyes were now shining, but not from the reflected light: they shone in wonder, and his heart tremored in complete awe.

*Faeries.*

At last his mind accepted the word.

*Faeries.*

It was impossible to deny. All the books he had read as a child were authentic, at least in part. The folklore, the faerytales, the songs, the poems, passed down from generation to generation, recounted to children whose minds and hearts were open, were based on some ancient truth. The stories his mother had told him when he lay in bed, or sat on her lap, a child without a father and with few friends and whose imagination compensated, whose imagination soared when he closed his eyes or played in the woods, a child who *believed* in faerytales, who understood their message, the constant battle between good and evil, right and wrong, who accepted the world did not belong to humans alone. But there was something more, something he could not remember; perhaps a knowledge – a *knowing* – which left all children eventually – no, once the *children* themselves left a certain state of mind.

*Faeries!*

Incredible. Unbelievable. Impossible!

Yet there they were, continuing to fly from the book, filling his kitchen with their sounds and radiance, repudiating all that adulthood had taught him, contravening the natural laws, contradicting sound judgement, and impugning every wisdom. They were not impossible, and they were in the room with him, flying about his head.

In the wonder of it all, he had almost forgotten the great hulking brute squatting on the tabletop, and only its bestial growl reminded him he was still in danger. At first cowed by this magical airborne fleet, the succubus was now enraged. It lifted one of its powerful arms to swipe at them, its rows of jagged teeth gnashing air, spittle flying out. The growl became a roar, a sound which rattled crockery on the dresser and made windows shiver.

Thom's head snapped round and he threw himself back from the table, his hips smashing against the edge of the sink behind him. He still held the beaker in one hand.

The beast screamed when the biggest of the flying creatures, an unclothed faery with tiny breasts and wings that were nearly twice her size, shot down from the ceiling and sprinkled what looked like silvery powder over its head. Another winged figure followed suit, its silky covering billowing between its wings, the wings themselves vibrating almost to invisibility. Then another, and another, until a whole squadron of these things Thom now knew as faeries was zooming in to attack, each one dispersing glittering powder like tinsel over the succubus until it started to sneeze, shoulders heaving, scaly feet almost leaving the table. If Thom had not been so scared and so confused, he might have laughed at its antics; as it was, he could only gape frozen-faced and wide-eyed.

More and more of the little winged people flew down and around in dizzying circles, bewildering the beast, taunting it, tormenting it, their soft but high-pitched voices crying out in both joy and anger, it seemed to Thom. The figures within the haloes of bright pulsing light were becoming increasingly discernible as each moment went by, as if once beheld, so their image was sharpened. The monster, the beast, the succubus, flailed at them with both arms, its movement clumsy, easily avoided, and the winged creatures, the flying stars – *the faeries* – were enjoying themselves immensely, their tiny voices still unintelligible, yet filled with high spirits, the game they were playing dangerous but exhilarating. Until one, the size of a pen top, became too bold and got too close, her speed just not fast enough. A huge paw caught her and Thom clearly saw one of her wings fold, then crumple, the faery spinning round and round like a damaged fighter plane.

Thom gasped, and the pixie-man next to him let out a sharp screech as the faery fell to the tabletop and lay there, either stunned or seriously hurt, her radiant aura pulsating, then dimming. The succubus roared in triumph and, ignoring its tormentors, who increased their activity, flying into its bulging eyes, flicking their wings against his face, raised both fists together over its head, making ready to bring them smashing down on the helpless creature. But the faery dust appeared to have slowed its movements, made the beast ponderous.

Thom saw what was about to happen and had time to dash forward and scoop up the would-be victim from the table just before the combined fists hit the wood with a mighty crash.

Thom was unable to hold on to the injured faery, his brushing scoop merely sweeping her off the table's surface, but even as she fluttered over the edge, one wing working limply, the other already beginning to unfold, two more faeries swooped and held her aloft long before she reached the stone floor. But he was left lying across the table once more, beaker clutched beneath him, his head and shoulders vulnerable to the beast towering over him. He just had time to look up, the big fists at their zenith, the beast's smoked-glass eyes gleaming, when something tugged at the waistband of his jeans and he was sliding backwards.

Again the joined fists shook the table and the succubus howled with frustration (and pain, too, Thom hoped) and Thom himself was upright, the little man letting go of his jeans and steadying him with an outstretched hand. The pixie-man was breathing hard, as if it had taken a great effort to drag Thom out of harm's way.

'*Runrunrun!Don'tletitgitit!*'

Although the words were spun together, the sound high-pitched and strangulated, Thom understood perfectly. Maybe it was the repetition, maybe he was just getting used to the dialect: it didn't matter, because he already knew what he had to do. The faeries – too many to count, but there were hundreds of them – were dive-bombing the succubus, who was lumbering like an ape towards Thom, knuckles grazing wood as it came, the fruit bowl and the open book and anything else still left on the table fiercely brushed aside, the air filled with swirling motes of silver. It was undaunted, its purpose very obvious.

Thom was suddenly near to collapse. He was supposed to be ill, for Christ's sake, not fighting off monsters from some neverworld that by rights, by all sane physical laws and common sense, could not possibly exist! He was running low on adrenaline, flight intercepted, defeat literally staring him in the face and getting closer all the time. But Thom *did* know what to do.

Ultimately, the faeries and the little man who never seemed to be the same size from one moment to the next – right now he was only six inches high, as though having wilted under the pressures of battle – were powerless against this great hulking beast, and so it was up to Thom to help himself. And he really *did* know what to do.

As the succubus reached the edge of the table, paws now raised shoulder-high as if to claw out Thom's eyes, huge muscles in its legs and shoulders gleaming with sweat under the ceiling light, he turned away and reached for the tap over the sink. The tap seemed to gulp and something in the pipes *clunked* before a jet of brown water burst out, splattering the sink, the work surface and Thom himself. Almost calmly he tilted the beaker over the drain and poured what was left of the whitish fluid away. Any that floated around in the whirlpool at the bottom of the sink, he guided into the hole with his fingers.

It seemed that everything had ground to a halt once more. The faeries hovered in the air like humming birds, the beast stayed its leap forward and the tiny man was now hanging from a bookshelf gawking at Thom.

It was over. Thom knew it was over. And so did the beast.

As he turned to face the succubus, Thom saw that something – spirit? Purpose? – had left it. It glared, it ranted, but it made no further move towards him. And as if encouraged by Thom's actions, the faeries resumed their attack, flying dangerously close, tickling its stubby nose, throwing dust like confetti, pulling at its ears, all the while ululating in their sweet, sing-songy way as the pixie-man called out encouragement.

With one last roaring howl, the succubus ran back across the table and leapt towards the front door, in its fury misjudging the distance and smashing into wood. It howled again, a wretched screech, and clumsily yanked at the door-handle. The door flew open and the beast was gone, out into the night. Darkness quickly swallowed up the shambling figure, but Thom could hear it crashing through the trees and undergrowth for long moments afterwards. The faeries' melodious cries reached a crescendo until they, too, went through the door and out into the deep indigo night, two of the larger ones, Thom noticed, carrying their injured companion between them. Like a silver-golden slipstream following the brightest comet, they swerved around the trees and obstacles and were soon gone from view.

Although relieved, he was also disappointed. The cottage felt suddenly empty. *Totally* empty, as though its soul had left with the faeries. Besides, he was still in awe of those wonderful ethereal flying creatures and, now that the fear had been removed, he wanted to learn more about them. He wanted to know their secrets, their genesis. But he was alone.

Well, almost alone. The little man suddenly appeared, sitting on the edge of the table.

# Chapter : Eighteenth

## CONVERSATION WITH AN ELF

THEY TALKED long into the night, Thom fascinated while sometimes doubting his own sanity. How could he be sitting here talking to a tiny man – who was sitting cross-ankled in the middle of the table, the old book closed before him, and who would have been at least a foot tall if standing – proclaiming himself to be an elf, keeper of the cottage, and guardian to Thom?

Thom had been dog-weary when the excitement was over – no, wrong, the danger was gone, but the conversation they now were having raised a different excitement – but as if from out of nowhere, the elf – the elf? Could there *be* such a thing? – had produced a pitcher of juice (the stone pitcher was not one Thom had seen before), containing the same kind of juice he had found waiting for him a couple of mornings ago. As before, although without the same intensity, he was suddenly refreshed, invigorated even, his mind clear, much of the tiredness gone. It was a delicious sensation, a natural one, as if toxins in his body had been removed. His troubled mind was calmed, his tension soothed, and the remnants of exhaustion still lodged within even became pleasurable. No drug could work this way, for clarity was its essence, the sense of wellbeing a by-product. He had downed a full glass in three large gulps, but the elf had refused him any more.

'Toomochanyeel – not want to sleep for a week.' The sentence had started garbled and had only made sense halfway through. 'Too much and ye'll not want to sleep for a week.' There was no accent, but there was a lilt in the voice, and most of what the little man said from then on was perfectly coherent to Thom.

Thom asked if there was something special in the juice, some magic ingredient, and it was odd that the word *magic* did not sound ridiculous, nor even imply trickery.

'Naw,' came the reply, the elf grinning from pointed ear to pointed ear, pixie eyes almost closed with the fun of it. 'Everyday herbs and things ye'll find in yer own woods, mixed with lake water and plum juice.'

'Lake water?' Thom examined the empty glass as if it still contained the liquid. 'I swam in the lake when I was a kid. It didn't taste special.'

The imp grinned even more, revealing tiny and almost pointed teeth. In the artificial light from above Thom saw that his face and hands were brownish, like parchment, and his hair, that which he could see sticking out from under the floppy, pointed hat, was black. It was impossible to tell the mysterious being's age because although his face was strangely wizened there was not a wrinkle in sight. With his tilted eyes and coffee skin he might have been Chinese, or even Mongolian, but in truth, he actually looked neither, something else about him that was weird.

Thom rested his elbows on the table, loosely clenched hands parallel but apart. 'Will you please tell me who you are?' he all but pleaded.

'*Dontchano?*' Don't you know? '*Kinchamemba?*' Can't you remember?

Thom shook his head and the minikin gave an exaggerated sigh.

'Y'all lose it.'

The more Thom listened, the plainer the words became. It was as if he were remembering a dialect rather than learning a new one.

'Y'all lose it an' some never be havin' it,' the man said.

'What? Tell me what.'

'The perception. It be deadin' as the 'magination fades.'

'There are people with fantastic imaginations,' Thom insisted. 'Artists, poets, composers . . . plenty.'

'Still their minds bint open no matter how theys tries. I think yous call it "maturity" when the knowin' goes. Never that simple though, there be much more to it.'

'You have to believe? You have to *want* to believe?'

'Don't be daft.' The reprimand was short, no-nonsense. 'If that be the case, there'd be millions seein' of us. Yous lose the magic.'

That word again. *Magic.*

'An' that's right an' proper, s'how it should be. Yous not be in the same spectrum, y'see, no, not at all. Yous lose the ability to move yer vision an' minds up a few notches. That's why, if we likes, we be come down to yer level. An' even then, yous might not be seein' of us.'

'I don't understand any of this.'

The little man rested his wrists on his raised knees. 'What d'yer want explainin'?'

'Oh, just about everything.'

'Well let's be makin' a start. I know yer doesn't remember me, but d'yer be knowin' *what* I am?'

'A pixie?' Thom felt no embarrassment in using the word.

'Elf, pixie, brownie, bwca – it be takin' too long to explain, and then yer wouldn't be understandin' anyway. Settle fer elf, that'll do fer now.'

'But elves aren't real, they only exist in storybooks.'

'Aye, an' so be faeries, an' yer've just seen 'em. An' so be the succubus, fer yer've just seen that evil thing too.'

'But ... but you're real. I can't believe what I'm seeing, what's just happened ...'

'We be real enough,' the – elf? – said gruffly. 'Used to be known as *fatae* – the fates – but that be changed through the centuries. Don't yer be rememberin' anything of us? Y'used to play with the faeries when yerself were wee.'

'Impossible.'

'Yeh, impossible. Just like me. An' yet yer be sittin' there talkin' to me.'

'I know I'm not dreaming.'

The little man chuckled and shook his head. Thom watched as he shrunk a couple of inches.

'Why do you keep doing that?' he asked, vexed.

The elf shrugged. 'S'up to ye, really. Yer've not quite settled on the size yer want me to be.'

'Up to me? I've got nothing to do with it.'

'Listen.' The elf leaned forward over his knees and spoke in a hushed voice. 'Humans be governed by the limits of their own spectrum. Yous do not see the infinite vibrations between. If ye like, we be exist between yer finites. Understand me?'

'Not a clue.'

Thom felt heady, either from the brew he had just consumed, or from relief that the terror – not just the beast, but the terror within himself – was gone. He was eager to learn, exhaustion for the moment allayed both by curiosity and the drink.

The elf-man sighed again, an almost comical gesture. He wasn't cute, not like the elves or pixies you saw in illustrated storybooks, but his size and features did lend him some kind of eccentric charm. No Disney character this, but bewitchingly intriguing all the same.

'Forget the senses yer know about – yer could when you

were little. Those five senses are too dense, they have no finesse.'

A strange thing was happening to the elf's manner of speech as he went on. Initially, it had almost been incoherent gobbledegook as far as Thom was concerned, then it had began to make sense and he could understand almost every word. Now it was becoming even plainer, the odd lilt still present, but the main inflections growing more like Thom's own. 'Yer' had become 'you' and the annoying 'bes' – it be this, it be that – dropped altogether. It was a relief, for the concept was difficult enough to follow without having to decipher every sentence as well.

'And because we choose to remain hidden,' the elf went on, his voice still a high tone but the words well formed, 'and because your senses are not in tune with ours, we remain invisible to humans. Most of the time, anyway. We live in different dimensions, you and I, but there is a link. To begin with, though, you have to understand that the cosmos consists more of energy and consciousness than it does of physical matter.'

Now Thom was convinced that his own subconscious was making sense of the elf's language, that the more he heard the easier it became to follow. He remembered the flutey-whistling sounds of the faeries, how they had gradually changed to little singing voices to his ear, as if familiarity were making sense of it all. His subconscious mind was the translator, the process . . .? Magical.

'Unfortunately, the more materialistic humans have become – the more civilized, you would say. Pah! – the more you've lost sight of the grand consciousness. If you gave it proper attention, you'd be amazed at how logical – and how wonderful – it all is.' He shook his small head sadly. 'You've chosen otherwise, though.'

Thom spoke up. 'I don't get it. Why *would* we do that?'

'Human contrariness. It's the way you are. Some of you

can't even appreciate fine music, art, beautiful prose – *some* of you even think the act of sex, that funny, exquisite pastime, should be conducted behind closed doors. Others have even forgotten the wonder in a baby's chuckle.'

'But that's different.'

'Not much so.'

'Most are a matter of preference, or taste. Or judgement.'

'It amounts to the same.'

Stumped, Thom closed his mouth.

'You've lost the ability, y'see, to understand that the consciousness is the thing *between* atoms and molecules and particles, the unseen glue that holds everything together. It has its own patterns – billions, trillions and whatever comes next . . .' (another hint here that nothing the elf said was going beyond Thom's grasp, for his own subconscious was the go-between; nonetheless, it was so, so strange to hear this funny little guy sprouting such things) '. . . and it's consciousness, which is energy, that binds the patterns and forms shapes, *matter*, if you like. Some of your scientists are getting pretty close to the discovery though, so it won't be too long before you have the technical skill to divine it. And boy-oh-boy, are you humans in for some surprises.'

The elf on the table slapped his knee and chortled.

'Wait a minute,' Thom pretested. 'How come *I* can see you? There's nothing special about me.'

The little man eyed him for a moment or two. 'Isn't there, now?' he said at last. 'You've an awful lot to learn, but it can't be done all at once. Try and think back, Thom. Remember when you were a boy.'

Thom thought long and hard, but was still perplexed. 'Bethan – that was my mother – told me lots of stories about faeries and little people like yourself.'

'Not people, Thom. Elementals.'

'Whatever. But they were just that – stories, made-up fantasies to amuse a kid.'

'Don't be so sure.'

'Come on. All mothers tell their toddlers faery stories.'

'And where d'you think those stories come from?'

'Myth, invention. Sure, part are folklore passed down through the ages.'

The elf shook his head. 'Memories, Thom. Most are race memories. Handed down from one generation to the next, like your genes. The little humans, your infants, believe, and so sometimes we show ourselves to them.'

'Why would you do that?'

'Because we like them and they're safe, no danger to us. For the same reason, we often reveal ourselves to your ancients. You call them senile when they speak of us.'

'I don't see how we can be a risk to you.'

Another laugh, a short one. 'You're even a risk to yourselves. One day it all might change, perhaps when you lose your cynicism and regain the simple knowledge. But I think the scientists will discover us first – or at least, discover the possibility of our existence. We'll see.'

Thom was desperately trying to absorb everything he had been told so far. It was difficult.

'Okay,' he said eventually, still leaning forward on the table. 'So why me? Why me now?'

'Because your life is in jeopardy.'

In jeopardy. Beautifully quaint, but still within Thom's own vocabulary.

'The thing?' he shuddered at the thought. 'What was it you called it?'

'The succubus. It's a sexual creature used by someone who wishes another harm. If you had been female, an incubus might have come to you. It wanted to steal from you, Thom.'

'But when I woke it was—'

'Stealing your life-juices.'

Thom slumped back in the chair, shocked.

'Why? Who—?

'Haven't you realized the peril you're in?' The little man's eyes were almost closed, so intense was their gaze.

Thom could only return the stare, his jaw dropped, mouth open. His hands gripped the edge of the table, his knuckles white.

'I don't understand.' He repeated it: 'No, I don't understand.'

A night breeze circled the kitchen and Thom moved to close the front door. He bolted it, then gave the handle a tug to reassure himself. The door rattled in its frame.

He came back to the table and faced the elf once more. 'Will you please stay the one size?' Thom complained. 'I've got enough to deal with without you shape-shifting.'

'I told you, my size depends on you. You can make it what you like, although I don't necessarily have to comply.'

Was this another hint that this was all in his own mind? Thom wondered. No, it couldn't be. He was neither imagining, nor dreaming. And he was perfectly sane (as most madmen choose to believe of themselves).

'I'll soon settle,' the elf assured him and, as an afterthought, added: 'They call me Rigwit, by the way. Sometimes they call me Philibert, other times Xerxes. But Rigwit is the name I've become used to. All right with you?'

Thom nodded, although he was not particularly interested in names at that moment. 'You . . . you said I'm in danger. From who? Who would want to hurt me?'

'*She* would. You know – the one humans might call a *hellhagge, ogress, midnighthagge, wiccawoman* – there are many names for them.'

'Witch.'

'Your most popular choice.'

'You're talking about Nell Quick, aren't you?'

The elf – Rigwit? all right: Rigwit, it was – nodded his coffee-coloured head.

'She despises you,' he said.

'She hardly knows me,' Thom protested. 'Anyway, earlier today . . .' he had not realized it was now well past midnight '. . . she tried—' He stopped abruptly. How did you explain seduction to an . . . *to an elf, for Christ's sake*? Instead, he threw a question back at his pint-sized companion. 'What makes you think she's a witch?'

'We know when evil is afoot. And we *always* know who the dark ones are. Nell is no mystery to us.'

'But what's she got against me?' True, he had felt uneasy in her presence since the first time they'd met, but he had assumed it was because her intentions were so clear. He wasn't against being seduced, it was just that she was so blatant about it. And there *was* something distinctly weird about Nell Quick; she was certainly attractive, even ravishing, with her wild black hair and scarlet lips, but there was a look in those dark eyes that was, well . . . wicked.

'We don't yet know the answer to that, Thom,' replied the elf. 'But this night she wanted your fertility to help work her evil against you. That's why she summoned the succubus and sent it to you.'

Thom just shook his head in confusion. Then: 'Who do you mean by "we"?'

'We the *faerefolkis*. Your neighbours. The forest dwellers.'

'That's crazy. I spent my childhood here – I know the woods. I used to explore every . . .'

His words began to fade as memories struggled to find their way through the layered veils of maturity. There came only unfocused and mystifying glimpses.

'Hell!' he said with an anger borne out of frustration.

'You can almost see, can't you?' Rigwit said artfully. 'You can almost conjure the pictures in your head. But you were very young then, and the dreadful shock of losing your dear mother damaged you in more ways than one. Life for you changed abruptly and you shed your innocence very swiftly. Grief and circumstance robbed you of the hidden knowledge and time stole its memory.' Rigwit gave yet another deep sigh. 'Unfortunately, it has always been so, not just for you, but for others who have known the secrets. I suppose it has to be that way, for the scepticism and distrust that comes with senescence would surely weaken and destroy us.'

It had become impossible for Thom to embrace any more. Tiredness, despite the nectar, the wonderful juice he had drunk earlier, was overcoming both body and mind, pure exhaustion defeating all further curiosity. He yawned.

'Time for you to rest,' Rigwit said kindly.

'No, no,' Thom protested weakly, 'there's too much unexplained, so much more to know.'

He was afraid he might never see the elf again should he let him go now. It was frightening, but wonderful too. Awesomely wonderful. Yet he could not prevent his shoulders sagging, his head dropping.

'You'll sleep soon,' the elf told him.

Thom's eyelids drooped.

'Very soon,' the voice now inside his head soothed.

Thom's weight felt too heavy for his elbows.

'Soon . . .'

As Thom's eyes closed the quiet voice said: 'I am the keeper of this place, Thom. I've always been present, even when the cottage was empty. I am here . . . to help . . . you . . .'

Thom's forehead was only inches from the table's surface.

'. . . fight your foe . . .'

His hair brushed the closed book before him.

'. . . the wiccan . . .'

He rested his temple against soft, aged leather.

'. . . who wishes you dead . . .'

Darkness. Friendly darkness.

# Chapter : Nineteenth

## JENNET

AGAIN HE had no recollection of ascending the spiral staircase to the bedroom, nor did he recall undressing and climbing between the cool sheets of the four-poster. He blinked several times, partly against the brightness of the day streaming through the windows, partly to bat away the gluey tiredness that cohered his eyelids. As was becoming usual these days, it was an extraneous sound that awakened him, a light tinkling from downstairs that took a few moments for him to register the doorbell. Although he had not cleared or oiled the bell since his arrival, its tone had lightened, its *clunking* clumsiness gone as if by ... magic. There was a clear and musical ring to it now, a happy cadence to its summons. Thom pushed down the top sheet with his feet and rose from the bed. He paused before the small settle on which his jeans were neatly folded, his cleared mind suddenly opened to the events of last night, the beast in his bed, the struggle for his stolen semen – *the arrival of the glorious, incredible faeries!*

His hand reached out for the arm of the chair to steady himself, his bent body swaying for a few moments as his legs weakened beneath him. *My God, was it possible? Had it really happened?* Thom was amazed and frightened by the possibility – *no*, the actuality! It had happened, right here in Little Bracken. It had not been illusion or an hallucination caused by some kind of brain seizure. It was all true, all *real!* He gasped at the assertion.

The bell downstairs again, persistent rather than insistent, its jingle too joyful to be otherwise.

And the elf! He remembered the elf, Rugwig, Rutwig, Wigpig, whatever its name was. Rigwit, that was it! He remembered their conversation long into the night after the battle between the succubus and himself and the faery hordes, the warning that his life was in 'peril'. What was *that* supposed to mean?

The bell, and its summons, could not be ignored.

Pulling on the jeans (he couldn't remember having folded them so carefully), left leg catching awkwardly as he pushed it through the straight-cut leg, he then grabbed a white T-shirt from the sideboard's top drawer. As he did so, he caught sight of himself in the free-standing mirror on top of the sideboard and paused, surprised to discover that his face bore no marks from the frantic scuffle that had taken place during the night. He distinctly remembered the succubus slashing his cheek with its claws, but there were no scratches or wounds in evidence save for the two thin scars that were already there. With no time to question it further, he padded bare-footed towards the stairs. Descending, he poked his head through the T-shirt's V-neck and glanced through the window on his left even as he thrust his arms through the sleeves. Changeable weather: dull and drizzly yesterday, today not a cloud in the sky; another scorcher, he reckoned. He pulled the hem of the T-shirt down over his chest and stomach as he reached the landing door, which was ajar, leaving it rumpled around the waistband of the jeans.

Thom didn't recall having locked the front door the night before (just as he could not remember going to bed), and he stretched to draw back its bottom bolt. On the other side the bell had stopped ringing as if his visitor had heard his bare feet slapping the wood of the stairs; or had assumed there was nobody home and had decided to leave. Thom suddenly felt anxious.

He quickly turned the long key and – perhaps incautiously, given the drama of the night – swung the door wide. And almost took a step backwards in surprise . . .

---

It was the girl from the lake. The slim, golden-haired, delicately beautiful nymphet he had caught – he had *spied* on – by the lake three – no, he had lost one day sleeping, recovering – four days ago. Only now she was fully clothed. Sort of. And still exquisitely beautiful, breath-takingly so. She was alone, no cohorts of faeries around her, brushing her flesh, trilling their ethereal tunes . . .

'I'm called Jennet.'

Her voice was as light as her stature suggested it might be, its high tone almost musical, yet with a strange kind of faraway huskiness to it that was entrancing as it was spine-tingling. She stood on the doorstep smiling up at him, for she was certainly no more than five feet tall, possibly less. The smile was playful, for it was defined only by its corners, and dipped for a moment, presumably to mock his dumbfounded expression. This day she wore a light green dress, pastel in shade but with shadows of purple within its folds; it was so sheer as to be transparent in parts, its satiny fabric of the like he had never before seen. It might have been spun from spider's silk, so fine and delicate was its structure. Cut

to the thigh on either side, an off-centre front hung almost
to her bare ankles, giving the garment a ragged appearance;
but the effect was subtly graceful. Like sewn stars, tiny,
practically invisible beads in the hem either caught the sun's
rays or were lit from within, and two small elegant knots tied
the material over her pale shoulders as if the dress were
casually fashioned. The cleavage was cut low, reaching
almost to her navel, and purple-bedded folds hid the flesh
beneath, lending a false modesty, for the effect was more
tantalizing than nakedness itself. Her breasts pressed small
but proud against the material and her skin was pale – oh so
pale – and unblemished.

The sun, shining from behind, (so how could the beads
catch the light?) outlined her slender figure, the gap between
her legs teasingly defined.

'Coming out to play?' she said and gave a mischievous
giggle, the fingers of one hand covering her lips.

---

He had no idea how to respond. She remained with her hand
over her mouth, her fingers long and thin, delicately pointed
at their tips, and he remained rooted to the spot, his own
mouth half-open. The surprise was not just because she was
unexpected, although that obviously played its part; no, the
surprise was mainly because of her waif-like beauty – her
doe-like beauty even, for she seemed vibrant and skittish
like a fawn. Her golden hair hung in long ringlets, tumbling
strands of it almost touching her breasts, but smooth on top,
parted in the middle, curls rising at the sides, backlit by the
sun. Her dainty feet were bare, toes, like her fingertips,
softly pointed; and when she smiled again, her hand dropped
to her thigh, so that he saw that her small teeth were also
softly pointed, like the elf's, not in a threatening, carnivorous
way, but in an oddly sensual way.

He still did not know what to say and she inclined her head to regard him curiously, amusement never leaving those eyes and lips.

'Good morning, Thom,' she said, as if starting again. 'Are you well today?'

That distant huskiness in her voice, he realized, was seductive as well as entrancing. Delicate fingers seemed to run up his spine.

'I – I don't think I know you.' It was feeble, but all he could manage. Of course he *knew* her – he had watched her by the lake taking pleasure in her own body in a most innocent and uninhibited manner. And they were both aware of it.

A little pleasing laugh. She really did find him funny.

'I mean,' he stammered on, 'I think I've seen you . . .'

'I saw you, Thom.' She looked at him coquettishly.

'I . . . How do you know my name?'

'Rigwit told me, of course. He's my friend.'

The elf was her friend? Then it wasn't a case of who was she, but *what* was she?

As if reading his mind (there was no sense of invasion) she said, 'We're all part of the same big family, Thom. You do believe in faeries, don't you?'

'I'm not sure any more,' he replied. It was all too fantastic to accept right now, right here on his doorstep and in the warm light of morning. 'And if I did,' he added, 'they wouldn't be like you.'

'Too tall, am I?' She sounded delighted.

Slowly, he nodded his head.

'Don't you know about faery sizes?'

Slowly he shook his head.

'Well, they come in all shapes and forms and dimensions, but there are only three kinds of height. The tiny ones you've seen, the medium ones – you've met Rigwit – and my kind.'

'Your kind?'

'Almost human, Thom. In many other ways too, actually, and it's because of it that we have to be extra careful when we hide.'

'From . . . us?'

She nodded. Then: 'Thom, why don't we walk? I've lots to tell you.'

She reached her hand across the threshold. And Thom – tentatively yet irrevocably – took it.

Both barefoot, she led him away from the cottage, into the woods.

# PART TWO

*In which we meet the
Faerefolkis of the forest and Good
confronts Evil when the greatest
Demon of all is disturbed.*

# Chapter: Twentieth

## FAEREFOLKIS

THOM KNEW this part of the woods she had led him to, but he had never known it like this.

Colour, smell, the very nature of the woodland itself, was more alive than he remembered or could ever imagine. Flowers seemed to vibrate with their own power, while other plants bristled with some unknown and unseen force, and their perfume assailed his sense of smell with such power and definition that his head felt giddy with it. Each single blade of grass was vibrantly individual, in perfect tune with its neighbours, existing apart from them yet remaining part of the whole. Trees, although motionless, sent out waves of energy that were so palpable he thought he could stretch a finger towards them and feel the currents separate and flow over his arm like a breeze; and he knew his skin would absorb some of that energy and he would be invigorated by it.

Even the animals appeared to have lost their shyness, for the rabbit, the fox, the vole and the woodmouse, all gambolled and ran around him, with no enemy lines drawn between them. The badger too had been persuaded from daytime slumber to observe Jennet pass by its sett. And then, there were the deer.

My God, he had never realized the woods were home to so many deer. Families of roe deer sauntered past, the buck leading the hind and kids. He even glimpsed the much larger red deer, with its long, twisted antlers, through the trees some distance away. Thom was thrilled by it all – by the tawny owl on a tree branch, who benignly watched their progress, by the young fawn that ate berries from Jennet's hand, and by the song thrush and chaffinch, who alighted on Jennet's shoulders to chirp in her ears and tug at her hair. It seemed that none was afraid, neither of him and the girl, nor of other species in the near vicinity.

Birds were everywhere, swooping and singing, disturbing the flights of fluttering butterflies, teasing animals on the ground, then soaring off high into the sky, as if celebrating the day.

But all this was later, for their stroll had began quietly, with no indication of what was to come. The two of them had moved further into the forest, following a trail that was not at first apparent to the eyes, while Jennet talked in her gently husky, way, explaining to Thom all that he might understand of faery life. She had spoken of their many forms, of ethereal queens and mystical enchantresses – neither one of which was she, Jennet insisted. She told him of the tiny spirits who lived among the fauna, in the undergrowth, or under mushrooms, in the hollows of trees, especially the older oaks, in the meadows, on the hillsides; she told him of creatures sinister and magical, secretive and mischievous, of elves and nymphs, gnomes and sylphs, elementals and earth-dwellers, all of whom existed in the mystic half-world just beyond human perception.

Some enlightened but, unfortunately, still misguided humans thought that the *faerefolkis*' habitat was somewhere between the paradise of Eden and the depths of Hell, between Light and Darkness, and this was wrong, for there was no such place. Rather, faeries dwelt within the spirit of Nature itself, a place imperceptible to mortal man, but nevertheless, very real (although she emphasized that *reality* was, itself, a false concept). Only a chosen few among humans – those with special ties, or a certain sensitivity – were allowed glimpses of the faery world. More often than not, most of those ties eventually were broken, or deliberately forgotten.

Of course, humans have always been aware of the existence of faeries – their mention in scholarly and religious works, in fiction or folklore, in Arthurian legends and fantasy tales, in poetry and soliloquy, philosophical treatise and contention, in alchemical explorations and in Jungian dreams, all bears witness to this fact. And even though no physical proof has ever been found, or at least, disclosed, the intuition that the *faerefolkis* exist lies deep within the human psyche.

'But you must beware of us,' Jennet had continued. And, when he asked why that was so, she replied, 'Because some of us are playful and some of us are wicked. The worst of us mean you harm.'

Again, Thom asked: 'Why?'

The answer was as simple as the question.

'For fun,' she said.

Further they journeyed into the woods and Thom soon realized he had lost his bearings. He had thought he was familiar with every inch of his woodland home, but now he found himself practically a stranger. Perhaps he had considered this part of the forest too dense to explore when he was younger; yet Jennet was leading him along an almost imperceptible path that was nearly as straight as it was true. A heavy clump of shrubbery ahead seemed to have an invisible path through it, the leaves easily parted, the roots set wide on either side; a fallen tree with a barrier of branches was easily cleared in three short steps; what appeared to be thick bracken was casually pushed aside with each footstep forward. Sometimes he had to follow close behind the lithe girl, but mostly they walked alongside each other.

'Sprites and goblins are the worst,' she advised him as they went. 'Try to avoid them, they'll only cause you trouble. Not all of them, mind.'

'How will I know the difference?'

'By their smiles.'

'Oh.'

'Brownies or elves are always helpful and usually good-natured. Rigwit is really a brownie, but he doesn't mind being called an elf.'

'You've spoken to him about me?'

She nodded, but continued as if it wasn't important. 'Brownies like looking after homes for people, especially when the owners are away a lot. They like you humans. But look out for the elves called cacodemon, afrite, deev, bogle, dwerger, pigwidgeon and flibbertygibbet – they can be very nasty. And also bogeys, boggarts, buccus, bugaboas, clob-bies and kelpies are bad spirits especially to be avoided. Fortunately, you'll rarely meet them, because they've been banished by our queens.'

'You've got more than one queen?' A few days ago, Thom would have felt foolish asking the question, but events had changed everything.

'Oh yes, lots. In these woods, it's Aeval, who used to be queen of Munster – that's in the country you call Ireland – but she left because of the Disharmonies and came here. Faeries just hate wars and famines because disbelief and lack of faith always abide with them.'

'And d'you have a king?'

Her expression became sad. 'Not any more. He and Aeval had their own disharmonies and, because her power is stronger, he was deposed. No one knows where he went.

It all happened over a hundred years ago, long before my time.'

'Really? So, how old are you, Jennet?'

'Our years aren't the same as yours. To be truthful, we don't even have them. Time isn't the same for us.'

'But you just said your king went away over a hundred years ago.'

'Yes, in *your* time, not in ours. I'm trying to make things easy for you to understand, Thom. A lot of what I'm saying would make no sense at all if I didn't interpret it for you.'

'Ah, so this is meant to make sense to me'

'Your own insights are helping. And our minds are working together so that you can sense my meaning, because my language is not entirely like yours.'

'I seemed to tune in after a while to the elf, this Rigwit.'

'You learned quite fast, actually. Mostly, you were remembering.'

'What?'

'You played with the faeries all the time when you were a child. Bethan allowed you to.'

He stopped dead among a group of tall ferns. 'My mother knew about the ... the ...' he could not help but stammer '... the faeries? She let me play with them?'

Slightly ahead, she turned to face him.

'Oh Thom, I didn't realize. It hasn't occurred to you yet, has it? Bethan was only part-human. She came from us and her lover caused her to change. It was of her choosing, but she really couldn't help herself. She was so much in love with your father.'

He almost sank into the ferns. 'That's impossible. I would have known, I would have remembered.'

'You did know, she kept few secrets from you. And you were too young even to question it, it was all perfectly natural to you. Before Bethan died, she made sure that all memory of that part of your life was erased.'

'Then she knew – ?'

'Your mother was on limited time once her lover, your father, was gone.'

He shook his head vigorously. 'No, that's impossible. It just couldn't be.'

Jennet reached out a hand once more. 'Come on, let's keep walking. There's so much more to explain than I thought.'

He moved forward, but this time he did not take the offered hand.

She walked alongside him. 'You never knew your father, did you, Thom?'

'You're not going to tell me that *you* did.' His tone was curt, his mood changed.

She laughed, that same tinkling sound that had charmed him before. It almost did again.

'I'm not *that* old, Thom, especially not in your years. Rigwit told me everything.'

'Then he was around even before my mother died.'

'He was there at your birth. Rigwit is a Venerable, he's always been here. He knew both your mother and your father.'

'Why didn't he tell me?'

'There was only so much you could absorb last night. You were confused enough.'

You got that right, he thought, but did not say.

'Thom, your father was a human. He and Bethan fell in love and were meant to be together. Their love was strong enough for it to be so.'

'Of course he was human. I'm human. My mother was human.'

Jennet was patient with her response. 'No, Bethan *became* part-human. *That's* how strong was the love between them. But our kind can only exist on your level when love is there to sustain them.'

'But I loved her. Wasn't that enough?'

'No. It isn't the same kind of love that a man and woman

can have for each other. That goes beyond blood binding, for sexual attraction plays its part to begin with. You humans *still* have no idea of how powerful the sexual magic is, how awesome is the alchemy involved, the force it gives to body and mind. Unfortunately, when your father passed on to *his* next dimension, Bethan was unable to return to her natural state. No faery who has given birth to a human can. And yet, she could not continue as one of you without her man's love. She had no choice but to leave you, Thom.'

His throat suddenly felt full, his eyes watery. 'My father ... who was he?'

'Don't you know? Isn't it obvious to you?'

He shook his head, sadly this time. 'Why would I ask?'

She was silent, but only for a moment or two. 'Perhaps I'll show you later, Thom. It would be the kindest way.'

---

Onwards they went and Thom suppressed the question of his parentage by embracing the wonders she revealed to him.

Jennet told him why faeries were invisible to most people, explaining that the human eye lacks the ability to see the more subtle shades that existed before and after the perceived colour spectrum, as well as those in between, that if Man could only 'tune in' to the infinite vibrations discharged by such 'neverworld' beings who themselves were composed of ethereal structures, then he might just begin to learn and eventually accept. Faeries could easily present themselves by changing their resonance and bringing their tones within the human-accepted spectrum, but rarely chose so to do; on the other hand, certain 'enlightened' humans could raise their own game and meet the faeries half-way. Although he was not conscious of it, this was precisely what Thom had achieved. Sometimes it happened by chance or freakish accident, other times the phenomenon was faery-inspired.

'You know those things you call Yufoses?' she said. 'The non-organic flying creatures?'

'You mean UFOs?' he replied.

'Yes, Yufoses.'

'Flying machines. Spaceships.'

'What ships?'

'Spaceships. From another planet in another galaxy.'

'Oh, I see. The things that cross the space between homes in the sky. But they don't have sails or oars.'

'It's just an expression, just a convenient name for them.'

'Spaceships. That's nice.' She thought about it, smiling delightedly.

'What of them? You're not going to tell me *they're* real too, are you? You know, most of us think they're a joke concocted by over-imaginative idiots or attention-seekers. Or nutters.'

'Nutters?'

'It doesn't matter. What were you going to say?'

'You don't believe in Yufoses . . . Yufose?'

'Why should I? I've never seen one.'

'You could now. Now that you're learning to perceive rather than just see.'

'Are you saying they work on the same principle?'

'Why do you think they appear, then vanish so quickly?'

'Well, we're told by the fools or hoaxers who claim to have seen UFOs that they fly off at fantastic speeds.'

'No. They appear to get smaller at fantastic speed. The Yufoses . . . Yufose . . . alter their vibrational pattern and disappear beyond your spectrum when they realize they're being observed.'

'But sometimes they're supposed to hang around for hours.'

'They're not so smart.'

He was dumbstruck. Then: 'Have faeries made contact with them?'

'Goodness no. Why should we?'

Thom shrugged. 'No reason. Hey, I suppose you're going to tell me they really are responsible for crop circles.'

She started to laugh, both hands held to her mouth as if to stop herself.

'What's so funny?' He was smiling and frowning at the same time.

'Crops circles are one of our games.'

'*Faeries* make them?'

She nodded vigorously through the laughter. 'Not to begin with. The Yufose caused the first magnetic patterns by mistake. The machinery of the ... spaceships?' She looked questioningly, waiting for his nod. 'The machinery of the spaceships attracted the magnetic lines and motifs that lie beneath the earth, bringing them to the surface so that the corn collapsed. That might have been deliberate, just to let you know they were around in the same way we faeries steal from you or play tricks just to tease you and hint of our presence. Like us, they think the human race is too dangerous for them to introduce themselves properly.'

She was still grinning as she went on and her eyes seemed to flash and sparkle with inner energies.

'But then, just for fun, the pixies – of all of us, they're the ones who make the most mischief – decided to make their own designs in the corn. Some were quite good to begin with, then they became too complicated even for us to understand. After that ...' she looked heavenward in mock despair '. . . after that, you humans started making your own patterns, which were even more mystifying than our own and beyond all logic. We never thought humans could be so funny.'

Thom was not as amused as his petite companion. They went on, Jennet sometimes skipping lightly ahead, wheeling round to face him with a remark or a new piece of information.

*What the hell is going on?* he wondered. *Am I going crazy? Do I really believe in faeries, me, a grown man, a pragmatist*

JAMES HERBERT

*in most things?* Motherless since the age of ten, fatherless even before his birth, Thom generally had had to deal with life and everything it brought with it alone. Sure, he'd had a generous patron – generous in financial terms, that is – but he'd had to cope with the traumas and stresses of growing up very much on his own. Realism had been forced upon him and coping had quickly become second nature. Perhaps it was that very aloneness and the necessity of getting on with life that had stifled fanciful notions and absurd memories; perhaps over the years they had been beaten into submission.

But still it was not cynicism that was now prompting him to doubt all that he had seen, heard, and learned over the past few days, for Thom was no cynic. Rather it was the sober voice of reason that was forcing him to think rationally.

Nevertheless, faint stirrings in his memory bank could not be denied, the sudden snap-visions of playing and talking with tiny folk in the woods, little people who resembled human beings, but who were different in so many ways, could not easily be dismissed. Yet they were just that, snapshots that had scant substance, for they were not complete, had no beginnings or end. Still he remembered the tales his mother had told him, stories of small people who loved to play and dance, who could be very naughty, but who often liked to help the 'big' people in their times of trouble. *Faery*tales of bewitchment and wonder, kindness and cruelty, magic and mischief, sadness and joy. He recalled them as fantasies; now he was not so sure, now he wondered if they were true accounts of another life that Bethan had known intimately, one which she had wished to share with her young son. *No*, he resisted. *Surely not, it just wasn't possible.* And yet . . .

As he and Jennet trekked further into the woods and he listened to her light sing-song voice with its peculiarly distant huskiness, Thom realized he was beginning to see and sense more clearly than ever before: the colours of the forest, its perfumes, the piquancy of its exhalation – yes, the forest *breathed* – and even the vibrations of its biomass, the trees, the flora, the vegetation, every goddamn single blade of grass and leaf, he could see and sense it all, and he could hear it *sing* its own vitality. It was almost overwhelming.

And there was still more to come.

---

Jennet, who was ahead once more, unaware that the assault on Thom's senses had slowed his progress, waited for him inside a small clearing.

'Are you all right, Thom?' she called back anxiously when she saw him frown.

'Uh, yeah. I think so. I seem to be getting a bit light-headed though.'

Her smile returned. 'Come on, catch up. Let's see what we can do about it.'

Again her outstretched hand invited him to her and this time, when he took it, she pulled him forward. A familiar charge of electricity ran up his arm and through his body at her touch and he shivered, not with shock, but with delight. She surprised him by raising her other hand to his face, palm flat and facing upwards, long slender fingers pointed at his stubbled chin. Before he could protest, she had pursed her lips and softly blown across her open palm.

If it had not sparkled as it billowed, the powdery dust that filled the air between them would have been invisible. Where it had come from he had no idea, but it filled his nostrils and open mouth instantly. He felt the minuscule particles being absorbed by his skin, a brief tingling sensation that was not unpleasant; the powder(?) carried no smell and its irritation – a tickling really – was minimal. But its effect was astonishing.

Like some fast-working, high-powered and highly illegal drug, it sharpened his senses – all five, plus one other – to a

223

degree that might have been frightening had it not also had a warming, calming effect. It was then that the world around him became almost surreal in its explicit reality.

He began to see things as they truly *were*, without the mind's own inbuilt proclivity towards conformity and order; he saw the world around him as it was meant to be (and perhaps, once was) seen had not the human brain become cluttered with assumptions and prejudices, development its enemy rather than ally, progression a blinding foe. Thom became aware of the wildlife not only in his vicinity, but well beyond his range of vision also; he could sense, hear and smell the woodland animals' presence even though they were far out of sight. And he watched the wildlife that was before him in the same way, seeing and *perceiving*, sensing and *feeling*, as if he were part of them, they were part of him. He saw the fox ignore the rabbit, the fawn dance with the hare, the mole's game of hide-and-seek with the wood-mouse, the moth encourage the late caterpillar, and he knew that as his view of these creatures had changed so, too, had their view of him. He was no longer a threat, he was of their kingdom, an accepted member of their habitat.

As Jennet quietly drew him on still further, he began to see the *faerefolkis* again, only this time they were even more lucid; they were also less inhibited, as though they, too, accepted him in their world.

Tiny coruscations of light emerged as winged faeries. They played together and with the sudden abundance of butterflies, several mounted on their insect counterparts, riding them as if they were flying horses, while still more trailed behind using silken threads as reins.

He almost tripped over a green imp who squatted on the poorly defined path, like a thin frog with 'human' limbs and features; stalks of grass grew from its back and otherwise bald dome of a head as part of its very nature. It watched balefully and made no effort to shift as Thom cautiously stepped around it.

Two muddy-green and brown pixies sat conversing on a fallen tree trunk, each of them about ten inches high and resembling wizened old men; wrinkles ravaged their thin faces and long pointed ears, and their slitted eyes were totally black. Tall brown hats of aged leather bobbed as they nodded their heads together in agreement and they hardly acknowledged Thom and Jennet as they passed by.

'Krad and Detnuah,' Jennet whispered leaning into Thom. 'They're *always* philosophizing about something or other without ever coming up with a conclusion. They get cross if they're disturbed, so tread carefully and say nothing.'

Bright silvery-blue faeries and imps played leap-frog together, jumping over a cluster of mushrooms, the former's fluttering wings making them master of the game. Their flutey high-whistling sound quickly became laughter and happy cries to Thom's ears.

As they approached an ancient oak that must have been growing in this part of the woods for the last three hundred years, Thom thought he noticed movement in its bark, but when he drew close he realized hundreds of tiny brown creatures were squirming and writhing on its surface in some mad slithering dance, their limbs intertwined, naked little bodies wriggling through gaps, tiny ugly faces grimacing as if each suffered their own private torment. Soft moans and wails came from them and he looked at Jennet in dismay.

She, herself, avoided looking at the oak and its moving cloak of misery and hurried on, urging Thom to follow quickly.

Her lovely face wrinkled in disdain. 'We call that the Punishment Tree. It's for all those elves and pixies who do harm that can never again be set right. It's their shame and despair that makes them wriggle so and each miscreant is there for a hundred years until they die and drop off like rotting bark. By doing that they make room for the next offender – the waiting list is enormous. If a human comes by, they freeze and become the oak itself, their torture interrupted until the unaware traveller passes by.'

Thom shuddered inwardly and they swiftly moved on. The sudden downturn in his mood lifted when he spotted a little fellow puffing away on a cornpipe while sitting almost invisible among the ferns. He was stroking his long brown beard, muttering happily to himself and taking no notice of Thom and Jennet until they were nearly upon him. Even then, he merely grinned and waved a hand in greeting, continuing to puff away at the pipe and talk to himself at the same time.

'Good-day, Ekulf,' Jennet bid him cheerily, and it was only then that Thom saw many, many other faces among the lush shrubbery, all eyes directed at the pipe-smoking speaker in their midst. Up close, Thom could make out faces and shoulders, and here and there almost complete bodies; all of the listeners, who seemed enraptured by the tale being told – Ekulf had not been muttering to himself at all – were green in colour and wore green and blue clothing, which was why Thom had not noticed them right away.

'Sometimes he's called Trebreh,' Jennet was saying quietly as they continued to walk, 'and sometimes Semaj, depending on what story he's telling. He claims to know all the old ones, the sad ones, the happy ones, and all the ancient riddles and songs, but sometimes I'm sure he makes them up as he goes along.'

Everywhere Thom looked there was some kind of activity, although more than once he had to concentrate hard to discern what was going on even with his heightened perception. Faeries, sheer wings sometimes twice as large as their own bodies, flitted among the trees and undergrowth, but particularly around the brightest of the flowers or coloured toadstools, chasing each other, calling out or singing, floating by hand-in-hand, in groups of three, eight, or a dozen, enjoying themselves on the perfect summer's day. Others copulated unashamedly together, their tiny bodies full of vigour and glowing radiantly, lights flaring outwards from their wingtips in fantastic fireworks displays as they achieved orgasm, all giving out their tiny ecstatic shrieks full of verve and melody. And although Thom's face reddened and his jaw dropped in momentary shock, he realized that, as orgies go, this was as innocent and joyous as could be.

Ruefully, he turned to Jennet, who gave him a beaming smile.

'Isn't it wonderful?' she said.

He could only nod his head in exaggerated fashion.

Further on, a bald-headed gnome sat in the middle of a stagnant shallow pond, his doleful eyes watching their approach, just his head and shoulders visible above the slimy surface, a single dewdrop hanging from his long, sharp nose; as Thom passed by an ivy-bound tree, a green face smiled out at him, only a slight movement and widening mouth revealing its presence; a creature with an extended snout for a nose and high-peaked ears, its head, neck and back bristling with quills so that it resembled a hedgehog, scurried across their path; more blue-coloured faeries, bodies sleek in their nakedness, played among a carpet of bluebells, while others, pink, silver, and purple, sat watching contentedly on plants and leaves, jabbering in their high-pitched but beautiful voices, many of them greeting Jennet with excited waves of their hands or fluttering of gossamer wings; there were even more in a vast golden glade they reached, both brilliant and pastel colours everywhere, some faeries wearing rich vibrant crimsons and mauves, others attired in graceful and transparent shifts, pixies and elves dressed in leather or cloth jerkins, while imps went about entirely clothesless, with inconsequential – and pointed, Thom noticed – genitals exposed to the air, no body hair on them at all save for long, unkempt tresses hanging from head to shoulders.

Jennet called out to all and sundry, reeling out their

names to Thom as she indicated each one – Srehto, Cigam, Hanoj, Obidiah, Titus, Rial, Ulick, Toby, Star, Enirhs, Noom, Philibert, Niamod, Rufus, the list seemed endless and most of the like he had never heard before – Osric, Erhclupes, Rovivrus, Troth, on and on it went, until he could only shake his head in defeat.

'Just don't ask me to repeat them all,' he said, holding up his hands.

Laughing, she pointed out the various types of *faerefolkis*, the goblin, the pixie, the elf, the bogle, the sylph, the elemental, redcap and boggart, until once again he protested, his head reeling from the scene itself let alone the names and variety. But he laughed himself as he watched these glorious (mostly) creatures enjoy themselves in the sun, the picture before him rich and dazzling with activity and vivid spectacle.

'Their forms depend mainly on you, Thom,' Jennet told him, in a way reaffirming what Rigwit had said the night before. 'Your own eyes and mind interpret their energies to whatever is acceptable to you.'

'But some aren't acceptable. Some are just plain horrible.'

'Those are cloaked in the nature of what they are and your thoughts are telling you so. You're also influenced a little by human depictions you may have seen in the past. Fortunately not too many of the nasty ones lurk in the sunlight – the night is their friend, the blacker the better. Some of them adopt their own version of the human shape, but because they're weak and nasty, they become ugly, distorted, parodies of earthly creatures.'

Thom shivered as he caught sight of a being that was hiding from them among the shadows of the surrounding trees; it was either too stupid to conceal itself properly, or it wished to frighten them with glimpses of its demeanour. Its body was a murky grey, its back hunched alarmingly, and its arms – and legs, Thom could only assume, because he could not see them – were as thin as matchsticks. It glared at them with evil yellow eyes and its muzzle of a nose quivered as it grunted and snuffled quietly.

'Gladback is one who shouldn't really visit the daytime,' said Jennet, glaring back at the creature, who seemed visibly to shrink. 'That's why he's keeping to the shade. He's a wicked fellow who likes to torment babies when the parents are sleeping. *Now shoo, Gladback! Go back to your pit until the sun's gone!*'

The ghastly dark brute was gone in a trice as though in fear of Jennet and her scolding.

'Its kind are usually cowards,' she said, lips set grim for a moment. 'And listen, Thom: don't ever believe those who say faeries can only be seen by humans through a good heart, because that's nonsense; as I told you before, you see us through your eyes and your mind – all your heart does is pump blood through your body.'

He grinned at the casual demolishment of romanticism. So much for poets and certain storytellers . . .

He and Jennet strolled hand in hand, like young lovers, deeper and deeper into the woods and, had it not been for the position of the sun high in the clearest of blue skies, Thom feared he would be completely lost. The woodland covered a vast area of the Bleeth estate, but he had thought he knew most of it; again he realized there were places here he had never visited. Yet occasionally as they wandered, he had a transient sense of *déjà vu*, as though once before, a long time ago, he had come upon these same places and some of these same sights.

By now he was beginning to recognize the disparate castes among the *faerefolkis*, a difference between elf and imp, sylph and elemental, boggart and bogle, and even more easily, those who were kind and those who were unkind; all were fascinating, all were incredible.

Two elves, both of whom resembled Rigwit, except that one had a flowing white beard that reached his plump stomach, while the other had merely a long white drooping moustache, sat round a sawn-off tree stump (sawn-off by whom? he wondered), using the rings and ray lines of its flat surface as some kind of circular chessboard, painted half-acorn shells as chequers. They frowned with concentration and, when one made a move, the other clapped heartily at the ingenuity of the play.

'Gof and Raeps,' Jennet said softly in Thom's ear. 'Always playing the same game.'

'Who usually wins?' he whispered back.

'No one yet.'

'What?'

She put a straight finger against her pursed lips, his exclamation a little too loud.

'They've only been playing for three years. No one's won yet,' she said. 'We're very privileged to see Gof make a move.'

Thom craned his neck to watch the two absorbed elves as he and Jennet tiptoed past, then turned back with a bemused expression.

'The previous game lasted twenty years,' his companion informed him gravely.

─────

They journeyed on, faery and human, strangely (for Thom) in communion with each other, glorying in the wood's very nature, the sun and then the shade on their faces, the constant activity around them and the hustle of animals, the man awestruck but gradually sinking into an acceptance of everything and the beautiful, neverworld nymphet delighting in her role as teacher. They trod lightly, unwilling to disturb anything they might come upon along the way, and although Jennet talked and Thom listened with occasional questions, they began to know one another just as surely as if it was of themselves that they spoke.

But among many other things, one thing in particular puzzled Thom.

'Why haven't I seen anyone else like you, Jennet?' he asked at last. 'I mean, your size, others that look like you. You could almost be taken for a human.'

She gave him a glance and, of course, a smile. 'You will, Thom,' she assured him. 'In good time, you will.'

# Chapter: Twenty-First

# PRELUDE TO SEDUCTION

NELL SAW that Little Bracken's front door was open wide even as she struggled to keep the black bicycle steady on the rough, rutted track that twisted through the woods from the main road. The bike's handlebars wobbled, its wicker carrier-basket heavy with plants from her own greenhouse, these dug from the soil so that they were complete with dusty bulb and stem. Nell tightened her grip to control the two-wheeler's direction, cursing under her breath at the struggle. The Raleigh's rear wheel had been reinflated (the tyre never had been punctured) but it wasn't the easiest of machines to handle unless the speed was up and the road was smooth. She squinted her dark eyes, the curls of her hair lifting in the breeze created by her pedalling.

Nothing unusual about the doors of country houses being left open, particularly on fine days such as this. Thom Kindred would be making the most of any cooling air drifting through. And if he had stepped out for a while –

his Jeep was parked, so he hadn't driven off anywhere – well, she could wait; she had all the time in the world this morning and she intended to make the most of it. Besides, how far could he go with that feeble leg of his? Okay, he had looked a lot better than she had expected when he had first arrived, but he was still debilitated. And soon he would be looking a lot worse. Oh yes, soon he would look very bad indeed.

Nell grinned as she steered the bicycle into the open area before the cottage, briskly stepping off while it was still in motion and bringing it to a short squealing halt alongside the Jeep. She pushed the bike along the broken flagstone path and leaned it against the cottage wall, just beneath the old bell that now looked polished and serviceable. The hem of the maroon cotton skirt she wore swung loose just below her knees and sandal-thongs wrapped themselves around her bare calves; her blouse was white, its short sleeves pushed gypsy-like down over her shoulders.

Lifting the flowers from the basket, crumbly, dried soil falling from the bulbs, and reaching for the small red purse that had lain beneath them, she called out: 'Thom? Are you there, Thom?'

No sound came from within the cottage.

Nell strolled through the open doorway regardless, calling again in case he was upstairs. 'Thom? It's Nell. I've come a-visitin'!' The last sentence was deliberately yokelized. She enjoyed the countrified image she portrayed with the flowers and off-the-shoulder blouse.

'Thom!' Louder this time and with some irritation.

'Shit,' she said quietly, glaring around the kitchen.

No evidence of breakfast having been eaten, no dirty plates on the table or in the sink. Either he had cleaned up after himself, or he had gone for a stroll before eating.

Dumping the freshly dug flowers on the table with the purse, Nell walked over and put her hand against the plastic kettle. Not even warmish. Good. He'd gone for a walk before breakfast, which meant he shouldn't be too long. Which was fine. She'd wait.

———— ✦ ————

She did not have to wait long. Nell was in the bedroom upstairs, mooching through the drawers and tall cupboard, not looking for anything in particular, just anything personal to Thom that might help her with her spells. His semen would have been best – how personal could you get? – but she'd been thwarted at the first attempt. She should be more fortunate today, for if all went as planned, she would carry home his seed inside her own body, the residue there to be collected within the privacy of her own bathroom. Even better, she would find an excuse – easy after lovemaking – to use his bathroom right here in the cottage. No need to plug herself until she got back, and she had a small plastic phial inside her purse.

Nell quickly closed the drawer she had been rummaging through when she heard the vehicle approaching and hastily ran to the stairs. Hurrying down, she heard the car's horn *beep* once and she glanced out the stairwell window as she passed. She caught a brief glimpse of a horribly green-coloured car drawing up in front of Thom Kindred's Jeep.

Nell carried on down the stairs and got to the open front door just as a woman with dark blonde hair tied at the back in a short ponytail stepped from the green Volkswagen. She was heavy-breasted, her yellow T-shirt tucked into grey tracksuit bottoms, white trainers on her feet, and she reached into the car's back seat for a large canvas bag, which she hauled out. Turning towards the cottage, she noticed Nell on the doorstep and stopped in her tracks.

'Oh, hi,' she said, smiling pleasantly and raising a hand in greeting. Behind the round thin-framed spectacles she wore, her brown eyes – as light and tawny-flecked as her hair, Nell noticed – were friendly. 'I'm Mr Kindred's physio-therapist, Katy Budd. He should be expecting me.'

Nell returned the smile, although hers was more viva-cious. She used it to hide her irritation, for she had planned on being alone with Thom.

Nice-looking, she mused, as Katy made her way up the broken path. Nothing compared to Nell, herself, but few were *her* equal. Just a little thickset, but still a good figure. Wearing nothing beneath the T-shirt either. Was that for Thom's benefit?

'I'm afraid Thom isn't here right now,' she said pleasantly as the girl drew near. Nell put her in her late twenties, a good, fit, vibrant woman. Very attractive, even with those plain glasses. Pert little nose, jawline a shade too heavy. A strong one, this. And no doubt, with strong urges.

Katy Budd looked disappointed. 'But Thom – I'm sorry, Mr Kindred – knew I'd be here at this time. We arranged it the other day.'

'P'haps he forgot,' Nell replied, leaning against the door-frame and placing a hand on her jutting hip. She was still smiling. 'Shouldn't think he'd be long though, not if he knew you were comin'.'

'I hope not. He really does need his exercises.'

'I'm sure he does. I'm Nell, by the way. I often look in on Thom just to see how he's gettin' on. Sometimes I bring him groceries, sometimes somethin' else . . .' Her voice trailed away.

'Do you know where he's got to?' Katy glanced down at her wristwatch, noting that she, herself, had arrived just a little late and that now it was more than ten minutes after the appointed time.

'Why don't you bring yourself inside and wait? His car is still here, so he's prob'ly only gone for a short walk.'

Without hesitation, Katy moved towards the doorway and Nell stepped aside, allowing her to pass. Nell closed the front door behind them, barely taking her eyes off the therapist as Katy wandered across the room to stop at the kitchen table.

'What lovely flowers,' the therapist said as she placed the sports bag on the floor and fingered the bright, speckled petals. 'Orchids, aren't they?' She glanced back at Nell, who nodded.

'Early Purple, they're called,' said Nell. '*Orchis mascula.* Common Male Orchid. I grow them myself.'

As Katy studied the orchids, noticing that the ten-inch stalks were still attached to their fleshy tubers, she failed to see the sudden gleam in Nell's dark eyes. The therapist wrinkled her nose.

'Can't say I like the smell too much, though,' she said. She turned towards the other woman. 'Have you known Thom long?' she asked, as if merely making polite conversation.

Nell, who had an instinct for such things, immediately knew it was not a casual question. *The bitch has taken a fancy to him*, she thought. *And why not? Thom is a good-looking man, quite a catch for any woman who doesn't mind an invalid for a lover.* Nell was surprisingly annoyed at the idea.

'No, not long,' she replied evenly, moving in closer to the therapist. 'I'm a trained nurse and Thom's friend, Hugo Bleeth, pays me to keep an eye on him.'

'Hugo Bleeth. Isn't he the owner of the big mansion, what's it called – Bracken?'

'Castle Bracken. No, his father, Sir Russell, owns the place and all the land around it.'

'How wonderful. I haven't seen much of the estate, but what I have seen looks brilliant. Are the house and grounds open to the public?'

'What makes you ask that?' Nell's response was unexpectedly sharp.

Taken aback, Katy replied: 'No reason. It's just that so many country houses and their estates are open to the public nowadays. The money from tourists helps keep these places viable.'

Nell caught herself and smiled back sweetly. *So, a nosy bitch too. Has a thing for Thom Kindred and wants to know other people's business as well. Attractive, though. In fact, the more you look, the more attractive she becomes. Thom might easily go for someone like this, 'specially when she is helpin' him get his health back. Nurse and patient kind of thing, and I know all about that.* Nell felt a mixture of emotions – it was she, Nell, who wanted Thom Kindred's undivided attention today, especially as she had already begun her plan (her gaze went to the flowers lying on the kitchen table). And there was something else, another emotion to vie with the others. It was attraction. Attraction for this girl.

The grey tracksuit trousers may have been a little baggy, but they did not disguise the impressive length of the legs inside them. And the tight T-shirt showed off the unharnessed breasts wonderfully. Why, the coolness of the kitchen had even encouraged the nipples beneath the yellow cotton to present themselves. Unless, of course, this Katy was also attracted to Nell . . .

'I was jus' goin' to prepare the flowers as a surprise for Thom when you arrived. Thought they might brighten up the place. Would you like to help me?'

Nell's voice was low, almost smoky in its huskiness.

Katy felt ill at ease. There was something weird about this woman and she was like no other nurse she had ever met. Darkly attractive, with the kind of overtly sexy looks many men went for. For a moment she wondered about Thom Kindred and this woman. Was there something going on between them? Was it more than just nurse and patient? Thom was single, his health was swiftly returning, he lived alone in this cottage, so who could blame him if such a voluptuous female with stunningly dusky eyes and a ravishing smile turned him on? Her figure was good – no, her figure was *great* – and her breasts were plainly ample beneath the low-cut blouse, the middle line of cleavage ... Katy checked herself, not fully understanding the disquiet she was feeling, the tension that was developing between herself and this woman.

For the sake of distraction, Katy said: 'Yes, fine. What would you like me to do?'

Irrationally, the question hung in the air between them for a couple of beats.

'Help me strip the tubers from the stalks first. I can use the paste from the tubers as a remedy for all sorts of things.'

Oh, Katy thought, so she's also some kind of herbalist as well as a nurse. Well, alternative medicines were the thing nowadays and there was no reason they couldn't work alongside the more conventional kind.

'Sure,' she said, going towards the table again (she realized that she had unconsciously moved a few steps away from the other woman as they talked). She picked up several orchids by their stems, noticing the dust that fell from them as she did so. 'What shall I do with them?'

'Take them over to the sink,' Nell instructed, 'and find a good sharp knife from the drawer. Cut the tubers from the stalks, then slice them. I'll find a pot to mash the remains in.'

Katy did as she was told, separating four orchids from the bunch and taking them over to the draining board beside the sink. She laid them down, disliking their smell intensely, and rummaged in one of the drawers for a sharp knife. While Nell looked through overhead cupboards for a suitable receptacle, Katy sliced into the first tuber, severing it from its stalk with one easy cut.

'Here,' Nell said as she placed an earthenware bowl in the sink. 'This'll do as a mortar. A big soup spoon can be a pestle. I should've brought a mortar and pestle with me, but I came out in a rush.' In fact, Nell had had no intention of bringing such implements, for the more fingers that came in touch with the tubers – those fingers originally were meant to be Thom's, but what the hell? This might be even more fun. It had been a long time, after all – and the mushy substance that came from them, the more effective the result. Nell moistened her lips with her tongue as she handed the small bowl to Katy, who had opened the same drawer again and brought out a heavy ladling spoon.

'Will this do?' asked Katy, holding the spoon aloft.

'Ideal,' replied Nell with a nod of her head. Her eyes held Katy's for a second.

What is *with* her? Katy wondered. Those glances of hers, glances that took in Katy's breasts and hips – what was *her* agenda?

'Slice them,' the dark-haired, dark-eyed woman told her.

'Sorry?'

'The tubers. Slice and dice. I'll get the other orchids.'

Katy mentally shrugged. Nell could have done this herself. She, Katy, was a physiotherapist, not a horticulturalist. And anyway, it seemed a shame to spoil such beautiful flowers, with their creamy petals and purplish spotted centres. Their scent wasn't too endearing, but the orchids themselves would make a wonderful centrepiece for the table. Urgh! The tubers had mushy insides. Her fingers were becoming sticky with it. Weren't these out of season? Katy thought she had read somewhere that they bloomed in spring and early summer, but these appeared to be at their best. Maybe Nell had her own greenhouse and green fingers to go with it. She, herself, had never come across this variety before. Hmn. The pulp was almost . . . well, almost sensual.

She continued to mash the cuttings and slices with their oozy pulp. There was a strange pressure in her breasts.

Nell, pretending to fiddle with the flowers on the kitchen table, kept a sly eye on the physiotherapist. Her gaze held a glint of expectancy and she, too, began to feel a stirring in her breasts, nipples stiffening, pushing against the soft material of her blouse. She picked out an orchid that sprang from a particularly large tuber base and artfully pierced the greenish-white skin with her long thumbnail. It bled pulp, which she spread over her other fingers, even dabbing some into her cleavage and on her neck directly below her chin. Why wait for Thom Kindred when there was such an enjoyable diversion so close at hand? Besides, if Thom returned soon, he might even be persuaded to join in without using this aphrodisiac. Nell's original intention had been to get Thom to help her prepare the orchids so that the extract from their tubers would swiftly and easily penetrate the skin of his hands. Called (by those in the know) Satyrion, the gooey substance was a fast-acting sexual stimulant, one so effective that its properties remained covert. There were other common amatory stimulants that she could have used – anything from hashish to avocado pears, nutmeg to broad beans, yohimbine to the skins of baby bananas; you only needed to know the recipes – but the Early Purple Orchid was the easiest for Nell's purposes. And its potency was astonishing.

She cast another sly glance at the therapist, who was busy at the sink; a red flush was creeping round the girl's neck, spreading from her chest.

'Here's a good one,' Nell said, walking over to stand beside Katy.

'What do you do with this?'

Was there the slightest quiver in Katy's voice?

'Oh, I can use it for lots of things,' Nell replied mildly. 'The ancient Greeks mixed it with goat's milk. I like to use it in ice cream.'

'Ice cream? Really?' Slimy goo covered her fingers.

'It's easy. Gelatine, brown sugar or honey, vanilla essence. It's delicious with chocolate ice cream.'

'Yes, but what do you use it for, just the taste?'

'Let's say it gives a sense of well being. It can be quite invigorating.'

Katy paused in her work. 'It's not some kind of drug, is it?'

Nell laughed. 'No, it's a natural chemical. Good for invalids. S'why I brought the orchids here for Thom.' Her voice had taken on an intimate tone, as if she was sharing a secret. 'We do want him to get well, don't we?'

For some reason unknown to herself, Katy blushed. Yes, Thom. She really did want him to recover from his illness. There was something about him, something she found very ... attractive.

Nell was handing her another orchid, holding it by the stem, her own skin slick with juices from the punctured tuber.

'Try this one,' Nell was saying, but oddly, her voice did not sound nearby. 'It almost burst of its own accord.'

Katy took it from her, grasping the split tuber because it was offered first. She felt its pulp on her skin. A prickly sensation was running over the surface of her body and she realized she was taking shorter breaths than usual. Thom. It would be so good to see him again. Now she was surprised to feel a slight dampness between her legs, as if juices of her own were seeping. She pressed her lower belly against the side of the kitchen working surface, relishing the pressure, but conscious that she was not alone. The points of her breasts were tingling.

She had to clear her throat before she could speak. 'D'you suppose he'll be long?'

'I already told you,' Nell replied softly, staring into Katy's dilated eyes. 'I'm sure he's only gone for a short walk in the woods. We can entertain ourselves while we wait, can't we?'

Nell knew she had to play it carefully. Be patient, give it time to work, she told herself. Don't frighten her off by making a move too soon. Had the girl any experience of other women? Not openly, Nell was sure of that. She seemed to be too fond of Thom to be attracted to someone of her own sex. But who knew, these days? Who truly knew of the inclinations of others at a time when shame was hardly a factor any more? These days boys and girls could swing any way they fancied without risking persecution. It was a good time for women like Nell.

She noticed that Katy's breaths were becoming shorter and harsher, the red flush from her chest very much in evidence above the T-shirt's neckline. She reached out a hand to touch the therapist's bare arm and sensed an immediate reaction.

Katy felt her flesh tingle at Nell's soft touch, and the sensation spread up her arm, seemed to invade her entire body, bit by bit, stealth its ally. And yet she did not recoil from the other woman's touch, for the feeling was pleasant and not unwelcome. What was happening to her? Good God, she was feeling aroused. She pressed against the low cupboard door, not daring to look at her companion at the sink. Every part of her felt tensed, strained, an exquisite feeling running with her blood, arteries widening at certain points in her body, increasing the awareness there – her groin, her breasts, the sides of her neck, the skin between her shoulder blades and inside her elbows, her thighs . . .

Katy dropped the spoon into the bowl of sticky juice and gripped the edge of the sink. What *was* happening to her?

The woman beside her spoke soothingly and yet her voice was still distant, almost as if Katy had created a shell around herself, but one that she wished – she *yearned* for it – to be broken, breached. Invaded. She needed to be touched and she almost sobbed with the uncontrollability of it all. She wasn't like this. She had only ever wanted another female's touch when she was very young, a schoolgirl's crush that had come to nothing. Nothing, that is, but her own touch, dreaming that her own hand belonged to the other older girl she admired so much. And then there was the other time, the *only* other time, the one Katy had shoved from her mind over and over again, for it had shamed her, made her feel less of herself, and its recurring memory was her penance.

Nell remained cautious, keeping her voice low, its tone soothing, persuasive.

'You're so pretty,' she said, feeling her own wetness between her legs, the wonderful irritation inside her vagina, the stiffening of her clitoris, the swelling of her breasts. Her fingers ran lightly around the back of Katy's neck. 'So very pretty.' The huskiness in her voice was emphasized.

Nell wanted to release Katy's hair from its restricting rubber band, but she was aware of how delicate this moment was. Anything that required effort at this stage could easily alarm the girl, bring her out of the mood she'd unknowingly entered so that she would reject any further advances on Nell's part.

Slowly, gently, stroke the neck, speaking quietly, softly, seductively . . .

It was of her own accord that Katy turned to face Nell. Behind the wire-framed glasses, her eyes were wide, confused, as if she knew what was happening but did not know *how* it was happening.

'What are you doing?' she heard herself say, and her own voice seemed distant to her now and there was no anger, no rejection, in its tone. She was burning and the fire was spreading from the flesh between her hips and thighs.

'It's all right,' came the other's voice. 'Everything's well, and nice. You are beautiful, you know.'

The next move was the most important of all, for it was invasive and would leave the therapist open, vulnerable – perhaps defensive. Slowly Nell reached up and gently, oh so gently, removed Katy's spectacles, holding them by their corners and softly, easily lifting, sliding the arms away from her ears. If Katy was going to object, if she was going to react negatively, then it would be now, as soon as those light glasses were gone, when her vision had softened and psychologically she was at Nell's mercy.

Katy did take in a sudden shorter and sharper breath, a kind of surprised gasp, but she did not utter another sound, nor did she grab Nell's wrist.

Nell's smile corrupted to a hideous grin.

# FROM ANOTHER REALM

THOM FELT wonderfully at peace.

He had become used – more 'attuned' – to the sights around him, yet was still in wonder at it all as he and Jennet slowly, leisurely, made their way through the deepest part of the woods. He saw many more sights that made him gasp because of their beauty, and many more that caused him to laugh out loud in delight, although Jennet assured him there was still more that went unperceived by him.

'On the deepest night do you always see every star?' she had asked him.

'I suppose it isn't possible to catch every single one,' he had replied.

'But you have little machines which have their own special eyes to record such things.'

'You mean cameras?'

'Kamras. It has a nice, capable sound. Doesn't it reveal to you much more than when you use only your eyes? Doesn't such a machine reveal many, many other stars beyond your own vision? But even so, this Kamras cannot capture them all. Yet the stars are still there, alive with their own energies, playing their part like everything else that exists on whatever plane or dimension.'

'Yes, but it's a matter of distance, isn't it? Humans are only capable of seeing so far.'

'Precisely,' she had said.

---

'There was a case early in this century where two little girls claimed to have photographed faeries. It was in a place called, er . . .' Thom racked his brain '. . . Cotting, Cottingley, I think. Before she died, as an old lady, one of them confessed it'd all been a hoax, they'd photographed paper cutouts of their own drawings.'

'And what do you think they based those drawings on.'

'Pictures from storybooks?'

Jennet shook her head. 'Memories,' she said.

---

Jennet had skipped lightly on to a fallen tree trunk and turned to face him. In answer to a question he had put, she replied:

'In the main, our function, or "purpose", as you put it, is to nurture nature itself. We are in the spirit of the woodland, the meadow, even in the gardens of humans. You'll find our essence in mountain ranges and in the wildest and deepest of oceans, in the hillside, or lake and pond. We are in the rain and in the rays of the sun. We are in the wind and fire. When people look at something that you have made with wood—'

*She knew he was a carpenter?*

'—be it simple or complex, they are aware it's come together by your effort and design. Yet when they take in a tree or plant, then they fail to see that this also has been accomplished by the work of others. Sun, seed and soil are our tools and our spirit stimulates the life.

'And when we work with humankind, itself, in the cultivation of crops and vegetation, in growing the perfect rose or finest corn, it's then that our mutual accomplishment is at its most glorious. But whereas Man always works from the *outside*, the faery works from the *inside*.

'Remember the flute uses the wind to play its notes, but it's the player who assembles those notes. A musical score is irrelevant without the musical instrument, and a musical instrument is nothing without the player.'

---

She had helped him cross a narrow but busy stream, steadying him as they used two small stepping stones to cross, and his whole body had tingled with her mere touch. In more ways than just the obvious she was unlike any other girl or woman he had ever known, her femininity mixed with mischievousness – she had deliberately unbalanced him on the second stone – her sensuality compounded by her sensitivity, her humour lightening her compassion for everything that lived and breathed.

On the opposite bank and as a flock of faeries had fluttered by, their tinkling laughter and light sing-song voices charging the air itself, he had asked about faery wings.

'They're not wings at all,' she had informed him, 'and they certainly don't use them to fly: they can do that perfectly well without them. Many faeries, especially the smaller kind, are almost all essence, spirit if you like, and what you see, or at least, what you *perceive*, is their spirit slipstream. The more vibrant and colourful they are, then the more vital and lively is that spirit.'

'But some are well defined and even disturb the leaves or blades of grass as they pass,' Thom protested.

'Of course!' She giggled at him. 'That's how potent the vibration of their essence is.'

———

'What about food or drink?' Thom had enquired. 'So far I haven't noticed any of you eating or drinking. So what is your diet – berries, wild fruits?'

Again, a small giggle. 'No, we don't need to sustain ourselves that way unless we take on human form, although we might sip water occasionally. Oh, and some of the pixies are fond of your ale when they can obtain it. We bathe in the rays of the sun to draw its energy, and we frequently take magnetic baths, absorbing the power of the earth itself. But mostly our nourishment is in the air we breathe, the smells we smell and the sounds we hear. Our power is derived from everything around us.'

Her small face suddenly became grave.

'But you humans are slowly spoiling that for us, poisoning the air and vegetation with your pollution and unnatural chemicals. Why do you think we keep more and more to ourselves, why we hide from you? It wasn't always like this.'

'I . . .' Thom had no idea what to say, had no excuse to make. How *did* you excuse the whole human race? Pleading ignorance wasn't an acceptable defence.

She touched his lips with two fingers to silence him. 'It's not your fault alone. But it's why we keep to the hidden places, why the secret territories unblemished by your kind are so important to our existence. We cannot survive in a tainted environment.'

Then, with the same two fingers she briskly tapped his nose.

'Besides,' she said, skipping away from him, 'you humans stink!'

———

He quickly caught up with her.

'I still don't get it. Where do you come from? Are you born, like us? And do you die, like us?'

'It's not quite like birth, Thom. We slowly emerge, we gradually *become* what we are. And rather than die, we return to a more subtle form of being, one that can only be revealed to humans when they, themselves, leave the life they know.'

'Do – can – others see you as I do?'

'Only a very few. Humans will have to change their ways and realize that the planet does not belong to them alone before the acceptance begins.'

She touched his upper arm beneath the short sleeve of his T-shirt and again he gave a little shiver.

'It's our hope that some day human consciousness will be elevated enough for them to first understand and then, when all is well, discern our presence. But if it should happen, it will be far ahead in your future. You have to learn so much and forget so much. You will be helped, Thom, I can promise you that.'

---

They had reached another smaller, shaded glade, one where beams of sunlight filtered through the leafy canopy overhead and whose dense smell of tree bark and vegetation was so powerful it seemed to sink into Thom's skin. He watched tiny lights, bright in the shadows, leave sparkly trails behind as they flitted in and out of the undergrowth. He and Jennet sat on the soft carpet of crushed leaves, Jennet with her knees raised, hands clasped together over them, chin on her thumbs, while Thom reclined before her, his weight resting on an elbow, his body stretched out.

'Tell me—' his words were hesitant '—is there . . . d'you know if . . . if there's a God?'

'Of course. We call many things god.'

'No. I mean, is there one true God?'

'Oh, the Creator Being. It's a mystery, isn't it?'

'You don't know?' Somehow he was disappointed; he had expected more.

'Yes, silly. I know God *exists*. But none of us have ever met the one we call the Creator Being, the Great Magician, and I'm very sure that none of you humans have either.'

'Well then, how can you be so certain He exists?'

'Thom, I am from the essence of everything. I am in the spirit of nature, itself, and I exist in the dimension between life as you know it and the one you're bound for. That means that at the moment I'm closer to the Creator Being than you and closer than some of your kind will *ever* be. So I know there is a one true God because . . .' she slowed the words for emphasis ' . . . it . . . is . . . so.'

---

'Do you know what happened to me last night?'

Incredibly, Thom had been able to dispatch the horrors of the previous night to a quiet corner of his mind, the wonders of the morning stroll into the depths of the forest almost overwhelming the worrying memory.

'Yes, Thom. The *hellhagge* sent the Night Thief to steal your seminal fluid.'

'My . . .? The elf . . .'

'Rigwit.'

' . . . said it was my fertility.'

'It came for your seed, that most intimate part of you. It was as if it was taking part of your soul.'

'But why? Rigwit couldn't tell me.'

'Because we don't know. All we can understand is that you're a danger to her.'

'I hardly know Nell Quick and I certainly wouldn't harm her.'

'Nevertheless, she wants your seed to help her sorcery. Such acquisition would be extremely powerful.'

'I don't get it. No way am I a threat to her.'

'You might be in the future and she's aware of this.'

Confused, bewildered – it was fast becoming a regular state for Thom.

'I wanted the elf to explain more to me, but, I don't know, I guess I was just exhausted. I fell asleep.'

'He knew you needed rest more than anything else right then. It gave your mind time to assimilate.'

'He made me sleep?'

'He helped the process. As you, yourself, said: you were exhausted. You might easily have become traumatized.'

'Believe me, I was already.'

'Which is why your mind and body needed to rest.'

There was silence between them for awhile, Thom brooding, Jennet watching him with both interest and concern.

Eventually: 'Why didn't you appear with the other faeries? I needed all the help I could get.'

'I cannot use the Book for entry. I can only enter by physical means and that wasn't possible last night. I would never have reached you in time.'

He digested this for a moment.

'I want you to tell me more about Bethan, Jennet. And my father. I want to – I *need* to – know more.'

She rose to her bare feet, a graceful movement, almost as if gravity meant very little to her. The diaphanous dress she wore was caught by a slight breeze so that it ruffled around her slender legs; that same breeze disturbed her bright golden hair, a curled lock tickling her cheek, delicate, fingers brushing it away.

'A little while longer, Thom. You've already had to learn so much.'

---

Soon they had reached the lake and the sight of it took Thom by surprise, for they had journeyed through unfamiliar parts to reach a destination he knew – or *thought* he knew – so well. He first glimpsed it through the dense trees, burning white behind their silhouettes, and when he and Jennet finally broke free of the forest to stand on its irregular grassy shoreline, he saw a million tiny glitters like daylight stars around its edges. He could not remember the phenomenon from his childhood days.

He knelt to examine the shiny speckles closest to him and reached for one particular object that shone diamond-like. It was a jagged and many-faceted stone, sharp to the touch and coloured silvery-white, with the palest of blues and pinks tincturing its angles.

'Coral,' Jennet answered to the question he was about to ask. 'Four hundred million of your years ago this place was a great barrier reef. If you dig just below the soil you'll also find seashells, and the bones of ancient sea creatures.'

He shook his head again in wonder. 'Why didn't I see this before? I used to come here all the time when I was a boy.'

'It's only today that you're beginning to see clearly again.'

Thom dropped the piece of skeletal rock and gazed across the lake's calm mirror surface. It was abruptly disturbed by a swooping heron, which dipped its beak into the water while still in flight to snatch an unwary fish. The big bird rose majestically, its body seeming too heavy for its wings, and the ripples its theft had caused spread outwards in ever-expanding waves towards the shoreline.

But if Thom expected those gentle tidal waves to fade, he was wrong, for not only did the growing circles become heavier, but they were joined by others all over that part of the lake as though something below had also been disturbed.

They first appeared singly, and then in groups of three or four, and they sang as they rose, beautiful siren songs that both enchanted and terrified Thom.

# Chapter: Twenty-Third

## WHAT KATY DID

NELL HAD led Katy up to Thom's bedroom.

The therapist had protested at first, but weakly, no commitment behind the protestation, for already they had kissed each other's lips, already Nell's fingers had lightly played around Katy's erect nipples before moving sedately, smoothly on to the nape of her neck, then down along her spine, fingertips soft, without pressure, their unimposing touch sending shivers through the therapist's body, resting at the elastic band of her tracksuit trousers so that she had wanted to implore Nell to move inside, to touch the dampness between her legs, but she had been too shy, too ashamed to voice her urges.

The first kiss had not even been tentative. The grin on Nell's face had frightened Katy, yet its scarlet slash was all the more alluring because of the fear, for it heightened the tension, the strangeness of the act exciting her senses almost to breaking point. What had happened to her? Katy wondered. Why was she feeling this way, all common sense abandoned, this sudden proclivity too intense, too fierce, to be denied? Her own lips had pushed hard against the other woman's without hesitation, although certainly with trepidation, but even this emotion served to increase the arousal. And her mouth had opened willingly, inviting Nell's intrusion, perhaps *insisting* upon it, and the tongue had entered with relish, meeting her own, tips curling against each other's, their juices mingling.

Even so, even though Katy had wanted this to happen, her hands never left her sides, did not reach around the dark-haired woman to pull her tight, for she was the lamb being led – not to slaughter but to ecstasy – and the guilt afterwards might be easier to bear if it remained so. It would be so much easier if she could cast the blame on another.

But her body, her own ungovernable desire, had let her down, imposed its own will, for she had found herself pressing her groin into Nell's, their hips touching as stomachs flattened, and they had both moved their bodies, squirming and thrusting, not wildly but insistently, moans rising from them both.

It was when Nell had drawn herself away, although remaining close enough for her warm breath to *burn* Katy's cheek, and said, 'Come with me,' that Katy had recalled the other time something like this had happened to her, although it had never been as exciting as this, and her part in it had been placid, almost docile.

She had been seduced – molested might have been a more appropriate word – in the home of a senior physiotherapist when she, herself, had been a mere seventeen-year-old. The older woman had been teaching her the art of body massage, useful in treating certain patients' ailments, and the session had gone further than anything Katy had expected. Only when it was over had she realized she had been duped, lured into loveplay (on the other woman's part) by being aroused beyond control by oiled and scented hands roving over her body.

She had fled the house in tears and never returned; neither had she ever seen the woman again, for she had promptly changed training schools. But still she had been left feeling abused and somehow unclean, even though such mores were considered unfashionable then as well as now. Why the guilt? What difference did it make to be made love to by either a man or woman? It was all experience. Yeah, right, Katy had said to herself. Tell that to my friends and parents.

But what had also confused and hurt her was that afterwards – and Katy had not even returned the other woman's touch – her seducer had proclaimed her a lesbian no matter how hard she tried to deny the fact. The older woman had said she had long suspected and this little episode had proved it. It was a cruel lie, of course, but Katy was too young and naive to know this, let alone understand her own sexual inclinations. She had soon begun dating boys and then men, and doubts about her sexuality came only on lonely nights when she had no other recourse but to pleasure herself, for that was when fantasy took over from reality.

And now, those long-stifled feelings and sensations had been aroused again by this beautiful woman and, it seemed, Katy could not stop herself from accepting – welcoming – the advances. The guilt was still with her – more so than ever, in fact – but this sudden and overwhelming rush of desire could not be denied. And, as before, perhaps it was that same old guilt that quickened and intensified the lust.

She lay on Thom's bed with Nell kneeling over her, the gypsy-looking woman's cotton skirt pulled high over her lightly-tanned thighs, breasts swelling against the low top of her white blouse. Nell's scarlet smile held challenge, daring, and her dark eyes seemed to blaze with her own passion.

'It's all right, Katy,' Nell soothed. 'There's nothing to fear. You want me as badly as I want you, so let it be.'

Just as she had all those years ago in the home of her

255

teacher-therapist, Katy wanted to protest, and she did, but exactly as before, her murmurs weak, without true conviction. She could not help herself, the lust within her was too demanding, too overbearing, too intoxicating. It was she who grasped Nell's wrist and directed her hand to the tips of her breasts, guiding it from one to the other, then back again, this time pulling it tight so that fingers – delicious, wonderful fingers! – clamped around the soft mounds and pressed their hardened centres.

Nell, of course, took full advantage, her lips descending to push against Katy's, parting them so that her tongue could dash through and explore the other girl's mouth again. Once more her tongue met and played with Katy's, once more they both drank in each other's juices.

Katy's head whirled, her thoughts as well as her senses spinning. Never, *never*, had she felt like this! Never had she been so aroused, nor did she care any more; she had to be *touched*, she had to be entered, and she had to find release before her impulses drove her mad.

'Please . . .' she managed to mumble between wild kisses. '*Please . . .*'

And Nell understood. She knew what was wanted. And she knew what she, herself, wanted, for not only had the natural aphrodisiac worked well on her own body, but this girl's primal need, her desperate yearning to be held, touched and brought to orgasm, had an aphrodisiacal effect all its own.

Nell reached behind Katy's head to slide off the rubber band that held the girl's blonde hair in a ponytail, freeing the tresses so that they spread out on the pillow, the action a form of release for her prey, a release to abandonment. Katy tried to pull Nell down on top of her, but Nell resisted, remaining in control, roughly pushing the girl's hands away, then pulling at the T-shirt Katy wore, tugging it loose from the grey tracksuit leggings and yanking it up over the naked breasts. Katy's nipples were almost red in their engorgement and the skin between her breasts was flushed. She moaned ecstatically as Nell lowered her head and took one tip into her mouth, drawing it in, lathering it with her own drool, circling and pushing with her tongue, driving Katy to frenzy. Then the other breast, concentrating on it alone, making Katy so aware of her nipple's reaction, its nerve-endings tingling almost as if invisibly sparking; back to the other nipple, her hand encircling the one her tongue had just left, kneading and rubbing, one moment gently, the next harshly, applying pressure so that Katy gasped with pleasurable pain. The valley between her breasts glistened with sweat and saliva and spittle escaped the corner of her mouth.

'Please ...' she said again, not as a murmur but as an ardent imploration.

And this time, Nell answered her. 'Yes, oh yes ...' she said huskily '... yes, my pretty ...' and she almost laughed aloud at the witchhag utterance.

She bent her head lower and drew her tongue slitheringly down to Katy's navel, lingering in its well, circling, moistening, while Katy slid her hands between their bodies and into the top of Nell's blouse, reaching for *her* breasts, touching the nipples, causing them to swell even more, pressing against the soft lush mounds until it was the other woman's turn to moan with delight. Katy's fingers stopped for a moment to crook around the blouse's elasticated top; she tugged downwards so that Nell's breasts, with their long points and dark rings, spilled free.

'Aaah ...' sighed Nell.

And then her hands were pushing at the waist of Katy's leggings, forcing them down, over her legs, along her thighs, forcing them easily over dimpled knees, rising momentarily to drag them over ankles and feet, tossing them aside when she was done, then returning her attention to Katy's quivering stomach, tongue once more taking up its eager and inciting task.

Katy felt like screaming with the clandestine joy of it all, every muscle and tissue and nerve seemingly stretched almost beyond endurance. Her lips were drawn back tightly over her teeth and occasionally her tongue would snake out to moisten them. She moaned and at times groaned with the pleasure, both body and mind lost to the wondrous sensations. She groped beneath Nell's shoulders, her arms stretched as far as they could reach, wanting to feel the other woman's body, her breasts, longing to move on, to feel more intimate parts, but afraid Nell's own tongue and hands would stop their work in order to relish the other's caresses.

She nearly cried out when Nell's moist lips and tongue travelled even further, descending to the waistline of her white cotton panties. The tip of the tongue shifted backwards and forward along the elasticated line, tantalizing, teasing, forcing Katy to push against Nell's shoulders to urge her on. Nell's tongue slid between flesh and cotton and Katy did cry out, a small sound that was uncontrolled, pleading.

Nell obliged, aware that the girl was nearing breaking point, that soon all restraint would be lost, the sensations would reach their peak; but Nell, herself, was not yet ready for that, her own yearnings also had to be fulfilled. She paused, but only to move up swiftly and kiss the girl full on the mouth, lowering the whole length of her body on to Katy's so that they were locked in tight embrace.

Katy allowed the harsh kisses – indeed, she returned them – but she wanted far more, she craved to be touched in her most sensitive place. Still, she pulled Nell close against herself, arms encircling her lower back, applying tension as she opened her legs, feeling Nell's thigh sink between them, the pressure returned so that Katy squirmed and writhed beneath the other woman. Both used each other's thigh to strain against, flesh filling cavity, juices in each now flowing freely.

Just as Katy thought she could stand no more, that the pressure within would quickly find its inevitable release, Nell slid from her and lay by her side. But before she had time for disappointment, Nell was shoving at her panties, pushing then dragging them down until her legs were free of them. She felt Nell's hand play along her leg, journeying upwards once again, past her knee, along her thigh, taking its time, allowing the expectation to build. She wanted to complain when fingertips bypassed her folded opening to play with her pubic hair, but knew it was part of the pleasure game, that the reward would come soon after. And she was right. Nell's fingers slowly dipped into the vale of her thighs, then gently, softly into the wet entrance to her lower body, parting the silky lips easily, then sliding, gliding, into the slick passage beyond.

Katy's ecstatic moan was long and loud, and her hips moved rhythmically, twisting, turning, helping the intruding fingers find places of acute sensation. She felt Nell turn her wrist so the fingers faced upwards, then the longest one curling inwards so that it touched her vagina's most sensitive spot, causing her to give out a small yelp of delight.

With her other hand, Nell reached beneath the ruffled T-shirt and found a point between Katy's shoulder and neck, applying mild yet nevertheless firm pressure to nerve endings there, making tantric connection between shoulder and genitals, her hand moving to the girl's breast between strokes, then back again, seeing to the needs of each part.

Katy's back began to arch, her heels digging into the bedsheet, her mouth opening wide, her teeth parted. Different sensations inside her began to swell, reaching towards bursting point, unable to be contained for much longer. A noise, a scream, travelled from somewhere deep inside her throat, rising as it came, growing louder along the way.

But Nell did not want the climax to come so soon, for she had other designs on this ripe pretty girl: she wanted to taste her.

She withdrew her fingers, ignoring the groaned protest, and ducked her head low, stretching her body so that her legs were off the end of the bed, her head and shoulders lying between Katy's spread thighs. She nuzzled the girl's brown pubic hair, tongue flicking in and out, mouthing the hard mound, so that Katy's desire rose again and her hands reached into Nell's raven-black hair, guiding her head, urging it further down, deeper into the cleft. And Nell willingly obliged, her darting tongue finding the open lips, sliding in easily between them, finding the hard little point just inside at the top, flicking around it at first, making it rise even more, teasing again before enveloping its peak, smothering it with the soft moist blanket of her own muscled flesh, flicking, then licking, sucking then driving further inwards, tongue stretched as far as it could reach so that Katy cried out again and again and again, her canal becoming hollowed, ready to receive all that could be given, her cries transcending to one long sighing moan, her hands fierce against the back of Nell's head.

Nell knew the girl was now beyond her control, that her climax was fast approaching and she quickly withdrew and threw her upper body towards Katy's feet, pulling up her skirt and pushing one leg beneath the girl's back.

Katy was too far gone to feel dismayed, her orgasm beginning to come in wave upon wave, and when she felt the other's vaginal lips against her own (for it was evident that Nell had been wearing nothing beneath her skirt) and Nell pulling down on her hips so that their secret lips sucked and crushed one another's and their vulvas flared open so that fluids flowed and mingled, Katy felt every part of her body, inner and outer, stretching to its limit. Her scream was loud, the feel of their mutual movement almost unbearable in its heat, sensations filling her body and mind, and the sound of Nell's own exhilaration, although more contained than hers, drove her to a new sublime delirium.

She screamed and thrashed her face from side to side as their bodies heaved and rocked together, then pushed the back of her head into the pillow as her neck arched and her legs quivered. Nell's ankle was hard between Katy's shoulder blades as they writhed against each other, both women frenzied, now extending every muscle as orgasm took them, both screaming as they were scoured by a filling and blissful tension . . .

Both shuddering and whimpering as the tides of passion came and went, each event softer, less intense, than the one before . . .

# Chapter: Twenty-Fourth
## THE UNDINES

SOME HAD dark hair, sleekly black yet not damp with lake water, while others were golden blonde like Jennet, sunlight framing their heads and playing on the edges of curls, thereby giving the deepest parts of their hair added darker texture. They rose to the surface, all facing in Thom and Jennet's direction, some smiling as they sang, others unsure, their expressions sombre. Several appeared nervous of Thom as they hung back in the deeper places of the lake, pointing at him with slender arms and long fingers, whispering to companions; others came forward to the shallows, some completely naked with small pointed breasts like Jennet's and hairless pubic mounds like a girl-child's, some wearing long or short shifts of material so sheer they might just as well have worn nothing at all. One, with dark frizzed-out hair like wedges at the side of her sweet face, the top decorated with small water lilies, giggled and held hands to her cheeks, watching him with apparent delight as she drew closer to the shoreline.

All resembled Jennet in that they had the same almond-shaped eyes, the same high cheekbones and delicately pointed chin; yet all were different, having their own character and other disparate features. Many were joined in song, a siren's song which Thom imagined could easily lead susceptible men out into the dangerous depths of the lake where currents were strongest. Every single pair of violet and silver eyes was on him and he felt mesmerized by them, the urge to swim out to be in their midst pulling at his will. It was his companion who broke the spell.

'Undines,' she told him. 'Waterfays, like me. Like your mother.'

It was those last words that interrupted his fascination and caused him to wheel towards her.

'My mother . . .!'

Jennet's voice was kindly, soothing. 'She came from the seas, Thom, from the oceans. Like us, she came from the waterfalls, the streams and . . .' she indicated the disturbed stretch of water before them '. . . the lakes. It was here, at this spot, that your father found her.'

'She never told me, she never mentioned anything like this . . .'

'Oh but she did. It was Bethan who made you forget.'

'What are you talking about? I've never known any of this.'

'Thom, you did. When you were just a child Bethan wanted you to know everything about herself.'

'Then why can't I remember?' He shook his head in exasperation, aware through the periphery of his vision that the water creatures – nymphs? – were moving closer to the shore. 'What are you telling me? I just don't get—'

'Be calm.'

His hand had gone to his brow and now she reached up and took his wrist, drawing his hand away from his face.

'Let's sit a while and rest,' she went on. 'You've had so much to take in recently and you're confused. Bewildered

263

too, no doubt. It's time for you to rest and let your mind absorb.'

'These . . .?' He waved a hand towards the undines, some of whom were emerging from the lake. He saw that several had skins tinged with green, others with blue. Very few seemed to have the natural if pallid colouring of Jennet herself. He wondered if she were something special among them.

'They wish you no harm,' she replied to his unspoken question. 'They're curious, that's all. Not many of them have ever seen someone like you.'

'So I'm the . . . oddity here?' He had almost said 'freak'.

'To us, yes. But we know your kind rule this world.'

Thom said little else. Instead he turned back to the advancing water-creatures, occasionally murmuring with wonder. Closer up they looked even more beautiful, their faces appealing, their bodies . . . God, their bodies were alluring, especially when seen through the diaphanous clothing that many wore. They remained cautious, but nevertheless moved nearer to him, stepping from the shallows while remaining by the water's edge as if ready to flee back from whence they came should Thom give the slightest cause for alarm.

The singing had stopped, although they made little chattering sounds at each other, their meaning gradually filtering through to Thom so that before long he could understand their words. Most of their remarks were directed at him, generally flattering comments about his height. (Some of these undines were the same size as Jennet, but the majority were smaller, so that if it had not been for their breasts, they could have easily been mistaken for children. Indeed, it did seem that there were very young girls among them, for these were even smaller than the smaller ones, their thin bodies hardly developed at all. It was these that drew the closest to him as if they had not yet learned proper caution, and their chattering was in higher strains, their giggles and chuckles much more free.)

'Sit here, Thom.' Jennet had taken both his hands in her own and was urging him towards the base of an old oak.

And suddenly he did feel tired, as though his body were obeying by auto-suggestion, his left leg growing weak as usual, his left arm becoming a little numbed. He practically slumped on to the mossy area beneath the oak.

For a moment, Jennet looked concerned, then she sat next to him on the ground, resting on a hand, knees drawn up.

'It'll pass, Thom. You're exhausted, but you'll feel better in a moment or two.'

With that, she raised her palm again and dust – *magic* dust – was blown into his face. This time he inhaled deeply, his trust in this wondrous being implicit, even though he could not quite take in all she told him. Instantly, he revived, the powder working, he imagined, like a coke hit, and he looked earnestly into her face.

'Please tell me everything,' he said and once again she was smiling at him.

'First you need to know about us.'

And with the words she spoke, a calmness descended upon him. Not only did he trust her and know she meant him no harm, but he felt she held the secret of his own past, a secret he hadn't even been aware of until this day. The area around him had come alive, not just with the girls and young women she had called undines, but with imps and pixies again, with faeries who played instruments that resembled lutes, although their tone was different, higher in pitch, less musical on initial hearing, but after a while *more* musical than any comparable earthly instrument. Its sound was oddly exhilarating and relaxing at the same time – he supposed it depended on the mood of the individual. A funny little man with brown skin and a peaked cloth cap sat at the edge of the lake playing a long thin pipe, its sound at once bleak, yet perfectly in tune with the other instruments. The music drifted across the water's surface, both haunting and sweet in melody and Thom felt an unaccustomed melancholy that was bitter sweet, as though he were being reminded of his mortal status, that he was not truly part of this strange otherworld. As for the creatures around him, the faeries that settled on leaves or in open flowers, the imps who stopped their frolicking to listen, and the animals that rested in the grass, the music seemed to render them reflective, more still. The undines, themselves, sang along with it, dulcet and ethereal, mystical to his ears.

He laughed when he saw beings so tiny that blades of grass towered over them; they wore snowdrops on their heads to protect themselves from the high sun and, on closer inspection, he realized they were toddlers, infant faeries, watched over by the older of their kind. Something arrived from the water with a splash that startled Thom and when he looked towards the grassy bank he spied an oddly beautiful creature – oddly, for although her face was vixen-shaped, her eyes dramatically slanted and closed almost to black slits, her ears long and also pointed, her flesh and bare breasts bluish, the unusual ensemble was strangely exquisite and perfectly formed. A garland of water lilies adorned her long black hair and her lengthy wings flapped languorously in the warm sunshine. She squatted on the bank studying him for a moment, no more then ten inches high but superb in every singular detail; it was only when she gave a kind of *squawk-croak* and leapt into the air from her haunches that he noticed the incredibly long webbed toes, the brighter blue mottling of her legs and feet. Her leap was high and arced, like that of a frog and indeed, except for the colouring, the lowest portion of her legs was amphibian.

'Christ!' he explained as she hopped out of sight beneath nearby undergrowth.

There was laughter around him.

'It's only the Frog Queen,' Jennet said, laughing with the others. 'Sorry she startled you.'

He should have been used to such queer sights by now, for hadn't he already seen a thing that was half-faery, half-hedgehog, and another that had shrubbery growing from its head and back? He'd been allowed a peep into a different dimension and nothing more should have surprised him. Even so, when he saw four tiny imps sitting astride a swift-moving grass-snake close by he could not help but wonder what else awaited him. The imps waved and went on their merry way, the one at the front holding a little twig which he used to tap either side of the green snake's head, evidently his way of steering the reptile. More laughter when the one nearest the tail fell off as the snake swiftly changed direction to avoid coming too close to Thom.

Many of the undines had now emerged from the lake to sit in a semicircle around Thom, although they remained at a distance; others preferred to sit in the shallows and watch from there. They were all beautiful, he noticed, each one in her own way, their faces generally wan in the sunshine, their bodies slender and supple. Whether naked or wearing the flimsy dresses and skirts, each one was incredibly erotic – and exotic – to Thom's eyes and it was almost impossible to subdue the stirring of his loins. He tried to cover his literally growing embarrassment by leaning forward from the tree trunk and resting his wrists on his knees. Even so, one or two of the nearest undines tried to smother their giggles with slender hands as they watched him coyly from the corners of their eyes.

Jennet scolded them with a look.

Flustered, Thom said: 'Tell me about the undines, Jennet. Are you one of them?'

'Yes, Thom, I'm an undine and so was Bethan.'

'She . . . she lived in the lake?' He was shaking his head disbelievingly even as he asked the question.

'She came from the lake. It was over there . . .' she

267

pointed '... by the willow that your father first set eyes on her.'

'And this is where she returned,' Thom said grimly.

'This is where she died.'

'Were there – are there – others like my mother? Undines or faeries posing as humans?'

'Not posing, Thom. Assuming the identities of humans. There is no pretence involved. But to answer your question, yes, there are several of us walking *your* Earth at this moment. Usually they are very discreet, but one in particular has already drawn too much attention to herself. She's quite famous?'

'Oh yeah? Who might that someone be?'

'She's an Icelandic singer. You humans think her a little eccentric, but in truth, she acts the way she does because she is still confused. She hasn't adapted yet, though she will in time. Meanwhile, most of you find her singing very strange; but persevere, eventually it will make sense to you.'

A green-silver-blue spark drifted between them and poised in the air in front of Thom. He could discern no regular shape to it, no form at all, and it surprised him by suddenly streaking off and vanishing completely before it had gone five yards. Another appeared, this one red and gold in appearance, a tiny fiery star that behaved in exactly the same manner as the previous one, although zooming off and disappearing in a different direction. Thom looked at Jennet quizzically.

'Little spirits,' she explained as yet another, and then another loomed before them. These were mainly purple and silver-white, although other fainter colours seemed to flare in their auroras. 'They're curious about you. It's not often that humans are allowed time to focus on them, so consider yourself privileged. Sometimes the eyes of your kind might catch their reflections, but rarely will they be seen properly unless by people who have very sensitive intuitions.'

'You mean psychics?'

She shrugged. 'We have no special word for them. To us they're just humans who see more clearly.'

'And these ... these things?'

'I told you, spirits, elementals. They are part of everything, the hidden life-force of all that exists. Their energies have wonderful powers.'

The three pulsing lights disappeared as abruptly as their precursors. But almost immediately a whole galaxy of similarly brilliant coruscations took their place, creating a glittering nebula between them. Thom had to squint against their combined glow, but he saw that they all comprised the same shades of light, twinkling blues to mauve and indigo, their nuclei a dazzling white that emitted streaks of its own essence into the halo of colours. Thom's shoulders hit the broad tree trunk behind him as he backed off.

'Don't be afraid, Thom.'

He heard her voice, her image hazy behind the shifting nebula.

'They're here for you. They're healers.'

Thom drew his feet up, pressing his spine even harder into the rough bark at his back. For some reason he was nervous of these dancing lights for, although other small faeries had eventually graduated into human-like figures, these remained dazzling little stars with no obvious form and therefore utterly alien to him, possessing nothing he could relate to as a human himself. Why were they here for him?

'Jennet, I...'

'Hush, now. Relax and let them do their work. Her bad magic is strong, Thom, because she comes from a long line of evil women.'

'Nell Quick is just a woman,' he insisted.

'Haven't you learned anything?'

His question came out of fear. 'Why should you care? Why are you concerned for me?'

She moved slightly so that now he could see her beyond the fainter fringes of the cluster. 'For Bethan's sake,' she said. 'And for ours.'

Like movie spaceships veering off to attack, the tiny stars arced towards him, each one taking its own graceful route, gliding forward to weave across his face and raised hands. They touched his bare skin, probes with no bite, scouting first before targeting. He felt their rays of light on the surface of his flesh, small beams of warmth that tickled, the soft heat sinking into him, disturbing his skin without hurting or even irritating. Some zoomed across his forehead and temples, peculiarly brushing without actually touching, while others reached his bare left arm to travel its length, down and then up, a constant traffic of energizing passes, their ethereal force entering his flesh, journeying with his bloodstream to be carried around his entire system.

He felt faint; he felt his body had been invaded by alien but friendly micro-organisms; and after a few seconds he felt a strength galvanizing every tissue, sinew and muscle. His blood seemed to rush through him with its vivifying cargo and he could almost feel its beat as it flowed in steady heart-governed shifts. The faintness soon left him as his body began to respond to the infusion.

It was miraculous. It was wonderful. It was a drug-free high that made him want to cry out with the pleasure it brought. His left arm was no longer numbed, his leg no longer ached. His chest swelled with the euphoria and, when he opened his eyes, for he had closed them in his joy, he saw that the water nymphs had moved even closer and were now joined by other imps and faeries, some of whom watched him intently, while others played and frolicked regardless of his presence. Several small animals had left the denser part of the woods to come closer and two roe deer were drinking from the lake itself.

He returned his attention to Jennet and when he

searched her lovely and bewitching eyes, they were slightly hooded, as if she, herself had become tired.

But Thom had mistaken the look she was giving him, for when she touched his upper arm he felt a palpable *frisson* between them, a charge that seemed to run through his limbs, his body, his heart, and rather than being unpleasant, it was exciting, arousing, a kind of tingling shiver that was stronger than before travelling with it. It was not weariness he saw in her, but uninhibited sexual hunger. Jennet had sensed his body's reaction to the micro-probes that coursed through him, instilling an energy he had rarely experienced. All sensations were heightened and he felt undeniably sensual.

As she sat on her heels by his side, Thom found it increasingly impossible to ignore her nakedness beneath the flimsy, translucent garment she wore, the delicate breasts and soft curve of her belly, the white unblemished flesh of her thighs, creating urges in him that were physically difficult to disguise. Oh God, he thought, embarrassed that his arousal was as transparent as her shift. He raised his knees higher to hide his swelling, his bare heels digging into the soft moss.

'Jennet . . .' he began to say, but suddenly she was leaning forward and brushing her lips against his cheek.

'So many questions, Thom, and all to be answered in time. How do you feel now?'

'Uh . . . I feel wonderful,' he replied, which was true enough but not quite all.

'Then let's walk on and talk further.'

She skipped to her feet and reached for him. Taking her hand and relishing the excitement of her touch again, he rose awkwardly. He shoved his fists into his jeans pocket, a weak attempt to camouflage the impudent bulge alongside. He felt ridiculously healthy and he prayed it would last. As they walked around the fringes of the peaceful lake, the other undines watching, some waving, his mind focused on the things Jennet had told him so far and he was soon lost in thought again.

'I used to think Bethan was the most beautiful undine I'd ever seen,' she said as they walked through the long grass that ran down to the very edge of the lake. 'Of course, I was only a faery-child, but even I could appreciate true beauty and wisdom. The undines wept when she left them and they mourned when she returned to us only to pass over into the next realm.'

Thom felt anger, confusion. 'But why did she have to die? And why did she leave me? I had no one else, no father, no relatives at all, and only one friend.'

'She had no choice. It's the way.'

'Not for humans, it isn't. We stick by our children mostly.'

'She had become almost human. We always do when we fall in love with your kind. Our magic slowly weakens as we begin to live as humans, although the powers never leave us entirely. Some magic remains but these amount to little more than the ability to create love potions, cures, ointments – nothing truly extraordinary.'

Birds nesting in boughs overhead sang of their approach; a red fox with an odd scar blemishing its small rascally face loped across their path, pausing only to look and bark crossly at them before going on its way.

'Goodbye, Rumbo,' she called after it.

'The fox has a name?'

'The animals we know all have names, how else would we address them? Rumbo was his name when he was a dog, then a squirrel. The name has travelled with him.'

There was already too much for Thom to consider without pondering over the apparent several lives of animals and reincarnation. 'So Bethan left me because my father had abandoned us both,' Thom said, dredges of bitterness clear in his tone.

Jennet stopped. 'Your father died. It was his death that

ONCE...

meant Bethan had to leave also. Just your love, a child's love, couldn't sustain her.'

'I never knew.' Thom was shaking his head. 'She never told me what happened to him. I just assumed he'd gone away before I was born.'

'Are you sure she didn't tell you about him, Thom?'

'I'm sure. I would've remembered.'

'You forgot everything else.'

'But not that. If she'd spoken of my father, I would have remembered.' He said the words deliberately, spacing them out.

'Then I don't understand. I'm sure Bethan had her reasons, though.'

'Yeah, he was no good. He ran out on us, but she was never mean-spirited enough to put it that way. Funnily enough, I don't ever remember asking about him as I grew older. I think he just didn't play any part in my thinking or existence.'

She took him by the hand. 'It's time you knew, Thom. Let me show you something that might help you understand.'

# Chapter : Twenty-Fifth

## A NASTY ACCIDENT

KATY SCREAMED. This was not what she wanted, what she'd expected.

The woman seemed crazed now, a wild thing taken by a perverse lust. Their lovemaking had been glorious, Katy could not deny that, and she, herself, had taken just as much a part as Nell, although initially the older woman had been the seducer. Katy had experienced sensations that she hadn't thought possible, certainly not between two women and rarely, she thought, possible between a man and a woman. The coupling had left her faint and she had lain exhausted on the bed, her T-shirt dishevelled above her tender breasts, an ache in her fulfilled loins that was not unpleasant. But satiated, she had began to feel shame, a guilt that nagged at her like some Catholic harpy, insisting that she had not just sinned but had sinned unnaturally. Stupid, foolish thinking, she knew, but years of sexual conformity and commonplace propriety were not so easy to dismiss. She had enjoyed it, though, she told herself, she had loved every illicit second.

While it was happening. Now that the incredible yearnings were gone, the intense desire satisfied (more so than it had ever been with any man) she was left only self-recrimination. She had come to Little Bracken to see Thom Kindred; it was the appointed time for his physiotherapy, exercises that eventually would mend him, would bring him back to the man he obviously had once been. Her interest in him was more than professional, she had no problem in admitting that; but this morning, when she had met the dark-haired woman, something – something she honestly believed was alien to her despite the single, and to her, singular experience all those years ago – had unleashed otherwise unfamiliar feelings in her. She had felt an overwhelming sexual passion and had willingly submitted to Nell's advances. It couldn't be so, she wasn't ... she wasn't that way ... it was an aberration, a *deviation*, and now she was left ashamed and ... frightened.

The woman, Nell, had changed horrendously. There was madness in those black eyes of hers! Perhaps she, Katy, would not have felt such mortification if the woman had shown some tenderness afterwards, some gentle caring, lying together and holding each other. It was what Katy needed, for sex was never just an act to her, it always meant something more, something fine.

Now this strange wild-haired woman, who at this moment personified Katy's vision of Rochester's mad Creole wife, escaped from her dungeon to wreak havoc on all and everything before her, knelt on the bed between Katy's naked spread legs, her hand closed in a tight fist, bringing it down, closer and closer, a lunatic's grin besmirching her stunning face.

Katy's realized what the other woman was about to do, for she had already treated her roughly, pushing her back down against the pillows when she had tried to rise, Nell's hand hard against her forehead, fingers clawed into her hair. The therapist had protested and received a vicious slap

275

across the mouth for the trouble; she tasted blood from a split lip and Nell's eyes only gleamed all the more. It was as if having submitted to the woman's seduction and indeed, taking a more than willing part in the loveplay, Nell considered Katy to be her chattel, her 'bitch', there only to receive whatever was dealt her. Well, Katy was nobody's harlot and was not about to let her body be defiled in the abhorrent way Nell Quick intended: it had been abused enough in their frenzied lovemaking.

As the clenched fist approached her exposed vagina, its move slow and deliberate, Katy bent one knee and kicked out at the other woman. The blow took Nell by surprise, almost knocking her off the end of the bed, and before she could recover, the therapist was scrambling to her own knees, one hand unconsciously yanking down the T-shirt still shrugged up over her breasts. Despite being a little overweight, Katy Budd was a fit girl, her very profession seeing to that (working with the generally unhealthy or infirm tended to make you more aware of your own body's condition), but there was something about this woman that truly frightened her. She had already felt Nell's strength and now she was witness to the crazed evil in her expression.

Nell had orgasmed with Katy, but that was not the end of the carnality for her: no, her demands far exceeded a single climax. Perhaps it was her nature always to want more, perhaps her sexual drive was insatiable; but more likely it was because of Nell's malign persuasion, her wish to hurt others and sometimes, when the mood was on her, be hurt herself. Whatever the reason, she was disappointed that Thom Kindred had not returned to find them both, herself and his little blonde-haired darling, in his bed making love. That might have altered his stupidly innocent but oh-so-beguiling expression, *that* might even have tempted him to join in the fun. The disappointment, charged with frustration, made Nell lunge back at the girl, who was on the edge of the bed, catching her flushed cheek with long fingernails, raking thin bloodied trails across the flesh.

Katy screamed. Loudly. It was the shock as much as the fear.

She fell to her knees on the floor, her own hand immediately seeking out the wound to her cheek. She did not wait to examine her fingertips for signs of blood, but tried to get to her feet. Now the offending hand was grabbing her shoulder, pulling her back so that her spine dented the edge of the mattress. Nell beat at her face, smacking her cheeks and temples, tugging at her hair so that she was unable to rise.

'*Leave me alone!*' she managed to shout, but the attack was merciless and she could hear the other woman laughing, a horrible cackling sound. '*Please!*' Katy wailed.

She felt her breasts being violated, cruel hands rubbing them, slapping them, pulling at the nipples that extended once more, this time because of manipulation rather than excitement. Then a hand tugged at her pubis, pulling the light hair there, drawing out some so that she screeched with the pain of it. Fingers dug deep between her parted thighs, this time no passion to them, exploration turning to excavation as the fingers plunged inside her. The violation caused Katy's anger momentarily to outweigh the fright, and she turned and struck back at her assailant who, only minutes before, had been her lover.

Nell was shocked, for the blow smashed into her nose, a splodge of blood jetting out to spoil her upper lip and tip of her chin. She gave a startled shriek, but immediately went after the girl again. Katy had stolen the moment to push herself off the bed and reach for the grey joggers she had so carelessly left just inside the bedroom door.

The dark-haired woman was swift of movement even though stunned by the punch and as she bent to retrieve the tracksuit leggings, Katy felt the rush behind her. She managed to straighten before she struck the door-frame and again she cried out, tears spoiling her already impaired vision. She found herself spun around, as if her pursuer wished to beat her face, but she felt warm moist lips against her own and tasted another's blood in her mouth. Then sharp teeth were biting her lower lip as she writhed in the woman's iron grip, trying to push her assailant away, trying to push *herself* away. Nell was ruthless, though, pinning her against the door-frame with an energy that terrified Katy.

She wrenched her mouth away and spat blood. Her head to one side, she implored, '*Stop it, stop it, please stop it!*'

No use: the attack continued. Nell's hands seemed to be all over her body, beneath the T-shirt, abusing her breasts, pinching the soft flesh of her waist, reaching between her legs again, and all the time laughing, spitting, squealing her lust and rage. Katy still held on to the tracksuit leggings and she kept them between their bodies, hopeless protection, but all she had, a psychological barrier of useless cloth. It was when she felt those invasive fingers with their wicked nails inside her once more that her terror turned to outrage once again.

*Enough!* she told herself. *Enough!*

But it was a reflexive action that saved her for the moment. A space had been created between them by the madwoman as she tried to push her hand further into Katy and the therapist swiftly brought her heel down hard on Nell's bare toes.

Air escaped her attacker in an explosive screech and for a second or two Katy was free. However, the rage was still with her, and that was good, that was positive, for it gave her the strength, the superiority over mindless panic, to bring one fist down hard across the other woman's face. Nell staggered and Katy's arms shot out, her other hand still clutching the joggers, to catch her attacker off balance. She thrust at her with all her might, sending Nell stumbling to the floor by the side of the bed.

Seizing the moment, Katy whirled and ran through the

open doorway, then down the staircase, her heart racing as if to beat her to the front door below. Her bare feet pounded on the boards, which groaned and cracked with the hurried pressure, and when she reached the small landing below, she did not pause, not even when she thought she saw something – a blur of movement only, a small animal perhaps that had crept into the cottage while she and the woman had been otherwise occupied upstairs – dart through the bathroom doorway that was slightly ajar. Besides, the maniacal screaming coming from the bedroom above easily overrode any curiousity she might have had.

Never mind that she was naked from the waist down, Katy flew out of the cottage on to the cracked path, spitting blood as she went, small stones sticking to the soles of her feet. She felt no pain then, only blind panic – almost literally, for without her spectacles her vision was seriously at fault – and the adrenaline that roared through her body overruled any notions of modesty. Because no one was likely to steal her car in this remote area of the woods, she had left the key in the ignition and gratefully she tore open the driver's door to throw herself inside; with virtually the same action and without waiting to catch her breath she switched on the engine. Then she quickly locked both driver and passenger doors.

There was not enough room in the clearing outside the quaint 'gingerbread' (her first thought on seeing it) cottage, so Katy had to reverse at an angle, go forward to the trees, then reverse again. It was a stilted three-point turn, but at last she was facing the rough lane leading to the main road.

At her second reverse, Katy had glanced back at the cottage, expecting Nell Quick to come chasing out after her, but the path had been empty. She had, however, looked up at the bedroom windows and there was the woman, somehow made pale, ghostly, by sun reflecting on the glass. She appeared to have one hand to her cheek as if soothing the blow she had taken; she also appeared to be grinning. A

279

flurry of wings as a bird took off from the parapet above distracted Katy for a moment, and then she was concentrating on the track ahead, pressing down hard on the VW's accelerator so that wheels spun and stones and small sticks shot up from behind the tyres. The green car roared off through the opening in the woods, with Katy jolting and bouncing inside, her naked buttocks slipping in the seat, loosened hair blown by the breeze coming through the open windows.

She drove fast, trees and branches rushing by on either side, the longer, leafy branches frequently scratching metal and scarring paintwork as she fought to keep control of the vehicle, the steering-wheel jerking violently in her hands each time the wheels struck a particularly deep rut. Even so, as she drove further away from the cottage, her heart still beating crazily, her breath coming and going in short sharp gasps, Katy became aware of her nudity. She slowed the car almost but not quite to a stop, manoeuvring the joggers down her legs, taking swift peeks to see what she was doing, pushing the left foot through first, then releasing the accelerator pedal for an instant to stab her right foot through. The car almost stalled, but she quickly stamped down again and it roared on. Then it was a question of pulling the grey joggers up to her knees, pressing back against the seat so that she could raise herself and slide the clothing all the way up. She did not notice the magpie circling overhead.

The track was difficult to see through the tears she continued to weep – out of anger as much as shame and fear – and her own poor eyesight hardly helped. She knew she would soon be approaching the busy main road that ran past the estate, but she increased speed again, wanting to be as far away from that dreadful woman as quickly as possible. The only other vehicle apart from Thom's Jeep at the cottage had been an old-fashioned bicycle leaning against the wall by the front door, and, assuming it belonged to Nell Quick, Katy could not imagine the woman pursuing her on such a heavy contraption, but still she did not slow the car.

Now though, despite Katy's ongoing panic, recriminations began to burn her again. What had she been thinking of? She wasn't a lesbian, even if there had been that one experience so long ago, so why had she given in so easily to this strange woman? She hadn't drunk or eaten anything, so she couldn't have been drugged with some kind of inhibitions-loosener. Yet she had felt so ... felt so ... *horny*. That was the only word she could think of. She, Katy, had not truly given in to seduction. More correctly, she had submitted to her own suddenly demanding sexual needs, the overriding – the *irresistible* – desire to make love with someone, man or woman, or *something*. She shuddered and wept freely.

*Oh God, how could it have happened?*

*And would Nell Quick boast of it to Thom?* Katy prayed not.

Regardless of her worsening vision, Katy put her foot down even further, the little two-door car's engine revving loudly. The steering-wheel bucked in her hand again as the VW hit ridges of hardened mud and sunk into dips, but she kept going, desperate to be away from that place, realizing despondently that she would never return, not even to see Thom, not even to carry out her professional duties. He would have to make other arrangement.

Katy wiped a hand across her eyes, trying to brush away the wetness there, but she sobbed again and more tears welled. The waistband of her leggings was beneath her hips, but at least she was covered, just a plumpish ridge of belly exposed. She felt uncomfortable, it was difficult to see, but she was not about to stop and calm herself, nor adjust her clothing: her emotions would not allow it.

The junction into the main road was less than fifty yards ahead, although she could not properly see the break in the trees. Only when something large and painted yellow – a high-loader transit van, in fact – blurred past the gap that was fast looming did she realize that she was about to arrive at the main road with possibly heavy traffic. Just before she could jam her foot down hard on the brake pedal, something appeared from nowhere in front of her, a flurry of movement between her and the windscreen.

It was a bird, of course, but Katy was too shocked to realize. It must have been travelling towards her at a good speed to fly through the open side window.

Strong black, blue and white wings flapped at her face and the bird's beak scored bloody lines down her forehead and nose, while feather tips stung her eyes. She tried to fight off the creature, but it was like battling a maelstrom. Katy's screams as she slapped and beat at it with hands and fists and the bird's own harsh squawking filled the car's interior with noise.

Katy continued to thrash out at the maddened thing, forgetting the steering-wheel for the moment, forgetting the footbrake, forgetting she was swiftly approaching the usually busy road. The VW shot from the small lane and into the main thoroughfare, unfortunately just as an articulated 'sheepdog', a carrier loaded with brand new Renault Meganes, fresh from the Continent, bright and gleaming on their treads, was approaching from the right.

Katy Budd had no chance. The vehicle-carrier smashed into her little VW Polo, knocking it a hundred and fifty yards further down the road, straight across a small ditch where it bounced back off trees that were part of the Bracken Estate's woodland, and into the ditch again.

When it did come to rest, concertinaed bonnet rising over the edge of the ditch, the car was no longer recognizable as the model it was deemed to be. And Katy was hardly recognizable as the girl she used to be.

# Chapter : Twenty-Sixth

## MARKER

THEY WALKED around the lake and Jennet led him even further into the forest.

'I never thought I could get lost here,' he remarked, 'but this is something else. I couldn't have come this far when I was a kid.'

'You did, but you were too young to know,' she replied, taking him through a tangle of brambles and undergrowth as if there were some secret path. 'When you did grow older, when you reached an age to understand and remember, she stopped bringing you here.'

'Wait a minute. How d'you know all this? You're younger than me. At least, you seem to be.'

'I am, Thom. Even in your years I am.' She lightly pulled him onwards. 'The story, almost a legend among us now, was passed down. A union between mortal and *faerefolkis* is something we could never forget.'

'Then why didn't she want me to know? Why didn't my mother tell me what she was? Or at least about my father?'

283

'You were too young for the burden. Besides, it seems, she'd made a promise.'

He came up short again. 'A promise? To whom? About what?'

'You'll understand much of it soon. Let's keep walking, Thom. I can only be with you for a certain amount of time.'

He could only brood over the secrecy all these years. Why, when she was alive, had his mother not told him of his father and these fabulous little people who lived in the woods? If she had, as Jennet had claimed, surely he would never have forgotten? *And what did Jennet mean, why could she only stay with him for a certain length of time, where the hell was she taking him?*

Jennet said no more to him for a while. They passed old oaks, venerable elms, sycamores, beech and many more that had grown undisturbed by man in this forest for countless centuries, alongside them new, leafy saplings that provided forage for fallow and roe deer. Animals, birds, insects too, appeared unperturbed by Thom and Jennet's intrusion as they journeyed through this perfect and self-contained eco-system, where each forest layer provided sustenance for every denizen – ground and soil, shrubbery and under-growth, lower and upper canopies. Insects, animals and birds dwelt here in a harmony that today, at least, not even human presence could disrupt. Birds and small animals might feed on insects, some birds on some animals, some animals on some birds, but at this wondrous time for him, there were no sudden scuffles as one species preyed on another, no squawks of birds diving for some juicy beetle, no squeals of rabbits captured by old enemies: today this world seemed at peace.

He continued to catch sight of little people playing among flowering hawthorn, elder, or spindle, none of them shy of him but all of them curious if only in a passing way. At the earthy, blackened end of a thick fallen tree trunk, where twisted roots slowly degenerated, he saw what he had first thought was a nest of termites, but on closer inspection discovered that they were hundreds of tiny faeries playing and bustling about, their frail red wings now giving them the appearance of minute moths or butterflies. He began to wonder just how many different types of *faerefolkis* there might be.

There were still hosts of lights, no more than bright specks in the near-distance, flitting between trees or disappearing into undergrowth caverns, although not as many as he had observed before; in fact, the deeper into the woods that he and Jennet went, the less he saw of both animal and faery.

The great green canopy overhead grew thicker so that in places they made their way in twilight. Silver shafts of light broke through the overhanging branches to speckle the mulch floor, or to highlight certain patches of ferns and wild plants, and in the very deepest parts of the woods they seemed like beacons to Thom, letting him know that the sun still governed the skies. Yet it was cool beneath this leafy pavilion as well as shadowy, the tops of the trees absorbing the sun's heat, a thin breeze below chilling Thom's flesh.

He shivered and wondered how much further they had to go? The girl walked on ahead, her movement graceful, snarled undergrowth no impediment, the sudden duskiness no disincentive, and as he was about to speak she pointed ahead.

'There, Thom,' she said. 'Do you see it?'

He followed her direction with his eyes and saw in the distance a bright oasis of light, a smallish clearing where the trees parted overhead to allow the sun full ingress. It was like a bright jewel in the sun-peppered gloom.

Her steps quickened as though she were eager for him to find out what lay ahead in the clearing and he followed close behind, trying to tread in her footsteps, for she knew the path that was all but invisible to him. Occasionally he stumbled, but hurriedly gathered pace again, feeling an excitement – one that curiously was mixed with dread – rising up in him. His mind had not yet tired of the phenomena brought by the day's events, but undoubtedly the constant shocks, delightful though they were, had been slightly numbed by his own brain defending itself from overload; but now his thoughts were racing once more, his imagination beginning to fly. Jennet had good reason for bringing him to this place, the confidence in her voice had reassured him of that, but so far she had not even hinted at the clearing's mystery. There was a quiver in each breath he took and he felt an unsteadiness in his stride.

She reached the spot that was like a forest grotto well before Thom and turned to wait for him, her lovely, if playful, smile encouraging, enticing. He hurried his steps despite the shaking of his legs and the accelerating beat inside his chest.

'Jennet . . .' he said, but could think of nothing more to add.

'It's all right, Thom.'

The soft-voiced words soothed him. He didn't know why, there was just something in this girl – her beauty, the stillness of her nature when she was quiet like this, the pleasing gentleness of her tone? Maybe it was her mystery, the idea that she was not as others he knew, did not possess the foibles and jealousies, and perhaps pride, so common in humans – something that made him trust her implicitly. He hardly knew her, yet he *knew* he already loved her. What normal and unattached man could fail to fall for one such as this?

He reached her, almost stumbling into the small clearing in his haste and she swiftly reached out to steady him, her movement fluid, her grip surprisingly firm. Like his mother's, he remembered.

The colours in this sun-blessed site were dazzling: bluebells, late-blooming like those close to Little Bracken, mixed with wild orchids, foxglove with balsam, cowslips with dropwort, and others whose names he did not know, a close-confined mixture he would not have believed were he not seeing it with his own eyes. An elder stood proud of the circle of ferns, shrubs with red berries and other trees, a fine, lush example thick with long tooth-edged leaves and creamy-white flowers, as though the soil here was rich in nitrogen – possibly a rabbit warren tunnelled through its roots, or badgers had built their setts nearby. Other elders, mere shrubs though, were in the vicinity, but only this one appeared to have flourished so well.

Thom looked at Jennet questioningly and she pointed once more, this time at the grass a few feet in front of the elder. He noticed the top of a stone or rock among the tall blades. Again he regarded Jennet.

'See for yourself,' she said, and when he went forward she accompanied him. He knelt on both knees before the stone – he could tell now that it had an uneven but generally flattish top – and parted the blades of grass. The stone had straight but roughly hewn sides too.

It was a marker. No, there was chiselled lettering on the rugged front. This was a headstone, for the lettering spelt out a name. It said:

## JONATHAN BLEETH

# Chapter : Twenty-Seventh

# INSIGHT

'SIR RUSSELL'S elder son? The soldier who was killed in Northern Ireland?'

Thom was stunned by the implication of this tribute stone deep in the woodlands of the Bracken Estate. Jennet did not reply to his question; she merely watched him.

'Jonathan Bleeth. You're saying . . . you're saying he was my father . . .?'

At last she spoke. 'It should have been obvious to you.'

'Why? Bethan never spoke of him.'

'Perhaps she thought it best. I can't really say, Thom, I only know the story that's been passed down through the years.'

He looked from her face back at the marker again. 'It isn't possible. She *would* have said. And surely when she died, Sir Russell would have let me know.'

Jennet gave a small shrug. 'Who can understand humans? Come, let's sit down and we'll talk.'

She strolled to the edge of the clearing and sank to the grassy floor, ankles crossed, the broad exposed tendril of a nearby oak at her back.

'Come on, Thom,' she entreated again.

Only after gazing at the rough and inscribed grey stone for several moments as if it, itself, would offer answers to the questions that almost swamped him, did he follow the girl. He dropped to the ground and leaned against the trunk of the oak, wrists on raised knees, eyes gazing back at the marker peeping over the blades of grass.

'Why? Why wouldn't my mother tell me? If I'd known . . .'

What? If he had known, then what? It was a question to which even he had no answer. But Sir Russell must have been aware. At last Thom began to understand why the old man, his mother's employer, had become his patron, sending him off to private school, giving him a small but helpful allowance to get by on. But why hadn't the old man acknowledged Thom for what he was, his grandson? He looked at Jennet uncertainly.

'You *are* telling me Jonathan Bleeth was my father, aren't you? That *is* why you brought me here?'

She nodded.

He was a confusion of emotions, glad at last to have the solution to the mystery that had vexed him for most of his young life. With it came some kind of relief, although the reality was perhaps more perplexing: why had nobody – especially his own mother – explained to him, told him of his heritage? He and Bethan had not been deserted by Jonathan Bleeth; his father had been blown to pieces by an IRA bomb. Why hadn't Sir Russell and Hugo acknowledged him as Jonathan's son? Because he was illegitimate? Was that much shame attached to the label in those days? Surely not? And what about now, when he was a grown man? Was he still to be rejected? It seemed so.

'*Godamnit!*' he said with force and Jennet reached out to touch his arm.

289

'Try to forgive her, Thom. Bethan must have had her reasons.'

'Oh I don't blame my mother. You're right, she must have had her reasons. She could never have kept the truth from me otherwise. But why didn't anyone else let me know?'

He thought of Hugo. Had his lifelong friend been aware all this time, or was it a secret kept from him too? In all the years Thom had known him, Hugo had never alluded to the possibility that they were kin of sorts, even if not in name. Thom tore a clump of grass from the soil and scattered it. Why? What was the purpose? Was Sir Russell really that upset at having a bastard grandson? Were his values still so set in the past?

As if having read his mind, Jennet said: 'I'm told they were married right here, Thom, in this part of the woods. A *faerefolkis* ceremony.'

'Then he, Jonathan Bleeth, knew about Bethan, knew where she had come from?'

'She was almost entirely human when she was with him. That's the way of it, it's faery law.'

'But he knew what she once was?'

'Of course. They met by the lake, Thom. Your father called to the undines and it was Bethan who came.'

A quick shake of his head. 'I don't understand. How could he know?'

'Who do you think owned the Portal Book in the cottage? And all the others you still have not bothered to look at since your return?'

'They belonged to Jonathan Bleeth?'

'As owner of the cottage, yes.'

'Bethan used to read stories from them to me.'

'And now you think they were only stories, faerytales to keep you amused.' She laughed and it was charming, not aimed at him. 'They were history, silly, and pictures and stories are always being added. The book is never-ending.'

290

At once, she became grave. 'Every master or mistress of Little Bracken has inherited the Portal Book and your father spent most of his time there, away from the big place, away from your grandfather. Weren't you aware that Jonathan Bleeth lived at the cottage from the age of sixteen, as soon as his father allowed it? And before that, even as a child, he was ever there, reading the books, seeking the faeries. It was the Portal, itself, that told him of us. Don't you see, Thom? Little Bracken has always been a place of magic.'

He reflected, thought of so many things, so many occasions that had been normal to him at the time, but now, given this new-found knowledge, could be explained as little pieces of magic. The time he had badly cut his knee falling from a tree he had been warned not to climb: Bethan had spread some sweet-smelling salve over the wound, gently squeezing the two sides of the deep tear together for a few moments; when she had let go, there had been no pain and the flesh had sealed over – the next day there hadn't even been a mark. In fact, he couldn't ever remember having seen a doctor or nurse as a child; all his ills – headaches, fevers, tummy aches, the normal kid things – all had been cured or 'sent on their troublesome way', as Bethan would tell him, by Bethan herself. He remembered the animals that had come through the always open doorway to the cottage, from young deer to squirrels, birds to butterflies; even the shyest of all creatures, the badger had found its way inside, unafraid, curious, and only sometimes hungry. How had he forgotten?

The cold winter evenings they had huddled together before the blazing fire in the old range, when Bethan had explained faery folklore to him, read him stories, parables you might even call them, from the big book and others; those summer nights, windows wide to allow in the slightest breeze, with tales of dragons and witches, themes to excite, sometimes to scare badly, but stories that always had happy, safe endings. And then, a few years older, the serious explanations of conjuring and enchantment, sorcery and magic, of bewitchment and potions, the natural medicines and the ancient laws of the *faerefolkis*, his young mind filled with so many things, so many treasures. How had he forgotten it all? *Why could he remember so much now?*

But yet another question begged. 'If Jonathan Bleeth was the kind of man who believed . . .'

'Believed in us, we the *faerefolkis*?' she finished for him, shaking her head at his hesitation. 'It was in his nature to believe, as it is in many other humans. As it is in yours.'

'But he became a soldier. That's what I can't figure. If he had the sensitivity – and I assume that's what it takes—'

'Among many other qualities, yes.'

'Then why would he become a man of war?'

'He didn't. He became a man of peace. His intention was for the good, Thom. He never took up arms to kill people, but to protect them.'

'By your own words you weren't even around. How could you know all this?'

'From Rigwit. He and Jonathan were great friends.'

The keeper of the cottage. Thom wondered just how long the size-changing elf had been around.

'Rigwit has told me much since we knew you'd be returning here.'

'You were aware that I was coming back? I didn't know myself until a few weeks ago.'

'It was predestined. It's why the cottage never deteriorated in its emptiness. We knew of your illness and we knew you would choose to recover here in the place that was always safe for you.'

'I was hundreds of miles away. How could you know about my stroke?'

'It still hasn't sunk in, has it? You're part of us, Thom. Not properly, you'll never be *one* of us, but you are linked. And there is another reason, but I don't quite understand it myself yet. It will evolve though, in time it will come through.'

A butterfly, wings of blue and gold settled on her shoulder. It spread those wings, as if proud of their regality, then fluttered away, its presence, its elegance made known.

'Rigwit told me that Jonathan was forced to make a choice by his father. Unless he took up a worthy profession, then Little Bracken would be destroyed. His father wanted him to prove himself a man, leave all "fancy notions and blithering books and nature study behind".'

Jennet's voice had suddenly lowered, become gruff, and the image of the formidable Sir Russell was sharp in Thom's mind. It was almost as if she had magically taken him back to the moment of father-son confrontation, for not only could he clearly see Sir Russell, almost as if he were standing there before him in the forest, but he visualized another, a younger, taller man, someone who resembled Thom himself . . .

'You have a younger brother,' Jennet's *other* voice was saying. 'You must be an example to him. No more day-dreaming in that bloody place. Take up a profession, or I'll have it torn down. It was never used for any good purpose anyway, nearly always tenanted by some mistress or other of whoever was the landowner at the time. I've never liked Little Bracken, can't stand its atmosphere. The choice is yours, Jonathan, but remember you have a half-brother now who will eventually look up to you. Show him a good example, make me proud . . .'

'. . . Make me proud.' It was Jennet's voice again, sweetly husky, light and somehow reassuring.

The vision was gone and now he doubted there had been one, or even that her tone and timbre had changed. She had put pictures into his mind, that was all, perhaps his enchantment with her making it an easy task.

'So he chose the services,' Thom found himself saying as he continued to rationalize his latest experience. 'I suppose the most macho profession he could think of, just to impress the old man.'

'No. He became a soldier because he wanted to protect people. Rigwit told me that your father—'

*My father. Jonathan Bleeth was my father.* It was a shock, yet surprisingly easy for Thom to accept.

'—intended to gain experience as a soldier, then join another force, some kind of worldwide army whose sole purpose is to act as a peacemaker in other countries' wars.'

'The UN,' he said.

She shrugged. 'I think it's something like that.'

'And instead he got blown to pieces in Northern Ireland.'

'Trying to protect others. He was a brave man, Thom, a good man.'

'But when – *how* – did he meet my mother?'

'Just before he left to take up his duties as a soldier. He'd believed in us for years and it was as if we, ourselves, realized we had little time remaining if we were to make contact. It's very rare that we choose to do so, but sometimes association with certain humans is beneficial to both sides. Sometimes we need someone like you.'

'Me? What have I got to do with all this?'

'You are the result of Jonathan and Bethan's bonding.'

'You mean it was planned just so that I could come along years later and help you in some way?' He was shaking his head in disbelief.

'Not planned, never planned. Foreseen, you might say. There is a difference.'

'But what can I do?'

'That we don't know. But there is a course for everything no matter how inconsequential some actions or events might seem.' She leaned forward and the flimsy material of her clothing hung loose, exposing her small but perfectly-shaped breasts. He had difficulty in checking his gaze, had to force it back to her eyes. 'Jonathan first gained access to us,' she was saying, 'through Rigwit, who showed him how to use the Portal Book. The undines cannot use the portal, it's only for those whose form is small and constant, but he was guided to the lake where he met Bethan.'

'You used Jonathan Bleeth for some future purpose? Is that what you're saying?'

She sighed, but remained gentle with him. 'Haven't you learned anything, Thom? Aren't you listening to my words, is your heart so closed to us? We do not use anyone, certainly not humans. We leave that to the bad *faerefolkis*, the black magicians and those you call wiccans or worlocks. Jonathan and Bethan's secret marriage was always meant to be, it was an association that could only work for the benefit of us all, humans and faeries. Without us, without our influence on nature itself, your world would soon be over, overwhelmed by the elements and the physical earth you abuse so much. Oh, you think you're very clever, you imagine you're learning to control nature itself with your technology, but you have no idea how wrong you are. Even when you feel you have complete power over the elements and the environment, you will not even be half-way there. You will eventually discover that you need our help. You'll discover that your yearning for material things and that the subjection of others is not the way, that it's these very faults that have led you away from us. Eventually – and this is our greatest hope – you will understand the emptiness of such desires and ambitions and begin to communicate with us once more.'

All this spoken in the same soft manner, nothing strident or chiding, nothing bitter, about her tone.

'Jesus . . .' he said.

'You both have something in common.'

'What?'

'The Nazarene was a carpenter too.'

'Well, there the similarity ends.'

'Not necessarily.'

The enigma of her comparison was breathtaking, for it

was not a mild aside, but Thom was already too perplexed to comprehend or question Jennet further. They both lapsed into silence.

Soon, wearied by images and words, and suddenly worn out by the long walk, Thom's eyes began to close. Perhaps the effect of Rigwit's tonic and the magical powder Jennet had blown into his face and the energy-giving lights were beginning to wear off. He lay down by the oak and slept.

---

Thom awoke and the sleep had been good, for it had been dreamless; nothing at all had disturbed his subconscious.

The angle of the sun had altered so that he found himself in shade; he was still warm though, comfortably so. And as he opened his eyes he realized he did not lay on the soft, mulch-covered earth alone. Jennet was nestled into him.

He was startled, but it was oh-so-pleasant, so reassuring. She still slept, her breathing shallow, her lips opened slightly. He could see the tips of gently pointed teeth.

She faced him and Thom took the opportunity to study her elfin face. The tilt of her dark lashes was somehow beguiling, as if they alone spoke of her other-worldliness. Her skin was very pale, but had a pinkish hue to it, and it was incredibly smooth and unblemished, somehow pure. Even in repose, the line of her neck was graceful and her hands, laid flat before her face, were long, the fingers slender and pointed at their tips. Her golden hair spread over the ground beneath her head like some untidy but soft blanket, and her knees were raised, one resting on the other. She was exquisite and Thom felt a stirring inside that, at this moment, was spiritual rather than sexual.

The questions still begged, but he was able to suppress them for now, while he drank in her presence. She was so *real*, beyond hallucination. Yet she claimed to be of the faeries themselves, a mythical being that the world today had little time for, save for tales told to children. And in their innocence, the children believed, so was that the key? Did you have to be pure of heart – pure of soul, Jennet might say – for these mystical creatures to take on form, become visible to human eyes? Yet he was no child and certainly no innocent. Even now he could feel desire awakening in him again, creeping through his body, arousing nerve endings, creating sensual sensations, quickening his blood flow, more questions easily put aside.

Tentatively, his fingertips touched her pale cheek and, like before, he felt a current run through them, a small shock that quickly encompassed his entire body. Perhaps he *had* doubted his own vision, perhaps he needed to touch her warm flesh to assert the reality; perhaps he just needed contact to placate his physical feelings.

Her eyes flickered open and he gasped at their silver-violet brightness once more. The pupils dilated when she saw him, blooming deep and dark, so that the irises shrank, their vivid colour subjugated a little.

'Thom . . .?' she murmured, aware of his hand on her cheek. She smiled and her fingers curled around his hand, pressing it firmly against her.

He remembered when he had first set eyes on her by the lake, the act she was committing upon herself, her unselfconscious audaciousness when she must have realized he was watching. Her pallid skin, her small breasts, her total lack of inhibition: could he be blamed for wanting her now that she was here, lying so near to him, close enough to feel the warmth of her breath on his face, close enough to touch like this . . .

He was almost afraid, but when he leaned his head towards hers, she came forward, met him half-way. Their lips touched and it was soft, hesitant, an exploration rather than bold contact. He tasted her, for her mouth was moist and sweet, momentarily withdrawing an inch or so, as if to seek unspoken permission. The permission came with her returned kiss, her own pressure against his, and this time the contact was firmer, more ardent.

Her mouth opened and he felt the ridges of those softly pointed teeth bite tenderly into his lower lip, nothing harsh or aggressive about the deed, rather an invitation to him, letting him know her passion matched his.

Thom's free arm swept down to the small of her back to bring her forward so that their bodies were in communion, pressed tight against each other's, hips to hips, breasts to chest. His fervour roared inside him, his hunger made him tremble, for it had been a long time since he had made such contact with any woman; yet a fear also nagged at him, for he could not know how the illness had affected capability. Had the stroke blunted his sexual drive? The growing hardness between his legs told him it hadn't, but desire was one thing, performance another. Thom despised himself for the doubts, but these were soon swept away by their mutual passion.

Jennet's hands touched his face, his neck, his shoulders, her fingers sliding beneath the short sleeves of the T-shirt to explore hidden flesh, the mere sensation of that alone causing Thom to catch his breath. And when the hand glanced down his spine to rest a moment before pulling him even tighter against her, he gave out a soft moan. Her legs parted and his thigh pushed into the gap.

He whispered her name and she cried out his.

*Dear God*, he thought, *this can't be happening*... But it was and it was overwhelming, all doubts of his ability easily vanquished by the growing ardour of their caresses.

Their kisses varied from harsh to tender and he felt a heated whiteness in his mind, one that usually came with climax and never before, never as this. Their tongues touched, their lips crushed each other's before drawing back to jab and peck, to moisten and savour, fervour giving way to soft murmurings, gentle responses, and then back again to more passionate kissing and fondlings. He felt his own wetness, a rising that would soon break loose and he was now concerned that it would be over all too quickly, but it was Jennet who calmed him.

'Wait, Thom,' she whispered close to his ear.

She pulled herself away and sat up. Lest he should mistake the movement, Jennet quickly reached for the hem of his T-shirt, tugging it up over his body and raised arms. Although they were in the shadow of the oak it was not deep shade and the air was warm against his bare skin; the sense of freedom he felt there in this secret little grotto deep in the forest was intoxicating. He reached for Jennet again, wanting to hold her in his arms and kiss her, to tell her of feelings that went beyond mere desire, but she held a hand against his chest.

Without speaking she unbuttoned the top of his jeans, then helped him pull them off. For the first time that morning, he realized he wore no shoes. As a child he had invariably played in the woods with nothing on his feet and the soles had soon hardened; but now he was surprised he'd felt nothing treading through the usual woodland debris of twigs, fallen acorns, stones. Entirely naked, he looked back at Jennet as she stood and slowly removed her only garment.

The sight of her slender body and cascading golden hair falling almost to her waist left him in awe.

As already observed, there was no body hair to conceal the delicate cleft between her legs and her small breasts stood proud, pink nipples erect. She sank to her knees, her legs parting so that nothing was concealed and he reached a tremulous hand forward to touch between her thighs. She was wet, the lips there open to him, and the thrill was almost unbearable.

He said her name again as he brought his whole body closer to kneel before her, his eyes gazing into hers, his body losing its shiver as she calmed him once more, this time just with her look.

'I love you, Thom,' she said quietly and his heart – his soul – soared again.

'But you don't know . . .' he found himself saying, as if unable to believe her words.

'I do know you,' she said. 'I know you're good and I know you're here to help us.'

He shook his head, unwilling to lose the mood, yet wanting desperately to be honest with her. 'What can I possibly do for you, Jennet? Until a couple of days ago I didn't even believe in the existence of your kind. Frankly, I'm not even sure that everything that's happened, including right now, isn't just some grand illusion brought about by damaged brain cells.'

She gave a little laugh. 'You think you're going mad? When I touch you here . . .' she leaned forward to touch his chest, her fingers pressing a nipple, and he almost yelped with the pleasure '. . . you think you're imagining it? And here . . .' she touched his stomach just above his groin and he drew in a sharp breath '. . . and here . . .' her fingers encircled his engorged penis and he almost cried out with the ecstasy of it. 'You think it's all in your mind, Thom?

'Jennet . . .'

'Yes?' Her smile was teasing. And so was her stroking.

'Jennet, this is all impossible.'

'Yes, Thom.'

'I mean, the faeries and elves, and witches and monsters, and tame animals . . .'

'And making love with an undine?' She continued to stroke him, a soft, easy movement that made him shudder with delight.

'Yeah,' he said, between short breaths. 'Impossible. But then . . .' his turn to smile at her '. . . to hell with impossible.'

He grabbed her by the shoulders and pulled her to him, his mouth crushing hers with wild, excited kisses that she returned just as enthusiastically, laughing when together they fell to the forest floor, their hands feeling each other, their lips seeking other parts – shoulders, breasts, any part of each other's body that was accessible.

She squealed when his tongue made circles around her nipple, and it was with joy; and he groaned when her tongue ran down his chest to his stomach, to linger in his navel, before journeying back up to his mouth. Once more, his hand reached between her legs, this time his fingers entering and becoming moist with her juices. It was Jennet's turn to groan and she arched her neck in a delirium, the feel of his strong fingers inside her wonderful. The tips of her own fingers dug into his back as she pulled him over on top of her, and then he was guiding himself into her, both of them murmuring each other's name and giving out small moans.

Although she was small in stature, his entry was easy and smooth, as though their body parts had been made for each other's, measured and apportioned by whomever planned such things – a silly notion that ran through Thom's head as he thrust so deeply and so effortlessly. She tensed beneath him, then relaxed with a pleased sigh. His hand found her breast and his mouth quickly followed, his back arched, their stomachs apart for a moment as she pulled at his neck, forcing his head down on her. His tongue smothered the nipple there, wetting it, making it grow hard, and when he withdrew his lips he blew air on to the moistened tip so that it swelled, grew even more proud of the fleshly little mound. Thom nuzzled his way over to the other breast to repeat the act and her hips writhed beneath his as she moaned and sighed and gave out small gasps as though she were short of air.

Resting his belly on hers again, Thom moved with her rhythm, the thrusts sometimes long, sometimes shallow, and her hips moved sometimes with him, other times against. Her hands were never still, palms gliding over his back constantly before moving to his buttocks, the backs of his thighs, pulling at him, pressing his flesh, urging deeper entry, then pushing him back, but never too far, never allowing him to leave her completely.

They kissed, and he had to bend his neck for their lips to meet, his hands at her waist, his knee digging into the soft earth; the kiss was emotional for both of them, not just affected by their mutual passion, although, in truth, that was part of it. Thom had never loved another before, not in this way. Certainly there had been girlfriends, lovers, but while his affection had always been sincere, he had never been *in* love with any of them. Now this. Falling fast, even instinctively, with someone who was from another realm. An undine she called herself. As was his mother, Bethan. How *could* it be true? Yet he knew, he just *knew*, that it was. And he gave himself up to it.

Jennet was whispering his name in between kisses, imploring him for more, for *all* he had to give her, and he was not about to deny her. He lunged into her, drew back, lunged again, and suddenly had no concern about anything: just being with her, inside her like this, was so intoxicating that stamina was no longer a problem and neither were questions about her very existence. It was … it was … *magical*. It was magical and for a moment he could not be sure if it was because of the circumstances, the forest environment, her elfin beauty, her uniqueness, or if it was because of love, genuine, startling, newfound love. He quickly realized it was for all these reasons, but it was what he felt in his heart – *no*, he chided himself, remembering her words, in his *soul* – that prevailed above all others. As he plunged even deeper into her, into this mystical girl who had taken on human or part-human form for him alone, he felt his whole *being* sink with his body, as though her physical opening was the entrance to her realm.

And that was when the magic really began.

He was aware of his own presence there in the forest glade, aware of his own skin as it were, but part of him had left, perhaps his persona, had travelled further than his intellect had ever before travelled, even in sleep, even in his near-death experience a few months earlier. This was a path journeyed by invitation only, for it took him into dimensions where even dreams did not belong. He was among stars and planets, a universe of white whose constellations glittered all colours and shades, many of those shinings surely never witnessed by mortal man before. Gases hung like gauze or sheer lace – except they were millions of miles in length – swirling among the stars in incredible ever-shifting patterns. There were other smaller shapes in the whiteness, gossamer forms that he instinctively knew were souls – spectres would have been the wrong word, for these were not apparitions, they were real entities, forces that were individual, yet somehow making up the whole.

And he, Thom Kindred, for a few brief moments that felt like eternity (for he sensed there was no time here in this place) floated among them, joined them in their euphoric exaltations, feeling their warmth, their peace, their quietude. But most of all he felt their devotion.

Then, having glimpsed the rapture, he hurtled back to the physical, back to the forest, back to the arms of Jennet, and he was stunned by the moment, stunned but not mystified, for he knew what he had witnessed. He knew he had been allowed a glimpse, a privileged insight, of something profound. Thom immediately understood that this had been Jennet's gift to him, that she had taken him to this place, and as tears dampened his eyes, he realized it was not casual, it had some future purpose and it was this that became the new mystery.

'Jennet . . .' he began to say, wondering about its significance.

'Hush, Thom.' She soothed his neck, his cheek, for he had lifted his face from hers so that he could study her eyes. 'No need for words. Just feel now, Thom. Let your mind and body soar again but together this time.'

303

And he did. He returned to the physical once more, driving into her, softly at first, then with more and more abandonment. And that was when the faeries joined them.

At first, he just felt their lightness on his bare back, on the flesh of his arms and legs, a brushing sensation that aroused more nerve endings that until then had remained dormant, not part of the lovemaking. These subtle touchings caused him to shiver, but it was with pleasure, as if his skin were exposed to tiny feathers, the faery wings beating against him and the vibrations of minuscule bodies that were comprised of pure energy prickling his flesh in a kind of tormenting bliss. He moaned with the delectation of it all and Jennet joined in with her own sighs of delight, for the exposed parts of her body were receiving similar attention.

Thom felt the turmoil inside his groin racing towards its peak; it felt as if everything inside his body, every sinew, nerve and all its juices, were being drawn to one central point, to congress and reach a climax that would release incredible energy, power even, in a union that was as giving as it was taking.

He began to cry out loudly, the feeling mounting inside beyond anything he had ever experienced, and Jennet's slender legs closed around him, hugging him tight without restricting his movement. His fingers dug into the forest floor, churning the earth, tearing the grass, as Jennet raised her hips towards him, almost lifting his body, her strength surprising. Thom burrowed, pushing himself into what seemed like endless depths, unaware that he filled her, that she felt there was no more she could take even though she pleaded for more as she consumed every inch of him.

The great tide began its surge and Thom almost screamed with its intensity; and as it came, as his juices broke free to pour into her, Jennet did scream, a shuddering sound that sent birds from branches into the air, caused animals in other parts of the woods to pause and look towards its source, drove the faeries surrounding the two naked writhing bodies into a last wild frenzy, their vibrancy brightening the shaded parts of the glade.

And with the mutual orgasm and the magic – *'The strongest magic of all,'* Jennet had whispered breathlessly to him – that was involved with it, combining in creating an ejaculation that was both spiritual and physical, senses, thoughts and feelings joining in one brilliant illumination of perception, Thom once again glimpsed the rapture of before and understood that this vision was the death experience. He had briefly perceived the beginning of life's end, the first stage of a new yet timeless and inevitable journey for his kind and every kind, an image of what was to come.

He had glimpsed the next doorway and the message was clear: there was so much more beyond.

# Chapter : Twenty-Eighth

## THE WRECK

THERE WAS something wrong with the cottage, but he could not tell what it was. Thom paused at the edge of the clearing, thick woodland at his back and all around. From where he stood he could see the other path that led to Castle Bracken, a bed of shaded bluebells crossing it, and on his left was the wider, rutted lane leading to the main road. His Jeep was parked in front of the cottage; nothing wrong there. The front door to Little Bracken was open, but then he was sure he had left it that way when he had followed Jennet into the woods earlier that day.

It was late afternoon now and Thom was tired from walking, from making love with Jennet, from all the new thoughts that besieged his mind. Reluctantly, he had left Jennet by the lake, their parting sadly sweet in the way of new-found lovers. He had wanted her to return to Little Bracken with him, but she had said it was too soon, she could not be free of the lake just yet, that nothing could be rushed. If he had been confused and mystified before this day, his thoughts were now in total disarray, some answers only leading to more questions, some questions – such as why Jennet believed he had returned to Bracken to help the *faerefolkis*, or why his mother had made him forget everything he had learned of them as child – remaining unanswerable, even by Jennet herself.

However, none of this bothered Thom too much on this warm late afternoon, for his day had been filled with extraordinary things, with love and insights into other realms that a few days ago he would have thought impossible. His whole concept of life – and death had been irrevocably changed and there was no going back, no retreat into the normal world of reason and commonplace things.

He frowned as he looked across the clearing at the turreted cottage. What was it, what was wrong? The place had an air about it that was cold – not lifeless, but somehow hostile, as if its very nature had changed. Maybe it was nothing. Maybe his nerves were on edge because of what had happened earlier. Or maybe *he*, himself, had changed a little – maybe circumstances had made him more perceptive. There was something wrong, he could feel it in his marrow.

Cautiously, he crossed the clearing, approaching Little Bracken as if it were some strange new place to him, one that held danger within. Although tired, his senses became alert and even his vision seemed to sharpen. He passed by the Jeep, glanced inside, checked no one lurked there. It was empty.

When he reached the short cracked flagstone path, grass growing through the breaks, he stopped once more and looked towards the cottage door. An area of kitchen was visible inside and all seemed normal. Yet still he felt a coldness about the place.

Then he saw the spots of blood on the stone path before him. A deep crimson colour as if almost dried out.

Thom went to the first stains and knelt by them, examining them closely without touching to feel their viscosity.

307

There were more spots on the next flagstone, and the next, a trail in fact, as if someone had walked or run along the path, perhaps fleeing from something inside the cottage. He looked back at the open door again.

What if that something was still inside?

He thought of the night creature that had tried to steal his fluids, the succubus. Was it that, a night – a *nightmare* – creature, a monster that could only skulk in the hours of darkness? Maybe something else had been sent against him, another monster commissioned, so he was led to believe, by Nell Quick. Even as he felt the dread, another thought struck him. Why did he think the blood was leading away from the cottage? Why couldn't it be leading into Little Bracken? Perhaps someone had been injured in the woods and had sought refuge inside. It might even be old Eric Pimlet, seeking his help after some kind of accident. Eric had a good few years behind him now, was well beyond retirement age, his legs not as strong and steady as they once were. That had to be it.

Thom rose to his feet and went warily, despite his sound reasoning, towards the front door, avoiding the blood on the flat stones. When he reached the open doorway he paused again, one foot on the step, a hand on the door's stout frame, unsure whether to call out or not before entering. He wouldn't want to alarm anyone inside nor alert an intruder. Mentally shrugging, he strode in more boldly than he felt.

The kitchen was empty, but there were new flowers resting in the sink. Orchids. He skirted round the table to reach them, his puzzled frown deepening. Who could have brought them in? Rigwit? Had the elf decided to brighten up the place? Thom doubted it, for the little man had shown no such inclination before. He looked down at the pretty flowers in the sink and saw that they had been plucked from the earth whole, tubers and all. But the tubers – the bulbs – had been split open for some reason, the mushy stuff inside oozing out, much of it lying in soft gobs in the bottom of the sink and on the draining board. Why would anyone do such a thing? *Who* would have done such a thing? Nell Quick immediately came to mind. What was going on here?

'Rigwit!' he called out as he turned to face the room again. 'Are you here, Rigwit? Can you hear me?'

There was no answer, not even the creak of floorboards, the movement of a cupboard door, tiny padding feet. Just the silence, the eerie silence.

Thom looked up at the ceiling and wondered. Could someone be hiding upstairs? Could Nell be up there, waiting for him? He felt anger beginning to burn. Was she playing tricks on him? Or did she have other ideas up there in his bedroom? Did she honestly think she could seduce him now? For Christ's sake . . .

He skirted the table again to get to the open doorway to the stairs, a firmness to his stride. Enough was enough. If it was Nell up there, she could take a hike, the faster the better.

But when he reached the small landing outside the bathroom and broom cupboard, he saw the white trainer on the first step of the spiral staircase, then its mate a few steps further up. Both were pointed forward, as if the person who had discarded them had been ascending rather then descending.

'Katy!' he said aloud. How could he have been so stupid to have forgotten? True, so much had happened that was way out of the ordinary he might have been forgiven for forgetting such a mundane appointment with his therapist, but he should have realized sooner. It had to be Katy, he'd seen her in these white trainers with the blue logo before.

'*Katy?*' This time it was a call. 'Are you up there?' He took the stairs two at a time, using the narrower end of the wedge shape, fingers curling round the centre newel to help hoist himself up. The drag of his left leg slowed him only a little.

Thom rushed into his bedroom and immediately took in

the rumpled bedsheets – he had left the bed unmade that morning, but it had not been as untidy as this – and the white cotton panties lying close by on the floor. There was also more blood near the open door.

For a while, he could only stare, comprehending nothing. Why had Katy been in his bedroom? Had she arrived at the cottage to find no one downstairs, but the front door open wide? Had she thought he might still be in bed and called up to him? On receiving no reply she might have suspected he'd had another, follow-up stroke and gone up to investigate. But why the blood on the floor, the panties by the bed, the tangled sheets? And why the orchids in the kitchen sink? The dread he'd felt before even entering Little Bracken grew even heavier, weighing him down, draining his strength. What the hell was going on?

'*Rigwit!*' he shouted again. '*Can you hear me? You've got to help me, Rigwit?*'

Only that cold foreboding silence still.

'Oh Christ,' he muttered to himself.

Going out on to the landing, he yelled some more, this time for Katy Budd as well as the elf. Before descending, he glanced back into the bedroom, looking around the walls, the windows, the furniture, as if for some clue, taking in the panties, the speckles of blood on the floor, even the rumpled bed again. What did it mean? Had someone attacked Katy when she'd arrived for their appointment, some stranger who'd wandered in from the woods? But wait, hadn't Katy left her card with him? It had her home number and cell phone number. He was about to return to the bedroom for his own mobile phone left on the sideboard/dressing table when a noise caused him to hesitate.

He listened, holding his breath. It came again, a snuffling, whimpering sound. Thom held on to the centre post and peered down the staircase, stretching forward to see around the bend. Once more, he listened. The sound. A quiet weeping. And it came from above, not below. Thom pushed himself back on to the landing, the old boards creaking under his bare feet.

'Katy? Is that you up there?' he called, this time his voice softer.

He stepped towards the second flight of winding stairs, took a few steps up, treading lightly lest the boards creak again.

'Katy?'

Thom peered into the gloom of the false belltower, trying to see through the shadowy rafters that criss-crossed the open space there. He thought he caught sight of a tiny face peering down at him, but it was gone in an instant, ducking behind a stout descending beam.

'Rigwit – it's you, isn't it?' Thom tried to keep his voice level, afraid he might alarm the little elf, who seemed scared enough already. 'It's me – Thom. What's wrong, why are you hiding up there?'

Still there was no reply and Thom climbed, going to the landing just outside the rooftop door. From there he had a clearer view of the fake belltower's interior, but it was still too dark and the beams too thick to see if a figure lurked there.

He softened his tone even more, speaking soothingly, coaxingly. 'Come on, Rigwit. You know me. It's Thom, Thom Kindred. No one's going to hurt you.'

There was movement among the shadows. The little face appeared again.

'*Shecomeshecomeshecome,didbadbadthings!*'

'Take it easy.' Despite the frustration, Thom kept his voice placid. 'I can't understand you when you talk so fast. Look, come down, let me look at you. It helps me understand your words.'

The elf was reluctant, but did as he was bid, swinging first from a crossbeam, then sliding down the centre post.

When he arrived at Thom's feet he was shivering so fiercely Thom thought he might be having a seizure. He quickly knelt before Rigwit and took him gently by the shoulders.

'*Turribleturriblethings,shedidshedid!*'

'Try and calm yourself,' Thom urged. 'I need to know what you're saying.'

Eyes wide – as wide as tilted eyes could be – Rigwit stiffened, forcing himself to gain control. He continued to shiver, but he began to speak a language Thom could comprehend.

'She-did-terrible-things.'

'Who did, Rigwit? The lady with blonde . . . with light-coloured hair?'

Rigwit shook his head violently, but bravely kept control. He was growing smaller before Thom's eyes though.

'Not Katy, not the fair-haired lady?' Thom willed Rigwit not to shrink any more and for the moment, it seemed to work. 'Who, then?' he asked, but was sure he already knew.

'The *hellhagge*,' Rigwit said with a sob in his voice. 'The *hellhagge* did bad things to the other lady.'

---

Thom's face was set grim as he climbed into the black Cherokee Jeep, his tiredness forgotten. He now wore soft boots and had pulled on a V-necked sweater over his T-shirt. He switched on the engine, reversing a little, then brought the Jeep round in one practised sweep into the lane leading towards the main road. He pressed down on the accelerator, picking up speed, going as fast as the deeply rutted track would allow.

A few minutes before he had tried calling Katy Budd on his cell phone, tapping in both her home number, and then her mobile, but, as he already knew, he was in a bad area for reception and all he got was heavy static. It occurred to him that if there was no link mast in the vicinity there probably should have been nothing at all, not even interference, but now wasn't the time to wonder about it. What Rigwit had told him had shocked him and although the elf had not used the word 'rape' – perhaps there was no such word in his vocabulary – from his description of events in the cottage that morning, rape was what it had amounted to. Female rape of another female. Weird, degenerate – and evil.

Rigwit had spied on the two women as they had shredded the orchid bulbs between them, the juices of the root a powerful love potion apparently, and Thom had began to understand. Nell Quick had brought the flowers to the cottage expecting to find him all alone. She'd found Katy Budd instead. But why use the extract from the orchid on the physiotherapist when it was meant for him? If it was her devious way of collecting his seed, some kind of aphrodisiac to turn him on, why use it on Katy? It didn't make sense. But then, what did make sense since he'd returned to Bracken? It could be that Nell Quick swung both ways as well as being an opportunist. She'd had the aphrodisiac on hand (so to speak), he hadn't been home, and Katy Budd had turned up out of the blue. Could Nell really be that crazy, that sick? Something told Thom she could.

Leafy branches lightly brushed the side of the Jeep as he sped along the narrow unmade lane and his hands remained firm on the steering-wheel as it tried to twist in his grip. He was angry, angry that the woman, whatever her gripe was with him, could use an innocent like Katy Budd in this way, and angry that someone who, until a few days ago, had been a complete stranger, could bear such evil intent towards him. What the hell had *he* ever done to Nell Quick? Had it anything to do with his new-found friendship with the little people, the *faerefolkis* who inhabited the Bracken Estate's woods? According to storybooks, weren't witches supposed to be the mortal enemy of faeries? He shook his head, still making no sense of it, bewilderment feeding the anger. There was only one way to find out and that was to confront the lady herself.

Yet another thought struck him. Hugo! Was his friend aware of the true nature of this woman? Thom was sure there was more to their relationship than employer and nurse – he'd sensed a frisson of some kind between them when he first saw them together – but was Nell using Hugo in some way? Thom's eyes narrowed as he continued to explore this fresh avenue. Hugo was single and the heir to a considerable fortune, even if these days it mostly amounted to the value of real estate. And what real estate! Castle Bracken and all its land, thousands of acres of pastures and woodland. Even if only small pockets of it were sold off, it would easily provide wealth to run the rest of the estate. And although Sir Russell's various business ventures were no longer the source of high revenue that they once were, selling his personal shares in them would yield sizeable capital. But again, what had this to do with Thom, why should he be any part of Nell Quick's plans? As an illegitimate grandson to Sir Russell – and not even acknowledged as *that* by the old man! – he was no threat to Hugo's inheritance. Thom thumped the steering-wheel in frustration. Whatever the answers, he had to confront Nell, if only over what she had done to Katy. Then, he would warn Hugo. He'd have no real proof about anything, but his friend surely trusted him enough to take his word. Maybe he was a little bit addled sometimes, but Hugo was no fool. Not a complete one, at any rate.

Up ahead, Thom saw the gap in the crowded woodland that meant he'd nearly reached the main road and he eased off the accelerator pedal, bringing the Jeep down to a safer speed. Traffic seemed even heavier than usual there and he noticed it was also quite slow, passing the gap almost bumper to bumper. He decreased his own speed even more.

When he finally reached the lane's junction with the main thoroughfare, he brought the Jeep to a complete stop, puzzled by the build-up of traffic blocking his way. First he looked right, the direction in which he intended to continue, and saw only the stretch of slow-moving vehicles; but then he glanced left – and froze.

A huge transport-carrier was parked by the roadside, red and white cones placed behind and along its right side, a patrol cop patiently waving on oncoming traffic. But from where Thom sat in the Jeep at the entrance to the lane, he could see beyond the carrier along the verge. A green-coloured car was angled in the ditch, its bonnet and part of its roof caved in as if it had bounced off a tree. He recognized the little two-door Volkswagen immediately.

'Katy!' he said aloud and quickly switched off the Jeep's engine. Then he was out and running – limping – towards the scene of the accident.

The transport-carrier was so close to the roadside's grass verge and ditch that Thom used its length to keep his balance along the uneven ground, careful not to slip into the shallow ditch itself. He saw that the front of the big carrier was badly damaged, but nowhere nearly as badly as the smaller vehicle, whose bonnet and side were completely smashed, although only the front of the roof was crumpled.

'*Katy!*' This time it was an anguished shout, and a figure who had been watching a blue-overalled man attaching a grappling hook beneath the wrecked vehicle, its twisted-iron cable running to the nearby breakdown truck, turned to look in Thom's direction. Another mechanic and a second police-man who were among the group of men hidden, along with the truck driver, from Thom's view by the transport-carrier, also looked towards the sound of his voice, but quickly returned their attention to the job in hand when they saw him.

'It's all right, Thom, it's all over.' Eric Pimlet said as Thom drew near.

He was too stunned to greet the estate manager right away.

'Terrible accident,' Eric said in his gruff burr. 'Poor young girl was badly hurt.'

'Was it Katy Budd?' Thom asked, already aware of the answer as he took in the terrible damage to the green car. Although the VW's rear end was closest to him, he could see that the windscreen was completely smashed and the front of the roof itself so badly dented its metal almost touched the front seats' headrests.

'It was a girl drivin' all right, but I wouldn't know her name. Policeman'll tell you though, he's had to look through her things.'

'It's okay. I know it was her. How badly was she hurt?'

'Can't say, but they tell me they took her out unconscious. The driver of this thing—' Eric pointed a thumb over his shoulder at the front-damaged transport-carrier '—tol' me she was pretty messed up though. They rushed her off to Royal Shrewsbury Hospital, didn't waste no time gettin' her there. Another ambulance took this driver off too, after he'd made a statement to the police, en'all. Had to be treated for shock, poor chap.'

'Did they tell you about the girl?' Thom was still eyeing the wrecked VW as if in shock himself. 'How bad were her injuries?'

'Don't know, Thom. They jus' said she was none too good. I came on it after it had all happened and stuck aroun' so's I could give a hand, bein' the accident occurred on the edge of the estate. Spoke to the driver though, managed to calm him down a bit.' Eric rubbed at his veined nose, then shook his head. 'He still seemed in bit of a daze to me, like he'd banged his head or somethin'. Kept goin' on about a bird.'

Thom at last took his eyes off the wreckage and regarded the gamekeeper curiously.

'Said the car appeared from nowhere, too late for him to stop,' Eric went on. 'Must've come out the lane to your place, Thom. One of your lady friends, was it? Someone up from London?'

Thom gave a quick shake of his head. 'What did you

mean, Eric? When you said the driver was talking about a bird?'

'Oh, I think he was just a bit confused, like. As I say, he must've taken a knock on the head. Couldn't make much sense of him, to be honest.'

'But tell me what he said.'

The old gamekeeper huffed, and shook his head yet again. 'He said that after the crash, when the other car had been pushed down the road and into that there ditch, he saw a bird, a black and white bird, he said, fly out from the windscreen. I reckon he was mistaken. I reckon if there was a bird, it was already in the ditch lookin' for worms or grubs, an' it flew up from underneath the car. I mean, it's not likely she'd be carryin' a magpie as a passenger, is it? Not likely at all.'

# Chapter : Twenty-Ninth

## OF BANES/SPELLS, & DECEPTIONS

HUGO HAD gone to the plate-glass windows of his father's bedchamber at the top of Castle Bracken, closing all the curtains so that the evening sun burned against their thick material. The spacious but now darkened room suddenly seemed claustrophobic, the air somehow heavier, and he felt his father's watery, old-ivory eyes watching him over the plastic oxygen mask, the invalid, as usual, propped up by pillows as he lay wasting away on the four-poster. He thought he detected momentary panic in them.

'Just giving you some shade,' Hugo called across the room.

Hugo grimaced at the sound of the laboured breathing in the shadowy room, for the initial sharp intake of air was like a grasp at life itself, the drawn-out rattling exhalation like final submission to the inevitable. A beastly noise.

'*Uuh – aaarrrghhhh . . .*'

Grasp, submit; grasp, submit . . .

And so on it went.

'You need to sleep, Father,' he called out again, wondering if the old boy even understood his words these days. Sometimes he thought he caught a spark of intelligence in those vapid eyes, but mostly Sir Russell continued to stare blankly, observing without reaction or recognition. And yet at other times, when his breathing was regular and there was no need for pure oxygen, Sir Russell could appear quite lucid. Well, the time had come for some plain, sensible speaking from the old man and Hugo hoped Nell's new concoction would do the trick. Their patience was running out.

He returned to the bedside, hands in the pockets of his creased trousers, and watched Nell tilt a vial over a small ball of cotton-wool as she stood by the trolley containing genuine medications and equipment.

'What is it this time?' he asked, impressed by her knowledge of potions and poisons. 'Hemlock?' He gave a nervous laugh.

'It was good enough to rid the Greeks of Socrates, but no, we don't want to finish him off jus' yet, do we?' Nell Quick was wearing surgical gloves to protect her skin as she liberally dosed the cotton wool. 'This is henbane, a close relative of deadly nightshade with some of my own ingredients mixed in, but I'm usin' only enough to loosen his tongue and impair his judgement. Too much and he'll be dead in a few hours.'

'It looks to me like his judgement is already impaired, although I do sometimes wonder if he understands what's going on.' Hugo eyed the frail figure on the bed, the sheet that covered his father more like a shroud.

'What does it matter?' Nell replied. 'He's too weak to do anythin'. Roll up his sleeve for me.'

Hugo was reluctant to touch the skeletal man. He remembered his father as he used to be, a small but powerful man, full of vitality. And, it had seemed to Hugo, always full of anger. 'But if he can hear us, if he can understand what we're saying, he'll be disinclined to tell us anything.'

Nell was short with Hugo. 'I told you: it doesn't matter. When this begins to work he won't know what he's sayin'. Jus' wish I'd used it earlier. But then he's been so weak it might've killed him. He seems jus' a little stronger tonight though, strong enough to take henbane, I think.' She bent over the sick man and dabbed the solution on the cotton wool into the skin of his forearm. 'I would have put it into his nose for quicker absorption by the mucous membranes, but he needs the mask right now. No matter, the pores in his skin will soon soak it up. It'll take a while to work though, so we'll have to come back later – unless you want to sit with him, Hugo?' Her grin was unpleasant, but to her companion, it was ravishing.

'I don't think so,' he replied hurriedly. 'I can think of better things to do with my time.' His leer was as ugly as Nell's scarlet grin.

*Even I've had enough for one day*, Nell thought to herself. *The little blonde bitch was strong enough to get away, but the fight was fun.*

She giggled and Hugo regarded her curiously. 'What is it?'

'Nothing to bother you, my lovely.'

Hugo was suspicious. 'You came across the bridge this morning. Had you been visiting Thom?'

'Yes, I called in.' She pulled the pyjama jacket sleeve back down over the emaciated arm. 'Kindred wasn't home though, so I pushed my bike all the way here along the forest path.'

'I think we should leave Thom out of this. He doesn't matter if we find what we're looking for.'

'We've been through all this enough times!'

By the light from a nearby lamp Hugo could see the blaze in her eyes.

'Until we're sure, we take no chances. We have to be able to control Kindred, otherwise we stand to lose everything.'

'But my father could die at any time.' Hugo spoke in a whisper now, as if the old man might hear.

'Not as long as I help keep him alive. But even if Kindred does go first, there's still no guarantee you'll get what's rightfully yours. Sir Russell might still despise you enough to leave you with nothin'. No, the only sure way is to find his last Will and Testament and destroy it. Count yourself lucky he wasn't well enough to make it in front of a proper solicitor, so there won't be any copies lodged in an office safe somewhere.'

'But his witness . . .'

She let out a sigh of exasperation. 'I told you before – it won't matter if there's no proper documentation. There has to be written proof. Soon as we find that we can make an end to all this.'

'Dear God, I hope so. I've had enough, Nell. We've searched the house so thoroughly these past months, I really don't feel I can carry on much longer.'

Nell's tone changed and her eyes searched his face. He was so weak . . .

'Jus' remember how good it'll be, Hugo. All the money you'll ever need, an' me on top.' She sniggered. 'Or beneath; or on my knees, the way you like it.'

Dropping the sodden cotton-wool ball into a plastic bag taken from the trolley, she sidled around the bed towards him. She sealed the bag as she came, her walk provocative.

'You'll have me, Hugo. Any way you want me. An' even when you're too tired, I'll mix you the brews you like, the ones that give you . . . energy.'

'Yes, Nell.'

'An' then we can do things, those things that make you feel good.'

He reached out for her, but she playfully evaded his

arms. She let the bag containing the swab fall to the floor where she would retrieve it later. She began to pull off the surgical gloves, slowly, almost like a stripper going into her act.

'An' there's always different potions for different things, Hugo. My, I've hardly shown you anything, there's so much more you'll appreciate.'

He made to move towards her again, but she stepped back, the movement languid, sensuous.

Hugo's bulging eyes were pleading and his thick lips were wet where his tongue had flicked out between them.

'Nell, please . . . just . . .'

He looked downwards, then up again and Nell groaned inwardly, knowing what the gesture meant. She would have to please him, otherwise he would be useless, sulking like a little boy refused his treat. She dropped the gloves by the plastic bag and went down on her knees.

'Come here, Hugo.' Her voice was low and she made it sound as though it contained pleasure. 'I know what you want. We must be quick though, Hugo. We've got a lot to do.'

He licked his lips again as he moved forward and his hand was trembling as he pulled down the zip of his trousers.

She delved inside, took him out, secretly disgusted by the flaccid penis that would take so much effort on her part to embolden.

And there, by his dying father's bedside, she leaned forward and took him into her mouth.

---

While outside the door in the antechamber of the rooftop quarters, a tall but stooped figure pressed close against the panels to listen.

# Chapter: Thirtieth

# THE SORCERESS' ROOM

THOM PULLED up before the broken picket fence and surveyed the creeper-covered house beyond it. Nell Quick's home looked empty; but then it had when he'd driven past yesterday and he'd known Nell was inside because he'd just left her. He realized the apparent emptiness was because the windows were so black, both downstairs and upstairs. The blackness seemed to represent an absence of life.

Nevertheless, he was here now and he was going to knock on that door – there were questions that had to be asked.

At the site of the accident Thom had used his mobile to call the casualty department of Shrewsbury's main hospital but, Thom not being a relative, the person he spoke to was reluctant to impart any information other than that Ms Budd was in a 'serious but stable condition'. Possibly tomorrow they would be able to give him a little more information.

He opened the Jeep's door and stepped out. He had to lean against the vehicle's roof for a moment as dizziness almost caused him to overbalance. Tired, he thought. Dog-weary beat. Too much had happened this day. He had learned so much, witnessed so much, and now this, Katy's accident. Accident? Thom wondered.

With an effort he pushed himself away from the Jeep and went through the gateless opening, his gaze skimming over the house as he limped up the short path. The dizziness receded, but the anxieties would not leave him alone.

He found himself in front of the porch, the shadows inside somehow discreet, as if hiding the front door. He stepped inside and pounded on the door with his fist.

The top section of the stable-door rattled in its frame, but there was no response from within the house itself. Thom cursed under his breath.

Stepping back outside the porch again, he peered at the upper windows, perhaps hoping to penetrate its blackness at that angle. There was nothing though, no sign of life at all. He went over to the downstairs window, treading through the long grass and weeds to get to it, and put both hands on the glass to form a darkened tunnel through which to look. He could plainly see the opposite window, the one that overlooked the back garden, but still detected no sign of life. Next he moved along to the kitchen window, shielding the glass against the glare with his hands once more. All he saw was the usual kitchen paraphernalia and shelves stocked with jars and tins, but no signs of life. Something – that sly little nagging voice of his? – told him not to give up. Even if Nell Quick was not at home, he might still find something useful inside the house, anything that might provide a clue to Nell's true nature and intention. Rigwit had called her a *hellhagge* and although a few days ago Thom would have scoffed at the idea, now he was inclined to believe. There might be something in the house that would confirm the elf's assertion; there might also be an indication of Nell's game plan. She appeared to have her hooks into poor old Hugo and Thom wanted to know why.

Moving stealthily, careful not to trip on weeds or tangled undergrowth, Thom turned the corner of the house and crept towards the rear. He hoped Nell's neighbours in the adjoining house had not noticed his approach along the path to the porch; with luck, they were not even home, for there had been no vehicle parked in front of their fence. Cautiously, he peeked around the corner, afraid that Nell might be sunbathing or attending her back garden.

And attending it needed. He had observed the garden once before, through the window of Nell's parlour, and had noted its cluttered disarray, but now it seemed even wilder. Yet ... and yet, there was some order to the mess. He could see that now, for what had appeared as total disorder – abandonment even – now took on some placement logic, for among the wild ferns and overlong grass there grew herbs of all kinds, screened by the brambles around them, but obviously carefully tended, for they appeared fine and healthy with space to allow in sunshine and for uninhibited growth. In fact, rather than neglected, the plants and herbs in this apparently fiercely overgrown garden were skilfully protected; or perhaps skilfully hidden.

Towards the end of the garden was the battered and flaky wood-framed greenhouse, its glass rendered almost opaque by rain-smeared grime. Out of curiosity, Thom made his way towards it, finding the cracked, broken remains of a centre path to make the journey easier, brushing aside tall ferns and taking each step with caution because of the slippery, moss-covered slabs of stone beneath his feet. Occasionally, he looked back over his shoulder at the house, half-expecting to see Nell's shadowy figure watching him from one of the windows. There was no one, of course – hadn't he rapped hard on the front door earlier? – but he could still feel eyes on the back of his neck. He realized it was the house, itself, that he could feel watching him. A silly notion, but one he was unable to shake off.

When he reached the greenhouse he saw it was in an even worse condition than he had first thought. Not only were the panes of glass filthy, but several were broken or cracked. Bird droppings decorated the slanted roof and bedaubed the side windows and the wooden-framed structure looked as if one strong push would send the whole lot crashing. There was something dirty, unhealthy, about it and Thom had no wish to enter. Instead, he found a broken pane and peered through.

Like the garden, everything inside looked to be growing wild, but he soon realized that this was only because the greenhouse was overcrowded with herbs, plants and fruits, most of which he did not even attempt to identify. But among them he did recognize the same orchids that he had found at Little Bracken earlier, the soil beside these disturbed and empty, as though their companions had recently been uprooted. Thom could not even guess at the significance of this; maybe Nell had thought they would make a nice gift, something to brighten up the cottage.

Okay, so what did all this tell him of Nell Quick? That she was an enthusiastic but untidy gardener? Or that she really was a maker of potions and herbal cures? He pictured Nell dressed in black, wearing a witch's pointed hat, stirring a huge cauldron of bubbling liquid, and he almost laughed aloud. What a stupid picture. But how far from the truth was it? Forget the black attire and ridiculous hat, forget the bubbling cauldron and broomstick in the corner; forget the heart of a frog, and puppy dog's tail, the black cat 'familiar', the book of spells, the ... wax ... the wax effigy with needles sticking into it – *no!* nonsense, forget that too. Forget all notions of witchcraft and sorcery. But remember the succubus, remember the battle for his own semen, remember Nell's own exotic allure, remember the uneasy feeling the magpie gave him each time he saw it – somehow he knew it was the *same* magpie each time – and remember a magpie had been seen flying from the shattered windscreen of Katy's ruined VW.

He straightened and slowly turned his head to look at the house again.

---

The back door had been left unlocked (not all the old country ways had died), and after a brief look around the downstairs rooms – the tiny kitchen, parlour and lobby – Thom found himself upstairs in Nell Quick's bedroom.

He felt guilty that he'd entered another's home this way, even ashamed, but he wasn't deterred in any way. In fact, he thought this surreptitious search was essential, even if he didn't quite know why just yet; he'd know when he discovered something relevant, God knows what. He was acting purely by instinct, Katy's accident jolting him from any reservations he might have. Besides, if Hugo was in trouble – blackmail was Thom's best guess, the blackmailer being Nell Quick, Hugo the victim – then it was up to him to help his friend in any way he could. Whatever Hugo had been up to, whatever indiscretions or transgressions he had committed – and there were any number of foolish situations Hugo could have got himself into – Thom would support him. They'd take on Nell Quick together. It was the least, and probably the most, he could do for his friend.

The ground floor rooms had not revealed much more than he had expected, for although his perusal of the parlour yesterday had been cursory, the room had no hidden secrets of any interest. An ancient, handwritten book on herbs and their properties for healing, a drawer full of bills, many of them red-inked final reminders, old letters still in their torn envelopes that he deliberately did not read – he was only prepared to take his snooping so far – and general accumulations that would not be out of place in any household.

The two upstairs rooms (not counting the tiny bathroom) were altogether different though.

The bigger one merely had a quilt-covered mattress on the floor's bare boards for a bed, a long oak sideboard set along one wall and opposite this a tall wardrobe featuring a full-length mirror on its door. Unlit candles stood on the top of the sideboard, sharing space with a few cheap jewellery boxes, make-up accoutrements and perfume bottles. Apart from another large mirror over the sideboard, its gilt frame chipped and flaked, that was the whole of its contents – no chairs, framed photographs or pictures, no books or magazines lying around, no flower vases or lamps, nothing at all to make the room more comfortable or personal. Behind him at the top of the stairs was the bathroom, its door open so that he could see inside. It was half-tiled with white squares, the rest of the walls a creamy shade of white; the bath itself was plain and small, the toilet and sink next to it equally plain and functional. However, the room next door to the bedroom was the very antithesis of its companions, for whereas they lacked clutter and colour, this room had more than enough of both.

Garishly painted in red and black – red walls, black ceiling and floor – it came as a shock. Thom gave out a quiet breathy whistle and remained on the threshold for several long moments. A gold pentagram, a five-pointed star, was painted on the floor, and when he glanced up he saw it was replicated on the ceiling. There were symbols or hieroglyphics painted at certain points, chiefly close to the apex of each triangular shape. However, whereas the five-pointed star on the floor pointed towards the window, the one above was reversed. At the far end of the room and beneath the curtained window there was what appeared to be a small altar covered in a black material, its surface littered with odd-sized candles, some black, some red, some gold, most of which were burned down to varying degrees, their wax molten-like, spilling over on to their stands or receptacles. There was also a medium-sized bowl on the altar, its contents hidden from Thom's view for the moment. Piles of dusty-looking books stood around the walls, and some that lay flat on the floor and whose pages were open, looked to be original handwritten manuscripts, their letters copperplate and inked in red. A bookcase occupied the corner to his right, but instead of books, objects filled its shelves: amulets, ointment jars, crystals, necklaces, unused candles, an ornamental hand mirror, an athame, which was a knife with a black handle and steel blade, both of which had lettering of some kind inscribed on them, a coil of red ribbon, cloves of garlic, and various pieces of small statuary and metallic symbols.

The combination of smells and scents was almost overpowering, the mixture unpleasant rather than pleasing.

There were daubings on the red walls, crude images of men and women copulating or performing lewd acts upon one another, some in groups of three or four, all badly executed in gold and black paint. A larger depiction was of a horned creature with the upper body and limbs of a man but with a distorted goat's head and cloven hooves for feet. A naked female knelt behind it and was lifting its tail to kiss its anus. There were names inscribed among the pictures, set out randomly it seemed and rendered just as unskilfully. CRESIL, MERIHIM, ABADDON, BEELZEBUB, LILITH, JEZEBETH, BELIAL, HECATE, MOLOCH, PYRO, SEMIAZ, ZAGAM ... the list seemed endless and there were far too many names to take in. But he recognized a couple, for years ago most of his boarding-school friends had taken a keen interest in horror stories and movies and, although he was never so inclined himself, it was impossible not to borrow such books or magazines in times of boredom, or to overhear snatches of excited conversations. Wasn't

Beelzebub the Prince of Demons, second only to Satan himself? And wasn't Hecate the Queen of Witches?

A looped cross made from twigs and straw decorated the opposite wall and close by it hung a fox's tail or brush, the reddish fur faded and matted as though many years had passed since the animal itself had roamed the countryside. Next to this was a horseshoe, open end downwards, the opposite of good luck.

Even though he knew all this was ridiculous, merely evidence of an obsessed mind – no, more than that: Nell Quick was plainly crazy! – Thom could not help making the sign of the cross on his chest. He was hardly religious, but this came as a reflex action, for there was something evil about this room, something that made him feel terribly vulnerable. He figured he might have felt the same in a high-security lunatic asylum where all doors were left unlocked.

Fighting the urge to leave immediately, Thom took two steps into the bizarre room.

And wished he'd followed his urge.

A heaviness seemed to fall upon him, a lumpen weight that had nothing to do with the physical. Rather it was like a sudden feeling of oppressiveness that sank over his shoulders, an ethereal mantle that hung heavily. Even the air he inhaled tasted thick. And the conglomerate aromas were like poison.

This is not a good place to be, he told himself. But still he lingered.

He walked to the altar.

Thick black candles at either end had been used, their frozen wax spilling on to the black cloth beneath; other thinner candles of gold and red were welded by their wax into tarnished holders. He thought there was a third black candle, but it was different from the rest, unburnt, its top curving slightly to one side, its surface smooth, lustrous in the light from the window behind. Curious, yet unthinking, his mind assaulted from all sides by other things in the room, he picked up the object. And quickly put it down again, for it had no wick and it was definitely not a candle. It was too heavy to be made of wax.

Why a black vibrator should be the centrepiece of an altar, he had no idea. But then, perhaps it wasn't an altar, perhaps it was a shrine, a shrine to eroticism.

Also on the crowded altar were three daggers, two of which had black blades as well as black handles, the third of normal steel and white-handled, a single but large rough crystal, a long, thin twig from a tree (Thom's experience with all kinds of woods and their origins told him it was from the willow), fairly straight along its length but unrefined, with no attempt to smooth out the knots. A wand of some kind? he asked himself of the latter object. Had to be, considering everything else that was on offer here. Nell honestly imagined she was a witch and this room held the proof! Christ, it was madness! But then, so was talking with faeries.

There were two receptacles on the altar he now realized, the smaller of the two hidden by the other when viewed from the doorway. The larger one was metal, a curved bowl with patterned holes around its rim, and its bottom was filled with broken pieces of charcoal and ashes. The smell of incense came from it, pungent enough to compete with the room's other odours. The second receptacle was of more interest to Thom.

It was made of dark-blue glass, broad at the top and curving down to a squat stem and base. It might have been a chalice, or at least represented one. There were oddments inside and it was these that caused Thom to catch his breath.

He picked up the container in both hands, hands that were not steady, hands whose grip was too wary, for the fingers cupped the midnight-blue glass lightly, as if it might burn. He raised it to chest height and a foot away from his body, and stared at the contents.

Each item was innocuous in itself – a white shirt button; a lock of hair, several strands separated from the main clump; a small set of steel dividers. Their bed was not the bottom of the receptacle itself but a crumpled photograph, and all conspired to create an identity.

The button might have come from one of his own old shirts. The hair had the same colouring as his own and could have come from his head. The small set of dividers had lost their shine, the needles at the end of each arm almost black with age, and they resembled the first set he had ever bought himself when he had left college and was preparing to take up carpentry as a full-time occupation (in fact he *knew* they were his, for he had measured wood and cuts and grooves with them for so long that it was impossible not to recognize the blemishes and scratches in their metal; because he'd had them for such a time and used them for virtually every job since day-one, they had become a kind of good-luck mascot, a familiar tool he held in affection, no big deal, but a simple and sentimental token of all the hard work he had put in over the years).

What held the items together and made him sure they were all from the same source – Thom, himself – was the colour print he now reached in for with one hand. The other objects slid off its rumpled surface as he drew the photograph out.

He placed the 'chalice' back on the altar and smoothed out the photograph with both hands. One edge was torn, as if it was merely half or a part of a whole and, although the photograph had obviously been taken many years ago, he recognized himself immediately. It was slightly blurred, as if the photographer had a shaky hand or had moved as the shutter had clicked, and there was just part of another's elbow showing on the torn side, as if he had been standing close to someone. In the shot, Thom was fresh-faced, a teenager, his hair too long, his clothes casual, and in the background was woodland. He could not remember exactly when the picture was taken, but he was fairly sure that the person who had been standing next to him, whose elbow was just in shot, was Hugo. Perhaps it was old Eric Pimlet who had taken the photo. Thom could not think of when he had last seen it, or if he had seen it at all, but assumed it had laid around in a drawer somewhere at Castle Bracken. Had Nell come upon it on one of her visits to tend Sir Russell? Or had she deliberately searched it out?

A button from one of his shirts wouldn't have been too difficult to obtain – easy to slip into the cottage while he was out and snip one off. The hair? His teeth bit into his lower lip as he reflected. Yes. The other day, on her sofa downstairs. She had sat next to him, an arm going round the back of the sofa. Hadn't he felt a slight tug at the back of his neck when he'd leaned forward? Had she had a small pair of scissors concealed in her hand? Easy to drop them behind the seat or leave them on the windowsill after they'd done their work. But the dividers?

He had never met Nell before he'd returned to Little Bracken to recuperate and the little tool had gone missing long before that; before his stroke, in fact. They had never been in daily use, but were kept in a special compartment of his tool box along with compasses, Stanley knife, vernier gauge, sliding bevel, squares and various other smaller tools of his profession. One day they just weren't there and he'd assumed they had been left lying around somewhere after a job and he had chided himself for such tardiness. They'd turn up sooner or later, he told himself, but they never had. Until now.

How? Why? It didn't make sense. He was sure they were his, but Nell Quick could never have had access to them. There was only one possible connection between his London workshop and Bracken itself. Hugo.

Thom shook his head in dismay.

Surely not. Yet Hugo had visited him a month or so before his stroke. And it was a short time after that that Thom had discovered the dividers had vanished.

But why? Nell might take all this witch – this *hellhagge* – nonsense seriously, but surely not Hugo? It made no sense at all. And what could Nell do with these personal items anyway? Did she truly believe she could cast some kind of spell on him? Thom remembered the succubus. And he remembered the stroke itself. Was Nell's magic the cause of that too?

Such a monster was hardly likely, yet Thom, himself, had borne witness to it. And the succubus had tried to steal the most intimate thing of all from Thom – his semen! Was that to be added to the contents of this glass? The very thought made him feel nauseous. And the idea that his lifelong friend, Hugo Bleeth, might be involved in whatever nasty scheme Nell Quick had in mind made Thom feel suddenly cold.

# Chapter : Thirty-First

## DETELS FROM THE BOOK

THE OH-SO-FAMILIAR sensation of overwhelming exhaustion had come over Thom only moments after the coldness and he had staggered from Nell Quick's house, footsteps heavy on the narrow staircase to the ground floor, heart pounding in a ponderous beat, his skin dank with sweat. He had to get away from there, in particular away from that red-and-black painted room that seemed to exude a peculiar degeneracy. Panic had set in with the fatigue and he realized that the thought of Hugo stealing from him to help this woman was its catalyst. He and Hugo had been friends since childhood, and even though they had not seen each other on a regular basis in latter years, Thom had always thought the bond between them remained strong. If he was wrong, if something had happened to change their relationship, what could it have been? Had Hugo discovered that they shared more than a long-term friendship, that they were related by blood, no matter how tenuously? Hugo had only been Jonathan Bleeth's half-brother, but the link was Sir Russell himself, for the old man was Hugo's father and his, Thom's, grandfather. Yet Thom had been virtually disowned, even though Sir Russell had paid for his tuition and board, so surely Hugo could not be jealous of him. And if Sir Russell was so ashamed of his illegitimate grandson, was it likely that Hugo had even been informed of his half-brother's congress with Bethan, or of the child who was its result? If he had known, surely Hugo would have talked to Thom about it when they were kids. Confusion, doubt, disbelief – all connived with the exhaustion to send Thom limping through the kitchen and out of the back door.

The fresh but warm air was a relief after the closeness inside Nell's house, reviving him enough to increase his speed. It was not exactly a run, more of a hobbling walk, but he was soon back at the Jeep and yanking open the driver's door. He drove back to Little Bracken erratically, once or twice losing concentration so that he had to jerk the wheel sharply to avoid leaving the road, the Jeep's speed rarely consistent, his foot sometimes too heavy on the accelerator pedal, weariness or lack of attention the cause. As he turned off the main highway into the lane that led to the cottage, he noted that the accident scene had been cleared, both transporter and green Volkswagen gone, only tyre marks on the road and a scarred tree trunk evidence of what had occurred. Brambles and thin branches lashed at the Jeep's paintwork as Thom fought to stay in control, and he was glad when Little Bracken's stunted tower finally came into view. He pulled into the clearing and parked the vehicle haphazardly, tumbling out and almost staggering up the short path to the front door.

Once over the threshold he leaned back against the door-jamb and called Rigwit's name. Response came there none.

He bolted the door top and bottom and ran his hands over his face, then studied the palms as if surprised at their dampness. Something else surprised him. He was hungry. He was so god-damned hungry. But then of course, he had eaten nothing all day. Just forgotten to eat, it hadn't been a priority. Now, though, despite the exhaustion, despite the incredible amount of information he'd had to absorb – Christ, that he'd had to accept! – throughout the long day, despite his fear for Katy Budd, his fear *of* Nell Quick, his body – in particular his grumbling stomach – was crying out for sustenance. He felt unwell, he felt as if the left side of his body was made of lead, yet his belly was demanding to be fed! Good to know there was at least some natural order to things left.

Thom made for the fridge.

---

It was getting dark outside and Thom left the kitchen table to switch on the overhead light. The plate and cup he'd used for his quick pre-packaged meal lay unwashed in the sink and he still wore the loose sweater over his T-shirt because of the chill that had crept into the evening air. He returned to the table and stared down at the open book.

Then he sat and began turning the pages again.

It was the same book that the faeries had used as a portal into his world, and this was the first time Thom had had a chance to study it properly. Earlier, the first pages he had searched for were those somewhere around the middle, half-expecting the faeries to come streaming through the moment he found them. Disappointingly, there was nothing but symbols and hand-drawn lettering in a language unknown to him. He'd left the book open on the table for several moments, simply regarding it and unconsciously fingering the small scar running from his lower lip as he did so. He'd tried willing the faeries to appear. Nothing. He'd placed his hands on the vellum pages in the way a spiritualist might place their hands on a seance table, his eyes closed, imagining the faeries pouring forth. Nothing.

Finally, Thom had given up and closed the book so that

he could examine its cover. There were no clues there. It was fashioned from plain, dark leather, its surface now worn and scarred but with no man-designed embellishment – no symbols, no title, not even a decorative border of any kind. It might have been some ancient idea of a scrapbook. In fact, on his initial perusal earlier, that had been his first impression, for although there were no cuttings inside there were sketches, more symbols, and lots of writing. Some of the latter went on for page after page, with no illustrations or adornments to break up the tedium, while other pieces were short, set out in stanzas as if they were poems, but again, all in a language Thom had never set eyes on before. There was nothing orderly about most of the writings – they appeared to be ideas or thoughts put down at random – and not all paid tribute to the particular author's penmanship, for there were blotches and scratchings-out, blobs of ink, or paint, or whatever the medium used, spoiling characters and often whole words.

Yet among them were scripts of pure beauty, their calligraphy alone a suggestion of inspired prose, while other examples were almost micrographic, barely legible to the naked eye even if the language had been comprehensible. But it was the illustrations that were the most astonishing.

Some were just rough sketches, and even these were stunningly beautiful, while others were wonderfully detailed, their colours still vibrant (God knows how they would have sung from the page had not time faded their pigment), and the depictions almost inconceivable had not Thom observed the real things – or at least some of them, for there were beings and ethereal forms represented here that were way beyond anything he had witnessed over the past night and day.

Some spread across the page in flashes of iridescent light, their shape indiscernible among the patterns, only the skill of the artist somehow conveying the invisible presence within (Thom had to blink several times at certain pictures, for their inner form seemed to be breaking through, the mysterious process hurting his eyes as surely as if someone was shining a light into them), while still more, smaller illustrations perhaps taking up a corner of a page or occupying what should have been a minor position among the script, leapt out at him in hues of green and mauve, violet and red, yellows and golds, often a combination of all these, and it took him only a short time to realize that what was being disclosed or unveiled to the reader of this tome was the recreated yet *true* vision of spirit creatures, elementals, energy forms that had more to do with the soul than the physical. He wished he could understand the words assigned to many of these miraculous renditions, for they might have explained their exact nature, but something told him that he was not yet ready for such knowledge. But nevertheless, that same instinct seemed to hint that some day . . .

There were other glorious but simpler and more recognizable depictions of the creatures he had recently been introduced to – elves, goblins, undines, sprites, various orders of faeries – and others he had not yet met – bogles, boggarts, kelpies, clobbies, *et al* – all named (their titles, or most of them, were at least comprehensible among the writings) and apparently with descriptions of their natures. There were many drawings and paintings of plants, flowers, herbs and toadstools, these apparently to illustrate long scripts relating to their properties and usages.

There were sections dealing with spells and potions, with component parts and recipes (it was easy to guess their text by their layout), charms, omens, rituals and even auguries. It was peculiar, but the more Thom concentrated on the writings and on the vellum pages, the more he seemed to become familiar with their intent, even though the individual words themselves meant little to him. He remembered how dialogue with Rigwit had become easier the more they talked and wondered if the book's text might work in a similar fashion. Perhaps the 'tuning in' was more complex in this case, but a basic understanding of the book's contents was coming through to him, the meaning of certain words or fragments of sentences seeming to spring out at him like clear jigsaw pieces, providing precise clues to the whole. Even so, he suspected it would take years of study, maybe decades, to fully appreciate the manuscript's full text and overall aspiration.

Now that Thom was looking through the book again, he noted once more that many different hands and minds appeared to have contributed, for handwriting and illustrative style varied throughout – from fine copperplate or calligraphy, with elegant flourishes and curlicues, to squiggles and clumsy scrawls – and Thom soon realized this was an ongoing project, as Jennet had told him, for when he turned to the back pages he found them empty, devoid of all markings as if waiting to be filled. Leafing backwards, he found there was something familiar about the penmanship and drawn images on the last twenty or so pages. He had seen this style before, although he could not recall ever having taken the leather-bound tome from its place on the highest shelf of the bookcase; oddly he could not remember having noticed the book itself before – it had always been one of many volumes and way out of reach for him as a child. Yet this particular text was familiar because he had witnessed much of its transcription.

His mother was both its author and artist and more than once he had watched as she had carefully penned whatever enchantment or piece of *faerefolkis* lore she thought might be a valuable and informative contribution to the volume. He now remembered she had explained the meaning of her words to him, the significance of the symbols and emblems, the names and characters of the little faery figures she drew with such devotion. Disappointingly, the telling lacked clarity, the explanations were dim recollections without detail or purport. Their discovery was both wonderful and frustrating at the same time.

Thom scoured these latter pages almost greedily, delighting not only in the knowledge that they were the work of his own mother, but also in their fineness, the beauty of their simple execution, the faithfulness to their cause which was manifestly evident. And then he found himself staring at a small pencil-portrait of a man, someone who bore a passing resemblance to the person Sir Russell Bleeth had once been, before the years of grief and his tragic illness had withered him. And which also bore a resemblance to Thom, himself.

Although, unlike Thom's, this man's hair was dark, the nose and chin line closer to Sir Russell's than his own, there was something about the eyes that Thom easily recognized, for they had looked at him all his life, reflected in a mirror. The portrait was from the waist up only, and the man wore a British army uniform. His name was spelt out below the sketch: Jonathan Bleeth.

Thom was dumbstruck. He gazed at the picture in awe and a great surging of love swept through him. He had never known his father, but he *knew* he would have loved him. He knew because of the picture and the compassion it revealed in the face of the man, and he knew because his mother would only have loved someone worthy, someone whose nature was akin to her own. Although still incredibly weary, Thom felt a lifting of his spirit and a lightening of his heart.

He continued to gaze at the picture, wishing he could properly read the words beneath the name, but not doubting for one moment that eventually – maybe not this night, or even in the days to come, but eventually, when he had absorbed knowledge from the book itself – he would be able to understand. Jennet would help him.

After a while, his eyelids dropped, his shoulders began to sag, his head felt too heavy for his neck. Soon, his cheek was on the open pages and he was asleep.

# Chapter : Thirty-Second

## BEQUEST

I N THE gloom of the first-floor landing Hugo's pale face
was a confusion of elation and despair.

'Is it . . .?' Nell asked in an excited whisper, her hands
clenched against her chest.

The trunk door of the old longcase clock was open, the
single weight and steadily swinging pendulum exposed in
the cavity like the living organ of an unsealed body. As ever,
the black hands on the engraved dulled brass dial declared
an erroneous hour and minute, but still its wheels and cogs
turned and clunked, for Hartgrove insisted on rewinding it
well before its thirty-hour cycle – eleven-hour cycle these
days – had expired, afraid the inner workings would seize up
completely if neglected. Dusty wall lights did not throw out
much of a glow along the lengthy corridor, and Hugo had
used his cigarette lighter to invade the darkness inside the
casing. He had almost squealed when he saw the envelope
propped up against the trunk's rear wall and his hands had

been trembling when he drew it out and slid a thumbnail under the sealed flap.

'It's the Will all right,' he said, eyes re-reading the contents as if they were a surprise to him and not a confirmation of what he and Nell already knew.

'I told you the henbane would work.' Nell said, moving round so that she, too, could see the single-sheet document properly. 'I told you he would talk and talk. All that was necessary was the right moment as far as his strength was concerned and the right questions.' Her heart was beating rapidly, spurred by the memory of how the feeble old man had rambled on once her brew had began to work, how Hugo had grimaced with dismay when he had learned just how low he was in his father's esteem, and now the thrill of finding exactly what they had been searching for since Sir Russell had mumbled on about a new Will in his drug-induced sleep. Now, at long last, they had it in their hands.

'So almost everything goes to Kindred,' she said, as if to twist the knife.

Hugo did not respond, but his hands continued to shake.

'The house, the estate – everything that rightfully should be yours.' Nell spat out the name. '*Thom Kindred!*' And what would *he* do with it all? Precisely nothing, Hugo. He's a romantic. Even if he followed our advice, we – *you*, Hugo, *you* – would not be part of it.'

Hugo was hesitant, troubled. 'Maybe—'

'*There's no maybe to it!*' she hissed back, immediately dismissing the vacillation she knew would otherwise come. 'You've been disinherited, cut adrift! Your father thinks nothin' of you, and you've always known it!'

'He *has* provided some financial arrangement.' Hugo's protest was weak.

'Nothin' like you deserve, you fool. You're his son, after all. And what's Kindred to him? A bastard grandson who isn't even aware of the fact.'

343

She snatched the paper from Hugo's hand, leaving him holding the envelope only.

'Here's the evidence and it can easily be destroyed.'

'It's witnessed.'

'That can be taken care of too. Everything's goin' to work out, Hugo, trust me.'

'I do trust you, Nell.'

'You have to be strong. I can take care of it, but you have to stand with me.' *You have to be part of it, Hugo,* she was thinking. *Your hands have got to be as dirty as mine, you must be an accomplice. That way you can't turn on me when it's over. And that way I can control you forever. Until it's your turn, of course.*

'I'll be okay, Nell, I promise you. It's just that, well . . .'

Her voice became softer, persuasive, for she knew how to play this weak idiot who depended on her for so much, knew what he liked, what it took to make him bend to her will. 'It isn't easy for you, Hugo, I know that. After all, he is your father, your flesh and blood. But jus' remember how he's treated you all these years. He's been a bully and a tyrant as far as you're concerned, blamed you for things you've had no control over. When has he ever shown you any respect or love?'

'Perhaps when I was a boy . . .'

'P'raps nothing! He's always treated you badly. And now he favours someone born on the wrong side of the blanket. What has Thom Kindred ever done to deserve your father's respect? He's jus' bein' used, your father's jus' gettin' back at you because he hates you so much. An' Kindred knows it. He's laughin' at you behind your back, Hugo.'

'I don't think Thom is even aware of the new Will.'

'Oh, don't you?'

'Well, I . . .'

'Get wise, Hugo. They're both in it together, Kindred and the old manservant, Hartgrove, the witness to the Will. Who else d'you think hid it in this place? Sir Russell couldn't have left his bed to stash it here. No, old Bones is in league with Kindred. Together they're tryin' to do you out of what's rightfully yours, don't you see?' Anger had returned to her voice, but it was an anger on Hugo's behalf not against him, used to stir up resentment towards his father and Kindred. And it seemed to be working. As it always did.

'You're perfectly right, Nell. I've already been too trusting. I've always liked to see the best in people.'

She gave a short laugh. What a fool, what a self-deceiving idiot. Everything Sir Russell had thought about his son was true. He was a lazy, self-serving ninny who had always been too stupid and too gullible to hold down a proper job. And then there had been the other things – the gambling and boozing, the drugs, the cheap hired women. The deceit. No wonder his father despised him!

She moved closer to Hugo, slid an arm around his ample waist. Her voice was low, conspiratorial. 'Listen to me. After tomorrow everything will be fine. I've got preparations to make that will take some time, but I'll be ready by tomorrow night. *We'll* be ready.'

Hugo grinned nervously. God, he needed this woman, and not just for her body, not just for the things she did to him. She was his rock. Without her he would never have the courage, nor even the will, to take what belonged to him. He sniffed her aroma, that faintly musky smell that excited him so much. He stared into those deep, dark eyes and felt himself drawn into her. The plan for Bracken had been his, but she was the driving force behind its execution. He remembered how aroused she'd become when he'd first mentioned the grand idea, how a fire had burned in those eyes. Her passion that night had left him depleted and bruised, but yearning for more.

'You'll see things you never thought possible.' she was saying, her voice breathy with anticipation, 'things that will make your father's heart freeze. But there won't be a mark on him, nothing that can be blamed on us. Now we have this . . .' she held the paper aloft '. . . there's no need to keep him alive. Ironic isn't it, how he would have been dead months ago if not for my medicines and care. No doctors would have saved him. But we don't need him any more, Hugo, his time has come.'

'I don't want him to suffer too much, Nell.'

'Ha! And what d'you think he's been goin' through this past year? It would've been kinder if I'd allowed him to die sooner, but that wasn't possible, not until we knew for sure. And you let him suffer, Hugo, you let it go on, so don't start weepin' for him now.'

She pressed her hips against him, a distraction that never failed. The thought of having her always prevented Hugo from thinking too deeply, not that his imagination could ever stretch very far anyway. For instance, the thought that one day – years to come, of course, when she, herself, was his partner both in marriage and in business – he might suffer a similar fate to his father would never occur to him. Poor, dumb Hugo . . .

He mistook her smile for affection, her tightened grip on his waist for desire.

'We should get rid of it,' he said.

Nell pulled her head back a little. 'What?'

'We should burn it. The Will. We should destroy it now.'

Her smile broadened to an unpleasant grin. 'Oh no,' she said softly. 'Oh no, I want the old bastard to see us do that. I think he should know that his rotten scheme to disinherit you will come to nothing. I want him to know that when his eyes shut forever.'

Hugo was silent, breathing in her smell, intoxicated by it; and excited, too, by the prospect of finally owning Castle Bracken and all its lands, to do with it as he pleased. If only the old boy didn't have to die in the way Nell planned (whatever *that* might be), if only he would just fade away naturally . . .

'Hugo.'

His attention snapped back to her.

'There's no turnin' back now,' she told him. 'Once Sir Russell is out the way and the Will destroyed, Kindred won't have a leg to stand on. And whatever happens tomorrow night will be his fault. He shouldn't have tried to do this to you, Hugo. D'you understand?'

Hugo mumbled something unintelligible, which Nell took as assent.

'Besides,' she said coldly. 'He should have died four months ago.'

Hugo shivered inwardly and, not for the first time, felt very afraid of this woman. But then, that was part of her allure.

---

She tore upstairs. How far had he gone? What had he seen?

Her bedroom first. She stood in the doorway, looking around wildly. Nothing appeared to have been touched, nothing moved. Yet the after-presence was as palpable as a lingering smell, a footprint in the sand, a fingerprint on a glass. She had felt it the moment she returned home.

Nell whirled and rushed down the short corridor to a room opposite. The door was open and Nell *never* left the door to her secret room open because to do so would be to allow some of its power to escape. Whoever had snooped around up here had obviously been worried enough to leave in a hurry, forgetting to leave the door the way they had found it.

She looked around quickly, taking everything in, her chest heaving in her anger. What had they touched?

She looked across the painted room towards the altar, at the blue chalice that stood among the other implements of her craft. She went to it.

And gasped when she saw that its contents were gone.

Thom Kindred had taken them with him.

Nell let out a screech of rage and lashed the air with clawed fists.

How dare he! How dare he invade her private place and steal from her! She knew it was Kindred who had entered her home when she was away, knew it the moment after she'd realized someone had been there, and that was the very moment she'd walked through the front door, for she sensed these things, she was aware of all intrusion and any negative thoughts directed her way.

She calmed herself, forced herself to breathe slowly and evenly; but her mind remained a ferment of rage.

So he thought he could play games with her, did he? He imagined he could get the better of Nell Quick, did he? Well, pity he wasn't aware that she enjoyed such happy diversions, especially when they could only end in horror for her opponent.

And before this night was through, Thom Kindred would know *such* horror.

# Chapter : Thirty-Third

## A DAMNABLE VESSEL

SOMETHING ROUSED Thom from his slumber. Arms still spread across the kitchen table, he lifted his head a few inches from the open book.

Holding his breath, he listened.

A gentle tap on the front door.

He lifted his head higher, his shoulders slowly straightening.

Another knock on the door.

He sat upright in the chair, watching the front door as if he might divine what was on the other side.

'Jennet?' he called quietly, optimistically. Wouldn't she have used the bell?

A great *thump* on the door, so that the wood seemed to strain against its hinges.

He jumped at the sound, fully alert now, the dregs of sleep startled away.

'*Jennet?*' he called. Then, quieter again: 'Rigwit, is that you?'

Silence the only response.

The chair scraped against the stone flooring as Thom rose to his feet.

The silence seemed brooding.

He looked around, searching for something to use as protection, a weapon of some kind. He went over to a drawer and took out a long carving knife.

He waited, eyes on the door, his breath held once more. The night seemed very still.

Lamely but loudly, he said: 'Anyone out there?'

If there was, they were saying nothing.

This is ridiculous, thought Thom. Why be afraid in your own home? Because horrible things have happened to you here recently, his inner voice replied. And that made him angry. Little Bracken was always a wonderful place for him, a home filled with love when he was small, a sanctuary now. Nobody was going to terrorize him here.

Thom limped forcefully towards the door, bravado dismissing any other course of action. Without hesitation, he drew back both bolts, top and bottom (insecurity had made him use both earlier), gave the key a swift turn, swapped hands with the knife so that it was in his right, pointing like a dagger, and flung the door open wide.

There was no one outside.

But something had been left on the doorstep.

Before picking it up, he looked off towards the woods, which were merely a darker mass in the general darkness. The night, itself, was very quiet. Unusually so, for even at that late hour there should have been rustlings, leaves or shrubbery moved by a breeze or any nocturnal creatures on the prowl, or the hoot of an owl, or the squeal of its victim as the predator swooped down for the kill. The woods were always alive, both night and day; but tonight they were hushed.

Stars and the three-quarter moon were bright enough and the clearing around the cottage was a silvery-grey, its shadows deep.

Only when he was satisfied that nobody lurked close by did Thom cast his gaze down at the object on the doorstep. Light flooded out from the kitchen behind him and it was by this that he realized that the object was a jar. A jar whose glass was very grimy.

He sank to his haunches to examine it more closely and saw that it was sealed with a tin screw-on top. Cautiously, he reached out and tilted the jar, shuffling his body to one side so that he did not block the light. Because of the smeared dirt and grime it was still difficult to see what was inside.

Thom picked up the glass container as he rose to his feet and, with one last look around, he closed the front door and turned the key in the lock, bolting it again for extra security. Then he took the unsolicited trophy back to the kitchen table, and put it down, leaning over it for a more thorough examination.

Elbows on the edge of the table, he peered into the jar, but was still unable to penetrate the dirty glass. All he could see was what looked like a mass of brittle hair inside, but he couldn't tell for sure. Wetting a fingertip with his tongue, he tried to wipe away some of the grime; it hardly helped, for the dirt was stubborn, as if it had clung to the glass long enough to be part of it. It was as if the jar had been hidden in the earth for some considerable time.

He stood up from the table, still pondering the dirty object, curious and fearful at the same time. It occurred to him that the jar might have been left by Jennet, or even Rigwit, some kind of gift to him. But then why hadn't they handed it to him personally? And where was Rigwit tonight? The elf was supposed to be keeper of the cottage, a mystical guardian, custodian, whatever it was he like to call himself, so why wasn't he on duty? Thom needed some guidance here, but apart from himself, the cottage was empty. God, it had never felt *so* empty.

Finally, it was curiosity that got the better of fear. Thom picked up the glass jar – it was surprisingly light considering it was packed tight – and began to unscrew its tin lid. He thought it might require some effort to open, but the lid turned easily and with a couple of twists it came off.

Thom yelped and dropped the jar back on to the table as its contents sprang out. It fell on its side and began to roll, stopped from falling off the table's edge by the open book lying there. He backed away, horrified and feeling faint as the long-legged spiders poured out.

---

At first, they flowed like black liquid, but as they spread each one became individual. Tiny, horrid, scurrying creatures, their thread-like legs carrying them swiftly towards the edge of the table. Out they streamed, more and more of them, spreading, scuttling, pouring over the open pages of the book, running in all directions, hundreds of them it seemed, now not all the same size, some among them with huge furry bodies and legs, while others were small, beetles with many, many, short legs.

Very soon the tabletop was one circular heaving mass of blackness.

Not for the first time that day Thom felt nauseous. The sight of them made his hair bristle and his spine stiffen. He backed further away until there was no more room, a wall at his back.

And still they poured out, thousands of them it seemed, which was impossible, for the jar that had contained them was not that big. He realized that what had looked like brittle hair when he had peered into the few less grimy parts of the glass had been their massed network of legs, all packed together in one hideous interlocking knot. The opening of the jar had caused the knot's undoing.

They spilled from the glass in a never-ending stream, fanning out immediately, joining the thick teeming crowds that were now overflowing the table, running down its legs or dropping on to chairs, then on to the floor to head towards Thom, who stood rigid with shock, his back pressed hard against the wall in a vain attempt to dissolve right through it.

They were not all black, these things. Their colours ranged from yellow, green, grey and brown to black and white striped. It was just that the predominant colour was black. Some, the striped ones, leapt or hopped over the backs of their companions. Thom felt his flesh crawl at the sight and the nearness of them.

His paralysis was broken when one of them sprang from the seething multitude on the table and landed at his feet. Automatically, he stamped hard on it, and although he must have been wrong, he thought he heard and felt the squelch. More were hopping off the kitchen table, while its legs were almost entirely covered by the descending little beasts. The stone floor around the table looked as if it were being laid with carpet, a black, holed, bubbling carpet.

It was impossible, but more and more surged from the cavern that was the jar's entrance, as if its interior did not follow the natural laws of physics, was merely the opening from another dimension, like the book the spiders now covered completely, a portal from a different world. In the stillness of the night, Thom could hear the faint *clicking* of their stick legs on stone and it was a terrible – a *ghastly* – sound that added to the nightmare. Unbelievably swift, the hordes drew closer and, having squashed one from existence, he had no qualms about embarking on a spider genocide.

He used both feet, stamping hard, his boots and the cuffs of his jeans soon becoming flecked with blood. Yet still they advanced, none seeking to avoid his crushing feet, kamikazes of the arachnid species. With renewed horror, Thom saw that one of the larger spiders, thick spiky fur covering its obese body and legs, swelling its size, was clinging to his leg just below the knee, slowly and determinedly crawling upwards, its stalked eyes weaving to and fro as it came.

Thom didn't quite scream, but the sound that escaped him was close to it. Timorously yet swiftly and giving himself no time to think, he brushed it away with his hand, just the fleeting feel of its hairy body enough to send shudder upon shudder through his body. It wasn't as if Thom had ever been afraid of spiders or any other creepy-crawly creature – although he had always been repulsed by them – but *en masse* like this, advancing like an ever-increasing army, was enough to make a coward of any man or woman. He pressed back against the wall again, irrationally standing on tiptoe, as if height would somehow make a difference.

Another striped thing hopped from the pulsating crowd on to his leg, followed by another. Others were scuttling over his books, disappearing beneath the stitched hem of his jeans so that he could feel the tickle of their wiry legs on his flesh as they climbed. He beat at himself with the flat of his hands, hopping from one foot to the other, screeching in disgust and dismay. He felt the wetness of their crushed bodies, but even as he danced, others were finding purchase, clinging to the rough material of his jeans. As if from out of nowhere, he found still more settled on his sweatshirt, two or three at first, but constantly multiplying. He never stopped beating at his own body, splats of blood staining his sweater and jeans as he moved from foot to foot.

And the blackness continued to expand with each passing moment, rising up the walls, creeping across the ceiling, the spiders, joined now by millipedes, centipedes, earwigs, woodlice, bugs, arachnids of all kinds, spilling from the glass jar, which never seemed to empty, the hordes spreading around the room to fill every space, cover every surface, swamp everything in sight.

Thom felt them inside his jeans, under his sweatshirt, and no matter how much he beat himself, there always seemed to be more in other places. Even as he slapped and punished his own body, he was aware that the kitchen was disappearing around him as the dark legions swelled in numbers and he began to cry tears of frustration and panic. Without even thinking, he ran towards the door to the stairway, squashing tiny bodies as he went, almost slipping once on the slime that he, himself, was creating. Something dropped on to his hair and he bent forward, cuffing his head with both hands in an effort to dislodge whatever nestled there. But even as he did so, he felt others falling on to the back of his neck, so that he squirmed and writhed, reaching back to brush them away. He knew it wouldn't be long before the spiders began to bite or sting his bare flesh, perhaps bloat their bodies on his blood, and the thought increased his panic.

He ripped open the landing door and rushed through, slamming it shut behind him. Even as he leaned against it, breathing heavily and continuing to brush himself with his hands, lifting his sweatshirt to get at the creatures, the ground floor landing lit only by the moon and stars shining through the window half-way up the spiral staircase, he saw the deep blackness flowing from the crack under the door like split blood. He pushed himself away and collapsed on the bottom few steps, looking at the sturdy barrier between himself and the spider army on the other side. Sturdy the door might be, but nothing could prevent the invasion through the cracks around the edges and the floor gap.

They swarmed through and in the moonlight it looked as if the wood was being eaten away at its borders.

'*Rigwit!*' Thom screamed in utmost terror. '*Help me, Help meeeee ...!*'

But the only response was the quiet scuffling of the spiders as they passed through the barrier and hurried towards him.

# Chapter : Thirty-Fourth

## AN ACT OF
## EXTREME VALOUR

MAKING HIMSELF as tall as he could so that his legs were able to take longer strides, Rigwit raced through the forest, crashing through shrubbery and scrambling over fallen trees, his little heart pounding, his arms pumping air.

He had left the Council of Elves without explanation, jumping to his feet so that the other eleven members rocked backwards in surprise. Although he had not heard his voice, Rigwit was suddenly aware that Thom was in terrible, perhaps even mortal, danger, for the subliminal cries for help were like stab wounds to the elf's heart. Important though the council meeting was – sinister and evil doings were astir and gatherings between the faery clans were taking place throughout the woodland that night to discuss where the threat might lie and what its nature might be – Rigwit could not ignore Thom's desperate pleas. Something dreadful was taking place at Little Bracken and it was Rigwit's duty to defend and protect not just the property itself, but also the dweller within. Nocturnal prowlers raised their heads in alarm as he sped by, while other night-creatures scurried off and hid in the undergrowth at his approach.

'*BebraveThombebrave!*' he called out on the run '*Bedaresoon, soonbedare!*'

He might have worn wings on his ankles, so swift was his stride, and before long he had the moonlit clearing in view, the light in Little Bracken's kitchen shining like a beacon. From outside and that distance, there seemed to be nothing amiss, but Rigwit's pace did not slacken, for it was his instinct for the ominous that spurred him on.

Scarcely checking his speed, the elf plunged into a burrow screened by thick foliage, moving along on all fours, scraping past the odd tree root along the way, dislodging loose earth from the tunnel's roof and walls in his haste. Although the secret passage, whose dimensions were big and wide enough to accommodate the biggest of badgers, twisted and turned to avoid occasional obstacles such as rocks and the more substantial tree root, its general direction was true enough, although it did become more and more narrow the closer it got to the foundations of the cottage, for this section was elf-extended. This was no problem for the elf: he merely allowed himself to become smaller and smaller so that eventually he was no bigger that the average dormouse.

In less than a minute since entering the burrow, he was climbing vertically and coming up through a hole in the cottage's bathroom floor, one that was beneath the raised bath itself.

---

Thom thought he might easily pass out. His left arm and leg were lead weights, hindering his progress up the spiral staircase, a burden he had to drag along. He had tried to flee up the stairs earlier, would have taken them two at a time, but the moment he turned away from the mass of spiders filling the ground-floor landing, seeping through the cracks around and beneath the door like black oil, the clicks and rustling of their movement like a language known only to their own species, he had all but collapsed against the curved wall.

His left leg had given way and when he had tried to reach the newel post for support, he found he could only lift his arm a few inches. Like a hammer blow, pain had struck his head, almost paralysing him, and even as he fell he had time to fear the worst.

*Not now*, he had begged. *Dear God, not now!*

This was how he had felt when the stroke had cut him down the first time, although the headache had raged for at least twenty-four hours prior to the collapse at the wheel of his car. Lying against the wall, he had sobbed when he felt the light prickling sensation of tiny needle-thin legs on the flesh of his right leg, the only leg that *had* some feeling. Almost in spasm, he drew it up and beat at it frantically with his right hand, mashing the spiders against his skin, killing those on the outside of his jeans as well as those that had found their way inside.

'*Bastards!*' he had yelled. '*Bastards!*'

But in the moonlight he saw there were more on his other leg, some of them way beyond his knee. They were pouring over the lip of the first step, dark liquid, thousands of them – *millions*, it seemed – with nothing to stop them, an army whose size was interminable and whose movement was perpetual. They flowed forward, covering everything in their path, easily surmounting any obstacle.

He kicked out and although his left leg was clumsy, it still had some strength in it. He pushed himself upwards, using his hands on each step to lift his buttocks, like a toddler negotiating a stairway that was too steep. Black spots were arriving on his lap and sweatshirt, leaping spiders eager to get at him. Something landed on his face and he quickly brushed it off, afraid to even glance at the wall above him.

The blinding pain in his head eased – or at least, adrenaline overrode it – and some power was returning to the debilitated limbs on his left side. Thom half-rose and, belly up, climbed more swiftly in awkward parody of the creatures that chased him.

Now the spiders covered every inch of floor space, with hundreds more on the curving wall and the newel post opposite, a thick advancing flood of long legs and tiny bodies that bristled and teemed, clicked and rustled, and in his despair Thom felt thousands upon thousands of minute greedy eyes on him, watching his every movement, impatient to engulf him, ready to defy nature and turn man-eater.

His shoulders were almost against the top step to the landing outside his bedroom door when the heel of his foot slipped off the edge of a lower stair and he slid down towards the oncoming tide. Thom gave out a short screech, fearing he would slide all the way down, right into their midst, but somehow he managed to stop himself. Nevertheless, they swarmed over his legs, crawling over each other's backs to get at him, and as much as he slapped them away, so more took their place.

In mere moments, they were up to his waist.

Thom's chest was heaving with the exertion of breathing and his hands were slick with gore and pap. He tried to turn over on to his side, tried to push himself upright, but the stairs were slimy with the spiders' juices, and he slipped again, slithering down even more stairs than before, one hand – his left hand, the weaker one – slapping against a higher step to halt his descent. He could only lie there for a second or two, trying to recover his strength and equilibrium, for his head was in a daze, the shock of his predicament making him dizzy, making him feel faint again.

Over the sound of his own fitful breathing and uncontrollable groaning, the combined quiet but feverish scratching of the spiders (nightmare muzak for the very afraid), there came the creaking of a door being opened, and even in his excitable state he knew it couldn't be the kitchen door, for that one and the front door were smooth on their hinges, almost noiseless when opened and closed. He couldn't see much because of the bend in the stairs, but the sound had to be caused by someone or some*thing* opening the cupboard or bathroom door. Oh dear God, what now? What fresh horror was on its way?

He heard light footsteps, soft scrunching of brittle-shelled bodies, like boots on snow, or faint squelching, bare feet crushing grapes, the sounds mixed inside his head and amplified because of the acoustics of the circular stairway and curving wall. Someone, some*thing*, was approaching.

A small shape appeared, one that seemed to grow in height, but not because it was mounting the stairs. It was becoming taller.

Thom knew it was Rigwit even before the elf spoke to him and even though the spiders and millipedes, earwigs, centipedes, countless others, climbed his diminutive body to cloak him with their mass, so that he was just a blackened shape in the moonlight shining through the high window.

'*DonbeafraidThom.*'

The elf's voice was calm, reassuring, but the words a gabble.

'Don't be afraid, Thom,' Rigwit said again, continuing to climb.

Spiders entered Rigwit's mouth and he turned his head to spit them out, casually, as if they were no more than apple seeds.

Thom tried to move away from him, for Rigwit was bringing more of the spiders with him, a troop-carrier for the enemy.

'Stay, Thom. Don't try to escape them. They really can't hurt you. At least, they can't hurt your body.'

'*Are you crazy?*' Thom pushed himself upwards, kicking out, feeling the prickle of their legs on the skin of his stomach, his chest, his arms, his clothing dark with them from the hips down. He slipped again, jarring his elbow. '*Help me!*' he pleaded.

'I will, Thom, I promise you, I will.' The camouflaged elf was just below him. 'But you must listen, you must hear me . . .'

'*Make them go!*'

'. . . you must obey me.'

Thom slumped, a paralysis that had naught to do with his illness taking over. He was rigid with revulsion and shock, like a rabbit frozen in a car's headlights, a gazelle shocked into stillness by a stalking lioness. He lay there helpless.

But Rigwit had climbed high enough to lean close to Thom's ear.

'You have to be brave,' the elf told him firmly without the slightest trace of excitement in his voice. Which did not exclude a grim urgency.

'Rigwit, make them go away! Use your magic!' Thom had turned his face to the stairs, an arm raised to protect his eyes.

The elf shook him by the shoulder. 'Only you can do that. They were sent to you, only you. Quickly, tell me how they arrived here. Were they in a sealed container?'

Rigwit persisted in shaking his shoulder, but more vigorously now.

Thom felt things running up his spine and he shuddered violently. In desperation, he looked at the elf.

'*Oh Jesus . . .*' he gasped.

Barely an inch of the elf could be seen, for his entire body including his head and shoulders seemed to quiver with a dark scabrous bustling.

Thom buried his head in both arms, but Rigwit would not let him be. Using two hands, disturbed spiders dropping from them, he wrenched Thom round, and before he could turn away again the elf wiped his own face, clearing most of the teeming layer.

Looking a little more like himself once more, if only for a few moments, he said sternly: 'You're the only one that can make them leave this place. The spell was meant for you and only you can break it. Can you feel them nip you, Thom? Can you feel their bites and stings?'

Before Thom could reply – and he was about to say 'Yes' – Rigwit jumped in. 'You can't. You can't feel a thing. Be honest with yourself. Now, can you feel anything other than their presence?'

Thom hesitated. He wanted to scream, wanted to tell the elf that, yes, of course he bloody well could feel them eating him, but he couldn't. He could feel their sickening bodies and legs brushing against his flesh, but there was no pain, no sharp stabs, nothing to cause him real harm. Surprised, unsure, he looked down at himself.

Which was a mistake.

For the moon outside provided enough light for him to see that webs were being spun over half his body, the silken strands creating a fine mesh over which the spiders continued to work, some of them spitting tiny jets of gooey substance – presumably a glue of some kind – to bind him. If he allowed it to happen, it would not take long for them to encase him in a tight cocoon of silver strands. And if he froze with the trauma, then they would spin their webs over his face and head, bind his eyes, seal his mouth and nostrils; they would stop his heart with the sheer horror of it all.

'Thom, Thom, you're thinking too much,' Rigwit insisted, a slight rise in his voice now, as if he was afraid he might be losing the battle. 'Lookit, lookit, see that they're nothing.'

He picked off a particularly large spider from Thom's neck and crushed it in his tiny fist. 'See? They can't hurt you. Let go of the fear and fight back.'

In fact, it was maintaining the fear that galvanized Thom – the fear of slowly being suffocated by these insidious thriving creatures. He kicked out, his left leg not nearly as agile as the right, but easily breaking the threads. He beat his body with hands and fists, slapping and punching, then brushing, long sweeping movements, ridding himself of the spiders and their clinging companions, sitting up on a step to make it easier for himself.

'Good lad!' encouraged Rigwit. 'Y'see how they're nothing. It's only their features that stop you from loving 'em.'

Even if he heard, Thom did not appreciate the humour. He was too busy shedding the rising cocoon, shaking, beating, flattening all that he could reach. He spasmed again when he felt them in his hair, then quickly swept his head with his right hand, his left too difficult to raise. Close to exhaustion, his actions became slower, more clumsy. He wanted to crawl further up the stairs, make it to the bedroom, seal the bottom of the door with bedsheets, only dimly aware that they would follow and enter anyway through other cracks and holes, relentless in their pursuit. As he turned, rising to one knee, Rigwit caught hold of him.

'It's no good running.'

Thom tried to pull away, but the elf's grip was surprisingly strong.

'There's only one way to defeat them, Thom, so you have to tell me – how did they get here? Was it in a box?'

Thom glanced fretfully over his shoulder before looking at Rigwit. *'In a jar!'* he blurted out. *'They were in a jar!'*

'Ah! And where is the jar now, lad?'

'I don't . . . the kitchen! It's in the kitchen.'

'Then you have to go down there.'

'Are you fucking insane?'

'Just a bit. But you already asked me that.' His light tone had no calming affect on Thom whatsoever. He smiled, thinking it might help, but a bug shot into his mouth. As before, Rigwit coolly spat it out and continued his conversation with Thom. 'We'll go together, but it's you that has to pick up the jar and throw it out.'

'I can't go down there!' Thom heard his own hysteria and wasn't proud. He started moving up again.

Rigwit caught him by his sweater, then hopped up two steps to get closer to Thom's face.

'Will you please listen. They cannot harm you unless you let them. Pretty soon you will start feeling their bites and stings, but it will only be because your own mind is allowing it to happen, and that's because it's what you expect. You have to fight your own thoughts as well as them. Come *now*, Thom, come with me. I'll be with you all the way.'

Thom felt a little hand grasp his and gently tug. As if in a dream, he allowed himself to be pulled, rising on trembling legs as he went.

'Close your eyes if it helps,' Rigwit advised.

'You must be kidding!' The stairs below looked as if they were covered in bubbling oil. With his free hand, he reached for the centre post and quickly withdrew it when the wood stirred and little bodies with long legs ran up his arm. The spiders were less dense on the curving wall to his left, but that freedom made their swift scuffling runs even more frightening to watch.

'I can't do this!' he shouted, shaking and thrashing spiders off his arm. He tried to turn back, but Rigwit, his arm and body stretched high, grabbed Thom's hand again.

'Y'can and y'will. Keep walking and think of pleasant things.'

Thom was in no mood for irony, but he could compare himself with this little man who clung to his hand like a toddler out for a stroll with his daddy. If the elf wasn't scared of the spiders, then why should he, a full-grown man, be? The logic of it failed to work. Thom felt the panic rising again, a volcano of panic, just waiting to erupt.

As if sensing Thom's thoughts, Rigwit uttered some soothing words. '*On the count of three, run like hell for the kitchen! One—*'

Thom was gone, racing down the remaining steps, praying he would not slip and fall into the fermenting mass and not for a moment understanding why the elf's last words had prompted him to take this course. Perhaps it was because fundamentally and deep down he knew there was no other way. There was no escape, neither in his bedroom, nor the roof. There really was only one course of action.

He imagined he could feel the crunching and splatting of their horribly tiny bodies and, at the bottom of the stairs, in the small landing where the doors to the bathroom, cupboard and kitchen were, the pile seemed to feel inches deep. It was both sickening and terrifying at the same time, and he tried not to dwell on it – not that there was time to do so anyway. Thom struck the big latch of the kitchen door and pushed hard, surprised there was no resistance, some-how expecting the multitude of spiders on the other side to shore up and hinder the door's progress.

The glare (compared to the moonlight his eyes had become used to) from the kitchen's ceiling light dazzled him at first, but he quickly acclimatized.

And almost became a gibbering wreck at the sight that greeted him.

---

They were everywhere. Literally, everywhere.

They coated the floor, the ceiling, the walls, the windows, every surface available. They even clung to the ceiling light, avoiding the bulb itself, which obviously was too hot for them. The sink, taps, chairs, ornaments, fireplace, the kitchen table, every possible piece of furniture, utensil, or object swarmed with them so that the room was decorated in a living, jostling motif.

And even so, spiders continued to rush from the jar's open neck, fanning out, the speedier of the species climbing over the back of the slower ones, the bugs, the millipedes, dominant larger ones – the raft spider, with its distinctive yellow ochre stripe and long hairy legs, the common garden spider with great swollen abdomen as if ready to give birth – pushing lesser ones aside as they rushed through the mob, while others dripped from the ceiling like the first heavy drops before a downpour, and still more hung from invisible threads, trapeze artistes swaying in the mild breeze created when the kitchen door had been opened.

Thom bent over and retched, a dry sound, the kind a dog makes before it vomits. Only silky drool fell from his parted lips and it soaked the backs of the tiny beasts thronging around his feet.

'*Keep moving!*' he heard Rigwit's command from behind. '*You mustn't stand still, not for a moment!*' Little hands prodded his calves.

When Thom straightened, his first instinct was to run out of the front door a few feet away, run out and keep running, into the forest, escape to somewhere they couldn't follow, but the elf seemed to have read his mind.

'*Don't even think about it, lad!*' Rigwit yelled. '*You'll never be able to return here unless you do as I say. Now get the jar, it's on the table. Get it and throw it out the door as far as you can. Do it now!*'

Thom moaned. The upturned jar was covered with spiders, as was the book next to it, as was the whole kitchen table, legs and all! 'I can't,' he wailed. 'I can't do it!'

'Sure you can. Just remember, they can't hurt you.'

'They're an illusion?'

'I didn't say that. But believe me, Thom, they can't hurt you unless you let them. Focus your mind on the glass alone. Try not to think of anything else.'

Something dropped on to Thom's head and when he lifted his arm to sweep it away, his hand contacted something much more bulky than he had expected. He sucked in a noisy breath and swept the spider away, using both hands to rake his hair, and stamped his feet like a child having a tantrum. He glimpsed the grey body and thick legs of a hunting spider falling into the bristling mass as he executed his unintended war dance. Again, he was spurred into action, his fear hiding behind a thick layer of revulsion and panic. Forgetting that his left arm and leg were supposed to be debilitated (the wonderful power of panic and adrenaline combined), he ran for the table, frantically sweeping his arms before him to knock away the hanging spiders in his path, skidding once and almost going down, but mercifully regaining his balance and rushing on.

It wasn't much of a distance between door and table, but it might have been a hundred miles as far as Thom was concerned, a gauntlet run that would have tested the bravest of men. He reached the table in no time at all – given the odd hundred years or so – and froze, his hands poised to grab, but his mind not quite prepared. Spiders crawled and slipped over the glass jar, the jar itself merely the entrance or exit, whichever way one chose to view it, of an endless tunnel through which tiny denizens of an underworld fled out into the light.

He could feel things dropping into his hair again, almost as light as snowflakes, as he considered the overturned jar, but his concentration for the moment was too fixed to swipe at them. Blunt needles scraped at his scalp. A tickle ran down his cheek.

*'Pick it up!'*

Not only was Rigwit's vexed shout in the room, but it was also inside Thom's head. As if mesmerized, he looked round to see a small kinetic structure made up of teeming black shells and minuscule brown bodies and thousands of moving threads, all in the shape of his little friend Rigwit. Only the slanted eyes that blinked and dislodged clinging spiders and the moving lips gave indication of any life beneath it.

Crawling things wriggled into the elf's mouth as he shouted, *'Throw it out, do it now before it's too late!'* The words were only mildly distorted.

Once again, galvanized, Thom leaned forward, flicked off

367

as many spiders as he could, then picked up the dirty glass jar by the upper rim of its opening.

Spiders – hundreds, vile, loathsome things – continued to spill from the top, but he took no notice of them – why should he? He was sharing a room with *millions* – and holding it out before him as though it exuded a nasty odour, he made for the front door. It was awkward to hurry across the piles (by the way his light boots sank into them, there had to be more than one layer) of crawling shells and bodies and his fear, among so many other suppressed fears, was that he would fall and land among them. What chance then? They would smother him in seconds, weaving their webs around him so that eventually he would be bound tight, unable to move, unable to swat them away ... He forced himself to stop that line of thinking, tried to go numb, halt his imagination in its stride. Not easy ...

Thom made it to the door and, with the glass vessel now in the crook of his arm (he shuddered and shuddered again until it became a constant shiver, for the spiders were still climbing over the rim, from there dropping to the floor or scuttling up his arm) he turned the key in the lock, grabbed the door-handle, and pulled. It jarred in its frame. He had forgotten it was bolted top and bottom.

He yelled in frustration and immediately two, three – God, it felt like a whole scrum! – maybe four spiders rushed into his mouth. Disgustedly and weepingly, he spat them out, not in the easy, cool manner that Rigwit had, but in a convulsive hawking, jettisoning them all like mushy pips, save for one which got caught between his tongue and the back of his teeth. He tasted its blood and the slop that was its juices and gagged, wanting to throw up but the vomit inside refusing to budge. Anyway, there was no time.

He reached up to the top bolt and lumps fell into his eyes so that he shied away, ducking and rubbing the lids before blinking them clear again. He was in a nightmare, only this was real and his mind knew it was so. No other choice but to keep on, keep moving, do what had to be done. Thom located the bolt beneath the rummaging infestation, closed his eyes (he felt drops of rain on his eyelids – drops of rain? He wished!) and yanked back the bolt. The door moved a fraction inwards, the top pressure off.

Wasting no time at all and refusing to believe his body was now entirely covered in jostling spiders – accepting that fact was the sure way to madness and again, he had no time for that – he sank to his knees and grabbed what he hoped was the end of the bottom bolt. His grip crushed the little bodies smothering the bolt's upright and he pulled hard so that the bar flew out of its supports. The door moved a barely perceptible millimetre, free of its restraint.

Something tickled the inside of Thom's ear and began to venture further. Thom stuck in a finger and mashed it, then dug it out with the nail. It was hard – oh God, it was so fucking hard – for Thom to maintain the numbness of mind, but really there *was* no choice, he *had* to move on.

He rose and pulled the door open, all in one movement, and it was good, so good, to breathe the warm summer air, to see the brightest of bright stars, even if he had to blink away irritating distractions just to clear his vision. It was invigorating, exhilarating – my God, it was *bracing!* – just to feel and look upon the outside world, the reality instead of the nightmare. But it wasn't over yet.

A stinging in his back. A bite to his neck. Pincers digging into his arm. They were becoming real! They had evolved from the phantasm to exist in the honest world, despite what Rigwit had told him. He realized that the longer the invasion had gone on, the more his belief in the normal had been weakened, so that the real had withered, finally giving in to the unreal. He was feeling pain, and if he didn't follow through quickly, then it would be too much too bear.

Thom grasped the jar in his other hand, his right hand, ignoring the spiders and bugs and God knew what else that scrambled from its opening, drew back his arm and threw.

The glass jar described a perfect arc, bodies spilling from it like a jetstream all the way, and landed almost at the forest's edge. All his strength and determination gone, Thom sagged against the door-frame.

And watched the hurrying creatures as they fled the cottage, forming a rippling stream that funnelled back into the dirty glass jar.

# Chapter: Thirty-Fifth

## BEFORE THE STORM

THOM AWOKE with a start, and overwhelming panic almost seized him yet again. He sat up in the bed and saw that he was alone in the bedroom and that it was daylight. The night was over, finished with; he was safe. The sight of the chest of drawers pushed up against the door reminded him of what had taken place the night before, the invasion of spiders, walking among them, throwing the carrier out of the cottage.

When the spiders had fled he had collapsed completely in the doorway, so weak again he feared another stroke was coming on. How long he had lain there, he had no idea, but it was the elf who had roused him and pressed a thimbleful of some sweet liquid to his lips, urging him with soft, kindly words to drink. Whether or not it was only in his mind, he had felt the potion sink into his body, then spread as though travelling through veins and arteries and even airways, reaching every part of his system, from toes to fingertips.

'It will help you as you sleep,' he remembered Rigwit had told him.

How he had got from the doorstep up to his bed was patchy – he'd insisted on locking, then bolting the front door, top and bottom, even though the elf had assured him the danger had passed for the night, and he remembered the long crawl on hands and knees up to the bedroom, Rigwit encouraging him all the way. But from there on, there was nothing. He had no recollection at all of pushing the chest of drawers against the bedroom door, nor of having climbed fully clothed into bed. He noted that his feet were bare and presumed Rigwit had pulled off his boots and covered his body with a bedsheet. Mercifully, sleep had swallowed him whole and had not even allowed a dream or two.

Thom rose from the bed, his body stiff, but his left arm and leg more mobile that he had expected. He drew circles in the air with his elbow, loosening the muscles of his left arm, then raised his left knee chest-high a few times, bending forward to meet it. The movement was awkward and hurt a little, but otherwise he was fine. Looking down at himself to examine his clothes, he saw the small dark patches, alien blood and squashed pulp, and his sweatshirt was torn in several places. He declined lifting the material to examine the skin beneath.

Instead, he went to the window and looked out at the woodland beyond. The day was grey, a vast blanket of light cloud filling the sky, covering the sun and dissipating its glory. The woods seemed very still, and when he listened, no bird calls came to his ears.

With some dread, Thom went to the stairs and looked down, expecting to see the small carcasses of spiders he'd killed; and see them he did. He was shocked, for another part of him had *not* expected them to be there, had thought all the spiders were imaginary, an illusion sent to the cottage by the wiccan, Nell Quick. And hadn't Rigwit said they couldn't harm him? Didn't that suggest they had been real only in his mind? Thom was confused. He had seen them, felt their scurrying legs on his own flesh yet they hadn't stung or bitten him. At least, not until the very end ... Lying in small scattered heaps was evidence of their existence. Maybe it was Rigwit's persuasion that they couldn't harm him that somehow nullified their effect at first. If the elf hadn't arrived in time to convince him, who knows what his own mind would have accepted.

Thom trod gingerly on the stairboards, his bare feet avoiding the splats and leg-curled bodies, and at the bottom he warily opened the door to the kitchen. It was the same in there, empty of any living creatures but the broken shells and pulp lying in heaps all around, a spider's graveyard whose sinister grimness was not lessened by daylight.

By the book – now closed, he observed – lying on the table was a jug containing the same juice that had revived him so well before; at least, he assumed it was the same. Rigwit, who obviously had closed the book, had left it there for him.

He called the elf's name, but there was no response. Thom was frustrated, but presumed that although he was the guardian of the cottage, Rigwit did not actually live there. It seemed he came and went as he pleased.

Guiltily (because he should have remembered sooner) he tried to ring the hospital where Katy Budd had been taken in Shrewsbury, but all he got on his mobile phone was the usual static. He resolved to drive into town later and visit the hospital. The next thing Thom did was to drink the juice straight from the jug, almost finishing it all before he felt satiated. He felt the same reaction as the first time, a sudden invigorating zest for life, his mind clearing of negativity, his strength returning. Unlike any hardcore drug, repetition did not appear to diminish the effect. With new-found enthusiasm, Thom swept the cottage free of squishy corpses, stripped and tossed his soiled clothes into the big rubbish bin hidden away round the back of the place, and took a long hot bath, scrubbing his skin hard with a brush, then soaking till the water cooled. Once dried, he realized he was famished, but quickly donned a midnight-blue short-sleeved shirt, medium-blue jeans, and soft black ankle-boots, before cooking a huge breakfast of bacon, sausages, scrambled eggs and grilled tomatoes. He finished off the remaining juice in the jug and, wiping his lips with a tea-towel, he thought he could now take on the world.

The feeling was not to see him through the whole day.

———

He called her name in vain.

Thom had left the cottage earlier that morning and gone into the forest in search of Jennet, walking through glades he had visited with her, along paths they had walked together, but there was no sign of her. In fact, there were no signs of faeries at all. Nor of the animals that they had come across in such large numbers.

The woods seemed empty, barren, devoid of life save the flora itself.

Thom needed to see her, needed Jennet's comforting arms around him, needed her to explain to him what was going on, for his return to Bracken had become a nightmare, the events of the past week beginning to weigh on him both in a mental and physical way. Whatever relief he'd had from the juice that morning was wearing thin, the enthusiasm and strength beginning to wane. But it wasn't the only reason he wanted to find Jennet.

He knew he loved her. He could hardly think of anything else but her: the terrible events, his suspicions, the monster that had nestled on his body to steal his vitality, the attack by wasps and its consequences, the spider invasion, all remained in the periphery of his mind when he thought about her, her loveliness, her nature, the mere image of her overriding all else. If it hadn't been for Jennet he might have easily packed his bags, climbed into the Jeep, and left Bracken for ever. Well, maybe not. Maybe he would have stayed on until after Sir Russell had passed away. He owed that much at least to the man who was, after all, his grandfather.

Sir Russell was of the old ways, respectable and duly respected, someone whose set opinions and traditional values would never allow birth out of wedlock to be acceptable. Maybe he was a relic of the past, part of an era that was never quite as pious and honourable as it pretended to be; anyway he was Thom's paternal grandfather and in the end that was all that mattered. Despite the rejection, Thom felt sure that Bethan – and perhaps even his father, Jonathan, Sir Russell's son – would have wanted him to be there for the old man as death drew close, or at least, to be around, even if at a distance. Besides, he was curious to discover just what game Nell Quick and, so it seemed, Hugo were playing. What had he, Thom, done to incur their rancour?

He went on with his search, continuing to call Jennet's name, his heart filling with dread as his echoes died away and only silence remained. There was no movement in the undergrowth, not even a shaking of leaves to indicate a fleeing animal, and no butterflies fluttered among the long flowers, no birds perched on branches or flew over the treetops. There was a strange quietness in the forest.

Finally, when he reached the lakeside, he cupped both hands around his mouth and shouted:

'*Jennnneeet!*'

Calm ripple-circles made by feeding fish spread here and there over the glass-still surface. But nothing rose from the lake's depths.

He called again:

'*Jennnneeeet!*'

Once more, in despair:

'*Jennet!*'

Thom sank to his knees, resting on his heels. He waited.

Disconsolately, he waited. Surely she hadn't deserted him? Not when he needed her so much. He leaned sideways, rested a hand in the grass. Eventually he sat, chin on his knees, hands around his ankles. He shivered. Despite the season, the forest felt cold. And he felt alone.

After an hour or so, he returned to the cottage.

# Chapter : Thirty-Sixth

# THE STORM

THOM HAD gone back to the cottage and brooded for the rest of the day, asking himself questions that appeared to have no answers, dwelling upon his relationship with Jennet, wondering about her unexpected absence that day. He thought of Hugo too, his so-called lifelong friend. Was he really involved in some kind of devious plot with Nell Quick? If so, why? And what was the purpose? It was as perplexing as it was tiring, and eventually Thom went upstairs and laid down fully clothed on the four-poster bed, his mind in turmoil, occasionally questioning his own sanity. Faeries, elves, witches, magic potions? *Was* he going crazy? He did not ponder too long, for soon his eyelids were drooping, his body relaxing. His last thought before sleep stole in and claimed him was that later he would drive to the hospital to see how Katy was faring. Then he was asleep . . .

It was the rumble of distant thunder that woke him. His eyes opened smartly, no flickering, no slow-rising from the depths of sleep, just sudden wakefulness. He was surprised to find the room in darkness and quickly turned on the bedside lamp so that he could look at his wristwatch. 9.45 pm. Shit! He had meant to drive in to Shrewsbury and check on Katy. He'd have to find a call-box and phone in, or drive to a better reception area for his mobile.

Thom left the bed to go to the window. It was late, but it shouldn't have been this dark. There were heavy clouds over the forest, but they didn't appear to be thunderous. Nor was it even raining. The sound of faraway thunder came again.

Curious, Thom left the bedroom and climbed the staircase to the roof. A strong breeze hit him as soon as he stepped out the door, ruffling his hair and clothes. The small figure of Rigwit was sitting on the parapet, looking outwards, over the woodland. Thom went to him.

'Where were you all day?' he asked, watching the elf's profile, his voice almost pleading.

Rigwit continued to gaze into the distance. He seemed agitated and even in the dusk of night Thom could see the distress in his expression. 'There have been many counsels throughout the woodlands today. The *faerefolkis* have been gathering to discuss what is to be done.'

'I tried to find Jennet.'

'You couldn't, not this day. The undines have gone to ground. Or should I say, to water. They're very afraid.' He turned his small face to Thom. 'As are we all,' he said ominously.

Thom shook his head. 'I don't understand. What's happening, Rigwit, what the hell is wrong?'

'It's the wiccan. She's unleashed powers she does not understand and cannot control.'

'Nell Quick?'

Rigwit nodded. 'She's a vain foolish woman who is not aware of her own limitations. She will wreak havoc this night. The *faerefolkis* are trying to find ways of restraining the malign forces she has released, but I fear it is already too late. I think all we can do is hide ourselves away until it has passed.'

Rigwit shuddered and Thom reached out to clasp his narrow shoulder. The elf was shivering.

'Why too late?' Thom asked, the breeze growing stronger so that his words seemed to be whisked away.

The elf turned away again and nodded towards the horizon. 'Look,' he said, his teeth chattering.

And Thom looked.

---

The wind hit him the moment he swung open the front door, pushing against him like some gigantic invisible hand, almost forcing him back inside the cottage. In the short time it had taken him to leave the rooftop and race down the stairs, the breeze had grown into a gale.

Bending into it, a forearm over his eyes, Thom ran out into the dry storm and such was the sound of the wind, he failed to hear Rigwit's cries from behind.

*'The book! You must take the book with you! It's your only hope!'*

Realising it would be quicker by foot, Thom ran across the clearing and on to the track that eventually would lead to Castle Bracken, the wind whipping at his clothes and hair, leaves flying across his path, and into his face, branches bending before its increased might. As he ran, the vision he'd had from the rooftop remained stark in his mind.

The clouds were heavier in the distance, with a thin light of yellowish-white from a sun that had long sunk from view silhouetting the low hills of the horizon, the light vignetting abruptly to dark grey the clouds themselves. But directly over Castle Bracken – he had seen lights in some of the windows – there hung boiling black clouds, their turbulent edges defined by flashes of inner lightning. Even as he had watched, a lightning bolt forked through the air to touch the mansion's roof itself. It was eerie and it was frightening, for it seemed that the big house had been singled out for attention, the dark rolling clouds directly hanging above it like a baleful portent. It was this and a dreadful feeling of impending disaster that had sent Thom down the stairs and out into the woods.

The wind set up a howling as he ran, growing stronger by the moment, bending not just branches but the young saplings also; it tore into his face like stabbing fingers, as if deliberately trying to blind him. He kept his right arm up, glad he knew the path so well, for it was growing darker by the second, the summer sun too far below the horizon now to have much influence. Already his breath was coming in harsh dry heaves and although his left leg was fine at present, he knew it would not be long before he was limping.

A leafy branch lashed at his face and would have struck his eyes had not his forearm protected them. Other branches waved at him from the sides of the path as though jeering his progress, their rustlings like angry voices. Crazily, the wind did not come from just one direction: one moment it was in front of him, slowing his stride, the next it was behind, speeding him along; at other times, when it appeared to come from all directions at once to whirl around him, it was like being buffeted by a whirlwind. There was moisture in the air – single raindrops constantly splattered against him – but there was no downpour. At least, not yet. He prayed he would get to the Big House before it did, for the track would quickly become slippery, the open field he would have to cross, a quagmire. Something tripped him and he sprawled headlong.

He rolled as he struck the earth, softening the impact, but still jarring his shoulder. When he looked behind to find out what had tripped him he saw a vine stretched across the path like a cunningly laid tripwire. Quickly, he pushed himself to his feet and set off again at a trot, gradually building up to a run.

Now even the thinner but more mature trees were bending or being rocked by the storm and occasionally, the whole woodland was lit up by distant lightning, the slow rumbling that followed growing louder each time. In the glare, the woods became a ghostly monotone, all greys and deep sharp shadows, the branches of many like arms held erect as if to frighten. Thom had never known a storm like this, had never known the woods to be so alien, so lowering. He had always regarded this place as his special homeland, but tonight he felt a stranger here, confused and fearful of what he might come upon. It was fortunate he knew the path so well.

He pressed on, panting hard, gulping in lungfuls of charged air when he could, beginning to tire, but determined to make it to Castle Bracken as soon as possible. To him, the jet-black clouds over the mansion presaged death and he could not understand why. He already knew that Sir Russell was dying, so perhaps it was a natural reaction; yet he had the strangest feeling of being called, almost as if a voice inside his head was screaming a warning, yet compelling him to come. As he ran he glanced up at the sky between the shifting treetops.

The clouds looked angry. They were a darker grey, not yet as black as those over the Big House, but barging into each other, pregnant with unshed rain. Something caught Thom's ankle again and this time he fell heavily, crashing to the ground, only his hands preventing serious injury. Oddly, as he tried to rise, he still felt a grip on his ankle.

He gave a small cry of terror when he caught sight of a grimy hand protruding from the earth, its short skeletal fingers curled around his leg. Another hand appeared near his face, bursting from the cracked soil as if on a spring, dirt flying off its thin flesh as the fingers wriggled in the air. Thom wrenched his foot away from the one clinging to his ankle, kicking back at the empty fingers as he did so. The

hand did not retreat; instead the whole arm, an undernour-
ished child's arm, rose from the soil, followed by the top of
a small, bald, grimy dome. Bleached hate-filled eyes that had
rarely seen the sun blinked away dirt as they came into view,
then the mouth, set in a vicious leer, spitting earth as the
complete face presented itself. Thom recognized it as one of
the brown creatures from the underworld near the lake, a
slow-moving thing with sharp claws and nasty intent. It, too,
received a smart kick from Thom's boot, but its expression
never changed and it continued to rise, emaciated shoulders
following a long thin neck.

Another lightning flash revealed a scene that might have
come from an old black and white horror movie, with hands
and shoulders appearing all around him, colourless except
for greys and blacks in the coruscation, a scene where the
dead rise gleefully from their graves. And just as corny,
thought Thom as he lashed out with his boot again.

The face leering next to him was just asking to be
smashed, and he duly obliged, only he used his fist for
added effect. The thing's head rocked back, but annoyingly,
the leering grin remained. Maybe it was because he had
encountered these earth-dwelling creatures before and had
easily eluded them that he was not as afraid as he should
have been, or maybe he was too intent on reaching the
house to take on more dread right then. As he rolled over to
get to his feet, two arms shot out of the ground on either
side of his head and pulled him down.

His face hit the earth with a definite thud, a whiteness
briefly spreading across his vision. He felt the hands tight
around his head and neck, yanking him down, the pressure
too strong to break. He tasted soil as his face began to sink
into the earth and he cursed himself for underestimating
these dirt-dwelling monsters.

He was losing breath, and no matter how hard he
struggled, the grip was not relinquished. Other hands
grabbed him in other places, all pulling, trying to force him

into the ground. As his face broke through the upper crust, he felt pressure rising beneath it, something below coming up to meet him. The shock caused him to yank his head back, the arms on either side rising with him. His face was only inches away from the dent he had made in the soil and, as he resisted the hands tugging him back again, the earth there began to erupt. The face that appeared, with its baleful pale eyes and gnashing clod-filled teeth, was grinning in a satisfied way, as if the creature knew it had him, that there could be no escape. The other hands around his arms, legs, his back and shoulders, renewed their efforts, dragging him down, welcoming him to their dark habitat, eager to bring him home, impatient to bury him.

And somehow, that enraged Thom. He had other things to do, more pressing matters in mind, than waste time here. With a fury that would have been intimidating had not these monstrosities been so dumb, he shot his head forward, striking his host below on its sorry excuse for a nose – mainly exposed cartilage around two narrow oval holes – a move he hoped hurt the thing as much as it hurt him.

Its grip relaxed and Thom felt a modicum of pleasure when he saw pain blossom in those eerily pallid eyes. He pulled free, then punched the other claws on his body so that bony fingers, with their jagged nails – good for digging? – uncurled. He had to prize off the more tenacious one with his own hands, but every time a leg was loose, so the other leg was grabbed. In desperation, he hauled himself to his feet, content to let his clothes rip so that all that the small hands clutched were bits of fabric or the air itself. He deliberately used a dome just breaking through the earth as a starting block for his continued run, stepping on it and pushing hard, the head sinking again, but slowly enough to give Thom impetus.

Ignoring the ground-dwellers that rose up on either side of the path like bizarre slow-motion Jack-in-the-boxes and hopping over those that appeared in front of him, Thom raced onwards, soon leaving them behind. He thought he heard their wails of disappointment, but it was impossible to tell over the noise of the wind. He was high on adrenaline now, energized by the short skirmish from which he had emerged victor, drawn on by thoughts of the impending danger to Sir Russell, which he knew, just *knew*, was not imagined.

There had been hefty individual spots of rain, but abruptly the rumbling clouds shed their full load. The sudden downpour drenched him immediately and, while to some extent it was refreshing, it bore down on his head and shoulders like a heavy load, making him hunched, his stride more awkward. It also made the path greasy within minutes, so that more than once he slipped, only keeping to his feet by good fortune rather than ability.

With the darkness of night, the howling wind, and the driving rain, the wood that had been home to him, his childhood playground, and was now his retreat, had become a hostile environment, the trees waving their arms as if to snatch him, thin leafy branches lashing at his face and body as if to punish him, and the ground at his feet with its hidden ruts and fallen debris, and now its mud, seeking to bring him down. A huge oak loomed spookily ahead as if to block the trail (in his feverish fright he couldn't be sure if the tree had always been there, or had craftily moved position), its great low boughs both formidable and foreboding. Lightning drenched the landscape in its uncompromising glare and, with a gasp, Thom came to a skidding halt. In the stuttering light, he had observed squirming bodies and hideous visages ingrained in the oak's bark, rough, moving, wooden shapes and countenances that resembled neither man nor beast, but which bore striking similarities to the monsters and demons that visited the worst kind of dreams.

An almost human head with an ugly disjointed face and the body of a slug turned to watch his approach; a thing with twisted horns and the black eyes of a viper slipped out a forked tongue from a lipless mouth to point in his direction; a female form with too many breasts and gorgon-like tresses for hair smiled wickedly at him as she thrust her naked hips provocatively forward; a pin-headed half-man (there was no lower body – perhaps his lower half was embedded in the tree trunk itself) with deepset holes for eyes and mouth squirmed around to 'see' who drew near. There were too many others to take in, sick rough-bark bodies that surely would only be recognizable under extreme circumstances, crooked shapes entwined and slithering among each other as if taking part in some kind of lazy orgy, some forms more horrendous than others, though all were unwholesome, and all appeared curious as to his presence on the path.

Thom, panting there in the darkness as the light died, body crouched, an arm outstretched before him, began slowly to edge sideways. No way was he going to go near that obscene oak tree, host to gruesome and loathsome parasites entombed in bark, even if it meant leaving the track.

Without a second thought, he plunged into the undergrowth to his left, intending to go around the distraction ahead, suspecting one of those great boughs might easily stretch itself to pull him into the writhing mob of peculiarities. Reality for Thom had become lost somewhere over the past few days.

Once among the bushes, he quickly became disorientated, the pounding rain limiting his vision, the woods themselves suddenly unfamiliar territory. He blundered around, cursing, biting into his lower lip, finally wheeling this way and that in exasperation, turning circles, utterly confused. There had to be a landmark nearby, something he knew, something that would give him his bearings. But there was just blackness out there, blackness and shifting trees and troubled skies.

Only when lightning next illuminated the landscape did he catch sight of the lone sentinel in the distance and realize where he was. It was the familiar long jagged trunk of the tree that had been struck by a lightning bolt long ago; it stood fiercely upright with its pointed, splintered top aimed defiantly at the clouds, easily visible among the other trees as long as the brightness remained. Thom took a quick bearing and made off in that direction.

He had to fight through bramble and rough undergrowth to reach it, sustaining more tears to his clothes as well as scratches and cuts to his hands and arms. But reach it he did, although by then he was beginning to limp and feeling was leaving his left arm. It wasn't too bad as yet, but Thom knew the weakness would grow worse the more exhausted he became. Nevertheless, he took no time out to worry about it: as soon as he spotted the trail again, he was off, lumbering towards it, relieved to know his direction once more.

Soon – although after more falls, more lashings from thin branches, and more shadowy sightings, none of which, mercifully, bothered to reveal themselves properly – he reached the edge of the woods and the great field opened up to him. He thankfully sank to his knees, his shoulders hunched, drawing in great gulps of wet air. The rain beat down on him even harder out in the open, but he didn't care, for it cooled him, refreshed him.

With a deep sigh, he was on his feet again and jogging across the grassland, a respite from the woods, no branches or bushes or unsightly things to stall him, nothing there to impede his progress. Except the muddy surface. And the grass snakes.

It seemed that every snake in the field and surrounding pastures had gathered to meet him, and instead of sliding between blades of grass, they stood half-erect, impossibly emulating the others of their species that had such power. Probably he would not even have noticed them in the grass had not he sprawled among them, tripped by an unseen slippery dip in the ground.

He fell only to his hands and knees, but immediately snakes coiled around his wrists like layered bracelets; he felt others nipping at his lower legs. They were not dangerous, merely unpleasant, and he ripped them away as he stood, then caught the others clinging to his legs by their tails and yanked them free, tossing them as far away as he could.

Even as he did so, he remembered the nasty little trick he'd played on Hugo all those years ago when they were boys, revenge for turning off the cellar lights and shutting him in. They were playing in this field and Thom had surreptitiously slipped a grass snake (which he knew was harmless, but Hugo didn't) down Hugo's shirt collar. Hugo had screamed and screamed and Thom had quickly pulled up his shirt and got rid of the snake. Too late, though. Hugo had gone into some kind of trance state, standing there like a zombie, but quivering, his eyes large and staring. When Thom had led him home, Sir Russell had hit the roof and Thom had been forbidden ever to play with Hugo again. Shortly after, his own circumstances had changed. So much for sweet revenge . . .

He kicked out at other snakes that endeavoured to block his path, their slim bodies visible only because the three-quarter moon had made a rare appearance among the stormy clouds, lightening the countryside in its fey glow, making the rain visible as silver streaks bombarding the earth.

He staggered a little as he went on, and wondered what else would try to hinder him reaching his goal.

Thom opened the gate on the far side of the field, leaning against it to stop himself collapsing. He didn't bother to close it behind him when he went on.

He was in the trees again, but the path was much wider, a lane almost. A rough lane leading to the bridge over the river.

Knowing he was so close to the Big House rejuvenated him to a degree, although he still limped and plodded rather than ran, his left arm hanging stiffly by his side, spoiling his balance. The wind seemed even harsher blowing through the tunnel created by trees meeting overhead, but at least he was shielded from the worst of the rain. The raindrops still came through the leafy canopy, but their power was reduced; they splattered against his head and shoulders with far less force and unity. The bridge was a short distance away and he blinked water from his eyes, not quite sure of what now lay before him.

Water was gushing over the bridge's low stone walls on either side, great waves that splashed on to its surface road, joining the rain to cause one huge rippling puddle along its length. What dismayed Thom, though, was that those towering waves that reached high over the walls were like watery arms and hands, throwing themselves at the bridge as if to catch anyone foolish enough to venture on to it. Another gauntlet to run.

Thom wondered what powers could create such a phenomenon. What was he up against? What forces *had* Nell Quick invoked to help her devious cause? It was all unbelievably insane – *everything that had happened to him this past week was unbelievably insane* – yet it was real, it was truly happening! Rainwater splayed from his hair as he shook his head vigorously, either to clear his mind, or refute the craziness, he didn't know. He felt fury rising in him again and he allowed it reign, aware that it was good, it made him less of a victim, it was the magic that would see him through this ordeal, a rage that was even *more* real than anything he'd been confronted by yet. With a hoarse cry he ran for the bridge.

He was already soaked through, so the renewed drenching did not bother him. However, those arm-like waves had unexpected force and they flew at his body, knocking him one way to the next, great blustering towers that rose high over his head to plummet down in a torrent, engulfing him, almost forcing him to his knees. He raised his voice against them, receiving a mouthful of gagging water with each yell, spitting it out, sucking in air again so that he could yell some more. His defiance, his wrath, was not purposeless, he was aware of that. Somehow it created a balance, man against the ... elements? No, this was rational man against unknown and irrational forces, powers that had no place, and no right to be in this world where the natural ruled and the supernatural was unacceptable – at least by those of pragmatic mind.

Thom roared again, the effect somewhat spoiled by the great rush of water that had him spluttering and retching, fighting for breath. Nevertheless he staggered onwards, buffeted by constant waves from side to side, his eyes stinging, his body bent like an old man's, his steps wide rather than long, as if he were on the deck of an ocean liner in inclement seas. Once, twice, he went down on one knee, and each time the river below seemed to renew its efforts, sending up even more lashing waves as if to wash him from the bridge entirely. And it almost did so.

The sudden great heave of water caught him off balance and sent him reeling against the wall on one side, his upper body crouched over the stone balustrade so that he was looking straight down at the raging river below. For a moment, he thought he saw figures and faces patterned in the surging foam, ghastly things that appeared to delight in his stress; even as he looked, a huge spout of twisting water shot up to meet him. He thought he would be dragged over the side and he clung tight to the parapet, knowing that if he fell into that churning maelstrom he would have no chance, he would drown.

The geyser sucked at him and waves from behind pushed – even the rain plotted against him by pelting his back, bending his shoulders – but still he clung to the stonework, pulling himself down, sinking to his knees, body bowed so that the wall offered at least some protection from the determined river. On all fours, he inched his way along, battered by more and more waves, their power dwindling as he drew nearer to the end of the bridge, as if the water had a mind of its own and knew it was losing the battle. One last surge, the river rising up on both sides together to wash him away, the waves boiling with rage and frustration (it seemed to Thom's own besieged mind), so that he had to flatten himself, press hard against the bridge's narrow roadway, choking on water as he did so, the bridge totally flooded, a surging river in itself.

For almost a minute he was beneath the water's surface, but still he clung there, fingers attempting to dig into the hard stone itself, willing a heaviness to his body; and then the water became shallow, was running away through drain holes cut along the bridge's length, leaving Thom heaving and spluttering, gulping in great lungfuls of rain-filled air. At that moment he knew he had won and the river appeared to realize it too; the water slunk away, withdrawing from the bridge, no further waves leaping over its ramparts.

Still choking, hawking water, Thom struggled to his feet and plodded through puddles, not stopping until he was once more on the muddy track leading to Castle Bracken. He did not linger long, giving himself just enough time to catch his breath and regain at least some of his strength.

It felt hopeless though. He felt sapped, most of his energy gone, the left side of his body a dead weight, a burden to be dragged along. What use would he be to Sir Russell even if he managed to reach the eyrie? He was exhausted, hurting, almost as weak as when he had come around after the stroke. What could he do to defeat Nell Quick with all these strange powers she possessed? He would not even be a match for Hugo in this state.

Thom wanted to sink to the rain-soaked ground and rest, even sleep, despite the storm. His body sagged. He almost went down. But something held him erect. Something he thought must be outside his own body, something that willed him on with silent encouragement. But on closer examination, on listening to his inner self, he realized that it was his own determination that was *instructing* him not to give in, anger at the wrong that was taking place *bullying* him to go on and do his best, whatever that might be, for his grandfather. He stumbled along the track, mumbling to himself that he had to get to the mansion soon, before it was too late. He was going to spoil their game. Or – he paused for no more than a second – die in the attempt. From then on, he wasted no more strength talking to himself. He concentrated on taking one step after the other.

And, almost taken by surprise, he soon found himself looking up the gentle incline towards Castle Bracken.

It stood tall and dark and brooding against the violent night sky, an imposing but ugly building in these conditions, a place, it suddenly seemed to Thom, where bad things were meant to happen.

Even as he watched, a jagged bolt of lightning split the air and appeared to strike the mansion. Immediately, the few inside lights that were on blinked out.

The immense roar of thunder that was instantaneous with the lightning, though lasting much longer, made Thom cringe, made him cower away from it – made him cry out in anguish.

# Chapter : Thirty-Seventh

# RETURN TO THE CELLAR

BY THE time Thom had dragged himself up the worn stone steps to Castle Bracken's huge single front door, the rain had ceased its torrent and the wind, while it still whipped his hair and snagged his clothes, had lost the worst of its wildness. The three-quarter moon, which was a long way off from the great black clouds that threatened the mansion and the immediate land around it, was now revealing itself occasionally, lighting the landscape with its queer metallic flush, then abruptly leaving it in darkness once more for long minutes at a time. Other clouds churned and rushed away – rushed away, Thom imagined, from the low deep cloud bank that loomed over Castle Bracken, the alliance between the black mass and the other storm clouds finally over.

Sodden and so weary his body was trembling, Thom smacked the flat of his hand against the brass doorbell set in the granite wall. He listened for its ring from within, but none came. The lightning. Of course. All fuses had been blown. Frustrated, he tried the door-handle, rattling against it in desperation when nothing happened. He banged on the wood with the heel of his fists, but there was no disturbance from within, in fact, no signs of life at all.

Taking a step back, he looked up at windows that were ominous and black. He cupped his right hand and called out Hartgrove's name, but the wind was still strong enough to carry away the sound. Why call for the manservant? Thom asked himself. Bones had to be part of it, in league with Nell Quick and Hugo. How else could they succeed? The manservant was always around, always close to Sir Russell. If, as Thom suspected, Nell was poisoning Sir Russell over a period of time to avoid suspicion that might be caused by his grandfather's sudden death – God, she knew how to do that with her brews and potions! – then Hartgrove was bound to know. Probably he was up there with her, in the eyrie, helping her finish the job.

Thom hobbled down the steps, at the bottom looking to left and right, searching for a way in. Break a window? That was the obvious choice. But wait, there was another entrance to the Big House. As a boy he had always known about it, but neither he nor Hugo ever chose to use it. Even now, the thought made Thom shiver over the trembling.

Reluctantly, yet resolutely, he made his way round to the rear of Castle Bracken.

---

It was a coal hatch primarily, although it was large enough to use for moving in boiler machinery, or anything else that had to do with the mansion's underground maintenance. The five-foot double doors were angled as though leaning against the building, and set in a concrete mount. As kids, Thom and Hugo would open one side and peer down into the gloom, Hugo usually daring Thom to climb inside, a dare he never took up, at least, not from that entrance. Thom remembered the last time he had visited these cellars and how he'd hidden in the darkness on hearing approaching footsteps. He had dreamed he was in the same predicament many times over since, nightmares that never seemed to fade with time.

In those days, the doors were never locked and he saw no reason why they should be now. Drawing in a deep breath, he slipped his fingers between the middle crack and pulled at one side. The door was heavy, but it opened with a loud creak.

The moon, still playing its tiresome hide-and-seek game, chose to reveal itself once more, bathing the land in a wintry light. It did Thom no favours, for the pit he was about to descend into looked blacker than ever in the contrast with the blanched landscape above. He wished he had thought to bring along a flashlight, but then he hadn't known his journey would end in darkness. He stood there for a while, a hand keeping the flap open, building up the nerve to step inside. Another lightning bolt from directly above the house whitened everything again, and its glare was strong enough to penetrate the cellar below. In its strobe-lighting effect, Thom was able to see the hill of coal that swept down from the opening, and with no further hesitation, he let go the door flap, so that it crashed to one side, stepped over the hatch's concrete base, and slid and tumbled down the treacherous slope.

He had tried to control his descent, but footholds only slithered away, and he crashed against the partition that held the great heap at bay. He sprawled there in total darkness, for not only had the lightning flickered away, but the moon had resumed the game and was now hiding behind the distant clouds. He tried to catch his breath and sucked in coal dust that caused him to cough. Dear God, it was so dark. Pitch black. Nothing to be seen. Its blackness almost tangible. If you stuck a finger into it, you would feel the darkness yield, flow around your hand like inky syrup. He lay there, one shoulder against the wooden partition, his legs splayed over the lower regions of lumpy invisible coal, swirling dust clogging his nose, and he was a ten-year-old again, supposedly hiding from a friend, but in truth hiding from heavy footsteps that came along the corridor outside this basement chamber, growing louder as they approached . . .

. . . As they did now, only these were scuffling footsteps, shoes dragging along the floor and, as it was all those years ago, a light came with the sound, a light that was warm but insubstantial, its arc widening with every step.

Thom felt the same panicky fear he had felt as a child, his heart seeming to freeze, then begin beating again, so loudly he thought it might be heard by whoever drew near. He pressed his temple close to the partition and moaned inwardly as the wood cracked, the sound like a gun going off in the stark, cold boiler-room. As he hid there, a ten-year-old boy once again, his mother's words came to him just as they had before in this sombre labyrinth of underground chambers.

Listen to your inner voice, it said. Go into that secret place that no one can touch. Draw strength from it. And that was where he tried to retreat in an attempt to escape the post-trauma of his terrible and difficult journey and now this reliving of a constant nightmare.

It almost worked. But when the scuffling footsteps stopped at the entrance to the boiler-room, the breathing that came with it heavy and rasping, the glow that travelled before it now stationary, he wanted to scream out his terror, let it loose, let the worst of it leave his body and echo around the walls; he wanted to precipitate whatever was about to happen, rush forward rather than hide from it. Wanted to, but found he did not have that kind of foolhardy courage. He wasn't a coward, just not an idiot. He waited there behind the partition, praying that whoever guarded the doorway would not think to look behind the wooden wall, wouldn't realize it was from there that the sharp sound had come.

Yet even as he cowered in the shadows, the hill of coal he had slid down had not properly settled. There were still precariously balanced lumps and they shifted for no other reason than that their equilibrium was unstable; one toppled and others followed in a small avalanche. Thom gritted his teeth and hunched his shoulders at the sound, which was not loud, but like a major rock slide to him.

Lumps of coal settled with the noise against him and when he listened, when he listened *intently*, he could no longer hear that terrible rasping breathing. He checked his own, wishing he could do likewise with his pounding heart. Then came a long, drawn-in sigh, as raspy as before, and the shuffle of feet on the concrete floor coming towards his hiding-place.

The scene was being played out almost the same way as before, but there was nothing repetitious about it; it was too bloody fresh and scary for familiarity to blunt its edge. Thom huddled into himself, that same child trying to make himself smaller, and the dragging steps on the other side of the partition grew louder, came closer. The cobwebbed ceiling above glowed orange. Now the creak of wood, someone leaning against the partition, the feeling of a presence above him, eyes cast downwards. Blindly, Thom reached into the pile beside him, his fingers closing on a good weighty piece of coal. He was no longer that child. He was a man who wouldn't be threatened any more by some unseen thing, who was only human anyway, for it walked (scuffled) and breathed (rasped) as humans do. Thom clasped the coal rock in his fist and made ready to leap up and strike out.

First though, he looked up. And it *was* the same scene as seventeen years ago, so for a brief and very insane moment he thought he was that child once more. The long cadaverous face. The dead eyes. All lit by candlelight. The same nightmare that had haunted him ever since. The only difference was that both he and Bones had aged, Bones terribly so.

The head slipped away and Thom heard Hartgrove's body slump to the floor on the other side of the thin wall. Scrambling to his feet and dislodging more coal so that the hill rushed in to fill the space he had just left, Thom stumbled around the partition and knelt by Hartgrove's collapsed body. The candle was lying on its side on the dusty floor, its small flame still alight so that its glow picked up the crumpled figure of the old lean manservant. He gave out a soft moan as Thom touched him between chin and neck to feel for a pulse.

The dry, chilled, parchment skin was abhorrent to the touch, but Thom persisted, not sure why he was suddenly anxious about Bones of all people. He had always been afraid of him, and even now, older and presumably, though not necessarily, wiser, he was still wary of the man. The pulse was weak, but the quiet moan and sudden raspy intake of breath informed Thom that the manservant was very much alive.

Hands beneath Bones's thin shoulders, he pulled him up as gently as he could, propping his upper body against the partition. Then he reached for the fallen candle and brought it closer to the semi-conscious man's face.

'Jesus,' Thom said in a low voice. 'What happened to you?'

The injured man tried to speak, but no words would come.

Thom persisted. 'Are your arms, your legs, okay? Can you feel if anything's broken?'

A mumble of incoherent sounds, nothing more.

'Let me get you upstairs. I'll call an ambulance.'

'No . . .' Bones muttered.

'You need—'

'No time.'

The hand tightened as if to hold Thom there.

'I think you're badly hurt, Mr Hartgrove. You need attention.' Thom made ready to pick up the old manservant, hoping he had enough strength left to get him upstairs. The rules dictated that an injured person should be left unmoved where they were until injuries could be properly assessed, but Thom did not like the idea of leaving Hartgrove down here in this dank, dirty place.

But again, Hartgrove protested. 'No time. You must help . . .' He seemed to lose breath once more, and the words trailed away.

'Who did this to you?' Thom asked, desperately concerned for the man he had never liked, had always feared.

'She . . . she did. They . . . both . . . did,' came the muttered reply.

'Nell Quick and Hugo?'

Hartgrove nodded his head as if that might be easier than speaking.

'Where are they now? Are they with Sir Russell?'

More slow nodding of his head. 'You must help . . .'

'I will. I'll get you upstairs. I'll call an ambulance.'

The hand gripping his arm left to grab his damp shirt. 'No. You must . . . you must help Sir Russell.'

'Is he in danger?' Thom already knew the answer, but watched as Hartgrove nodded his head yet again.

'They threw me down the stairs.' His voice became stronger with anger. 'They wanted me out the way while . . . while . . .' Hartgrove groaned and tried to touch the bruises on his face, but his hand fell away uselessly.

'Mr Hartgrove, you know me, don't you? It's Thom, Thom Kindred.'

Hartgrove's fingers fluttered in the space between them. 'I know . . . you.'

'Can you tell me what this is all about? Why Nell Quick and Hugo have hurt you, and what they're going to do to Sir Russell?'

'Threw me . . . down . . . cellar . . . stairs . . .'

'I know, I know. But why? Just take your time and try and tell me why this is happening.'

'I hid the Will from them. Sir Russell's last Will and Testament. It left . . . left everything . . . to you.'

Thom was stunned, not sure he'd heard correctly. 'Surely everything will be passed on to Hugo on Sir Russell's death?'

Hartgrove shook his head from side to side and the effort was too much for him. He seemed to lapse into unconsciousness.

'Hartgrove? Can you hear me?' Thom gently cupped the manservant's cheek in his hand.

Hartgrove's eyelids flickered, opened. He regarded Thom in silence for a few moments, then seemed to summon up whatever strength he had left.

'Hugo is not . . . a good . . . son. He has hurt . . . his father in many ways. Let him down, disgraced him. And now . . .' his lipless mouth formed a half-smile, half-sneer '. . . and now he wants to sell Bracken Estate to developers. Do you know . . . what kind of developers?'

He began to cough and the spittle on his lips was pinkish. It turned red as the coughing went on uncontrollably and Thom guessed he had sustained internal injuries. Maybe a broken rib had pierced a lung.

'Don't try to talk.' he told the manservant. 'Rest here while I get help.' Now he knew it would hurt Hartgrove even more if he tried to take him up upstairs.

But when the coughing had stopped, Hartgrove continued, as if anxious to impart as much information as possible before it was too late.

'The developers, Thom. Do you know what kind? Can you . . . can you guess?'

Thom shook his head and added, 'I've no idea,' in case Hartgrove's vision was not too clear.

'They're . . . they're experts in things . . . what do you call them? You know, Thom, don't you?'

And suddenly, Thom did know. This ancient country

mansion, set in beautiful acres, with its own woodland, river and lake: Nell and Hugo could only have one thing in mind. Open up Castle Bracken to the public, certainly. But that wouldn't be enough, it still wouldn't bring in enough income for Hugo. No, they probably wanted to turn the whole estate into a theme park of some kind. Jesus, that's what it was all about. And Sir Russell knew, somehow he had found out. Perhaps Hugo and Nell had even discussed their plans in front of him, thinking him comatose at the time. Sir Russell had then changed his Will in favour of Thom, who was, after all, his natural grandson. My God, how could Hugo even think of such a thing? To turn this wonderful countryside into a theme park, to tear away its privacy, its stillness, its beauty. Hugo must be desperate. And Sir Russell must have hated Hugo for it.

Thom had room to feel wretched. It was not what he wanted. Hugo had always been a good friend . . . hadn't he? Thom thought of the item that had gone missing from his London home, the pair of dividers he'd had for years so that they were almost a mascot to him, a talisman even. Probably the shirt button too. And the photograph had been Hugo's. Hugo must have taken the items and supplied the photo. To Nell Quick. Who, no doubt, would soon become Hugo's wife. Yet Thom still had no desire to come between father and son. As much as he loved Bracken's woodlands and the cottage, they did not rightfully belong to him. They were Hugo's inheritance. Maybe it wasn't too late to talk to him, make him see sense. He had to try, he felt he owed it to his friend. His one-time friend? Even if the estate was left to him, Thom, they could share it. He could persuade Hugo there were better things to do with the land.

Hartgrove was stirring, clutching at Thom's shirt again.

'It . . . must . . . go . . . to . . . you,' he gasped. 'Only you . . . will understand.'

Even in his pain, there was a special gleam in Hartgrove's eyes. Thom was curious. What exactly did the injured man mean? There was a knowing look in his tired old eyes, one that went beyond words, an understanding that the manservant obviously assumed was mutual. And probably, it was.

'The ... land must stay ... privately owned, Thom. *They* ...' he emphasized the word '... depend on it.'

He knew of the *faerefolkis*? And if he did, then Sir Russell must also know.

'You must keep ... their secret, Thom. They will count on you.'

Thom was about to speak, to question Hartgrove, find out how he knew of the others that lived in the woods and the lake, how long he had known, but Hartgrove raised a faltering hand.

'You must go now. Sir Russell, you ... must ... you must ... stop ...' His words trailed away and he slumped down the partition, his body stretched out.

Thom wanted to stay and help him, but was aware he could not waste another moment. Something bad was happening up there in Castle Bracken's roof room, and only he could prevent it.

If there was still time ...

# Chapter: Thirty-Eight

# STAIRWAY TO HELL

H E'D HAD no choice. Thom had had to leave Hartgrove lying unconscious on the cold dusty cellar floor. The old manservant was in a bad way, his breathing shallow, the full extent of his injuries unknown. By candlelight, his thin, cadaverous face seemed to have a deathly pallor and his eyes were mere slits, neither open, nor quite closed. His stillness had something of death about it.

Thom reached the top of the creaky cellar stairs and he saw the bank of light switches by the door. He flipped a couple, but nothing happened. Now he was sure the mansion's main fuse had blown, but he didn't have time to locate and fix it. He had to get to the roof room.

He twisted the handle to the cellar door, half-expecting it to be locked – in which case he would kick it open, regardless of noise – but as soon as he pushed, the door opened. He went through, the candle's flame creating unsettled shadows like darting spectres in the great hallway. The eyes of portraits around the walls seemed to be watching him

from the surrounding darkness, statues on plinths seemed
to agitate because of the wavering light. The inset doorways
contained deeper, concealing shadows. The house's familiar
smell came to him and it was stale, degenerative, different
from the stronger smells of the dusty cellar, but even so,
somehow more intrusive. There was a corruptness about
this odour.

Thom did not linger. He quickly moved to the stairway
and began to climb, the candle held before him like a
weapon against the dark. His left hand swept along the
curving banister, ready to grip tightly should he stumble, or
should anything emerge from the gloom above to throw
him back down. He was not quite sure what he expected –
a lunatic Nell, the succubus again? – so was ready for
anything.

The darkness retreated before him on the first-floor
landing, but only so far: the candle was a weak champion
after all. He could just make out the tapestries on the half-
panelled walls, the longcase clock at the far end, for some
reason its trunk door left open. Pausing only to catch his
breath – his left leg had to be dragged up every step so far,
his left arm felt like a dead weight on the rail, and although
the shock of seeing Bones down there in the cellars had set
adrenaline on free-flow again, exhaustion had returned like
an unwelcome guest – he went on. The smell of corruption
was even stronger here. It wafted down from the stairway to
the floors above, becoming more odious with every tread of
the stairs. And it was unlike two days ago, when he had
ascended this stairway with Hugo for, although pervasive
and unpleasant, the smell had been bearable; now its pun-
gency almost made Thom retch. He began to question his
actions. In his present state, what would he do, what *could*
he do, when he reached the 'penthouse' room? He was weak,
badly debilitated, and no match for the two of them, Nell and
Hugo, let alone whatever evil *she* had conjured. If he had
thought to bring his cell phone, he could have called the

403

local police and they would have at least have been on their way by now. Then again, he couldn't be sure the mobile would work in this area; it hadn't at the cottage. Find a phone here. Go back downstairs and find a phone. The power cut wouldn't affect the telephone lines. Even as he considered retreating (and in his heart he knew he was looking for an excuse not to venture up those stairs any further) he realized if he wasted time it would be too late to help Sir Russell, that only he could prevent any more harm coming to the sick old man. He had to keep going. Besides, it was probably already too late. There were noises, quiet noises, quiet noises combining to make a fuller sound, coming from the floor above.

Coming his way.

He stopped climbing.

He looked upwards.

---

They poured over the lip of the top stair like a rippling river, a mass of blackness flowing from the greater darkness, hundreds – thousands, *millions* maybe – of them.

Spiders. A fluid multitude. Legions of dark scuttling bodies. Streaming towards him.

He was too aghast to scream. Too shocked to move. Not again! Oh dear God, not again! But they couldn't hurt him. Rigwit had told him that. They could crawl all over him, they could get inside his clothing, skitter over his flesh, *but – they – could – not – hurt – him!*

In a second they were swarming round his feet. In two seconds they were climbing his legs. Holding the candle in his left hand, he swatted them, squashed them against himself, his jeans turning darker with their blood. But they were inside the material, they were crawling over his bare flesh. And – *Christ!* – they were biting!

This couldn't be! Rigwit had said they couldn't hurt him!

And they hadn't before! At least, not till the very end of their attack!

He cried out as his calf received a particularly vicious nip. Jesus! It hurt! He slapped at the back of his leg and felt something pulp against his skin. Others were climbing higher, he could feel them racing up his thighs! More bites, more nips. A stinging. Like a needle pushed into his knee. No! They shouldn't – A cry again. Oh God, something on his neck, puncturing the skin there! They moved so fast. And there was no end to them. More and more swept over the tip of the top stair, rippling over lower ones, a great tide of spiders, all headed towards him, re-igniting the conflict.

Involuntarily, he stepped backwards, missed his footing on the stair, and went down, at first falling against the rail, then bouncing off it, tumbling down the rest of the stairway to the flat half-landing below. He lay there, stunned and in terror, the candle on its side a little way off, out of reach, but, fortunately, still burning. Even as he raised his head from the floor, the scuttling hordes streamed down to him and within moments they were all over, in his hair, inside his shirt, his jeans, everywhere. He felt their jabs, their stings, their bites – he felt them eating him!

Thom rolled over in an effort to crush as many as possible, but still they came, a seemingly endless flood of them, covering him, swarming over every square inch, finding their way into his ears and nostrils and, when he opened his mouth to scream, into his mouth. The pain was terrible, like red-hot needles pricking his skin and he had to close his eyes as they poured over his eyelids. He rolled this way and that, hitting himself, rising enough to press his back against the wood-panelling of the wall, killing as many of the little bastards as possible, squashing them so that they were no more than gooey bits of mush and gore that could no longer bite. It was no use though, there were just too many and their stinging jabs were too much to bear. Thom felt himself swoon with the intensity of the pain, for although the bites were nothing in themselves, painful but tolerable, combined they were overwhelming. He spat bodies and dismembered legs from his mouth, swiped tormentors from his face, and felt what remaining strength he had left fast draining from him.

Only when something tugged at his shoulder did he open his eyes, immediately closing them again to blink away spiders. He brushed a hand across his eyes again and saw the anxious face of Rigwit staring up into his own. The little man had comparatively few spiders crawling over him – Thom apparently was the main target – and to those there were he paid no mind.

'You're allowing them to hurt you this time.' The elf said, cross rather than anxious. 'Your mind is tired, weak, as well as your body, and because you're not resisting them, they have power over you.'

'I am ... I am resisting them.' Even as he spoke, Thom feebly swatted spiders crawling over his raised knee.

'No, you're believing in them too much. It's not your fault, you're too exhausted. But you must resist, Thom, you must tell yourself they cannot hurt you.' Rigwit's voice was not even raised. It was as though he, himself, was not unduly bothered by the spiders. As if to make the point, he flicked off a particularly large and nasty-looking individual with a gross furry body and heavy furry legs and which had appeared crawling over his shoulder.

'*But they are hurting me!*' Thom yelled back at him.

'Go into your mind, tell yourself otherwise,' Rigwit patiently urged.

'*It's no good, I can't! They're killing me!*'

'Try. Try harder.'

Thom did try, but he could still feel those prickly legs all over him, still yelped at any particularly stinging bite, of which there were many.

'Keep trying, Thom. I'll be back.' With that, the elf sprang up the stairs, crushing spiders with his feet as he went.

'*Don't leave me! Come back!*' Thom's disbelieving gaze followed the climbing elf – each step was like a waist-high shelf to the little man until he disappeared over the edge of the top stair and spiders dropped from Thom's hair into his eyes again.

In desperation, he scrambled for the candle lying a short distance away, its flame still burning. He picked it up with spider-infested fingers and brought the flame close to his body, touching it to the tiny specimens that had now become slow, content to nest and feed on their prey. They shrivelled up under the fire and he could almost hear – only in his imagination, of course – their dying screeches. There were still too many though. Blinking hard again to dislodge those on his eyelids, he looked down to see his body was thick with them.

A light patter of feet on the stairs, the occasional *squelch* of a larger-bodied spider as it was flattened underfoot, and then Rigwit was by his side again, the same dirty jar (so Thom assumed) that Thom had hurled from the cottage the night before in his small hands.

'Throw it, Thom,' Rigwit said close to his ear while proffering the jar. 'Cast it away. The spiders must follow wherever the vessel is cast.'

Like a drowning man grasping for a lifebelt, Thom took the jar from the elf and raised it over his shoulder, ignoring the parasites that nipped and ate his body, making ready to throw it down the stairs.

'*No!*' Rigwit commanded urgently. 'Through the window. It must be cast outside for it to work.'

Thom aimed at the window overlooking the stair-landing, and pitched the jar as hard as he could, using up whatever strength he had left. The window shattered and the jar disappeared into the night just as lightning flared outside.

Thunder seemed to rattle the building.

He collapsed against the panelling and the spiders instantly began to leave. They seemed to drain from him as one, flowing towards the wall beneath the broken window; up they rose, a thick throbbing mass of them, climbing on to the glass in lower frames and then through the opening, where the wind howled and whistled in. The stream on the stairs bypassed Thom and the elf, pouring to the wall and up to the smashed windowpane. It took surprisingly little time for them all to go by, and quickly the numbers began to dwindle, the stream becoming narrower, a trickle.

A strange thing – that is, another strange thing – happened to the last few hundred or so. As they reached the wall and began their journey upwards, they began to dissolve, to fade away, as though they had not really been there at all, until finally, there were none left to see. Only Thom and Rigwit remained on the mansion's stairway.

---

Thom closed his eyes, but this time it was with relief. He drew in great gulpfuls of the fresh but charged air that blew in from the hole in the window. He was finished. He knew he could do no more and a tear spilt down his cheek. He could not save his grandfather. He was too used up. Although he no longer felt any spider-caused pain, his body ached with fatigue and he knew he would be bruised from the fall downstairs. He was cut and marked from his race to get here, but that was all, there was no other hurt. It was as if the episode with the spiders had never happened, although he knew it had and that it was something he would never forget.

Opening his eyes, he searched for Rigwit in the candle light, but the elf had disappeared from view. He soon heard the soft patter of small feet again, and there was Rigwit, climbing back up the stairs from below, the book from Little

Bracken clasped in his arms. The elf laid it down next to Thom.

'It's no good, Rigwit,' Thom told him wearily. 'I can't do any more. I can barely move.'

'That's why you need this.' Rigwit raised a loop of leather over his head and one shoulder; attached to it was a tiny leather bag that held a container or vial of some kind – Thom could just see its top sticking out from the bag's open end.

Rigwit undid the top and held the bag out towards Thom. 'Drink this,' he said 'You'll soon feel better.'

'What is it? Another magic potion?'

'It will make you feel strong again. I brought it from the cottage with the book. I'm sorry I couldn't catch up with you, Thom, but the book is heavy and my legs were never meant for running too far.'

Thom's head sank back against the oak panelling. He closed his eyes. 'How did you get in here?' he asked distractedly, wanting only to lay down on the floor and sleep. 'Through the cellars, like me?'

'There are a hundred ways for my kind to get into this place,' Rigwit answered, pushing the leather-encased container against Thom's lips. 'Now come on, you must drink. If you're to be of any use, you must be strong again.'

Reluctantly, Thom opened his mouth and allowed Rigwit to pour in the liquid. It was not only his strength that had left him, but his spirit too. How much more must he endure?

The potion flowed like treacle, thick, glutinous, but it tasted like nothing he'd tasted before. It had a sweetness that was subtle, an aftertaste really; he had an odd image of drinking deep red velvet, it was the only way he could describe the sensation. And he could feel it sinking into his throat rather than it being swallowed, flowing smoothly and instantly beginning to spread into his system like the brew he'd drunk before, but somehow different. From the main arterial that was his throat, it seemed to follow lesser tributaries he hadn't known existed so that his whole body was replete. The small bottle or vial contained no more that a thimbleful of the potion, medicine, whatever, and it was gone in one long gulp.

'That should see to it,' said Rigwit when he was satisfied that every last drop – in actuality, it was all one large drop – had been consumed. 'It's very powerful stuff, lad, extremely potent, and, I might add, 'tisn't easy to come by. Had to do a lot of bargaining to get this much. I'll be working off the consideration for the next hundred and fifty years or so. Not meant for humans, y'see, only for the *faerefolkis*. However, in *your* case there was a lot for the counsel to consider.'

Thom was only half-listening, for the sensation spreading through his body was too wonderful for him to concentrate on other things. It wasn't too dissimilar from the other juices he'd taken, but its effect was far greater and even more immediate if that were possible. His strength returned in a matter of seconds and his spirit lifted in equal amounts. The numbness went from the left side of his body and the exhaustion became barely a memory. What the hell was he sitting here on the stairs for when all that mattered was that he reached the roof room before Nell Quick had a chance to murder Sir Russell? He pushed himself to his feet and turned back to the next flight of stairs.

'Wait, Thom.' Rigwit had caught hold of his leg. He leaned down towards the little man, holding the candle near his face. He saw a lot of fear, a lot of anxiety there now. 'You must take care,' the elf told him. 'What you find at the top of this house might destroy us all. It will be the most terrible thing you have ever had to face.'

'After what I've been through lately? I doubt it.'

The grip tightened.

'If you're not dead by the end of this night, you might at least be mad. Use caution, Thom, and listen to your inner voice, because it's always true.'

The inner voice again. It hadn't really helped so far.

As if reading his thoughts, Rigwit said, 'You must believe in the voice. Your only real power is in your conviction. Faith is both your shield and your weapon. There is only so much we can do to help; the malign forces have moved into your realm now.'

Thom considered what he had been told for a moment. Naturally, he did have a choice. He could run down these stairs and out into the stormy night, call the police from a safe distance. But he was feeling good, strong, confident, not quite eager for battle, but not adverse to it. He was still afraid, but the fear was surmountable. Again, he turned to go, but the grip held.

Rigwit's voice was grave. 'Remember, you will see and feel things that will make you doubt your own sanity, and I mean it when I say madness, indeed, might soon follow. You think that over the past days and nights you have witnessed the very worst that nightmares may bring, but this I can tell you: they were nothing compared to the abominations that await you in that loathsome room above. They will be insidious and sly, cunning and dangerous. And unless care is taken, they will be fatal. You will be afraid, Thom, so afraid you'll feel weak again. Even the effects of the potion will not help you.'

'Thanks for the pep talk.'

'*You must believe me!*'

Thom was taken aback by the sudden anger.

More calmly, although his little body was trembling, Rigwit went on: 'Take the book with you. Use it as you used it last time. That and your faith is all you have.'

Thom lifted the heavy book, briefly wondering how the elf had managed to carry it through the woods. It must have weighed more than Rigwit himself.

The thought, he knew, was a deliberate distraction, his own mind's way of deflecting further consideration of what lay ahead for him. Rigwit's warning had roused his nervousness again, despite the feeling of wellbeing induced by the potion, and maybe that was the idea, maybe he had begun to feel too bold, too incautious, and the elf knew that could be just as dangerous as fear, in an odd way, maybe even more so.

Once again he looked into the darkness of the next landing, and once again he felt terribly afraid.

He really did not want to go up there.

He took the first step.

# Chapter : Thirty-Ninth

# THE HORRORS THAT BIDE

**T**HOM STEADIED himself. He stood before the double doors to Sir Russell's great bedchamber, candle in one hand, the book under his other arm, its base resting against his hip. Sounds came from the other side of the doors, moanings, wailings, the kind of sounds he thought only distressed children could make.

The antechamber was in darkness, but there was a soft glow from beneath the doors. It wavered gently as candlelight would.

He swapped his small flame over to his right hand, awkwardly pressing the book against his body with elbow and wrist, and reached for one of the door-handles. He stayed his hand. It was shivering badly.

The problem was putting Rigwit's hints about the horrors that lay beyond these doors out of his mind. He grew angry with himself, cursed himself, called himself a wimp, a wuss – and yes, a coward. He was just plain scared.

*And who could blame me?* he asked himself and that, at

least, gave him some satisfaction. Reality had shifted around him, dimensions had become interlinked. This past week he had witnessed both wondrous and abhorrent things, had made love to an undine, had been scared witless by a monster, had discovered his own birthright. He'd been amazed and abused, overawed and terrorized. Too much had happened, too many new concepts had besieged his fragile mind, to go through the list right now. Yes, he was profoundly afraid, disorientated – *even in love, for Christ's sake!* – and what normal man or woman would blame him for bailing out right there and then?

Only himself, came the wordless reply.

A muffled shriek from next door, an old, quavery voice. Sir Russell.

Oh shit. Thom steeled himself. Twisted the doorknob, nudged the door open a little. Then, expecting the worst, stood back and kicked the door wide.

---

He stopped on the threshold, open-mouthed.

Nothing.

No monsters.

No coven of witches dancing around a bubbling cauldron.

No demons.

Nothing.

Except for the dim figure of Hugo Bleeth cowering in a shadowy corner, knees drawn up, his arms before his face, Nell Quick standing rigid in the centre of a crudely drawn five-pointed star within a circle, a *pentagram*, a candle burning at each apex. She clutched a piece of paper in one hand and faced the room's big drapeless four-poster bed on which Sir Russell Bleeth, a frail and sick old man, sat upright, oxygen mask and tubes still in place.

But nothing else.

Except for black candles placed around the room, all of them lit, each a separate island of brightness in singular struggle with the surrounding darkness, their waxy smell mingling with a smell that was so rank, so foul, that death – or its corruption – seemed to occupy the room.

Nothing more than that, though.

Except . . .

Except for the other shadows that now began to emerge from the overall shadows, coming from the corners, the ceiling, from beneath the bed . . .

Emerging as if they had hidden when the door had burst open *or* as Thom's own mind and eyes began to perceive the insubstantial entities that filled the room, a crowd, a host, of vaporous beings that loomed and shifted, that were part of the darkness as night itself, forms without real form, amorphous configurations that depended on the intellect for definition. Already Thom was imagining cowled hunched figures, enormously tall as if they were mere shadows cast against the walls by the candle-glows. Only they were not confined to the walls; they roamed the room itself.

Then they bunched together and became something else. No longer shadows, they became countless serpents, intertwined and weaving, fanged heads rearing over the four-poster bed and the man in it, darting down as if to strike, but never touching, although Sir Russell flinched each time one came near.

Still at the door, Thom realized almost at once that this was their true horror: they could be whatever abomination the individual's mind could conceive. And because their attention was on the sick man, it was Sir Russell's mind that created their being. He further reasoned, all in the space of seconds, that if they were figments of the imagination, then they had no substance and could do no physical damage. Unless you believed implicitly, that is, as he had discovered with the spiders.

415

Dropping the candle because it was of no further use, he rushed into the room shouting, '*Get away, get away from him. You're nothing, you're phantoms, you're not real!*'

And then three of the serpents' heads lunged at him, sending him crashing back against the side of the double doors that was still closed. It rattled in its frame and he slid to the floor, stunned by the impact.

*Impossible.* He didn't believe in them, they were creations of Sir Russell's mind. Yet they had hurt him. Fuck it, they had *hurt* him!

But at least they were leaving him be. The three trailed away to regroup with the mass. Then they squirmed as a whole across the room, towards the crouching man there in the corner, Hugo, who had peeked from behind his raised arms to see their advance. He let out a piercing shriek, a child's high-pitched cry, and ducked back behind his hands, his body seeming visibly to shrink as he bunched up, tried to make himself as small as possible, foolishly imagining he might go unnoticed there in the shadows. It was pointless though. The snakes struck out at him, taking it in turns, sometimes one flicking a long forked tongue at him, other times two or three together, a chorus of reptiles.

Jesus, thought Thom, Hugo, who had always abhorred snakes, now to be tormented like this! It then occurred to him that this vision – vision? He had been physically struck by the creature's snouts – had not just manifested when he had opened the door to the room. No, they were already present, but it had taken his own mind time to adjust, time to bring them into focus. And if that were so, then they truly were figments of the imagination, a vision that leapt from mind to mind, like a disease might leap from body to body, the force so great that even he had believed they could touch him; with the belief came the physical response. But whose vision was it? He guessed he had been wrong in thinking it was Sir Russell's, for Hugo was the one who had the phobia of snakes.

'*Hugo!*' he called across the room. '*They can't harm you, not if you don't let them! Get rid of them, get them out of your mind!*'

He might just as well have been advising a terrified passenger on a crashing jetliner to whistle a happy tune and think of nice things. Hugo continued to shriek, flinching each time a serpent stabbed at his head or shoulder.

Thom knew he had to get to Hugo, pull him from the room if necessary, slap some sense into him, bring him back to reality. But would it really be that simple? Somewhere in his mind – perhaps his inner self, that canny but elusive voice? – he was being told there was *so* much more to all this.

And when lightning outside washed the room with its stammering radiance, there were a new set of shadows occupying the room. They wavered as they grew, taking time to form, but when the glare died and the thunder settled to a rumble, they began to emerge, their forms lit by candlelight. They were huge cowled figures, the silhouettes of giant monks, it seemed to Thom, although each one was bowed, hunched, and their extraordinarily long fingers were curled. It was impossible to tell how many of them there were, for like the serpents that continued to torment Hugo they merged, were as one body, gradually filling half the room, their malodour a poison in the air. They were made of blackness, only their outlines giving sense of form and movement.

In the gloom, Thom caught sight of Sir Russell again. He was a diminished man, a frail husk, his withered body trembling as if gripped by ague, the face behind the plastic oxygen mask gaunt, hollow-cheeked, the eyes both deep-set yet shiny and bulging in their dark caverns like the haunting eyes of a famine victim. And it seemed that this new manifestation was concentrating on him alone for, as one, the amalgamation of cowled hunchbacked figures moved towards the drapeless four-poster bed, floating around, or moving *through*, Nell Quick, who maintained her stance near the centre of the room. They advanced on the sick man like some dense drifting fog.

Sir Russell saw the movement, saw their coming, and his skeletal hands clutched the bedsheets, holding them to his chest like a maiden aunt disturbed by a prowler in the night, the thin material her only protection. Curling and lurching, the sinister clan came closer and Sir Russell backed away, squashing the pillows behind him against the oak headboard.

Thom, who was still rising from the floor, shouted a pointless warning and, crouched, made ready to go to the sick man's aid. But his movement was slow, a bad dream's motion where limbs were hampered by the thickness of the air and a dull sickness in the gut caused by fear. Somehow, it was as if the stroke of months before had taken charge of his whole body. He struggled against the apathy, his arms moving but only lethargically, his legs pushing but only feebly. He could do no more than watch as the massed shapes drifted over the bed towards Sir Russell.

Muted sounds came from behind the transparent oxygen mask, the old man protesting against this stealthy invasion, his shiny eyes burdened by terror. There were screams, but these came from Hugo, who was going through his own ordeal.

Thom could only look on as the black mass of weaving figures rose over Sir Russell, who had sunk down in the bed, his frail old arms now raised as if to ward off these unworldly predators. The oxygen mask suddenly began to darken as if filling with thick liquid. Its colour gradually filtered through the transparent wall of the mask and it was red. Deep red. The deep red of blood. Oh dear God, thought Thom, the man was about to drown in his own blood.

But that was not Sir Russell's only problem, for even as Thom managed to find his feet, the shadows were bearing down on the horrified old man, black claws reaching from the mass to sink into his chest, to clutch at his heart. The swelling drift descended like some heavy crushing load sent to smother Sir Russell with its weighty blackness.

It was too much for Thom. His mutinous body responded as if commanded by some greater force than his own frightened self. Rigwit had told him to listen to his inner voice and now it seemed that voice had become impatient, was screaming at him, propelling him forward despite the reluctance of his limbs and body.

Just as Thom staggered towards the bed, lightning flared again and simultaneously thunder shook the ceiling and rattled the big windows. The roof door that had been open when Thom had entered the room swung shut, its crash barely perceptible over the thunder before it swung wide once more.

Thom cringed as though he thought the ceiling might cave in, but he kept moving, his legs unsteady, his actions still slow. But just before he reached the edge of the bed – he could see the oxygen mask was quite full with blood, red rivers running from its edges down Sir Russell's hollow cheeks and scrawny neck, and he could see the massive bulk of blackness and reaching claws just inches away from the old man's prone body, bearing down, the space between gradually shrinking as though the descent were deliberately drawn out to maximize the terror – something appeared in the periphery of his vision, something tall, lumbering forward from a dusky corner of the room.

His head reflexively swung towards this new shadow, for it was he that it approached. He gasped. He almost fell to the floor. Inside his head, he screamed, *No, no, it can't be, not him!*

For it was *Bones* who came at him from the flickering shadows. But somehow, he was taller, much taller, his thin cadaverous face wavering way above Thom's own. And his shoulders were hunched, his elbows bent, his long, thin-fingered hands reaching . . .

For a moment or two Thom thought he had been

419

betrayed by the manservant, his injuries a fake, a ruse to send Thom up to this room alone. Then he realized that this was an exaggerated figure from a nightmare, an apparition whose resolve was to freeze Thom's heart.

But it *was* from a nightmare, even though it towered over him, a sickening triumphal grin on its skull-like face, eyes piercing Thom's own like sharpened needles, sliding through eyeballs, muscles and bone to sink into the brain itself and causing pain beyond belief.

The great bedchamber was a maelstrom of activity and sound, each person – apart from Nell, who still stood as though in a trance – terrorized by their own particular nightmare.

*Nightmare* ... The word, the thought, repeated itself to Thom over and over again as those long, thin fingers grabbed his throat and began to squeeze, their deadly grip unremitting. And Bones was laughing, literally laughing in his face, spittle shooting out between stained teeth to speckle Thom's cheek and nose, the hands squeezing, squeezing, squeezing the life from him.

Until a voice broke through the uproar. An external voice this time. A calm voice, a gentle voice, that could be heard without it being loud.

Although in 'Bones's' clutches, Thom was nonetheless able to see the double doorway, both sides of which were now open, two figures standing in the opening, one very small, the other taller.

Jennet, her anxious but sweet face lit by candlelight, called to him again.

*'Thom. Your inner voice. Listen to it. It will tell you what this is and give you power,'* she was saying.

His inner voice. Vision was beginning to haze over, the fingers around his throat ever-tightening, but he remembered Rigwit had told him to listen to his inner voice. And Bethan, his mother, had told him to listen to his inner voice. But it had not worked before, so why should it now?

The room was spinning, he was blacking out; somehow though, he listened, but to Jennet, not to this elusive so-called inner voice, for her call was clear above the hubbub, still insisting that he go into himself, escape this place by retreating – no, by sinking, that was her word – into himself. Difficult, though. So difficult to do when ... he ... was ... being ... throttled ...

In fact, it was the violence of the assault that allowed him to find the 'voice', for he was losing consciousness, *sinking* deep. And the inner voice was awaiting him, for it was not far below his conscious level. *This* is *the horror*, it seemed to say. *This is the nightmare that has haunted you for so long, this is your worst fear* ...

And it was right, for this was the voice that could only speak truth, no matter how much his brain or conscious mind railed against it. It was the voice inside every man, woman and child, the voice that drew the line between right and wrong, the conscience, if it pleases, the voice that no outside force can deter or overcome. The voice of reason, the voice of the soul.

He listened. Thom 'heard' its unspoken words. The alien things in this room, the manifestations conjured by Nell Quick in her aberration of the wiccan craft, were truly from nightmares. His: recurring dreams of Bones coming to get him since the incident in the cellar all those years ago. Hugo's: a lifelong fear of snakes, these no doubt dreamt or thought of in times of stress. Sir Russell: his claustrophobia, his dread of enclosed rooms, confined spaces, the reason he insisted all doors inside the house remained open, his refusal to have a lift installed even though he loved this rooftop eyrie and its wonderful views, the room where even in his dying days no curtains were allowed to be drawn, where every bit of daylight was used and welcomed.

And because the visions – the manifestations – present in this room came from within the mind, because they stemmed from each person's own psyche, so then they were all the more powerful, their effect all the more horrendous. These horrors were the substance of each individual's inner phobia; quite literally, they were their worst nightmare come into being.

Here was the evidence of their private fears all brought together on this night when Nell Quick had sought to raise but one – Sir Russell Bleeth's greatest horror, conjured to cause his last and fatal heart attack. His last Will and Testament had been, or would be, destroyed, its single witness put out of the way permanently (if not earlier, then later after they had finished with Sir Russell). It was iniquitous, it was evil. It was vicious.

Sir Russell was to die this very night, but Nell had unleashed more forces than she was capable of controlling. She was a fool, a modern-day wiccan who practised some kind of voodoo and conjuration, but had no idea of how to govern or contain the powers that came forth.

The grip around his throat became less firm, as though truth was a tool that could be used against an enemy that dwelt within his own darkest thoughts. Yet the hands did not let go completely. The apparition that claimed to be Bones, who in reality was at this moment lying unconscious, perhaps even dead by now, on the hard, cold cellar floor, did not vanish with the dénouement. It remained poised over him, still visible in all its ghastliness. And the serpents continued to terrorize Hugo, the cowled figures relentlessly beaming down on Sir Russell.

Thom turned away from further thought in favour of action. His wrists shot up between the apparition's and spread in one quick, strong movement, and the grip was broken. Still dismayed that the doppelgänger had not vanished in light of reason, he looked towards Jennet at the doorway.

She and the elf had ventured further into the room, but seemed reluctant to come any closer.

'*Now you must use the book, Thom,*' she said, her lovely face grave with concern.

She said something more, but lightning flared and thunder boomed so loudly it might have been in the room with them. It rolled around the chamber, reverberating off the walls and windows, and Thom clapped his hands to his ears. Even after it had died away (almost as though leaving by the swinging roof door), he remained deafened.

'Bones' and the other manifestations, however, were unaffected: they proceeded with their attack, their intimidation.

Thom realized he'd dropped the book that Rigwit had given him when he'd been knocked over by the serpents. It lay beside the wall in the uncertain candlelight, open, its pages flicking one after the other as though a wind had entered the chamber.

Thom lunged for it just as the spectre representing Bones reached again for him. It missed its grab completely, for Thom was already on his hands and knees, scrabbling for the book. His fingertips found it, he picked it up, he frantically leafed through the pages.

The phantom lumbered in his direction.

'*Any page, any page!*' shouted Rigwit and, at last, his little voice could be heard.

'*Just choose a page, Thom, and then think of them,*' called Jennet, still some distance away. '*Will them to come to you.*'

His back against the wall, Thom sat cross-ankled, the book lying open between his knees.

'Bones' towered over him. Began to stoop towards him; malicious grin, evil, lunatic eyes, hands crooked like claws.

'*Hurry, Thom!*'

He concentrated.

Nothing happened.

He willed the faeries to come through the aged pages.

Nothing happened.

The hands of 'Bones', as material as any solid object, grabbed his shirt and began to pull.

'*Don't think too hard,*' Jennet cried. '*Just will it to happen.*'

'Help me!' Thom yelled back as he felt himself lifted from the floor.

'*I can't. You have to do it alone.*'

With a control that surprised even Thom himself, he blanked his mind, not quite shedding the fear, but shielding himself from it for a brief time. In the not quite empty space of his consciousness, a space that was besieged from the periphery, he simply said silently:

*Come.*

And they did. They burst out of the open book as though they had been waiting for his call, flying into the room and whizzing everywhere at once, sprinkling that same starry powder Thom had witnessed before.

The spectre gripping his shirt let go and sprang back, a look first of consternation on its face, then doubt, then fear, then even loathing. More and more came, magical lights pouring forth, bringing with them a new energy. Thom felt his heart lift again, his own fear slacken. And the better he felt, so the more the thing before him was diminished. It started to fade, its blackness turning to grey. Soon Thom was able to see through it.

The faery hordes, increasing by the moment, quickly numbering hundreds or more, swept through the black mass hovering over Sir Russell's prostrate body; so close were these cowled figures and so heavy-looking their mass that it seemed the old man would be crushed rather than smothered.

But now the black amalgamation was disintegrating, being torn apart by tiny but fierce opponents of all things evil, who swooped into its darkness, brightening its murk, striking at the nucleus that was the darkest part of all. Gold, silver, violet, blue, red, purple, indigo, green and pure white – all these brilliant colours dissipated the central solidity, breaking it down so that it began to deteriorate, decay into smaller pieces, while the cohorts, the shadows resembling hooded monks, yowled their anguish, their screeches filling the air as if they were in true despairing agony – which Thom sincerely hoped they were.

He saw his chance. Sir Russell had been reprieved, his body beneath the sheet freed of its tormentors. But still his shiny eyes were filled with horror and his thin body continued to shake.

The oxygen mask was dense with blood and Thom realized the old man was choking, drowning, his infirm hands too feeble to rip the mask away. Thom swiftly laid the book down, making sure the pages were flat and open as the little creatures continued to emerge, fluttering like butterflies now, spilling out at a more leisurely pace, their high-pitched jabbering and singing filling the room as if their voices, too, might defeat the darkness. Thom knew there was still great danger in this place though, and he pushed himself to his feet to run through the diaphanous image of Bones, his own body completing the dream figure's final disintegration. All that remained were wisps of grey matter floating in the air behind him.

He leapt on to the four-poster bed and snatched at Sir Russell's oxygen mask, digging his fingers into its edges and whipping it away, snapping the restraining straps. The blood flooded over the sick man's already bloodied face, staining the parchment skin a glossy red. Sir Russell belched the blood he had swallowed and a dreadfully thin hand clutched Thom's wrist. The emaciated body spasmed in the younger man's arms and the eyelids flickered as though fighting unconsciousness. Those weary old eyes suddenly focused on Thom.

Thom thought he might be wrong, it might just have been the effect of the shifting light as iridescent colours swept around the room and candle flames wavered in their breeze, but he thought the old man's lipless mouth had formed a smile – a frail one, but still a smile – and that there was the faintest look of recognition in his watery yet oddly luminous eyes. A piercing shriek drew his attention to a corner on the other side of the bed.

Hugo was on his feet, his body covered with slithering snakes. They were smaller than before, but looked just as deadly. Arms that seemed to beseech Thom wore bracelets of writhing serpents. These creatures were dark green, almost black, in tone, and they bore little resemblance to the small grass snakes Hugo had feared so much as a child and ever since. They slid across Hugo's chest, around his waist, finding their way into his clothes so that moving shapes bulged beneath the cloth.

Hugo shrieked again as a snake stole across his face, over his mouth, muting the cry. His eyes looked as though they might pop from his head. He tore at the snake on his face with his serpent-laden hands in an effort to rip it away, stumbling back into the corner as he did so, only the walls preventing him from falling. The snake nipped at his fleshy fingers, then bit down hard with venomous fangs, hanging on when Hugo desperately tried to flick it away. He shrieked again, and again, and again.

'*Help me!*' he managed to plead in between the shrieks.

But his whole body was now a dense but unstable knot of glistening serpents. They coiled around his neck, drawing themselves tight, forming a noose that smoothly squeezed his throat.

Thom had no idea what to do, how to help him. The commotion continued around him – the hundreds of shooting stars and their unearthly chants, the *moaning* of the withering shadows, for the darkness itself had voice – and he saw Jennet with the elf against the wall by the door, their eyes wide, Rigwit quaking. More and more winged lights flew from the open book on the floor, funnelling out to join the fray, their brightness fierce, but not yet overwhelming the umbra. In fact, although pierced by the zooming lights, the shadows seemed to remain as thick and looming as before.

Jennet caught his eye. Even from that distance and with all that was going on in between, something passed between them, an emotion that excluded all else in that fearsome room. In Jennet's expression there was much anxiety, fright also – as Thom felt sure there was in his own – but even in such circumstances, there was tenderness too and it was for him alone.

He pointed at Hugo and she understood.

Jennet called to the swooping faeries using their language, their voice, and many came together before her, swarming like electric bees. It was her turn to point at the serpent-bound figure in the corner and a whole squadron of tiny and not so tiny sprites swept from the main body to the far corner of the room. They made a slight diversion on the way though, swerving around the pentagram chalked out on the boarded floor where Nell stood transfixed. Their glittering jetstream trailed across the room behind them and none of its floating motes settled within the boundary of the symbol's circle either.

The faeries hovered over Hugo and his living bonds and scattered and blew their dust. The snakes reared their heads and bared dripping fangs, many of them uncoiling to drop to the floor in a languid heap, some of these slithering into the cavernous gloom beneath the bed, while others headed towards the crashing terrace door. Those still clinging to Hugo began to shrivel, their scaly skin wrinkling, became brittle so that bits flaked away. Hugo appeared incapable of fending for himself: he swooned in the corner, his face pale and drawn even in the warm light from the candles and faeries alike, his eyes glazed as they stared directly ahead. He seemed to have retreated into his own world, a place where nothing could touch him, even though the nightmare of serpents was from deep within his own mind; perhaps he

had locked himself away in the place beyond both consciousness and subconsciousness (perhaps even between them), a
hideaway where nothing – no inner conflict, nor outside
influence, and certainly no physical threat – could ever enter.

An incredible rage of thunder erupted from above, the
lightning itself strobing for several long seconds. Thom was
sure the roof had been struck and so fierce was the impact
that he automatically shielded his grandfather's skin-and-
bones body with his own. The ceiling held, although dust
drifted down to mingle with the twinkling particles strewn
by the little people. There was a series of sharp cracks over
the thunder's roar and he looked up in time to see several of
the plate-glass windows crack from top to bottom.

As the last of the snakes dropped from Hugo's immobile
body, the faeries resumed their attack on the darkness,
because strange forms could be observed moving inside its
inkiness, a brief and non-defining outline here, the warped
curve of some impenetrable creature there – for the battle was
far from won. Although weaker, the darkness prevailed, the
quick-darting lights mere shooting stars in a black universe.

The wind howled through the roof terrace's restless door
so that candle-flames danced at an angle. Even the flying
mites, with their lustrous but fragile wings, were buffeted,
the dust they scattered, blown across the great bedchamber
in eddies and swirls. As Thom's hair was tugged, his shirt
snagged, he saw that the wind had caught Nell's long black
hair, tossing it around her head and shoulders, flapping
the piece of paper he'd noticed in her hand on entering the
room, whipping at the long loose skirt she wore so that it
twisted and snapped in its currents. He also observed (it had
been hidden before) that in her other hand she clutched a
black dagger, an athame. It was now clutched to her breast,
above which hung an ankh, a strange cross with looped
upper arms held there by a silver chain around her neck.

She was rigid, still trance-like, even though the wind
flayed hair and clothes. Her eyes were closed.

Despite all that was happening and despite his terror, Thom still had time to note how stunningly beautiful she was in the shadowy and perhaps muting candlelight (for some reason, reflections from the faeries did not touch her), more beautiful than he had first realized. She stood as a silent siren in her rough chalk pentagram, exotically and erotically alluring – but deadly. He blinked as if to break a spell cast between them.

And as he did so, her eyes opened. They were confused, switching this way and that, finally coming to rest on him and the invalid he held in his arms. Her face changed. It became ugly in its loathing. Her crimson lips corrupted to a sneer, her black eyes blazed with a passion whose genesis was hate. The hand bearing the dagger moved away from her breasts. Towards Thom.

He readied himself. He gently lowered his grandfather on to the bed and, remaining half-sitting, turned back to Nell and her vicious gaze. The potion he had drunk in the stairway appeared to have worn off, for he was close to exhaustion once more. Maybe it was the terrible dread in his heart that had had time to wear down the magic, or maybe it was because continual horror inevitably debilitated the soul itself. Whatever the answer, and whatever his condition, he was not going to give in to this monster. She would have to kill him first to get to his grandfather. As she had tried to kill him once before by causing his stroke with her magic witchcraft.

But that was the moment when something else happened. Something extraordinary.

## Chapter : Fortieth

# FROM NIGHTMARES

THEY CAME from the darkness. And they came as if to claim her. For their ragged nebulous arms reached out to her alone.

At first, Nell was not aware. Her eyes still burned with black-hearted hatred, and her gaze was still fixed on Thom. But she frowned when Thom was distracted by something behind her and because of the undoubted fright in his expression, she knew it was no trick. And then, she stiffened.

The hate left her lovely yet dangerous eyes, to be replaced by alarm. She spun around. She cried out.

They were formed from all the things that had hidden in the murk, grossly misshapen entities that amalgamated to create more substantial configurations, a gathering that had found form through Nell Quick's own incautious and mis-guided practice of the Black Arts. Through her vain callings. Through her recklessness.

And they had risen from the depths to discover shape and substance in vengeful caricatures of ancient witches.

*These were the true hellhagges.*

These were the sorceresses of old writings, destroyers and malefactors all, furies each and everyone. Never themselves of human breed, they could only exist in human dreams and legends, reviled by the worthy, revered by the wicked.

They were Nell Quick's evil externalized, beckoned from places adjacent to Hell, idolizers of everything sinful, everything cruel, everything perverted.

Followers of the Dark Lord himself.

---

They edged apart, a shambling movement, the gait of the very old and crooked, for they *were* aged and bent, their crone faces, which were only half-concealed by great hoods like the monk-figures before them, rutted and wizened, their sored withered skin grey and unappealing. The more they shuffled forward, the more plain in image they became, ancient hags of diabolism, whose scabby countenances somehow told of eternal misery and depravity. Although their figures were not solid – they were amorphous, subtly shifting in pose and the blackness that had birthed them sometimes imposed itself through their garb – they seemed as real as any person in the room, and their stink was far worse than the chamber's general malodour, which even the furious wind was unable to dispel.

Nell cringed before them, even though they were what she aspired to be. These grim creatures were both her superior and her goal. But she had not yet understood that corruption of the soul would always lead to the eventual degeneration of the flesh.

Their wicked eyes gleamed as their semicircle around Nell drew close.

She looked about her wildly. This was not right, not how it should be! Why did she feel threatened by them? Why did they look at her that way? Why did they grin, why did they mock? She did not want those scaly and leprous hands to touch her, did not want to be drawn into them! She threw the black dagger, and they absorbed its metal. She screamed and they chuckled and drew ever nearer.

Nell's back was turned to him, so Thom could not see her face. But he could imagine the horror there. She was retreating from the creeping hags and soon her legs were against the end of the bed. She still clutched the piece of paper that he suddenly guessed was his grandfather's last Will and Testament, presumably handwritten by Hartgrove from Sir Russell's dictation, and he briefly wondered if she had brought it here to gloat in front of the dying invalid. Her other hand was stretched out before her to ward off the advancing coven and for a moment – it was a very short moment – he almost felt sorry for her. This was her nightmare come into being and she could not control it, just as she could not control anything that had gone before on this hideous night. She had only meant literally to frighten Sir Russell to death, to cause another heart seizure that would be his last. It seemed that she was about to pay the price for her folly, her vanity in thinking that not only could she summon such unearthly creatures, but that she could command them also. But of course all she had invoked was the personal nightmare of each individual in the room, *including her own*.

For as the taunting hags crowded her, pulling at her clothes, lifting her skirt, pinching her flesh, they let the cowls fall away to their crooked shoulders, revealing countenances that were even more unfavourable than already imagined when mostly hidden from view. The skin of their scalps, from which hung scant wisps of white hair, was covered in crusting scabs and sores, their wrinkled faces full of lesions and wounds that oozed yellow pus. Their grey eyes had no lids, condemned always to see, even in sleep. Some had but a single eye, an empty, livid, red-puckered socket evidence that the other eyeball had once been torn free; some had noses that had been eaten away as if by disease, only fragments of bone and gristle remaining. Grinning and lipless mouths were mainly toothless, merely black holes that gabbled ceaselessly in some unknown language.

They seemed pleased to see Nell (or perhaps they were just glad to be free of their own hell for a while), for they cackled gleefully as they prodded her with thin ulcerated hands, their fingernails long and curved like talons.

Their indications were evident, for between pokes and prods, they pointed at themselves, and Thom – as did Nell, herself – began to understand their garbled message.

This, in her vanity, in her blind ambition, in her wickedness, was what she was to become. Eventually, her abuse of the wiccan craft in unleashing forces that were beyond her skills and her right would lead her to the corruption of her own physical body, the inside mirrored by the outside, the price of pursuance of the occult and the powers she sought. The price that they, themselves, had paid in other lives.

Nell's terrified but nimble brain grasped the significance of these embittered creatures that were more than mere apparitions and she started to scream. And scream. And scream . . .

But there was far worse to come.

---

Just as the *hellhagges* were about to overwhelm Nell with their jabbing and goading, their slaps and their pinches, lightning whitened the room and thunder shook the walls and ceiling. Every window on the west side of the room suddenly shattered inwards, millions of scintillating fragments and shards spewing into the room, an explosion of glass that blew Hugo to his knees and caused the others – even the witches – to cower. The wind roared through the new openings.

Thom threw himself over his grandfather's prone body again, and felt the bed beneath them vibrate.

Everything was bleached. Even the lights emanating from the faeries were subjected to the greater fulguration, for it had gained entry into the rooftop room itself and it was constant for a few seconds, an intense, dazzling flood of brightness that froze everyone present into colourless sculptures. The airborne faeries became still, many of them dropping to the floor like chemically-sprayed insects. The thunder continued to reverberate and Thom clapped his hands to his ears to muffle the sound.

And even as the light flickered away and the thunder's roar diminished, the coven of *hellhagges* turned away from Nell Quick to look as one towards the open terrace door, for they had sensed the presence even before it had revealed itself.

The wind suddenly dropped, although the darkness itself continued to swirl like a dense mist. No longer dominated by the other light, the brilliance of the faeries nevertheless dimmed, became soft, insubstantial. The flames of the many candles also dulled, the glow becoming weak, ineffectual. Shiny glass littering the floor became lustreless.

It was Jennet who screamed, a spare sound, but one of absolute despair.

And the faeries began wailing, a feeble cacophony of dread.

The old crones, all in disordered shape but dark in robe and aura, raised their gnarled hands to their disfigured faces, shielding their lidless eyes from the being that filled the doorway across the room. Some turned away and howled and whimpered, while others beseeched the new interloper, hands reaching out towards it, then snatched back as if burnt, short shrieks coming from the crones's toothless mouths.

Nell, her body half-crouched, wary of her tormentors, slowly turned her head towards the door.

Thom followed her gaze.

As yet it had no formal arrangement. It was pale in the darkness that flowed around and *into* it, merely snatches of form that suggested, but *only* suggested, a figure. It was of average height – unless the parts that were suggested rather than made visible were required to knit together to make the whole – and appeared, so far, to have human form; that is, suggested eventual human form, for it was too scattered and too ill defined at that moment to tell. And of all the noxious smells wafting around the room, this was the most foul, for it clogged the nostrils and caused the throat to constrict. It was a stench not of this realm.

The *hellhagges* stepped back from their intended victim, leaving Nell standing alone in the inverted star-shape. They set up a low moaning as they shrank before the visitor, leaning away with cruel-nailed hands raised in dramatic gesture. The faeries, their beacons no longer bright, gathered against the far wall, close to Jennet and Rigwit, who clutched at each other (the elf held aloft in Jennet's arms). Darkness seemed to pulse around the mutable vision as it entered the room, gliding rather than walking.

It moved towards Nell Quick, pale and spectral parts of a whole that might resemble human form when assembled – no, not assembled, for the proportions now seemed correct; it was just that the swirling darkness interfered with the overall shape, concealing elements so that those visible appeared adrift – and the closer it drew, so the fluid bulk that was the coven backed away. Thom could see their shapes in the gloaming, unsightly visages that would forever haunt him, long, claw-nailed hands waving in the air above the mass, and he could hear the reverential terror in their howls and moans. He sensed a kind of fear-struck awe in them.

The as yet unformed entity stopped before Nell, the darkness around it like a ruffled cloak caught by the wind. And indeed, the wind had returned so that the tiny flames around the room sputtered and leaned, the shadows ever-moving, the smells whisked away but others taking their place.

Thom could see Nell's profile and strangely her face was in rapture. There was a luminous shining in her dark eyes as she regarded the blurred vision that remained unmoving in front of her. Her breasts heaved and her breath came in short, sharp gasps; perspiration beaded her brow and trickled down her cheeks like tears. Her teeth were bared, her scarlet lips drawn back from them; her body trembled. To Thom, it looked as if she were in some kind of paroxysm – or even an orgasmic trance.

But the unclear figure finally began to take on a more stable and defined form. Features drifted through. A limb, thin, white, blurred at its edges. The chest, again thin, scarcely muscled, but a man's chest. That is, it resembled a man's chest, for this thing could not possibly be human. The stomach and waist became more solid, for they had already been present as a variable lightness in the dusky mists. The rest emerged – or semi-emerged; they were not yet complete, nor binding, their arrangement remained insecure and vignetted – together, the naked legs, the rest of the second arm, the genitalia – a man's genitalia that conformed to any other man's, neither overdeveloped, nor undersized, merely an ordinary penis over an ordinary scrotum – except there was no pubic hair. The feet, the shoulders, the hands were all vague and ambiguous, shimmering softly.

Then, last of all, the head began to appear.

---

*'Thom, look away!'*

Jennet's voice cut through the sound of the wind that had now gentled to a breeze and the howls that had risen to a roar.

*'Don'tlookatit, don'tlookatit!'* came Rigwit's screeched warning.

But the assembling visage held a mesmeric fascination for him. As it did for Nell Quick also, for she regarded it with anticipation, her breasts still heaving, her lips open and wet, her eyes lit by some inner fire.

The slow transfiguration continued.

---

Thunder cracked overhead as if it were splitting the heavens, and in the instant flare of light he saw that the form had grown and the pale flesh had become dark and leathery. It held up its scaly arms as if to take Nell in its embrace, and all the while its features were forming. The misshapen bunch that was the *hellhagges* shrieked in adoration and wretchedness. The *faerefolkis* flooded back to the open book that lay on the floor, many of them plummeting before they made it, their lights burned out, their tiny, woeful cries lost in the jabber of their fleeing companions.

Even the staccato lightning could not banish the darkness entirely and there were now a multitude of other vaporous creatures skulking in the shades, raw-looking things that could only be demons, cohorts of the ghastly manifestation that towered over the woman inside the pentagram. The candles at each point of the five-cornered star snuffled out, but others around the room retained their dim glow which was as nothing against the blinding whiteness of the lightning's stammering flare. This time it did not die away, but stayed, an awful strobing glare that half-revealed beings that could only have arrived from some sinister and bizarre source.

But then Nell screamed, a sound so full of hysteria that Thom could only wonder at the state of her mind. The thing before her had a face and – *something hurled itself at Thom, knocking him over on the bed.*

Jennet smothered him with her own body as the lightning finally stopped and the thunder rolled off into the distance. Her small hands covered his eyes.

'*You mustn't look! You mustn't see its face!*' she cried. '*To see the Diabolus is to invite him into your soul!*'

Thom tried to rise, but she pushed him back again so that he lay alongside his grandfather. Something clung to his legs, adding its weight, and he knew it was Rigwit.

'*But Nell . . .*' Thom's words were lost in the wind that had returned in full force. '*We've got to help her!*'

'It's already too late,' Jennet murmured close to his ear, sadness and pity for the foolish woman whose dubious ambitions had led to this confrontation in her voice. 'She belongs to him now.'

Jennet took her hands from Thom's eyes and he blinked them open, pushing himself upright as he did so, unable to control the impulse, stubbornly curious to see the Diabolus for himself.

It was gone though. He caught its final fading, a pallid blurred shape once more, a fearsome and chimerical image that dulled and was soon consumed by the shadows around it. Shadows from which the *hellhagges* re-emerged, for they were not yet finished with Nell Quick.

Thom felt a stirring beside him as Jennet and Rigwit released him and he turned to see Sir Russell gazing up at him with eyes that had lost their earlier trance-like shine. A quavery hand closed over Thom's wrist.

The wind tore through the shattered windows and open doorway, unsettling flames and shadows alike, seeming to form a kind of vortex around Nell, whipping at her skirt and blouse and tossing her untamed hair. So strong was its force that the ankh at her breast was wrenched away, chain and all. Nell turned, twisted, raised her arms to the maelstrom, the piece of paper still gripped tightly. The witch crones taunted her and, curiously, pulled at their own robes to reveal their dried-up wrinkled bodies to her. Their ugliness caused Thom to wince – their flat drained breasts hung low over their bellies, their sallow flesh was ulcerated and blistered, tormented further by vivid unlanced boils, the lips of their hairless vaginas were distended and horribly puckered – and he wondered why they would cavort and display themselves in this way.

Then he understood.

They were showing Nell Quick what she was to become.

She started to scream again, for the realization had come to her instantly. She knew this was the price to be paid for her ambitions and the corruptness she had embraced, for it was revealed to her now by those who had followed the same path. And despite their taunts, they welcomed her, for they gloried in this dark side, celebrated her summoning, because it meant that she, too, would share their eternal misery.

Nell ran. To escape her self-constructed nightmare? To escape her tormentors? Who could say? Perhaps it was to flee from her own descending madness. But it was the terrace door she headed for, as though the night itself might offer refuge, and Thom thought she might even throw herself from the parapet in her panic. Glass shards and fragments crunched beneath her feet and shadows swirled around her as if giving chase; her mouth and eyes were wide with horror. Thom leapt from the bed to follow her, barely registering the sound of Jennet's voice calling him back over the noise of the rushing wind.

'*Nell!*' he yelled uselessly. '*Stop, Nell!*'

He passed through the doorway and the rainless gale struck him with its full force. He struggled against it, bending low, the wind carrying away his shouts.

She turned as if she had heard him – or perhaps it was to see if the dream-hags had followed her – and looked directly at him. The horror was still there on her face and

439

her lips moved incessantly as though she were mumbling some protective incantation.

Something fluttered beneath the parapet behind her and Thom could just make out the flapping wings of a bird. A magpie. The *same* magpie? The creature, he suddenly realized, that was Nell's familiar. It *shrieked* at her.

But Nell ignored its cry. Buffeted by the wind, she stood on the rooftop terrace with legs apart, and slowly lifted a hand to examine it in the poor light thrown from the room behind Thom. He lingered in the doorway, unsure of her, scared for himself. The commotion inside seemed to have stopped and he felt other eyes watching Nell Quick, although nothing tried to get past him.

Nell's hand went to her face. Her fingers felt her skin. Her body sagged.

But her head slowly lifted to the skies.

He thought he heard her wail.

Then lightning streaked from the troubled black clouds to strike her.

Nell's poor marionette body spasmed as the violent bolt of electricity seared her flesh and roasted her innards. Her meat sizzled as she jerked and smoke rose from it; smaller blue-white charges danced over her skin and her hair and clothes, and the crumpled piece of paper in her other hand flamed as her arms shot high in the air and her feet turned black.

There had been no time for her to scream, and in that brief initial flare Thom had witnessed something more to haunt him for the rest of his days.

The lightning had revealed a sudden change in Nell, for her body had appeared old and withered, the skin ravaged by ruts and blemishes, the once-beautiful face a hideous mask of deep-etched wrinkles and weeping sores. Her nose was crooked, her teeth blackened and stunted, her lidless eyes filled with madness. Even her breasts had become formless pouches.

That was why Thom had observed her studying her own fingers and arm by the dim light. In the few moments preceding her death, Nell Quick had finally become a *hellhagge* herself.

———•⊕•———

The rain returned, but it did not have the same force as earlier.

On the rooftop terrace, the charcoaled husk that had once been a beautiful, if devious, woman became spattered with raindrops.

A solitary and bedraggled magpie flew off the roof to disappear into the night.

# ENDS TIED

T HOM BROUGHT the Jeep round in front of Little
Bracken without having to use the steering device on
the wheel. He looked along the short path towards the
cottage door where Rigwit sat on the stone step. They waved
at each other.

It was a gloriously bright day, with the clear blue skies
that tend to follow a storm. He opened the car door and
stepped out, leaving the walking-stick discarded on the back
seat. He paused to listen to the birds' chatter, a small smile
on his face. A bee droned by. Flowers along the path
somehow seemed more vivid than he remembered.

He had just returned from the hospital in Shrewsbury
where Katy Budd lay conscious but sedated in the intensive
care unit. She was going to be okay. The duty doctor
explained to Thom and Katy's parents, who had travelled
up from Hampshire to be with her, that while Katy had
sustained many broken bones and bruises in the accident,

including a fractured pelvis and a left lower ribcage that was pressing against a lung, there were no serious head injuries, even though she had taken a hard knock that had left her concussed. Her body would heal in time (ironically, given her profession, she would require a substantial amount of physiotherapy).

Katy's parents had thanked Thom for his concern, telling him that they had spoken with their daughter twice during the night. She had not even complained about the pain she was in, but had seemed drowsily annoyed that she could not remember how the accident had happened. As soon as she was well enough, they informed Thom, they would take her back home to Hampshire to recuperate. They had let slip that hopefully, when Katy was fully recovered, she would stay with them, or at least find somewhere nearby to live. They missed their daughter very much.

It had left Thom relieved, but still saddened that Katy had been caught up in something that had had nothing to do with her. He had told the physiotherapist's parents that he would be a constant visitor while she remained in hospital and they seemed delighted to hear it.

Thom walked up the cracked stone path, the half-smile still on his face, his limp hardly noticeable.

Rigwit rose from the step and grinned at him. '*Howsdegil Katty?*' he garbled.

'Slower,' Thom told him, even though he had caught the elf's drift.

'How's the girl Katy?'

'She'll mend. It'll take a while, but she'll be fine.' He sat on the step and Rigwit clapped him on the shoulder. 'I don't think she'll come back to this place though. When – or *if* – she remembers what happened,' Thom added.

'Probably for the best,' the elf said with a sigh. 'Jennet is waiting for you in the woods.'

'She was here?'

'No, but she's waiting for you.'

443

Thom made ready to get to his feet, but Rigwit's little hand now exerted pressure on his shoulder.

'Wait,' Rigwit said. 'I've got something for you, something that will help to make you well again.'

'I feel fine.'

'I know. But it's time for you to speed up your recovery. There's a lot of work ahead of you.'

Thom turned his head to follow Rigwit as the elf went through to the kitchen. What did Rigwit mean by that last remark? Had he read his mind? Thom was only just formulating his plans, so how could the elf know? *Magic*, he told himself, not for the first time over the past few days.

Rigwit was soon back and in his hand was a small round bottle with a longish neck, a hazelnut pressed into its top as a stopper. The elf removed the nut and proffered the bottle to Thom. The thick liquid inside was a deep green.

'Drink half of this now,' Rigwit advised him, 'the rest tonight when you go to bed. Leave the empty bottle by your bedside and it'll be full for the morning, when you'll drink half again, the rest at night-time. Same routine after that.'

'It'll fill itself?' Thom asked in surprise.

'Don't be daft. I'll refill it during the night while you're sleeping.'

Thom held the liquid up to the light and regarded it uncertainly. There appeared to be bits floating in it.

'Looks like corked chartreuse,' he remarked.

'Whatever that is, this isn't. Come on now, one good swallow, but only drink half.'

Thom raised the bottle to his lips and, after a moment's hesitation, drank from it. Immediately he tasted the elf-made medicine he tried to take the bottle away, but Rigwit would not allow it. The little man pushed against the bottle's flat bottom until half of the green liquid was gone.

'Swallow,' he ordered Thom, whose cheeks were filled with the concoction.

Thom gulped it down and pulled a face. It tasted foul.

'What's it made from?' he asked, staring disgustedly at the remainder of the medicine left in the bottle.

'You really don't want to know.'

Rigwit had not used these precise words in his reply, but this was the interpretation in Thom's mind. Sometimes, especially at the beginning, talking with the elf was like watching a badly dubbed Italian movie; the words were not quite in synch with the movement of the mouth. At least Jennet could actually speak the language of humans.

'How long do I have to keep taking the stuff?' he asked resentfully.

'One month of your time. No more than that.'

'Well, that's something to look forward to.'

Rigwit chuckled. 'You be on your way now. Jennet will be getting impatient. There's something important she has to tell you.'

'You're not coming along?'

'It's about time I got down to some serious housework. The place has become a pigsty with all that's been going on. Mind you, certain goblins of my acquaintance enjoy living in real pigsties. One other thing before you go . . .'

He popped inside again and reappeared brandishing a rusty and weathered-looking horseshoe that was half his present size.

'Iron,' he told Thom unnecessarily. 'I want you to keep this on your doorstep from now on.'

Thom regarded him quizzically.

'Iron before the threshold prevents witches from passing through.'

'I could have done with it a week ago. It would have kept Nell Quick out.'

'It was too late for that – she'd already been inside Little Bracken long before you arrived home. Once a witch has gained entry, the spell doesn't work any more.'

'I guess that's handy to know, although I don't expect

any more trouble from witches, or wiccans, whatever you call them.'

'Wiccans. You never know, Thom, m'boy, you never can tell. Be prepared, has always been my motto, a saying that has been stolen by your Boy Scouts, I believe.'

Thom chuckled. 'I don't think Baden-Powell knew it belonged to you.'

Rigwit chuckled with him, then, abruptly: 'Now shoo! Jennet's waiting.' His pointed face turned grave. 'And Thom . . .'

'Yeah?'

'Please. Be prepared.'

---

Thom made his way across the clearing to the edge of the woods, puzzled by the elf's concern. He paused by the first trees and looked back towards the cottage, with its walls and turret of warm red stone. Rigwit was no longer on the doorstep.

Everything looked fresh and sparkling after the fierce storm of the night before, although small branches and leaves were strewn across the clearing, torn loose by the winds. Jewels glittered in the grass and the tree leaves, dewdrops not yet absorbed by the sun; flowers abounded, reds, yellows, blues – especially blues for, to his right and crossing the track that led to the river and Castle Bracken, the bluebells flourished, a vibrant carpet of near-impossible beauty. Soon they would be gone, for they bloomed only a few weeks at a time, and he would miss them. But there were other flora to catch his eye, wild flowers and plants that lifted the heart and made the spirit sing.

He took one last look at the tranquil scene – the sand-stone cottage with its stunted but nevertheless proud tower, the broken stone path with dazzling flowers on either side leading up to it, the verdant clearing itself and the trees behind the building, their shades of green too numerous to take account of, and the clear blue skies where birds playfully wheeled and dived above it all.

Thom filled his lungs with fresh air, the purest anyone could wish to breathe and, for a moment, lost in the gentle splendour around him, he forgot Rigwit's last words of advice. He felt satisfied, content even. Maybe it was because of the contrast between the past few days and the present, the lull *after* the storm (quite literally in this case), but Thom felt at peace, a feeling that had eluded him for many long years. Since Bethan's death, in fact.

He turned and entered the forest's cool shade.

Tiny faeries fluttered around her like excited butterflies as she sat on the overturned tree-trunk waiting for him, their colours dazzling as ever in their varied vibrant hues, while brown and red coated pixies darted in and out of the blades of grass, squeals of laughter and sweet singing mingling with birdsong. She wore the same sheer green dress, with its folds of mauve and purple, and her hands were clasped together in her lap. Jennet raised one and waggled her fingers at him as he approached.

Thom increased his pace, the slight limp no impediment as his heart palpitated and his spirits rose even higher at the sight of her. His excitement grew even more when she rose and skipped towards him.

They kissed. They kissed and the faeries whooped with glee, swooping around them, catching their hair, brushing their clothes. They kissed as if wanting it to go on for ever, each reluctant to break away, neither of them wishing to be the one to end it.

At last, Thom needed air and their lips drew apart, although they still clung together.

'I was coming to see you anyway,' Thom finally managed

to say, 'but Rigwit said you had something important to tell me.'

Her smile faded. 'Let's walk to the lake, Thom, and you can tell me all your news.'

He frowned, but she had already turned and was leading him by the hand. It only took one step to be by her side and, still holding hands, he looked down at her. He loved her yellow ringlets that became golden when the sun struck them; he loved her petite face with its delicately pointed chin and almond eyes that shone a silvery violet; and he loved the gentle slope of her nose and he loved the pinkness of her soft lips. He squeezed her hand and she returned the pressure.

It was like the first time they had strolled through the woods – although now they were strangers no longer – when she had made him aware of the secret life around them. Animals played together and with the *faerefolkis*. A faery glided by holding silken reins drawn by a yellow and black butterfly. Two sprites were engaged in a mock swordfight, using long, birds' feathers as soft weapons. A pixie rode a snail, while another cavorted on the back of a dormouse. A group of green-coated elves threw a red berry about as if it were a ball, while others were happy merely to sit on leaves and inside flowers and chatter, or to dance around toadstools and raise their little voices in song, accompanied by an elf playing a clay pipe of some kind, while one of the faeries plucked at a tiny instrument that looked like a lute. Some were gathering sticks and twigs that had been blown from trees and bushes in last night's gale, carrying them off over their shoulders, or in their arms, to build homes (Jennet explained) for themselves and their families, or for friends whose habitats had been destroyed by the harsh winds.

Thom found the company around him intoxicating and he laughed aloud at their antics. It was difficult to think of last night's events as real; they felt like a very bad nightmare.

Jennet, who had remained silent for some while, suddenly prompted him.

'Tell me what happened after Rigwit and I left the Great Place. And this morning. There must have been much to explain.'

The prompt brought him up short. Suddenly he was no longer paying attention to the woodland activity.

'It was a long night, explaining everything and making statements to the police. You know what I mean by police? Don't you?'

'Of course.' She was mildly indignant. 'We are more aware of your world than you might think. The police are the ones that come and scold you when you've done something very bad.'

He chuckled. 'Well, something like that. To begin with, Bones – I mean Hartgrove – the person who looked after Sir Russell . . .'

'I'm aware of that.'

He regarded her curiously.

'Thom, I told you. We know much more than you think. Your grandfather has lived just beyond the woods for many, many years. The *faerefolkis* know of everyone who ever lived in the Castle.'

Thom considered that for a moment, then went on: 'By the time I returned downstairs to the main hall, Hartgrove had managed to crawl up from the cellar. I must admit, I'd expected to find him lying dead on the cellar floor, so it was wonderful to find him sitting at the bottom of the hall staircase. He was in a bad way though, and the first thing I wanted to do was phone for an ambulance. By then the storm had passed, but there was still no electricity, although the phone lines were working.'

'The witch-woman invoked the storm. When she died, so the storm abated.'

'Hartgrove wouldn't let me call *anybody* until I had told

him everything that had occurred upstairs. He was still in a daze and hurting quite badly – apart from the serious blow to the head, he'd managed to fracture several ribs. But he's tougher than he looks, and very determined.'

Thom took in another deep breath, remembering the foul stenches that had poisoned the air in the eyrie room.

'So, I told him everything, didn't leave out a thing, and you know what? Nothing surprised him, nothing at all fazed him. It was as if he already knew about witchcraft and faeries, and all that stuff. He wasn't even put out when I told him of the demons.'

'But he has always been aware of us,' Jennet said patiently, 'just as his father and his father's father were before him. Each generation of Hartgroves knew the estate's secret.'

'He knew all along? Even when I was a kid?'

'It was he who helped your own father, Jonathan, explain who and what he had fallen in love with all those years ago. The man Hartgrove tried to smooth the way for Jonathan and Bethan. He eventually told your grandfather everything about the *faerefolkis* who lived on his land.'

'Then why didn't Hartgrove ever say anything to me when I was younger? Why didn't Sir Russell?'

'Because the master of Castle Bracken did not approve. He hated the *faerefolkis* because they were not human. He called them freaks of nature, the Devil's children. He forbade Jonathan ever to speak of your mother in his presence.'

On this serene day, and after all he had been through, Thom could not feel anger. He was concerned, disturbed by the new information maybe, but not angry.

'Sir Russell wouldn't accept my mother into the family, but he did give her a job as a tutor and governess to his other son, Hugo. And he did allow her to live in Little Bracken.'

'Where she had already lived with Jonathan for more than a year. Neither she nor Jonathan cared about a formal marriage – it certainly isn't *our* way, love alone is enough for us and never an arrangement – and your grandfather would never have let it happen. Jonathan feared for the forest dwellers – us, the *faerefolkis* – concerned that his father might devastate the woodlands with those awful machines you have. He was afraid Sir Russell would authorize homes to be built and roadways to be put in. We would have had to leave this place, but where would we go? More and more, humans are changing the landscape, destroying the natural countryside. We often wonder if you will ever learn.'

Tiny laughter interrupted her. A ring of faeries was listening to their storyteller – Thom could not remember the elf's odd name – and they clapped their hands together with joy, a quiet pattering sound.

'After his son's death, Sir Russell promised to take care of Bethan and her son, *you*, on one condition.'

Thom bought them both to a halt on the obscure track.

'What did my mother have to do?' he asked gravely, even though he had already guessed.

'She had to promise never to tell you who your father was. When she had to return to the undines after your tenth birthday – oh, she didn't want to leave you, she begged and pleaded with the Magicks, our leaders, but there was nothing that could be done: it was our natural law, something even we have no control over – he made her vow something more. He would take charge of your welfare if she made you forget everything you had learned of the *faerefolkis*. She had no choice but to agree, although she did hide the Book among others on a top shelf in the cottage, with the hope, I believe, that some day, when you were older, you would discover it.'

'The—' He was about to curse his grandfather's memory, but held back. Too much had passed between them last night and things had changed in more ways than one.

On the roof terrace, Thom had sunk to his knees in

the rain, appalled and sickened by what had just befallen Nell Quick. Her blackened corpse lay on the stone floor, smouldering and steaming in the downpour, and the smell of her cooked body had caused him to retch.

Eventually, Thom had returned to the rooftop room with its burning candles and glass-strewn floor, where Jennet and Rigwit were waiting for him, the plump figure of Hugo sitting among the glass fragments, staring directly ahead, his mind in some other place entirely.

'You saw what happened,' Thom said to Jennet as they continued walking through the woods. 'After we held on to each other and Rigwit set about erasing the chalk pentagram.'

'It's an evil thing, especially when drawn by one such as the witch,' Jennet interrupted. 'Rigwit knew its power.'

Thom nodded, understanding the symbol's significance only too well by now. 'I went to my grandfather. I ... I thought he was already dead. But his eyes opened a little as I sat next to him on the bed. He took my hand, Jennet ...'

'I saw.' Jennet pressed close to his side as they walked.

'Did you hear what he said? His voice was very weak.'

'I heard, Thom.'

'He called me Jonathan. He called me by my father's name. But then his eyes opened a little more and I saw recognition in them. I saw something else too. For the first time there was ... there was affection there.'

'No, Thom. It was love. I saw it, I felt it.'

He was silent for a few moments. A sparrow hopped across their path and then was gone, into the undergrowth.

'He called me Thom.' He looked at Jennet and she smiled sadly. 'He called me Thom and his grip tightened on my hand, just for a moment, a squeeze that told me more than words. And then he said: "Take care of them. The world needs them more than ever." His hand fell away from mine and my grandfather died. It was only when I spoke to

Hartgrove later that I understood who he meant. He wanted me to take care of the *faerefolkis*.'

Thom caught a glimpse of the lake through the trees ahead.

'I asked Hartgrove what had changed Sir Russell's mind about your kind and he told me that it happened after he became bedridden. My grandfather's illness was not caused by any magic spell of Nell's, by the way. I guess she kept that for me. It was a genuine illness brought about by a diseased heart. That's the irony of the whole situation. Nell and Hugo were trying to keep my grandfather alive, at least until they'd found his last Will and Testament, or I was dead. And all the time I thought they were slowly poisoning him, or Nell was using some kind of voodoo magic, as she had on me. But they were prepared to finish him off last night by more practical means if his heart did not finally give out with all the horror Nell had invited to his room. I'll get to that in a moment though.'

'You said you'd asked Hartgrove what had made your grandfather change his mind about us,' Jennet said.

'It seemed his condition had made Sir Russell rethink a lot of things. He truly missed his son, Jonathan, and regretted his harsh treatment of both him and my mother. Hartgrove told me that Hugo had completely failed his father, in more ways than I was aware of, in fact. Hugo had not been sacked from his insurance company for incompetence, but for sharp practice and embezzlement. He was cheating his personal clients out of the full dividends they were owed. Only Sir Russell's intervention and repayment kept the scandal out of court. Hugo also drank too much and he was into drugs. Cocaine is expensive, which might have accounted for the shortfalls in profits owed to his clients. But it gets worse.'

Thom was slowly shaking his head as if still astounded by the revelations.

'There was the small matter of his gambling – dogs, horses, roulette; apparently he did the lot.' Thom sighed. 'I'm just amazed I wasn't aware of all this, even though I never saw much of Hugo. Too busy getting on with my own career.'

A cool breeze met them from the lake and Thom undid his shirt buttons to make the most of it. The hem of Jennet's thin dress ruffled and locks of golden hair tickled her cheek. The breeze soon passed.

'Anyhow,' Thom went on, 'Sir Russell began to regret his treatment of his eldest son, comparing him to Hugo, I suppose. It was wrong, but at least it served to soften his general attitude. His heart disease caused him to open his mind. That's when he asked Hartgrove to help him make his new Will.'

'Which Hugo caught wind of and finally found.'

'Hugo must have eavesdropped on them both when they were discussing the Will, or Sir Russell murmured something about it when he was in one of his semi-conscious states. Nell could have overheard and started the search.'

'And the Will was destroyed last night, burnt by the lightning.'

'Hugo and Nell didn't know, but there were two of them anyway. Hartgrove copied out another, which Sir Russell signed and, obviously, Hartgrove witnessed. Hartgrove kept it on him at all times. Seems he had always been suspicious of Nell and her relationship with Hugo. Hugo just brought her home one day, by the way, and announced she was to be Sir Russell's full-time carer to ease the burden on Hartgrove.'

They came out of the woods to stand by the lakeside. She pointed to a patch of lush grass beneath a willow tree, whose branches drooped into the calm waters. They strolled over and sat side by side.

'Rigwit and I left before the policemen and the doctor people arrived,' Jennet said, again as a prompt.

'Right. And I closed the book once the faeries had returned inside and left it in the antechamber next door. The medics took a look at Sir Russell and advised me to call in his doctor to formalize time of death and all that. The ambulance took Hartgrove away, but left Hugo there for the doctor to examine when he arrived. Of course, the doctor called another ambulance for Hugo as soon as he examined him. I learned this morning that he's still in a catatonic state, but there's no other physical damage, not even cuts from the glass from the shattered windows.'

'What will become of him?'

'His condition is only just being assessed, but the family doctor told me that Hugo is in shock. His mind has closed down and it might stay that way for a long time to come. Or he may never recover. Whatever the outcome, I'll take care of him. If the worst happens, I'll make sure he's kept in the best kind of home or hospital that deals with that kind of thing. In some ways it'll be unfortunate if he does remember what happened.'

'If that should be the case, Rigwit has the means to make him forget last night and his involvement with the wiccan. But he did help Nell Quick in her efforts to murder you. Don't you at least blame him for that?'

'What's the point? Okay, he isn't the best person in the world and, as it turns out, he wasn't the best friend to me either. But I believe he was corrupted by Nell in the end and learning he'd been deprived of his inheritance sent him over the edge.'

'That's generous of you, Thom.'

'Not really. Believe it or not, I still like Hugo. Seems crazy, I know, but I can't forget when we were kids. Besides, it looks like I'm going to be reasonably wealthy once I've sold off all the shares Sir Russell still has in various companies, so I can easily afford to pay for Hugo's care.'

'But isn't he in trouble with your policemen?'

'I kept Hugo out of it. Before I called the police I made

455

sure Hartgrove was comfortable, then went back upstairs and removed all the candles from the room. The wind had dropped by then, but there was still enough breeze coming through the smashed windows to clear the air of that waxy smell, as well as all the others that had come with . . . with, well, those apparitions.'

'They weren't apparitions, Thom.'

'I know, but it's how I prefer to think of them. When the police finally arrived I told them both Hartgrove and I suspected Nell had been trying to harm Sir Russell and I'd gone over to confront her that night. Naturally, Hartgrove backed me up and told them, before he was carted away in the ambulance, that Nell had deliberately pushed him down the cellar stairs. Hartgrove and I had already agreed – Hartgrove a little reluctantly, I must admit, but he knew Sir Russell, himself, would have approved – not to mention Hugo's part in all this.'

Thom had expected to see undines emerging from the lake on this beautiful day, but there was no sign of them. In fact, even the faeries and elves had vanished.

'Now this is where it all fits perfectly. Nell *was* going to poison Sir Russell if the fatal heart attack failed to happen. The police were mystified when they found pieces of coral on the medicine trolley by the bed. One of them was astute enough to remember something he'd read or heard during the course of his duties. The coral that's found in these parts is the same kind as sea polyps found in the Pacific Ocean.'

'And it can be used for making poison. We've always known this.'

'I spoke to the police this morning, and they had a small bottle of liquid that stood next to the coral on the trolley analysed overnight. It contained polytoxin, taken from the coral by whatever process Nell was able to use—'

'It isn't difficult if you know how to extract the poison and the rites that have to be performed.'

He looked at her blankly for a moment. 'Okay. Anyway,

it seems this particular toxin isn't traceable in the body's system. No post-mortem would ever have found it. Nell didn't even have to apply for the polytoxin from any biochemical firm, because she processed it herself. She had it covered all ways.'

This time, Thom's sigh was deeper. He found it difficult to credit such wickedness. 'I told the police that I'd confronted Nell over my suspicions and she'd run out on to the terrace in panic. She'd already tried to kill Hartgrove and hadn't quite managed it, so the game was up. Outside on the roof, lightning had struck her as well as blowing in the windows. Hugo had witnessed her electrocution and had been traumatized by it. It was a lot for them to swallow, but with Hartgrove's statement and the result of the analysis this morning, they seem to have accepted the story.'

Thom leaned back on one elbow, relieved to have got so much off his chest. He knew he should have been exhausted by last night's and the early morning's events – he calculated he'd had no more than four hours' sleep – but he wasn't: he was elated instead; peacefully elated, if that were possible. And yes, he was saddened too. Nobody's death was good news, not even Nell Quick's. Thoughts of his grandfather, Sir Russell Bleeth, were with him also. To discover he was related to the man he'd always regarded with respectful awe, and not a little fear, then to lose him just when his birthright was acknowledged was tragic. At least the last few moments with the dying man had redeemed some of the past.

And then there was poor Hugo, struck speechless, shocked into a zombie-like state that might possibly last for the rest of his life. Thom fervently hoped it wouldn't. He looked out across the lake, so still, so placid.

'Thom?'

He turned back to Jennet and her expression was serious.

'What will you do with the Castle and all its lands?' she asked.

He gathered his thoughts before replying, his gaze

returning to the still waters. He smiled a sad smile. 'I had an idea when I visited Katy Budd at the hospital today.'

She raised her eyebrows at him, but he was still watching the lake.

'I passed a children's ward,' he went on, unbidden, 'and looked in. There were some pretty sick kids, lots of them with no hair, many of them so thin it almost made me weep. I realized I was in a cancer unit. Those kids were suffering from leukaemia and various other forms of cancer, and many of them are going to die. That's when I had the idea.'

There was an excitement in his eyes when he turned back to Jennet.

'I'll find the best medical staff possible, people who see medicine and nursing as a vocation, not just a career, and then I'll turn Castle Bracken into a hospice for terminally ill kids. The grounds will be their adventure playground, nothing too grand, just a few swings, simple roundabouts, sandpits, that kind of thing. And seesaws, kids love seesaws. I'll make them myself – I've already got some fun ideas. Government grants and whatever money's left over from my grandfather's share options will be ploughed back into the house to open it up, let the light in, convert it into a suitable place of care. And the top room with its wonderful views, will be the special place for those closest to death.'

'And the woodlands?'

'Kids that are fit enough will be brought here on organized walks, just a few at a time guided only by me – and, I hope, by you.'

In his eagerness, he did not notice the shadow that passed over her face.

'I know it sounds high-minded, crazy even, or maybe just too ambitious, but I know it could work. Think of it, Jennet. They can come here and, in time – we'll plan it very carefully – perhaps they'll see the *faerefolkis* for themselves. Who knows, you might indulge them in a few miracles. If Rigwit is anything to go by, you know more about medicines and cures than'll we'll ever know.'

A tear trickled down her cheek and Thom frowned. 'What is it?' he asked, concerned.

'It's what you were meant to do, Thom. It's why you're here, why you came back.'

'I came back because I was ill,' he said gently.

She shook her head, wiping away the teardrop from her chin with the heel of her hand. 'No, you were always meant to return. Remember when I compared you to the Nazarene?'

'To Christ?' He gave a short laugh despite the sadness of her face. 'Yeah, I'm a carpenter too, but that's as far as it goes.'

'You're more than that. I wasn't that sure, but I understand perfectly now. The Magicks were right.'

'Jennet, I think you're—'

She put her fingers to his mouth to prevent him saying more and he couldn't help kissing their tips. 'Listen to me, Thom. Bethan was an undine and your father was a human. You have the blood and – what is it you call it nowadays? the genie—'

His puzzlement turned to another laugh. 'The genes. You mean the genes.'

'All right. You have them too. Don't laugh, Thom, listen to me.'

He checked himself. 'Sorry. Slight hysteria after yesterday.'

'You have the power to unite us. Humans and *faerefolkis*. You could be the emissary, the go-between, if you like. Starting with the children.'

He was silent, perplexed. Then: 'The children, maybe . . . But the rest? Jennet, I don't think the world is ready to accept life from another realm just yet. There's too much cynicism around, too much materialism. Even the normal religions are failing miserably.'

'That's why you need something more. I promise you this, most of the other religions will gain a new and more correct perspective once mankind comes to know and *understand* us. The religions will begin to make sense and there'll be no need for blind faith. As for cynicism and materialism, that was here two millennia ago when the Christ appeared among you.'

'And look what they did to him,' Thom muttered.

'But *you* will begin with the children, and there will be miracles, Thom, please believe me. If that's how we can get through to others, then that's what will happen.'

'You've spoken about this with your, uh, Magicks?'

'It was they who spoke of it to me.'

Thom pondered. He looked away, he looked back at her, and away again. He considered. *No it was impossible. He'd be a laughing stock.* He mused. *I'm just one person.* He deliberated. *And yet . . . and yet . . . if the children began to be cured of terminal illnesses . . .*

'Maybe . . .' he said finally. 'Maybe with your help . . .'

'That isn't possible, Thom.'

She cast her head down and he suddenly felt a dread looming inside him.

'Jennet . . .?'

'There's something I have to tell you,' she said quietly and Thom felt his heart begin to beat faster.

# Chapter : Forty-Second

## LAST WORDS

H E DIDN'T want to hear. The sad look on her face, the tone of her voice . . . He really did not want to hear.

But Jennet told him anyway.

'I have to go back, Thom,' she said simply.

'Back? Back to the undines? Why? I thought . . .' He was panicking.

'Hush. I have to go back for you. I have to go back to save you.'

He shook his head.

'It has to be done.'

'I don't understand . . .'

'Poor Thom. You've had to learn so much. I have to return to the moment of your car crash. Don't you remember the bright light?'

'Yes, but—'

'Now is the time for it to happen.'

'For what to happen? I'm alive, Jennet, I'm okay.'

'Because I went back to change Nell's bad magic. If I

461

hadn't, you probably wouldn't have survived the accident, let alone the blood interruption inside your head.'

He remembered the blinding light at the time of the crash and was lost for words; he could only stare at her.

'To do this, I must have your help.'

'But I don't want you to go.'

'Please, try to understand. It's a deed already done. Neither of us can change things now.'

'I don't get it.'

'Because you're not trying. If I hadn't gone back to save you, then you wouldn't be here now, talking to me.'

'That doesn't make sense.'

'It does if you think about it. We're only wasting time, because it will happen. But I need all my powers and the powers of the undines. You, too, can help make it work. Remember I also told you about the power invoked by the act of love? I said it was the greatest magic of all.'

He saw where she was going with this. She began to push his unbuttoned shirt off his shoulders.

'Jennet . . .'

'No more words, Thom.'

'Just one last question, grant me that.'

She nodded, but she was weeping again.

'What happens after? Do you come right back as if you've never been gone?'

'I have to go to the Waiting Place.'

He caught her wrist. 'What did you say?'

'I have to leave you for seven years.'

'No! No, that can't be. I can't let that happen!'

'We have no choice. It's the price I have to pay for using such strong magic.'

'I won't let you!'

'I already have. But listen again to me, Thom. Listen and *hear* what I'm telling you. After seven years I will return to you. I will be like Bethan, mostly human. And as long as you live I can remain so.'

'But the Waiting Place – where is it?'

'Don't you remember? I showed you once before.'

'The vision. The constellations, the great clouds. The spirits. But I thought it was the new beginning.'

'For most it's the start of the journey onwards. For others it's the dimension humans call Purgatory. The Waiting Place. Some return to this world from there, but only those who have more to do here, or who have left certain things undone.'

He stared at her in disbelief, while in his heart he knew she would only speak the truth.

'Do you recall the fox we met in the woods, the one I called Rumbo?' she asked and Thom nodded. 'I told you that once his life was human, and that he came back as a dog, and later a squirrel. Now he's a fox.'

'You're saying humans go through some kind of reincarnation?'

'No, not all. Just special cases where it's necessary for the individual's growth and awareness. Most of you – and most of us – journey onwards because you've learned all that's required of you on this Earth. Some might go on immediately, but for the majority there is always the waiting time that eventually leads to a condition of near-perfection. A state of grace, some of your religions call it.'

She squeezed his hand.

'I have to be there for seven years in your time. It's the price I have to pay for challenging the natural laws. But it's all right, Thom, it's a wondrous place to be.'

He fell silent once more. Jennet had shown him the Waiting Place so that he would not be afraid for her while she was gone. But he felt there was another reason too, that some time in the future when the terminally ill children came to Bracken, to the hospice he would create there, she would also show them this wonderful place and death – if that was to be their fate – would hold no fear for them. He understood now and realized it was pointless to argue. Besides, to win would be to lose anyway.

He shrugged off his shirt. 'Jennet, I love you so much. I don't know how—'

'Seven years will soon pass, you'll see. And you will achieve so much during that time.'

She slipped the flimsy dress from her shoulders and the top fell to her waist. Her small breasts were proud in the dappled sunlight, their points softly pink and extended. The sight of her beneath the willow, with the lake behind her, the backdrop of forest, was exquisite; her flawless skin seemed to glow with a serene kind of energy and, not for the first time, Thom was lost in awe of her. How could he be without her now? He could not let this sweet, unique being escape him, not for seven years, not for one moment.

'There must be another way,' he said determinedly.

'There is, but it would mean losing each other for ever. This is the only way, Thom, and you must help me.'

She bent forward and kissed his brow, then his lips, and he returned the kisses with desperate passion. Jennet responded, equalling his fervour, and quickly, with her help, he was naked. Jennet, however, remained wearing the diaphanous dress around her waist where it rumpled over her lap and upper thighs. Somehow, the partial nakedness made her even more alluring as she knelt before him, resting on her heels. He drank in the vision, allowed it to sink deep into his mind, an indelible image that would last all his days.

She pushed him back gently with one hand so that he lay prone on the mossy forest floor that felt like velvet against his skin. She leaned over him, the aroused tips of her little breasts almost touching his chest, and they kissed again, softly, tenderly at first, then more firmly, her tongue exploring his lips, entering his mouth, pushing past his parted teeth to be met by his own tongue. Firm, but then hard, pressing against each other, their mouths becoming moist as they savoured one another.

His hardness was intense as he thrust his naked hips towards her, and she responded by moving her smooth pudenda against him, wetting herself with the slick moistness that was seeping from him. He groaned and reached for her breasts, gently running his fingertips over their elegant smoothness, covering the nipples, pressing softly until her hips became more active, drove against him, her kisses becoming wilder, her long golden hair falling over both their faces to create a momentary curtain that enclosed them in their own world. He returned her kisses, his passion easily equalling hers, although his touch never once became rushed or clumsy.

Jennet lowered herself so that her nipples could touch his. She smeared her breasts over his chest, the movement less and less gentle as her body began to lose control. Thom reacted to the increasing roughness, thrusting himself hard at her, his arms encircling her back, fingers running down her spine, fingertips exploring the cleft at its base, kneading the dip so that nerve endings sent a shiver through her.

She suddenly straightened and reached a hand beneath the flimsy rumpled material of her skirt to guide him inside her, her own dampness making the penetration easy. Thom drew in a brief gasp of pleasure as he felt her melt around him and as she loomed over him, the sun behind her highlighting her flowing locks and curls, outlining a golden sheen around her body, he saw the dazzling lights approach, small irradiations of pure energy that concealed the beings within. Their colours dazzled the eye as they glided around Jennet, brushing her skin, sending waves of power through her, titillating her flesh, descending so that they crossed her stomach and swept over her stretched thighs to reach him as he lay there, exposed and vulnerable on his back.

The sensation on his skin, with their wings fanning him, tickling him in their sensuous way, was stimulating and he felt his senses drawing together, sinews and muscles tightening, nerve endings tingling with excitement. Out of the corner of his eye he saw more of the *faerefolkis* arrive to watch and cheer their approval and joy at this most natural of acts. He no longer felt exposed lying there, and was neither intimidated, nor embarrassed by their gaze, for their thoughts were pure, their reaction innocent. Somehow he knew they were there to encourage, not to leer. He saw the beautiful creatures rising from the lake, neither their hair, nor their bodies, not even the thin fabric that some wore, wet or dampened. They were some distance away, yet he could see their smiles and feel their benevolence.

The lights increased, pulsating with individual power, so stunning in their brightness that he was forced to close his eyes, or shield them, with a forearm when they came too close to his face. He absorbed their potency, drew their vibrancy into his own body, and the elation was incredible.

Jennet moved against him, raising and lowering herself on him with a steadily mounting rhythm, occasionally breaking to writhe her hips, drawing from him all that she desired, for he was rigid, strong, meeting her every demand, and soon she was breathing in short, sharp gasps, her straddled legs pumping, her hands now behind her, pulling at his thighs, taking every inch of him, and never had he felt so hard and powerful, never had his juices seethed so wildly inside him, rising to cause small eruptions, before receding only to rise again, and again . . .

Until both their bodies were caught in the shuddering paroxysms of ecstasy.

The noise around them – the light flutey singing, the tiny shouts of joy, the dainty clapping of hands – reached its peak also as the little people danced and copulated among themselves, some in groups of three or four, five or six, but mostly one-to-one, celebrating their own as well as Thom and Jennet's union, for there was no shame in such behaviour for them, nothing about it that should be secretive or hidden. Lovemaking was their supreme delight and they saw no reason why it should not be shared with as many as possible.

Besides, this was their way of helping Jennet work her magic, a mass consortium of energies that drew forces beyond her normal powers. Good forces. The forces of purest rapture . . .

The ascendancy for Thom and Jennet was perfectly timed and both cried out as one, over and over, bodies swelling with the supreme ecstasy.

Thom opened his eyes to watch Jennet in her last blissful throes and saw that her arms were thrown upwards and spread wide as if in supplication. Lights zoomed around her dizzyingly, their splendour now so harsh that he had to squint to protect his eyes. He could just see that her eyes were shut tight and her mouth was set in a euphoric smile; her bare arms trembled as she arched her spine and neck so that she faced the skies through the overhead canopy of willow leaves. Her cries turned into a moan and he could not tell if it were one of joy or despair.

Suddenly, a blinding light radiated from her, a shining far greater than that which emanated from the flying sprites and even greater that the rays of the sun. He had to throw both hands up to shield his face and eyes. The heat burned and even from behind his own palms he could see that the light throbbed, although it never once grew less fierce.

And then it was gone, waning a little before blinking out completely. It was as if a light-switch – one that controlled the most powerful light in the universe – had been flicked off. It was as amazing as it was confusing and, when he dropped his hands away, Jennet was gone.

---

Thom took his time walking back through the woods. Beneath the willow tree on the banks of the lake, he had silently wept, but the tears had not lasted long. There was so much to be done, so much to get ready for Jennet's return. For return she would; he had no doubts. And when she did, he would find his peace again.

As he strolled, watching the enchanting *faerefolkis* caper, the animals and the birds of the forest still undaunted by his presence, he lost the numbing ache in his leg; he could even swing his debilitated arm without impediment despite his general fatigue. He wasn't entirely cured, he was aware of that, but the harm had been lessened, and with Rigwit's medicine and daily exercise, he knew he would soon be back in shape.

Both joy and a peaceful kind of sadness were his companions on his walk back to the cottage, but at least he had a purpose now as well as something to look forward to, a dream that could only come true.

For as Jennet had vanished into the blinding light, her voice – it was not a self-thought, for this voice had sound and inflection – had come into his head.

She had said: 'Expect me.'

# Epilogue:

# A MURDER OF CROWS

T HE BIRDS gathered in the trees surrounding the hidden forest clearing. Their feathers were sleekly black, sinister in the shade afforded by the thick leaves around the edges of the glade, their bills long and pointed, these also black.

*Kraaaa!* they called to one another, and the sound was harsh in the quietness of the woods.

The crows – a gathering that was known as *a murder of crows* – watched the black-and-white bird skip haltingly through the grass below. The magpie, shabby and tattered wings flapping weakly each time it tried to lift them, seemed disorientated as it hopped from one spot to another as if searching for something (although it never ventured into the shadows of the trees). It opened its bill as if to call, but no sound came forth, and occasionally it would peck uselessly at the soft mulch between the blades of grass.

The crows in the branches began to bustle on their perches, their feathers seeming to bristle, the long and strong

JAMES HERBERT

wings rising and lowering, a few strokes at a time. Their calls became more strident, the communication more intense.

The magpie on the ground did not seem to notice. Round in rough circles it went, each skip more feeble than the last.

The crows waited, their mood growing keener by the moment. It only took one to leave its bough, and that soon happened, for them all to swoop from their branches, their great wings spread as they plummeted.

The magpie finally found voice when the first two crows pecked out its eyes. And it managed a last shriek as others ripped out its throat.

Its agony did not last long. The crows soon tore it to pieces and the forest was peaceful once more.

CONCLUDED.

**James Herbert** is not just Britain's No.1 bestselling writer of thriller/horror fiction, a position he has held ever since publication of his first novel, but is one of our greatest popular novelists, whose books are sold in thirty-three foreign languages, including Russian and Chinese. Widely imitated and hugely influential, his twenty novels have sold more than forty-eight million copies worldwide.